PREDATORS

Terry Hodges

PREDATORS

MORE TRUE GAME WARDEN ADVENTURES

TERRY HODGES
AUTHOR OF SABERTOOTH,
TOUGH CUSTOMERS & SWORN TO PROTECT

PREDATORS
More True Game Warden Adventures
By Terry Hodges

Copyright © 2002 by Terry Hodges

ISBN 0-9634092-3-9
Printed in the United States of America

Published by T&C Books
P.O. Box 1126
Oroville, CA 95965
(800) 499-8420
rv6@cncnet.com   www.gamewarden.net

All rights reserved. Except for use in a review, no portion of this book may be reproduced in any form without express written permission of the publisher.

Neither the author nor the publisher assumes any responsibility for the use or misuse of information contained in this book.

Cover artwork and design by Sherri Dobay
www.dobayart.com

To my father, Tharen R. Hodges,
who was always there for me.

The stories in this book are true, presented with as much accuracy as memory and existing records permit. I have, however, changed many of the names to protect the privacy of those who have already paid the price for their misdeeds.

Terry Hodges

ACKNOWLEDGMENTS

I would like to thank the following people for their help and support on this project:

My wife, Cathy, who is first to read my stories and whose comments and suggestions I greatly value.

Alexia Retallack, editor of OUTDOOR CALIFORNIA magazine, in which most of these stories first appeared. Alexia served as my editor for this book.

My friend Barbara Malloch Leitner for her final proofread and polish of my typeset manuscript.

Joan Prince, for her infinite patience in yet again preparing my manuscript for print.

Sherri Dobay, for her excellent artwork and cover design.

James Wictum, for his comments in the Foreword to this book and for being as fine a supervisor as a warden could ever hope for.

Special thanks to Dave Dick, the previous editor of OUTDOOR CALIFORNIA, who gave me my start as a writer.

CONTENTS

Foreword	iii
Trash Can Joe	1
Callous Hearts	15
Lucky Breaks	27
Rascal's Road to Justice	43
True Remorse	55
Turkeys	69
A Weekend With "Starsky and Hutch"	81
The Natural	93
Lobster Jake	103
Dirty Harry and Ape Island	117
Cold, Cold, Hearts	129
Davie Crockett and the Bush Baby	153
Tiger's Revenge	163
Smooth Operator	173
Time Bomb	187
Cheaters	199
A Calculated Risk	211
Killer John	223

New Talent 237
Slow Learners 249
Predators 261
Then Came Speedy 277
Delta Ghosts 291

FOREWORD

There was a time when I supervised Terry Hodges, the author of this book. He was a new warden then, and he and I worked together in the Delta for four intense years. I knew from the start that he would be a good one. Not only did he have the dedication, commitment and courage necessary to be good at his new profession, but he had a variety of skills and abilities that set him apart.

He was an accomplished small boat handler and an expert with canoes. He was a trick shot with a rifle, and became first among the warden force to qualify as Grand Master with a pistol. He was a record-holding SCUBA diver and a private pilot, and at six-feet-one, over 200 pounds and hugely strong, he was a difficult package for the bad guys.

Yet what I most remember about Terry is his imagination and ingenuity, his inventiveness when facing challenging problems. To combat hard-to-find dove and waterfowl poachers in the Delta, Terry devised a way to use maps, magnetic compasses and plotting tools to triangulate on the sound of distant shooting, enabling us to quickly locate the culprits. It worked well.

He has a quick mind and is a master of the bluff, a tool

he employed often. On one dark night in the mountains, using only his patrol vehicle and radios and aided by his wife, Cathy, he managed to bluff a veritable rat's nest of hoodlums into believing that they were surrounded by a score of wardens. He then arrested one deer poacher from their midst, seized one illegally killed doe and captured an armed and wanted felon. Not bad for a lone officer.

In short, Terry is a game warden, one of the best I have ever known. It came as no surprise to me when he began to write, for not only is he an excellent story-teller, but he has a wealth of stories to tell. The compelling tales you are about to read are the real thing, true game warden adventures just as they happened, for Terry has walked the walk and talked the talk. When you read his stories, he'll take you there, to California's wild places, in pursuit of real outlaws. Enjoy the trip.

> Deputy Chief James Wictum, Retired
> California Department of Fish and Game

TRASH CAN JOE

It was *him* again. Snooks, the toy poodle, had spotted him first, almost invisible as he stood amid the scrub oaks and brush at the mouth of the canyon.

"We see you!" shouted Thelma Hobbs defiantly as little Snooks lunged against his leash, yapping furiously. At this, a dark figure, clad head to toe in camouflage, emerged into the early morning sunlight. He carried an evil-looking, camo-painted compound bow with all its complicated wheels and levers. Slung across his back, Robinhood-style, was a homemade quiver of razor-edged broadhead arrows.

"You can't hunt around here," said Hobbs, standing her ground as the man approached.

"I'll hunt where I please," said the man, glaring at her with the fierce eyes of ancestors who had spear-hunted leopard on the plains of Africa. "And you'd best mind your own business," he growled as he strode away.

Hobbs later described the encounter with a neighbor who had, herself, encountered the same disturbing man on at least two occasions.

"He threatened *me* with a *gun*," said the neighbor. "Well, he didn't actually point it at me, but he was wearing it, and he made sure I saw it."

Both women were senior residents of Altadena, at the

base of the San Gabriel Mountains near Los Angeles, and they enjoyed walking their dogs on the old fire road in El Prieto Canyon. But often of late, encounters with the man in camo had discouraged them from venturing too far from home.

"Agnes saw him riding into the canyon on a motor scooter the other day. He was carrying a bunch of lumber and stuff," said the neighbor. "What could he be building up there?"

"I don't know," said Thelma. "But I think I'll call the sheriff."

She did, in fact, call the Sheriff's Office that morning, and a dispatcher there immediately referred the matter to Fish and Game. The information ultimately reached Warden Mike Conely who took one look at it and said, "This sounds like Trash Can Joe!"

Joseph John Bass was well known among the game wardens. First captured years earlier with a deer out of season, he had later earned his nickname when one night he illegally shot an arrow into a bear that was rooting around inside a trash dumpster. Warden Emmett Lenihan got wind of the matter, drove to the scene and followed a blood trail from the dumpster to a large pile of entrails in the forest. He also located a broken and blood-stained arrow and found witnesses who provided a description of the violator and his vehicle. The investigation ultimately led to Joe Bass, who one morning found his home surrounded by game wardens with a search warrant. The search of Bass' home yielded the bear, plus enough evidence for a slam-dunk case against the man. State law clearly forbade the killing or pursuit of bears near dumps, dumpsters, trash cans or any other bait that would attract bears to any certain spot, and it was also illegal to hunt bear at night, which clearly was the case with Bass' "trash can" bear.

While Bass was thereafter known among the wardens as *Trash Can Joe*, he regarded himself in other terms. He was well known in and around the community of Altadena, and he enjoyed introducing himself as *The Black Robinhood*. During the search of his home, the wardens had found a stack of business cards which read, *Black Robinhood Guide Service — Trophy Bear and Deer Hunts*. Lenihan checked with the Fish and Game records people and found that *The Black Robinhood* was indeed licensed as a hunting guide.

Warden Conely, upon reflecting on Joe Bass' past, was well aware that reports and rumors persisted that the man continued to illegally hunt bear and deer, and that he was regularly accused of intimidating people who objected to his outlaw ways. Many of these reports came from the archery community, for Bass often visited archery ranges and passed around his guide service business cards and photos of various bears he had taken with bow and arrow. The archers were generally nervous around him, well aware that he was not only a frequent violator of Fish and Game laws, but that his practices on the archery shooting range were dangerous to others. He always kept his compound bow adjusted to a draw weight he could barely handle, and he could manage it only by beginning his draw with the bow and arrow pointed straight up. Then, with muscles straining, he would simultaneously draw back the bow string and lower the bow in a shaky, dangerous-looking maneuver that would send onlookers scattering.

Just two weeks earlier, an anonymous informant had told Conely that Bass, who drove a battered black van, had been hunting in El Prieto Canyon using bait, and using a motor scooter or bicycle to travel from the locked gate at the trailhead to tree blinds he had constructed somewhere in the canyon.

With these things in mind, Conely now decided that it was time to take a closer look at Trash Can Joe. He phoned his friend, Steve Ulrich, another local warden, and the two of them decided to take a hike one morning into El Prieto Canyon to see what they could find. They parked their patrol vehicle at the locked gate at the trail head and started in on foot.

It was cool in the canyon beneath a canopy of giant oaks and sycamores which shaded El Prieto Creek, a tiny stream of clear water that bubbled down from the higher San Gabriel Mountains. Wild things thrived in the canyon. A doe with a spotted fawn peered down from a brushy canyon wall. Gray squirrels scurried along tree limbs. Cottontails zigzagged for cover amid sage brush and poison oak. A mother valley quail hurried across the old fire road, pursued by a dozen tiny fuzz balls on legs. There were bear tracks on the road, mingled with those of hikers, horses and mountain bikers, and Conely paused at one point to examine what appeared to be old mountain lion tracks.

It never ceased to amaze the wardens that wildlife was so abundant in the hills and mountains around Los Angeles. Despite the proximity of literally millions of people, an incredible variety of wildlife thrived in numbers far surpassing mountainous areas elsewhere in the state. It was therefore not surprising that "city wardens" there dealt with more wild animal problems than their more rural counterparts elsewhere—bears raiding outbuildings and parked cars for anything edible; bears in swimming pools and hot tubs; mountain lions dining on pet llamas, cats and dogs; deer snacking on expensive landscaping; possums in attics; snakes in basements; raccoons in swimming pools; "something black on my ceiling" calls; there was no end to it. It was therefore not surprising that these same city wardens dealt with more outlaw hunters and fishermen than most wardens elsewhere.

A quarter-mile up the canyon, the old fire road crossed El Prieto Creek. Here the wardens left the road and followed a faint trail that paralleled the stream deeper into the canyon. Shafts of sunlight filtered down through the trees as they picked their way up a narrow, poison oak choked trail. As they gained altitude, the canyon opened up a bit, and suddenly the wardens encountered something odd—a long strip of masking tape stretched across the trail, knee high, anchored at each end to trees. Attached to the tape, at one point, was a beer can with pebbles in it. The wardens were amazed, having never seen a warning device quite so crude. Stepping over the tape, they continued on and soon encountered more of it, another strip with an attached beer can. Then they noted more of the devices on game trails that converged at this spot.

It was then that Conely spotted a man-made structure high in an oak tree. It was a tree stand—a platform of plywood and two-by-fours. A crude ladder of short boards nailed to the tree trunk provided access to it. The ground at the base of the tree was littered with beer cans. Conely gingerly climbed the 15-foot ladder and examined the stand. It measured about 10-feet by 10-feet and was carpeted. On it was an old radio, a blanket and an old Styrofoam ice chest. But the structure appeared abandoned and unused in recent months and was so termite infested as to be unusable by any sane person.

Continuing another 75 yards up the trail, the wardens found more masking tape warning devices and another tree stand. But it was in much the same condition as the first, obviously unsafe to use. The wardens filmed both tree stands and the surrounding area, then hiked out of the canyon, puzzled over the apparent absence of anything newly constructed.

Reports of suspicious activity on the part of Joe Bass continued, and six weeks after locating the tree stands in El Prieto Canyon, the wardens returned for another look. All was the same. There had been no change. But a break in the case came one evening nine days later, the day after the opening of archery bear season. Warden Ulrich spotted Bass' black van parked at the El Prieto Canyon trailhead. Ulrich radioed Conely, who immediately set out and joined him there shortly before dark.

"There's his motor scooter," said Ulrich, as they peered through the van's windows. But Trash Can Joe was nowhere to be seen. After stashing Conely's patrol vehicle, the wardens climbed into the camper shell of Ulrich's unmarked pickup and began a surveillance of Bass' van that was to last all night.

At 8:30 a.m. the next morning, when Bass had still not returned, Conely set out on foot into the canyon while Ulrich remained with the vehicles. Upon reaching the point where the fire road crossed El Prieto Creek, Conely sat down and waited. A half-hour later, he heard the clatter of a bicycle approaching from up the creek. Sure enough, it was Joe Bass, in full camo, with his bow, a quiver of arrows and a duffle bag slung across his back. Conely watched from cover as the man pedaled by.

"He's coming out," whispered Conely into his radio. "He's carrying a duffle bag, but it looks empty." When Bass reached the trail head, Ulrich had a camcorder running, filming his every move.

When Bass had loaded his bicycle into the van and driven away, Conely discussed the situation with Ulrich. They concluded that they had apparently not gone far enough into the canyon when they had searched for Bass' hunting spot before. This proved to be the case, for upon hiking into the canyon again, beyond the second blind, they located a faint trail leading up a hill. As they followed it and topped the hill, the brush began to close in on them. But someone had begun trimming the brush at this point, stacking the cuttings neatly beside the trail. And then they encountered fresh masking tape across the trail, this time with tiny brass bells clipped to it.

"Can you believe this?" said Conely. "The bears must think he's crazy!"

Then the terrain opened up a bit, and they encountered more masking tape. And at a place where several game trails converged, each with its strip of warning masking tape with either beer cans or bells hanging on it, they spotted a third tree stand. It was immediately apparent that this one was new.

"Here's his bait pile," said Conely. Ulrich followed the other man's gaze and spotted a pile of bakery goods—mainly donuts, old loaves of bread and dinner rolls. But there was rotten meat in the pile as well and a variety of rotting vegetables. Conely wrinkled his nose at the stench.

"I'll bet he was hauling bait in that duffle bag," said Ulrich. Conely agreed.

Upon climbing the 18 or so feet up to the blind, Conely concluded that not only had Bass been there only a short time earlier, but that he was soon to return. There was a small ice chest that still contained ice and a number of unopened beer cans, a tiny barbecue with charcoal, several fresh apples, a tub of butter, a can of sardines, a camera, a flashlight with extra batteries, and several packets containing chemical light-generating devices called "glow sticks." There was also a shelf built above the platform on which was a blanket, a camouflage hat and a can of bug dope.

"He's comin' back tonight," said Conely. "I'd bet on it." Ulrich agreed with him. After thoroughly filming the area with a camcorder, the wardens departed. But they would not be gone for long.

At 5 p.m. that afternoon, after collecting the gear they would need for the operation, Conely and Ulrich returned to the trail head at El Prieto Canyon. Awaiting them there was Warden Bruce Toloski and Lt. Tony Warrington, having arrived a couple of hours earlier to assist. The four of them now made a formidable team—four superb wardens who enjoyed working together. Toloski, at Conely's request, had hiked in and located the new tree stand and collected a sample from Bass' bait pile. After moving the marked patrol vehicles out of sight, Toloski and Warrington settled down to wait. Conely and Ulrich grabbed their gear and set out at a brisk pace for the tree stand.

It was cool in the canyon beneath the trees, the still air fragrant with the spicy scent of sage and chamise. Upon arriving at the stand, the wardens found everything as they had left it a few hours earlier. They spent most of an hour studying the lay of the land, planning for their ambush of Trash Can Joe. But it was a tough place to work. Due to the steep canyon walls and the heavy brush, there was no good place from which they could watch at a safe distance.

"We're gonna have to be right on *top* of him," said Conely with concern. It was true. It was crucial that they see

Bass do something to associate himself with the bait pile, but to do so they would have to be but a few feet away. Neither warden was comfortable with the idea, but there was no other way. So they chose their ground with care, and when Lt. Warrington called to alert them that Bass had just arrived and was on his way in on a bicycle, Conely and Ulrich knew exactly what they had to do.

Conely, wearing camo pants and a green, nylon "raid" jacket, quickly lay down amid some low, sparse vegetation beneath a scrub oak, a mere 20 feet from the bait pile. Ulrich then covered him with leaves and leaf mold until little more than his nose and eyes were visible. Ulrich then stood back and regarded his work.

"You'd better not sneeze," he said. "And if you so much as wiggle, he'll spot you." He then hurried into thick brush and burrowed into a spot they had selected for him. He would be able to see nothing from there, so they would be relying entirely on Conely's observations.

Now it was time for silence. The wardens ceased all movement and conversation, becoming like statues. And the wildlife in the canyon grew quiet as well, as though sensing the tenseness of the situation. Two large coveys of quail on opposite sides of the canyon had been calling to one another, their clear, melodious little voices ringing back and forth through the evening air. But now, even *they* were still.

Beneath his covering of leaves, Conely was fighting a battle with himself—his self discipline pitted against his natural reflexes. Insects had discovered him. A pair of large carpenter ants were exploring his face, and something had entered his sleeve near his wrist and was creeping up his arm. *Probably a tick*, he thought. He gritted his teeth, his eyes squeezed shut as time crawled by.

He sensed the presence of Joe Bass before he saw or heard him. Opening one eye ever so slightly, he saw a sight that chilled his blood. Bass was at a crouch, eyes burning, sneaking toward him, his bow and arrow at the ready. Conely had never experienced such peril, and he knew with certainty that were he to sit up at this moment, Bass would instantly drive a broadhead through his chest. He held his breath.

Then, to Conely's vast relief, Bass, having determined that no bear was sampling his bait pile, relaxed and set his bow on the ground. He then removed a duffle bag from his back, and drew from it several smaller sacks. Conely, with the utmost of care, turned his head slightly so as to better observe Bass' actions. He was in time to see Bass dump the contents of three bulging plastic bags onto the bait pile—mainly donuts. Bass then grabbed an equally bulging burlap sack and walked with it out of Conely's sight, but to some point very close to Conely. The warden now heard climbing sounds and the limbs of the small oak tree above his head began to shake. Then suddenly a terrible smell washed over him, the unmistakable stench of rotting fish. *More bait*, thought Conely. *He hung it in the tree.*

Bass reappeared at the bait pile again with a slender object the length of a pencil in his hand. This he shook vigorously until it began to glow with an eerie green light. He then hung it from a piece of twine over the bait pile. *Light to shoot by when it gets dark*, thought Conely. Bass then gathered his bow, strode to the ladder on the large oak tree bearing his stand, and climbed. The wardens now heard him, 18 feet overhead, busying himself in his stand.

Near sunset, when it appeared certain that Bass was settled comfortably in his tree stand for the night, Ulrich made a careful, whispered radio call to Warrington and Toloski. Within seconds, they had left the parking area and were headed in. Five minutes later, when Conely could bear his torture no longer, he and Ulrich made their move. They burst out of hiding.

"JOE BASS! STATE FISH AND GAME! YOU'RE UNDER ARREST! GET YOUR HANDS UP!" shouted Conely.

Bass leaped up, his hands high above his head. "OK! OK! No problem!" he said, but then he ducked down again, doing something with his hands near the floor of his blind.

Almost instantly, two fully loaded, 16-shot Glock semi-automatic pistols were brought to bear on him.

"GET YOUR HANDS UP, JOE BASS!" repeated Conely.

"OK, man! It's OK!" said Bass, standing briefly, but again he ducked down, doing something the wardens could not see.

"GET YOUR HANDS UP!" shouted Conely again, and *this* time there was sufficient menace in his voice that Bass did as instructed.

"Now climb down from there," said Conely, and Bass descended the rickety ladder to the ground. He then began to subtly resist the wardens, as though to test them.

"Put your hands up and turn around," said Conely. Bass put his hands up, but didn't turn around.

"TURN AROUND!" shouted Ulrich. Bass turned around, hands in the air, but immediately turned back to face Conely, lowering his hands. Bass' passive resistance continued for a minute or more before the wardens finally had their fill of it. They grabbed him and took him down to his knees, but suddenly they noticed smoke and flames up in the tree stand. Both wardens were horrified. The foothills were dry as old bones, and a fire now, at this place, would mean disaster.

"The tree stand!" shouted Joe Bass. "Come on, man, somebody go to the tree stand!"

In a flash of realization, Conely saw it—Bass' plan, his diversion. Conely acted immediately, pushing Bass face down on the ground, cuffing his hands behind his back. He then scrambled up the ladder to the tree stand as Ulrich radioed for the fire department. The blanket and carpeting were fully in flames when Conely arrived on top. He first attempted to smother the fire with an unburnt part of the blanket. When this failed, he grabbed the ice chest and splashed water and ice onto the flames. This knocked down the fire to the point that he was able to finish the job by pouring canned beer and soda on the hot spots.

Finally, it was over. Conely sat back, panting, sadly examining the scorched and blackened holes and melted spots in his new Fish and Game "raid" jacket. Then he noticed the small barbecue. It contained hot coals. Conely was certain that Bass had intentionally put the blanket over the hot coals to set the tree stand on fire so as to create a diversion that would allow him to escape. Sorting through the smoking debris, Conely found a fully loaded .38 caliber revolver, certainly illegal for a bow hunter to possess.

Joe Bass, of course denied everything. "I wasn't huntin', man, I was just scoutin'."

It took the four wardens hours to tag and log all the evidence and to lug it out to the patrol vehicles, and by the time Conely arrived at the county jail and delivered Trash Can Joe to the booking cage, it was crowding midnight.

"What's your name," demanded the jailer.

"I'm Joe Bass, The Black Robinhood."

"The black what?" asked the jailer, peering up from his paperwork.

"The Black Robinhood."

"Yeah, right."

*   *   *

Maureen O'Brien, of the L.A. County DA's Environmental Crimes Unit, was more than a little Irish. She was also more than a little brilliant. Totally confident, superbly articulate, a master of environmental law, she was viewed by the local wardens as the absolute best at her profession. Her method of dealing with wildlife-abusing criminals was simple: She went for their throats. Red-haired, green-eyed, with a ruddy complexion, she had the harmless look of an Irish farm girl. But she could, and often did, verbally destroy unwary defense attorneys. The wardens, upon learning that she would be prosecuting the Joe Bass case, were delighted.

"Wait a minute," she said to Conely, glancing through his report. "Let me get this straight. This guy was dumping donuts in the woods? He was gonna shoot bears eating donuts?"

As she always did, O'Brien pored through the wardens'

reports and became an instant expert on the case. But the Joe Bass case would never come to trial. Bass' first attorney, a large, arrogant man who liked to intimidate shorter, smaller adversaries, attempted to employ this tactic on O'Brien during a pre-trial hearing. When he limped from the courtroom 10 minutes later, he looked as though he had been body-punched. He withdrew from the case. Bass' second attorney, sensing his peril early on, convinced Bass to plead guilty to most of the charges.

During sentencing, an event attended by Joe Bass' wife, O'Brien made a compelling argument for heavy penalties against Bass. The judge saw no reason to disagree, and promptly sentenced Bass to seven months in county jail, fined him $6,000, and ordered his archery gear destroyed. Trash Can Joe blinked his eyes in astonishment, then glanced at his wife, a fierce-looking woman whose unpleasant mood had just turned distinctly ugly. Only an hour earlier he had assured her that he would get off for four or five hundred dollars.

"But you're in luck, Mr. Bass," the judge continued. "Assuming you pay your fine, I'm going to suspend all but a month of your jail term . . . providing, of course, that you comply with the terms of your probation. Those terms are as follows: You are hereby placed on three years probation during which time you can neither hunt nor guide." Bass just stood there, stunned, withering beneath the malignant glare of his wife.

"Let me make sure you understand this, Mr. Bass," the judge continued. "Not only can you not hunt for three years, but you are not to be with others who are hunting. In fact, for three years, you are forbidden to be in any forested area where bear or deer are hunted. Now, do you have any questions?" Trash Can Joe just stood there, looking like a man facing execution.

But when it dawned on him that he was to be immediately taken to jail, his mood perceptibly brightened. When a large bailiff approached him with a set of handcuffs, he gladly thrust out his wrists. And as this same bailiff escorted him

from the courtroom, handcuffed and manacled, he shot one final glance over his shoulder at his wife.
"See you later, dear!"

CALLOUS HEARTS

Antonio Francisco Diaz, eyes smarting from caustic vapors, grimaced as he poured acetone from a gallon can into a large beaker of cloudy liquid. He then leaned close and studied the resulting reaction as an off-white powder began to appear and settle to the bottom—the same addictive, mind-bending substance that in earlier years had destroyed his teeth, reduced him to a walking skeleton and otherwise aged him far beyond his 34 years. Remarkably enough, he had weaned himself from the drug that he now produced only for sale to others. In so doing, he had saved his life. But it would be but a temporary reprieve, for he had breathed the killer fumes of too many homemade drug labs, and even now the first mutant cells had begun to multiply deep within the dark recesses of his meth-cooker's lungs.

Walking out of his cabin, he lit a cigarette and stared vacantly at the snow-covered slopes of Mount Shasta as he considered his immediate future. He then turned and called out to a companion.

"Hey, Paco! Call Julio and the others. We need to go get some meat!"

It was now time for slaughter, for tomorrow, he would make the six-hour drive to sell his dope and visit his mother, and he had learned that venison, like methamphetamine, would convert easily to dollars in the barrios of San Jose. A few minutes later, he grabbed a .22 rifle and stalked toward his pickup.

* * *

James Robertson, at his home on the Gazelle Callahan Road in southern Siskiyou County, was at work at his wood pile when he first heard the popping of small-arms fire. *Not that far away,* he thought, peering in the direction of a low hill that blocked his view. *About six shots from a .22 rifle. Probably ground squirrel shooters.* He had barely resumed his labor with a splitting maul when he heard a vehicle coming his way down the road. He paused again as a blue and white pickup went by. *Probably the shooters*, he thought. About 10 minutes later a sedan approached and turned into his 100 yard-long driveway. He set the maul aside and walked over to meet the vehicle. It contained two strangers, one of whom rolled down his window and spoke.

"Sir, we were just driving by and noticed two deer down in your pasture back up the road. Looks like they've been shot."

Robertson thanked them for the information, considered it briefly as they were driving away, then hurried for the house. From a business card taped to his refrigerator, he read a number, then grabbed his telephone and dialed. Two rings later, he had Warden John Dawson, Department of Fish and Game, on the line. Dawson listened with great interest as Robertson related the information.

"Had to have been the guys in the blue and white pickup," said Robertson, concluding his report.

"I'll be right there," said Dawson. "I'll leave right away." Before leaving, however, Dawson phoned Warden Herb Janney and advised him of the situation. Within five minutes, both wardens were on the road.

Dawson headed south out of Yreka on Interstate 5, then

west, through mixed farm and rangeland and through the tiny community of Gazelle. It was approaching dusk when he rolled into the long driveway on the Gazelle Callahan Road. Robertson climbed into the patrol vehicle with him and directed him back onto the road and to a sharp bend a half-mile beyond the driveway. What first caught Dawson's eye, as he stepped out of the patrol vehicle, were three spotted fawns, all eyes and ears, in high grass in the field beyond the fence. Dawson's heart fell, however, when he saw two still forms near their feet. He climbed through the fence, revulsion rising in his throat like bile. Upon his approach, the three orphaned fawns retreated but a few feet, reluctant to leave their dead mothers. Dawson examined the lifeless does and found small-caliber bullet wounds in their heads and necks. He shook his head, teeth clenched in anger. *Who would shoot does with fawns?* He then regarded the fawns. To Dawson they were a pitiful sight, for suddenly on their own at no more than five months old, their survival was very much in doubt. But at least they looked healthy, except that the smallest of the three had been slightly wounded and bore a bloody, perfectly round bullet hole through her left ear.

Back at the patrol vehicle, Robertson spotted a fired .22 cartridge casing on the road. He pointed it out to Dawson, who picked it up and noted that it had not yet been crushed by traffic. Dawson then placed it in an evidence envelope and turned to face Robertson.

"I think the bad guys will be back tonight," he said. "I'll drop you off, then I'm gonna pick a spot and wait for them."

And so it was that by nightfall, Dawson was in position on a sage-covered hillside where he could see the sharp bend in the road near the dead deer. Fifteen or so miles to the west, Herb Janney was watching the Callahan end of the road, ready to assist in whatever way he could. Both wardens were veterans of many long and usually fruitless stakeouts, but they were to have better luck on this night. Things, in fact, started happening almost immediately.

Dawson saw the headlights off to the west about the same

time he heard the far-away sound of an engine. Other vehicles had passed since dark, but Dawson sensed instantly that *this* one was the one. For one thing, it was traveling unusually slow for the existing conditions, and its exhaust system was a bit louder than normal. To Dawson's disappointment, however, it didn't stop at the sharp turn. But it didn't go far. At a driveway a quarter-mile beyond, it turned around and headed back. This time, as it passed the sharp turn, it slowed nearly to a stop, and Dawson heard two distinct clunking sounds that puzzled him. *Doors slamming? No, it hadn't been that,* he thought. The vehicle then accelerated and continued on. But something had happened. The horses in Robertson's pasture had, for some reason, begun whinnying loudly. When the vehicle had been gone and out of sight for about five minutes, Dawson began to worry. Had he missed something? Had they somehow got away with the deer? Then he heard the vehicle returning, and it soon passed him again, heading towards Gazelle.

When five minutes had passed, and the vehicle had yet to return, Dawson's stomach was again tied in a knot borne of indecision. Had he blown it? Had he waited too long? It was always the same gut-wrenching problem—when to make your move. When to pounce on the bad guys. A wise old warden, years earlier, in response this very question, had provided Dawson with an answer he would never forget: "You trust your instincts," he said. "You make the best decision you can, based on the available information, then you never look back." Dawson had always followed this advice, but it was *never easy*.

On *this* night however, Dawson was spared such a decision, for a radio message suddenly changed the ball game. It was the dispatcher, advising him that a citizen, calling from a phone booth at a gas station in Gazelle, was reporting having seen two Hispanic males dragging two deer through a fence at the Robertson Ranch, toward a blue and white pickup. Dawson was stunned. *How can this be?*

"Tell 'em I'll meet with them there in about 10 minutes," said Dawson into his mike.

Upon his arrival in Gazelle, he was met by a young man, Allen Phillips, who reported that he and his two friends had been driving past the Robertson Ranch and had seen not only the two Hispanics dragging the two deer, but a third Hispanic male behind the wheel of a blue and white pickup parked nearby.

"We stopped and talked with the driver," said Phillips. "We asked him what they were doing, but he said he didn't speak English. I just took down his license number and we left."

Phillips then stated that he and his friends had seen a total of four deer lying along the Gazelle Callahan Road. Dawson was again amazed. How could all of this have been going on right under his nose? But there would be time enough later to piece it all together. For now, he needed to act. It took little convincing on his part to persuade Phillips to ride with him and hopefully identify the suspects. Phillips hopped in, and as they drove, Dawson called in the license number Phillips had given him. It came back to a 1971 Ford pickup, registered to a Julio Nunios, showing a residence in Weed.

Westbound down the Gazelle Callahan Road on this moonless night, Dawson and Phillips overtook another vehicle, a brown Chevy pickup drifting from one side of the road to the other, its driver apparently having trouble navigating.

"Just what we need, a drunk," said Dawson, but before he could take action, a Fish and Game rig appeared, coming from the other direction. It was Janney. Stopping window to window, the two wardens discussed the situation. Dawson related what Phillips had told him, and Janney reported seeing dead deer along the road. Janney, however, had seen no blue and white pickup.

"So, it looks like we have four poacher-killed deer, and the suspects have vanished," said Dawson in frustration. "But my witness here, Mr. Phillips, says that the blue and white pickup never made it to Gazelle, so it still has to be somewhere near this road."

The battle plan now called for Janney to search out the few short side roads which branched off of the Gazelle Callahan Road while Dawson continued searching farther west. As Dawson passed the sharp bend where the deer had been, he was surprised to see that they had been dragged down to the road. He then recalled the clunking noises he had heard earlier in the evening as the blue and white pickup had driven by. *Had someone jumped out of the pickup bed? Or perhaps even two people?* Dawson continued driving west, and it wasn't long before he and Phillips again overtook the brown Chevy pickup. But now, it was parked along the right shoulder, and a Hispanic man was standing near the rear of the vehicle. Dawson pulled in behind it and stopped.

"Good evening, sir," said Dawson, stepping out. "Are you having trouble?"

"No, man. No trouble," said Antonio Diaz, taking measure of the warden.

"Then what are you doing out here tonight?" Dawson inquired, noting an unnatural stiffness in the man.

"We're just on our way home, man. He had to take a leak," said Diaz, indicating a second man who appeared to be urinating near the front of the pickup. A third man sat inside the cab, behind the wheel. Dawson didn't like the feel of the situation, noting an almost palpable tension in the air. Sensing a potentially lethal situation, and shielding his action from Diaz's view, he edged his right hand back to the holster of his 16-shot Glock pistol and popped the safety snap. He was certain he had found his poachers, and he intended to survive the experience.

"Sir, can I see your ID please?" Dawson asked. Diaz dug out his driver's license and handed it to Dawson, who briefly studied it.

"What are you stopping us for? We didn't do nothin'," Diaz complained.

"If you live in Weed, Mr. Diaz, and you're going home,

then why are you going in the wrong direction? Weed's the other way." Diaz's answer was a shrug of his shoulders.

Dawson edged back to the window of the patrol vehicle and spoke to Phillips.

"Do you recognize any of these guys?"

"The guy in the green shirt was driving the blue and white pickup," said Phillips indicating Diaz. "I recognize his voice, too, from when I spoke to him."

Dawson returned to Diaz and called out for the man near the front of the pickup to join them. The man, he would soon identify as Julio Nunios, reluctantly complied, but did his best to remain in shadow. The reason for this soon became apparent, for when he came into harsh light of the patrol vehicle's headlights, Dawson spotted a rust-colored smear on the man's shirt.

"What's that?" said Dawson. "That looks like blood."

After a few seconds of silence, Diaz answered, "So what, man. He cut himself shaving."

Dawson then spotted a much larger smear of blood and what looked like deer hair on the man's pant leg.

"That's it," said Dawson. "You're both under arrest. Turn around and put your hands on the tailgate."

Nunios complied, but Diaz spoke low words in Spanish to Nunios, then began walking toward Dawson, talking as he came.

"Man, I'm not even from around here. What's the problem?"

Dawson took a step back, assumed a combat crouch and shouted, "HOLD IT!" his left hand held up in warning, his right hand resting on his gun. Diaz stopped.

"Now you do *exactly* what I say. First, turn around," and there was more than enough menace in Dawson's voice to convince Diaz that to do otherwise was to risk death or serious injury. He slowly turned until he faced away from Dawson.

"Now, get down on your knees," said Dawson. "NOW!" Diaz complied.

"Hey, man, we didn't do nothin'."

"Just do as I say. Now, cross your ankles and put your hands behind your back." Diaz complied, and Dawson stepped cautiously forward, handcuffs in hand, and snapped them onto Diaz's wrists. Keeping an eye on Nunios and the third man still in the pickup, Dawson hurried back to the patrol vehicle and grabbed two extra sets of handcuffs. He stuffed one set into his back pocket, then approached Nunios. Seconds later, Nunios, too, was handcuffed behind his back, and Dawson turned his full attention to the third man.

"HEY, YOU IN THE TRUCK!" he shouted, maintaining a relatively safe position near the rear of the vehicle. "OPEN THE DOOR AND STICK YOUR HANDS OUT WHERE I CAN SEE THEM!" Perfilio Cabral complied. "NOW STEP OUT SLOWLY!" Cabral complied, and soon found himself handcuffed like his friends.

Returning to the patrol vehicle, Dawson found Phillips beaming with excitement.

"Wow! That was great!" said Phillips.

Dawson grabbed the radio mike and called Janney, advising him that he had three of the suspects in custody, but that the fourth was still at large. He then went to the pickup, made a quick search for weapons and found none.

"Where's the rifle?" he demanded, facing the three men.

"What rifle? We don't have no rifle," said Diaz. "You don't have nothin' on us, man."

"Where's the fourth guy that was with you?"

"Fourth guy? I don't see no fourth guy. Do you?" And so it went. Diaz, becoming more and more hostile and disrespectful, also denied any knowledge of the blue and white pickup.

When Janney arrived, Dawson discussed the situation with him and they agreed that Janney would take Phillips back to Gazelle and collect, on the way, the four dead deer still lying along the Gazelle Callahan Road. They agreed also to call Siskiyou County Sheriff's Office for assistance in transporting the three suspects to the county jail in Yreka.

Soon thereafter, Deputy George Walsh, Siskiyou County

Sheriff's Office, responding to assist the game wardens, passed two Hispanic males, on foot and walking toward Gazelle on the Gazelle Callahan Road. He mentioned this a few minutes later to Janney, upon meeting with him, and Janney, highly interested, set out immediately to contact the two men. Janney, followed closely by Walsh, caught up with the two men about a mile outside of Gazelle. Janney immediately spotted fresh blood on the clothing of both of them, and a pat-down search of the two produced a large folding knife in the pocket of one of them, one Nicholas Avila, a resident of Gazelle. Janney folded the knife-blade out and noted fresh blood and deer hair on it. Avila and his friend soon found themselves handcuffed and seatbelted securely in back seat of Walsh's patrol car.

Dawson, upon learning of the two additional suspects, was delighted. Not only was the missing fourth suspect now accounted for, but there was a bonus fifth suspect as well. But there was still the matter of the missing rifle and the missing blue and white pickup. While Dawson arranged for the towing and impounding of the brown pickup and for a second deputy sheriff to transport suspects, Janney drove by Nicolas Avila's residence in Gazelle. To his delight, the blue and white pickup was parked in the driveway, beside a white pickup.

When the suspects were on their way to jail and the brown pickup was on its way to the impound yard, Dawson joined Janney in Gazelle. Together, they went to Avila's house in hopes of locating the rifle. They first took a preliminary look at the blue and white pickup, and while they could see no rifle, they were surprised and saddened to find, in the bed of the vehicle, the lifeless bodies of two more freshly killed deer—one doe and one fawn. Dawson gave a low whistle.

Upon knocking on the door of Avila's house, they got no response. But there were lights on at a neighbor's house, so they went there. A resident of this home turned out to be Nicholas Avila's landlord, and he was full of information. The landlord claimed that late that afternoon he had seen

Avila and several other subjects standing between the two vehicles, and that one of the men was carrying a rifle. He said that the white truck belonged to one of the other men in the group and it appeared as if all of them had just returned from squirrel hunting. Dawson asked him about the rifle, and the landlord said that he thought it had gone into one of the two pickups.

Following a thorough, but fruitless, search of the blue and white pickup, Janney turned his attention to the white one. Behind the seat, he found a fully loaded Winchester .22 caliber rifle. The wardens also seized Budweiser beer cans from both vehicles. They had found Budweiser cans at the crime scenes as well, where deer had been dragged down to the road. On the bottoms of all of these cans were lot numbers. The lot numbers on *all* of the cans matched perfectly—more evidence against the suspects.

The blue and white pickup also went to the impound yard that night before the wardens were finally able to knock off. Both seized vehicles would be thoroughly examined and photographed by the wardens the following morning in the light of day. And there would be bullets to be dug from the deer carcasses, and bloody clothing to be photographed and reports to be written. But for now, at least, their work was done.

"Six deer, five suspects. Not bad!" said Dawson to Janney as they parted company and headed home. But for Dawson, at least, sleep would not come easily on this night, for he found himself haunted by the eyes of the orphaned fawns, suddenly left alone to fend for themselves in a very hostile and unforgiving world.

* * *

One chilly morning, weeks later, Dawson pulled into the parking lot of the courthouse in Weed. As always, when an important case of his was to be heard in court, he had a feeling of foreboding, for anything could happen. On this day the five suspects were there, looking meek and repentant, in stark contrast to the defiant, remorseless men he had observed the night of their crimes. But when he caught Diaz's eye for a brief moment, he knew it was all an act. He felt his anger rise, and it rose higher as he remembered his return to the scene of the poaching on the morning following the arrests. Two fawns had been struck and killed on the road there during the night, a stone's throw from where he had last seen the *orphaned* fawns, and the memory of dragging the small carcasses off of the pavement tore at his heart. *But what of the third one?*

As it happened, Dawson left the courtroom that day in a better mood, feeling that justice had in fact been done. The judge, it seems, had ignored the poor-ignorant-us routine the defendants were trying to sell him and had correctly concluded that he was facing some particularly callous-hearted violators. Like the wardens, he was particularly offended by the killing of does with fawns. He expressed his displeasure by sentencing each of the five men to 15 days in jail, a $1,500 fine, plus the loss of hunting and fishing privileges for three years. Additionally, they were to be subject to warrant-less search by the wardens for three years, and should they break any laws during this time, they would automatically receive an additional 90 days in jail.

Despite the sentence, Antonio Diaz flashed Dawson an insolent smile as he and the others were led away by the bailiff. But it was a smile cut short by a fit of coughing, a deep rasping hack that had begun a few weeks earlier. It seemed to be growing worse.

* * *

It was about a month later when drug enforcement officers from Siskiyou County Sheriff's Office raided a suspected drug lab in a cabin just outside of the town of Weed. They found no significant quantity of actual methamphetamine there, but there was a staggering amount of glassware and chemical byproducts from the manufacture of the drug—enough to send the resident of the place to prison for a long while. The resident, however, was not there at the time, and he at least temporarily avoided capture. According to a neighbor, the man was in San Jose, visiting his mother.

* * *

It was a year and a half later when Dawson again found himself near the Robertson Ranch on the Gazelle Callahan road. It was a particularly nice day in early summer, and the fields and hillsides had not yet lost their green. As he rounded a bend, he was in time to see a doe dash across the road pursued by two spotted, spindly-legged fawns. With an easy bound, the doe sailed over the barbed-wire fence, and the fawns dove between the lower strands. Then they stopped on the hillside beyond the fence and looked back. Dawson felt a pang in his heart, a bittersweet thing as he recalled other fawns he had seen near this spot. But then he looked at the doe and something caught his eye. Could it be? Sure enough, and his spirits suddenly soared, for as she stood there, statue-still, backlit by a blue summer sky, he could clearly see, in her left ear, a tiny hole the diameter of a pencil.

"Good for you, girl," said Dawson. "Good for you!"

LUCKY BREAKS

Senior Trooper Walt Markee, at his desk in the Salem office of the Oregon State Police, sat pondering a handwritten list he held before him. The list, which consisted of the names of 16 of the most despicable game-law violators in the Western states, was the result of months of hard work—interviewing informants, debriefing undercover operatives, poring over arrest reports, piecing together the countless bits of information that came his way from an endless variety of sources. Markee, an aggressive investigator with a gift for total focus, pursued his work with OSP's Fish and Wildlife Division with the same fierce intensity that in college had won him back to back Pac-10 wrestling championships.

Running a finger down the list, his attention was drawn to the name Rodney Charles Grogan. Rod Grogan, an outlaw houndsman and bear guide, was an Oregon resident and had at one time contracted with the state to hunt stock-killing bears and mountain lions. But those days ended when he came under the scrutiny of the State Police. He was now into the exploitation of bears and mountain lions for money. He usually guided Asians who responded to the ads for *guaranteed bear hunts* that he ran in the Korean Central Daily Newspaper in Los Angeles. Most of these clients had little interest in actually killing a bear, but would gladly pay Grogan's $800 to $1,000 guide fee simply to get their hands on the bear's gallbladder. Grogan himself was often the trigger man, illegally shooting the bear after his pack of well trained hounds had run the animal up a tree. Grogan would then perform minor surgery on the bear and present the animal's gallbladder to the happy client. Sometimes they would take the paws of the bear as well, which were also valuable, or the head and hide. But usually nearly all of the animal was left to spoil.

It was a growing problem. Greedy men like Grogan had discovered the high value of certain animal parts and were slaughtering wildlife at an alarming rate to reap the profits. Dried bear gall, for instance, was worth more than cocaine. It was to this problem that Markee had applied his full attention for more than two years, identifying the players, zeroing in on the worst of the worst. And now it was time to put the screws to them. In the case of Grogan, who had been operating mainly in northern California of late, Markee decided to get help from his counterparts in California.

In August of 1997, at the State Police office in Medford, Markee met with John Dawson, a highly respected veteran California Fish and Game warden. Dawson, like Markee, was a superb investigator and had considerable experience in dealing with the likes of Rod Grogan. Markee briefed Dawson on what he knew about Grogan and two other suspects who often hunted with the man. Markee also spoke of an Asian man in Los Angeles whom he suspected was a main buyer of bear parts from Grogan. Dawson then advised Markee of potentially useful contacts he had in the Los Angeles Police Department.

Upon returning to California, Dawson approached his Captain, Doug Buchanan, and briefed him on the situation, asking for support. "It could be expensive to do this right," said Dawson.

Buchanan thought for a few seconds, then said, "Go for it! Do what you have to do. I'll cover you."

Dawson began his investigation by confirming through

Fish and Game that Rodney Grogan possessed not only a valid non-resident hunting license, but was licensed as a hunting guide in California as well. Dawson then checked with the U.S. Forest Service in Yreka and determined that Grogan had not bothered to apply for the commercial use permit that was required of hunting guides operating in national forests. This was important, because it appeared that Grogan was fond of hunting in the national forests.

In mid-September, two weeks prior to the opening of bear season, Dawson flew to Los Angeles and met with two very specialized L.A. cops. Ron Kim and Ross Arai were assigned to L.A. Police Department's Asian Crimes Investigation Unit. Kim was a first generation Korean-American. He spoke heavily accented English and appeared to Dawson to be perfect for the job at hand. Arai, Japanese-American, lacked Kim's natural accent, but he was a veteran undercover operative and very good at it.

Concerned over the possibility that Ron Kim, because of his parent's culture, could be sympathetic toward bear parts dealers, Dawson asked him outright, "Are you sure you won't have any problems with this?" Kim returned a steady gaze and said, "No problems."

Kim began by telephoning Grogan in Oregon, answering the man's ad in the Korean newspaper. Within minutes he arranged with Grogan an October date for a guided bear hunt. Kim then asked Grogan if he could bring a friend along just to watch. Grogan agreed.

On a cool morning a month later, Kim and Arai met with Grogan and an assistant at a mini-market in the mountain town of McCloud. Both Dawson and Markee were nearby to observe what they could. The two-day hunt went down much as Dawson had predicted it would. Kim and Arai rode in a pickup driven by the assistant, Billy John Hicks, a big, dirty hillbilly with body odor like rancid grease. Upon reaching the hunting place, a rough and heavily forested area in the Shasta-Trinity National Forest, Grogan set out on his own, with his dogs, on a quad-runner equipped, front and rear, with dog boxes. On the second day, upon finally locating a fresh bear track, he released his dogs and radioed Hicks by CB.

"I've got a good one goin'. Go ahead and turn loose."

Hicks, who had already heard the distant baying of Grogan's dogs, hurried to the rear of his pickup, dropped the tailgate, then removed four more hounds from the pickup's built-in dog boxes. As he did so, he checked that the radio collar on each dog was transmitting. The dogs milled around only briefly behind the truck, then dashed away to join the chase, their own melodious bawling ringing off the canyon walls.

Two hours later, Kim and Arai stood at the base of a huge pine tree, peering up at a bear in its dense, needled branches. Grogan and Hicks first tied up the dogs, then Hicks handed Kim a rifle, a big, lever-action, .45-70 equipped with a scope, to shoot the bear. At the shot, the bear tumbled down, crashing through the lower branches of the pine tree and striking the ground with a loud thump.

"Here, take this," said Grogan, handing Kim a big, stainless steel, .44 Magnum revolver he had drawn from a shoulder holster. "Shoot it again!" Kim handed the rifle to Hicks, then approached the bear cautiously, took aim and fired a bullet into its head. When it was clear the bear was truly dead, Grogan pulled a small folding knife from his pocket and began skinning the animal. He left the feet and head on the hide so that it could later be made into a rug. With this done, he opened the body cavity, located the gallbladder, tied off the bile duct with string, then sliced the organ free from the liver.

"Here you go!" he said, presenting it to Kim. Held by the tied-off bile duct, the gallbladder looked like a large, greenish-blue-colored fig.

"I would like to have one too," said Arai, facing Grogan. "Can you get me one? I will pay."

Grogan studied him closely for a few seconds, then said, "It's against the law to sell galls."

"OK. I understand," said Arai, turning away.

But later, Grogan caught Arai alone and told him, "If

you really want some galls, I'm comin' to L.A. in November. How many do you want? Small ones cost $500. Big ones are $800."

"I just want one for myself, a big one," said Arai. Grogan said he could deliver the gall, but he asked Arai to not mention the deal to either Kim or Hicks.

Before leaving the woods that day, Grogan fed a small part of the naked bear carcass to his dogs. He also carved out a small roast from one of the bear's hams and gave it to Kim, telling him it was the best part of the bear. They then hiked back to the vehicles, leaving over 100 pounds of bear meat to rot on the forest floor.

That night, Kim and Arai met with Dawson and Markee and turned over to them the gallbladder and the bear head and skin. Dawson unfolded a map of the national forest in hopes that Kim and Arai could determine where the hunt had taken place and the location of the wasted bear carcass. But it was soon clear that neither man had any idea where they had been. And they were both exhausted from what had been something of an ordeal.

Upon the departure of Kim and Arai, Markee and Dawson discussed the situation and agreed that there was little to do now on the Grogan case except to wait. At worst, they could already charge Grogan with waste of game and illegal guiding in the national forest, but with luck he would sell Arai a gallbladder. In so doing, he would commit a felony under California law.

With the Grogan case on hold, Dawson resumed his duties in his own patrol district in Siskiyou County. Bear season was still open, and there was much to do for a hardworking mountain warden. One chilly morning in mid-November, Dawson was patrolling the forest roads above McKinney Creek, following fresh vehicle tracks. It had rained the night before, obliterating all previous vehicle tracks on the roads. The first set of tracks he followed led to some wood cutters, hard at it with chain saws. The next set, however, led him up a side road where he encountered a blue pickup that he recognized instantly. Hicks had been driving it the weekend of the hunt with Kim and Arai. It was a hound-rig, with Washington plates and built-in dog boxes, parked at a locked gate. When Dawson pulled to a stop behind it, a large, big-bellied man he recognized as Hicks climbed out and faced him nervously.

"Good morning, sir. State game warden. Are you doing some hunting?"

"I'm just waitin' for my friends," said Hicks, who went on, at Dawson's urging, to explain that he and three others had released their dogs on a small bear early that morning and that the other three men were now looking for the dogs.

"We finally got a weak signal on 'em that-a-way," said Hicks, pointing up the road beyond the gate.

Dawson gently prodded the man for information and soon learned that one of the three men out looking for dogs was Rod Grogan. Dawson wasn't surprised, but he greeted this information with mixed emotions. He was intrigued by the possibility of catching Grogan in the act of some kind of violation, but he didn't want to spook the man from the felony crime of selling a gall to Arai.

"What about you?" said Dawson. "Do you have your hunting license and bear tags?"

"I got my license, but my tag's already on a bear back at our camp. Can you validate it for me?"

Dawson consented to validate Hick's bear, and he followed the man a mile or so to a substantial camp hidden back in the trees. Dawson took advantage of the drive to the camp to radio Warden Jake Bushey, advising him of the situation and asking that he come and drive the higher roads above McKinney Creek where the outlaws had probably struck the bear's trail. Dawson fully expected Hicks to communicate with Grogan by CB radio during the drive to the camp, but he knew this would happen sooner or later and there was nothing he could do to prevent it.

The camp consisted of a large military-surplus tent pitched in a small clearing. Dawson noted two pickups there, including Grogan's, and a small utility trailer. The quadrunner Grogan used, however, was missing. Hicks brought out a bear head and skin, and Dawson was surprised at the huge size of it. It was legally tagged, however, and Dawson signed his name on the tag and pulled a small tooth from the massive head. Biologists would use the tooth to age the animal at some later date.

"That's the biggest bear I've seen in a while," said Dawson as he grabbed a camera from his truck. "Here, let me get your picture with it. I'll send you a copy." Hicks readily knelt beside the huge head and skin, and Dawson snapped a photo. He now had Hicks on film.

Dawson questioned Hicks further concerning his and Grogan's plans and learned that they intended to strike camp and depart for Oregon later that day. When it appeared there was nothing more to be gleaned from Hicks, Dawson left the man in camp and returned to the locked gate for a closer look at the area. He had advised Hicks of his intention, and Hicks had said that he, too, would return to the gate to pick up his friends.

At the gate, Dawson stepped out of his patrol vehicle and examined the ground. He immediately identified three fresh sets of man tracks leading around the gate and up the road. Each track was distinctive in size and pattern, and as Dawson followed them up the road, he made mental note of more subtle things concerning the tracks, like the relative lengths of each man's stride.

About this time, he heard Hicks' pickup return to the gate and shut down. Concerned that Grogan and friends might return to the gate by some different route, Dawson took a position close enough to the gate that he could hear them should they return. While he waited, Bushey radioed and advised him that he had located a quad-runner that was undoubtedly Grogan's. Soon thereafter, Dawson heard Hicks start his engine and depart, and not long after that, he heard what was probably the same vehicle on another road deeper in the canyon. At one point he heard it pause, and he heard a door slam. *He picked 'em up*, thought Dawson with certainty.

In assessing the situation, Dawson concluded that

Grogan and the others were intentionally avoiding him, and that Hicks had indeed communicated with them. They had obviously been up to no good and had committed some crime against wildlife, and Dawson had no doubts about what it had been. He knew, based on the totality of the situation, including what Markee had told him about Grogan, that they had probably killed a bear somewhere, most likely a small one, and had taken only the saleable parts of the animal and left the rest to rot. He was certain of it. Sensing that no good would come from his contacting Grogan and the others at their camp, Dawson set about the staggering task of locating a dead bear in 30 or 40 square miles of forest—a needle in a haystack. He therefore picked up the trail of the three men again and began what were to be several hours of serious and difficult tracking.

The sun had reached its zenith in blue sky to the south as Dawson left the road, following the three sets of tracks up a skid trail. It was more difficult now, the skid trail being covered with a blanket of fir and pine needles. But it was when the tracks left the skid trail and continued out through the forest that Dawson's considerable tracking skills were taxed to the limit. For there were no longer tracks to be seen, but only small disturbances to the forest floor—a slight scuff here, a disturbed leaf there. For a while, it became easy again when the trail led over ground covered with tiny brown mushrooms, some of which had been kicked over by the hiking men. But more often it was a painstakingly slow process, the trail often simply vanishing. He would then return to the last definite sign he had found, mark the spot with his hat, then search outward from there in ever expanding circles until he again found some small sign of the trail.

It helped, however, that Dawson had by now determined the general direction Grogan had been heading. And Hicks had said, probably truthfully, that Grogan had picked up a faint signal from the radio collars on the dogs. A faint signal could mean that the dogs were very far away, or it could mean that they had been down in some deep canyon. But the dogs could have still been moving at that time, in which case they could have ended up miles away.

Hours passed. At one point the trail led to the intersection of two small canyons. Dawson was confused here for a short time until he determined that there were tracks leading up one canyon to his right and more tracks leading down the one to his left. Believing that he must be close to his goal, he continued, staying to the right. Soon these tracks left the bottom of the canyon and started up toward the ridge top that separated the two canyons. Upon reaching the top, the going got tough, for the ridge was covered with dense stands of manzanita. At times Dawson had to crawl along under the canopy of brush, but at least the marks of passage left by the outlaws were easy to follow here, for they, too, had been forced to crawl. Upon emerging from the manzanita, the trail vanished. The ground was hard now, mostly exposed rock, and Dawson, after spending considerable time searching in the now dwindling daylight, had to face the sad fact that he would have give it up and start back. The sun was well below the timbered ridges to the southwest when he arrived back at his patrol truck.

The next day, Dawson returned to the area, checking first the road leading to the locked gate. His own tire tracks from the evening before had been the last ones. No one had driven the road since then. He then drove the other roads in the area, and determined that none had been driven since the day before. The camp was gone, the outlaws having apparently cleared out the night before. They had not returned. This was a bit surprising to Dawson, for he felt strongly that the outlaws had killed a bear and taken its gallbladder. And because Grogan had been aware of Dawson's presence in the area, Hicks having undoubtedly warned him by radio, he would not have risked bringing a gallbladder out of the woods. It had to still be there somewhere, probably hanging in a tree, and Grogan would likely return for it. But he hadn't, at least not yet.

On day three, following Dawson's encounter with Hicks,

Dawson again returned to the area, this time accompanied by Warden Herb Janney. They went directly to the ridge top where Dawson had lost the trail two days earlier. They searched for tracks farther up the ridge and could find none. After pondering the situation for a while, Janney had an idea.

"Maybe they came up here on this ridge just to listen for the dogs or try to get a better signal on their tracking box."

"Certainly possible," said Dawson. "Lets go back down, and I'll show you the other tracks I found coming out."

It was on their way down the opposite side of the ridge that they encountered a single set of man tracks apparently leading into yet another canyon. As they began their slow descent into this canyon, following the ever-so-faint trail, Dawson spotted a tree that drew his immediate interest. It was a huge sugar pine, standing somewhat by itself, the type of tree that Dawson had learned were often chosen and climbed by closely pursued bears. Upon approaching it, he knew instantly that his search had ended, for the ground around the base of the tree had been torn by the feet of a number of excited dogs.

"They treed here," said Dawson as Janney approached. "Here's where he went up." Dawson pointed to the tree trunk where claw marks and torn bark marked the bear's ascent. Upon careful examination of the ground around the tree, the wardens found man tracks and smears of blood, but an initial search of the surrounding area failed to turn up the remains of the killed bear.

"It has to be around here someplace," said Dawson. And then he noticed a shallow gully not far away. Something there didn't look quite right. He walked to the spot and found rocks and sticks covering something at the head of the gully. It took him only a few seconds to clear away enough of the rocks to reveal the carcass of a bear buried there. The wardens quickly dragged it into the light of day.

"The gall's missing," said Dawson, examining the slit in the bear's belly. "And they obviously hacked some meat off to feed their dogs."

"This thing's been half skinned," said Janney. "Why didn't they finish the job? It's a nice hide."

"Hicks probably called them on the CB right about then," said Dawson. "That would also explain why they tried to hide it so carefully."

Needing other equipment, the wardens made a round trip hike to their vehicles, returning with a camera, extra film and a metal detector. While Dawson took a series of evidence photos, Janney began passing the metal detector back and forth across the carcass. In the area below the bear's left ear, the detector suddenly let out a squawk, then again as Janney pinpointed the spot. Dawson drew a small knife, sliced open the hide and flesh at that spot and found a spent bullet. It was a heavy, copper-jacketed pistol bullet, now mushroom-shaped.

"Probably .44 Mag," said Dawson. He left the bullet in place, pointing to it with the knife as Janney snapped a photo.

The wardens concluded their investigation by taking a meat sample for possible DNA testing. They then hiked back to their vehicles. They were standing by their patrol vehicles, both men in full uniform, when they heard a vehicle approaching. When it appeared around a bend, its driver spotted the wardens, hit the brakes, hurriedly turned around and sped away. Dawson recognized it instantly as Rod Grogan's green pickup, having seen it in McCloud and again two days earlier at the camp with Hicks. Dawson leaped into his vehicle, spun it around and took off in pursuit.

It was a three-mile chase at dangerously high speeds for the primitive road before Dawson was able to stop the vehicle with his red light. He then approached the driver's window and got his first face-to-face look at Rod Grogan. A second occupant of the pickup was a man Dawson had never seen before.

"Why are you guys runnin' from us today?" demanded Dawson after identifying himself.

"We weren't runnin'," said Grogan, highly nervous.

"We're just out lookin' for a lost dog."

When Janney arrived, the wardens separated the two men and questioned them concerning their activities two days earlier. But the men had obviously rehearsed a story and they stuck to it. They denied any knowledge of who might have killed a bear, claiming that their dogs had failed to tree a bear on that day. With plenty of probable cause to search Grogan's pickup, the wardens did so, hoping to find a .44 Magnum pistol to match the bullet they had found in the dead bear. But there was no pistol or other conclusive evidence. The wardens had to let the two men go on their way.

That night, Dawson called Markee and filled him in on the events of the last three days. Markee was at first aghast to learn that Dawson had intentionally tangled with Grogan, the subject of an ongoing undercover operation. But Dawson's logic was undeniable: Grogan would have thought it highly suspicious had Dawson acted any other way. Markee was intrigued about the dead bear and the pistol bullet, but quickly concluded, as had Dawson, that there was no way, based on the current evidence, to connect Grogan with the death and wanton waste of the McKinney Creek bear. They would need more evidence, some lucky break.

The lucky break came two days later when Markee made a follow up call to Ron Kim, in Los Angeles. As Kim was again relating what had taken place during the guided hunt with Grogan, he happened to mention that he had finished off the bear with a pistol, a fact that he had failed to mention to the wardens before.

"Wait a minute!" said Markee, straightening up in his chair. "Run that by me again!"

Kim explained that he had thought it unimportant before, the fact the Grogan had provided him a pistol for the final shot.

"What kind of pistol?" Markee asked anxiously.

"Just a big, stainless steel revolver," said Kim.

Following his conversation with Kim, Markee immediately

called Dawson, who was overjoyed to learn of the possibility that a bullet from Grogan's gun might be in the head of the bear Kim had killed during the guided hunt. Dawson immediately retrieved the head and hide from a cold-storage evidence locker and was dismayed to find that it had been frozen, head down, in an ice chest and was now a solid block of ice. Three long days later, when the head and hide had finally thawed sufficiently, Dawson stood by as his captain, Doug Buchanan, prepared to run a metal detector over the head of Kim's bear. Dawson leaned close as Buchanan made the first pass with the detector. And when the machine let out a cheerful squawk, Dawson leaped into the air, shouting "YES!" at the top of his lungs. He then sliced into the flesh near the bear's left cheek and revealed a perfectly mushroomed pistol bullet that was the identical twin to the one he had found in the McKinney Creek bear.

The following day, Dawson drove the two evidence bullets to the Wildlife Forensics Laboratory in Ashland, Oregon. Senior Forensics Scientist Mary Mann, a world-renowned expert in ballistics, took one look at them and said, "Those look like .44 Magnum Noslers, partition style hollow-points, probably 240 grain." Dawson was impressed with her instant assessment which would later prove correct, and he looked on as she peered through the twin barrels of a dissecting scope, examining the bullets under high magnification. "Left twist," she said. "Probably fired from a Smith & Wesson revolver."

But there was a *third* bullet to be examined on that day, the result of a remarkable coincidence. During the time Dawson had been anxiously awaiting the thawing of Kim's bear, Walt Markee had a chance phone conversation with a friend of his, Scott Salisbury, an OSP trooper on the Oregon coast. Markee mentioned the Grogan case to him, aware that Salisbury knew of Grogan's past contract hunting for the state. Salisbury, upon learning that a bullet, probably from Grogan's gun, had been found in the McKinney Creek bear, astounded Markee by announcing that he, too, had a bullet from Grogan's .44 Magnum handgun.

"About two years ago, he hunted a stock-killing lion for us, and when I skinned the lion, I found a bullet. I saved it. It's in my evidence locker."

Markee, astonished over yet another lucky break, had immediately driven to Florence, Oregon, picked up the bullet from Salisbury and took it to the lab in Ashland.

As Mary Mann examined the three bullets, she made a preliminary observation.

"I think it's highly probable that all three of these bullets were fired from the same gun," she said. "But I'll need to test the gun to make a definite match."

"Highly probable," however, was not enough to convict Grogan in court. Markee and Dawson later discussed the situation at length and made a decision. For whatever reason, their hoped for sale by Grogan of a gallbladder to Arai had not happened, and they lacked enough evidence against Grogan to convict him of the killing and wanton waste of the McKinney Creek bear. But they had more than enough probable cause to go for a search warrant for Grogan's house. They would search for not only Grogan's Magnum pistol, but for evidence of his trafficking in bear gallbladders.

Because Grogan was an Oregon resident, the demanding task of writing the search warrant fell upon Markee. But Markee could write search warrants in his sleep. He was, in fact, at that moment, putting the finishing touches on 15 other search warrants for the homes of 15 other Oregon scoundrels nearly as bad as Grogan. Because many of the worst of the bear-killing outlaws were in close touch with one another, Markee wanted to hit them all at the same time. It was a typical Markee operation—16 search warrants to be served simultaneously, his philosophy being, "Why take singles when you can flock-shoot 'em?"

And so it was, on the appointed day, at the appointed time, over 100 law enforcement officers from eight agencies descended upon the homes of the 16 unsuspecting outlaws. Dawson was among those who hit Grogan's place. Grogan's surprise was complete, and he could only watch, sickened, as cops and wardens searched every inch of his house. Dawson had no trouble locating the big Smith & Wesson revolver on a shelf in a bedroom, and he seized this and all the ammunition for it into evidence. And there was paper evidence of Grogan's outlaw practices as well, various guide's documents, all apparently falsified. All in all, it was probably the worst day of Grogan's life.

A week later, the report returned from the forensics lab in Ashland. Mary Mann had concluded, beyond any doubt, that all three of the evidence bullets had been fired from Grogan's revolver. Grogan was now securely tied to the McKinney Creek bear, and Dawson's remarkable determination had paid off. But as it turned out, the hopes of Dawson and Markee that they would end up with a felony bear case against Grogan never materialized. He never sold a gall to Arai, and the search of his home yielded no further evidence that he was dealing in bear parts. What remained was a collection of misdemeanor violations against the man, charges that would ultimately cost him nearly $10,000 in fines and loss of his California hunting privileges for three years—just enough punishment to turn an outlaw like Grogan into simply a more careful outlaw.

But as often happens, real justice for a serious violator comes from some unexpected quarter. In Grogan's case, it came as a result of the search of Grogan's home, when a deputy assigned the task of drawing a map of the house noticed a discrepancy in wall measurements. This resulted in his discovery of a false wall in a large closet. Upon removing the false wall, officers found a ladder leading up into a secret room in the attic. The room was equipped with everything necessary for the indoor cultivation of marijuana—grow lights, fans, reflectors, fertilizer and a watering system. And in a refrigerator at the far end of the room were several carefully weighed Ziploc bags of green leafy plant material.

Months later, following long days with judges and attorneys, Grogan emerged from a courtroom a genuine felon, convicted of the sale and cultivation of marijuana. But he might as well have been convicted of selling bear galls, for the result was the same. If he chose to hunt again, he would either have to shoot arrows or throw rocks, for as a convicted felon he was now forbidden forever from using or possessing firearms.

The benefit to wildlife from such a conviction is beyond measure. But at the very least, in Grogan's case, his guiding days were over, and the 18 to 25 bears he would have killed each year for their gallbladders would now be spared. To Dawson and Markee, this was quite enough.

RASCAL'S ROAD TO JUSTICE

"You gotta be kidding," said Lieutenant James Halber. "Rascal McRoy? That's really his name?"

"Well, that's what everybody calls him," said the informant. "I know the McRoy part is right, but I think his first name might really be Rosco."

"And people really pay to hunt ducks with him?" said Halber.

"That's right," said the informant. "He's a good duck caller. In fact, he claims to be the best duck caller in the world."

"Now, tell me again what he's doing," said Halber.

"Well, he always takes the plug out of his shotgun, and he always uses lead shot. He hunts in the rice fields east of Richvale where the land's really flat. He can see a warden coming from a long way in any direction from his blind, and he keeps a sharp lookout. If he sees a warden, he tosses his lead shells, and he puts his plug back in."

Halber was well aware of this type of violator. State and federal law, years earlier, had banned the use of lead shot shells for hunting waterfowl due to the high losses of ducks and geese to lead poisoning. Outlaws like McRoy, however, continued to use lead shot because of its range advantage over the legal steel shot. The McRoy types were also apt to remove the magazine plugs from their shotguns so that their guns could hold five shells instead of the maximum three allowed by law. This gave them another advantage over honest hunters.

"And he shoots over his limit whenever he can and brags about it," the informant continued. "He keeps a little hibachi grill in his blind. He likes to breast out some of the ducks he shoots and he cooks them right there in his blind."

Halber was aware of the hibachi trick as well. With a four-duck bag limit, a pair of unscrupulous violators could breast out and eat a limit of ducks without leaving their blind. They could then stomp the carcasses into the mud and shoot another limit, with little risk of being caught.

"He also brags that you wardens will never catch him again," said the informant. "He says he's too smart for you," and at that moment a pair of tiny cross-hairs in Halber's brain shifted, as on a gun turret, until they were trained directly on his mind's-eye image of Rascal McRoy.

That same day, Halber climbed onto a four-wheeler ATV and visited the rice ground between Richvale and Highway 99. The vast, harvested rice fields in the area were flooded now, separated from one another by tiny earthen levees called "checks." It was on these checks that waterfowl hunters, surrounded by duck and goose decoys, shot from sunken steel blinds they called tanks. Halber spotted two sets of tanks in the area that the informant had described as being McRoy's hunting grounds. Of these, each skillfully camouflaged with grass and tules, Halber eliminated one, due to the unskilled placement of its decoy spread. The other had to be McRoy's.

The ground there was indeed difficult for the wardens to work, open and flat, with no cover. But there was always a way, Halber had learned. It was just a matter of how much time and money the wardens were willing to invest to catch one violator. In *this* case, he decided, a single piece of equipment would do the trick—a piece of equipment worth about a half-million dollars.

Upon returning to his office, Halber picked up the

telephone and dialed Sgt. Ron Chaplin, a helicopter pilot for the Butte County Sheriff's Office. Chaplin was always willing to assist another agency, and Halber smiled at the recollection of some of the adventures he and Chaplin had shared. A mere two months earlier, when he and Chaplin were returning in the helicopter from a salmon survey on the Feather River south of Oroville, they experienced some memorable action. As they were passing over the Oroville Wildlife Area, a state recreation area closed to all off-road vehicles, they spotted two young men racing along, tandem, on a dirt bike motorcycle. Not only was this a clear violation of state law, but visitors to the wildlife area had of late been plagued by vehicle break-ins. The thieves were thought to be using dirt bikes and making their getaways off-road. Chaplin, at Halber's urging, immediately swung the helicopter around in pursuit.

It was a chase of which Hollywood would have been proud, with the dirt bike speeding along through the off-road trees and brush, zigging, zagging, spinning brodies to reverse direction, the terrified passenger peering skyward as the helicopter careened along in close pursuit. Unwilling to lead his pursuers to his home, the dirt bike driver kept to the wildlife area where he finally aimed the bike into heavy brush, laid it down, and he and his passenger fled on foot.

"Can you set us down there," said Halber pointing to a small clearing.

"No problem," said Chaplin, and as soon as they touched down, Halber leaped out and dashed into the brush. He soon found the motorcycle, but the suspects were well away. He paused only briefly to consider the situation, then pulled the motorcycle upright and wheeled it back to the helicopter. He pushed it astraddle of the helicopter's skid, leaned it against the hull, then climbed aboard, belted himself in and nodded to Chaplin. The engine whined, the rotors thrashed the air and the craft lifted skyward, with Halber leaning out the door, hanging onto the motorcycle's handlebar with one hand. From hiding, the suspects could only watch in dismay as their dirt bike departed without them.

Unwilling to risk dropping a motorcycle through someone's roof, Chaplin chose an uninhabited route back to the Oroville Airport, where they landed, had a good laugh, and stashed the captured dirt bike in a hanger. Two days later, a sheepish young man came to claim the bike. Halber, unable to link him with the car burglaries, returned the bike to him, but not before issuing him a citation for its illegal use on the wildlife area.

Halber was still grinning at the recollection as Chaplin answered the phone.

"Are you in the mood for some adventure?" said Halber.

Chaplin, who lived a steady *diet* of adventure, said "What do you have in mind?" Halber filled him in concerning Rascal McRoy.

"You gotta be kidding," said Chaplin. "That's really his name?"

Halber, in putting the finishing touches on his plan, had discussed the matter with Agent Joe Sandberg, U.S. Fish and Wildlife Service. Sandberg was a tireless protector of wildlife and one of the best undercover operatives Halber had ever known. Halber was surprised to learn that Sandberg not only knew all about McRoy, but had actually walked up on the man in his blind a year earlier in the fog and had caught him with the plug out of his shotgun. Sandberg readily accepted an invitation to help with the helicopter raid.

The plan to capture Rascal McRoy was executed the following Saturday. Cold wind and rain pelted the valley during the early morning hours, but it cleared somewhat a little later. When Sandberg spotted McRoy's pickup parked near the hunting area, Halber and Chaplin decided the operation was a go. As Halber pulled a camo parka over his uniform jacket and climbed into the helicopter, Sandberg and two state wardens on ATVs deployed to their assigned positions. Chaplin went through his checklist, and soon, accompanied by the whine of an accelerating engine, the rotors began to turn. They were up and away in seconds in a steel-gray sky, and Rascal McRoy was within a few minutes of one of the major surprises of his life.

Skimming along at low altitude, the last vestiges of the Sierra foothills flashing below them, they soon reached the vast patchwork of winter-brown, flooded rice ground that was the Sacramento Valley. A minute later Halber pointed, Chaplin made a course correction and the targeted tanks appeared, clearly occupied. Chaplin slid the helicopter in close, but not too close, as Halber made the radio call to the other wardens.

"NOW, you guys! Come in NOW!"

Chaplin was holding them in a hover, 40 feet off the ground and about 50 feet to one side of the blind so that he and Halber were looking right down the throats of the three occupants. The plan was to so distract McRoy and his hunting companions that they would not notice the ATVs racing toward them from three directions. Looking down, Halber saw a sight he would never forget. The men in the sunken tanks were peering up, wide-eyed, like a trio of prairie dogs regarding a falcon. Then they looked at one another, totally puzzled, then back up at the helicopter which bore the words SHERIFF'S DEPARTMENT painted in bright orange letters on its white hull.

Halber could see the total bafflement in their eyes as the seconds dragged by. It was taking longer for the ATVs to arrive than Halber had anticipated, and he was getting nervous that McRoy would start looking around. To further confuse and occupy the suspects, Halber began directing hand signals at the three men—gestures that meant absolutely nothing. They now cocked their heads first one way, then the other, like puzzled puppies, as they tried to make sense out of Halber's gestures. Then the one on the left cast a glance off in the distance and suddenly froze as he spotted an approaching ATV and the realization was upon him.

Good morning, Rascal, thought Halber, as the man suddenly turned an about-face, ducked down into the tank and came up with a full box of shotgun shells in each hand.

Without looking back, he tossed the shells behind him, over his shoulders, hanging onto the boxes so only the shells flew out. Four dozen shells splashed into the foot-deep water and vanished.

"Can you believe that?" said Chaplin.

The two other men in the blind were having a hard time believing it as well, as their guide again ducked down, grabbed more of his shotgun shells and flung them out into the water. Next, he grabbed his shotgun, jacked the shells out of it and flung those away as well. This was too much for Halber.

"Can you put me down on that check?" he asked Chaplin, who without hesitation swooped down over the long berm of earth separating the two vast flooded fields of rice stubble. Halber jumped out and scrambled over to the sunken tank where McRoy was now busily putting the plug back into his shotgun. He was half hunkered down, attempting to shield his actions from view. Halber reached down, grabbed a fistful of the man's parka and jerked him upright. McRoy now turned and faced Halber, and in a remarkable attempt at nonchalance that astounded Halber, he flashed a big grin and said, "Been seein' any ducks?"

About this time the ATVs arrived. Sandberg was first to step off and approach the blind. "Hello, Mr. McRoy," he said.

"Just call me Rascal," said McRoy, as Halber assisted him from the blind.

Wardens Leonard Blissenbach and Terry Libby were now on hand, and Halber pointed out the area in which they should search for the tossed shotgun shells. Most of the shells had landed about 12 feet out from the tanks, in about a foot of water. Blissenbach, his sleeves pushed back over his elbows, searching by feel, was the first to find a lead shell, then another and another.

Libby, who had only a week earlier received a beautiful Cabelas Cold-Weather Parka as a Christmas present from his wife, took a minute to remove the garment and lay it carefully on the check near the tanks where it would be safe. He then began groping for shells and soon began finding them. Then he happened to glance up and was first horrified, then enraged, to see Rascal McRoy, in muddy hip boots, standing right in the middle of his new parka. McRoy, upon seeing the murderous look in Libby's eyes as the warden started for him, quickly took cover behind Halber.

"I'm sorry! I'm sorry!" he cried, arms raised defensively. "I didn't see it." Libby glared at him, then returned to his search.

Halber, in the meantime, had examined McRoy's shotgun. McRoy had successfully gotten the plug back into the gun, but he had only managed a turn or two with the magazine cap before Halber had grabbed him. Halber now removed the cap and examined the green plastic magazine plug. While the magazine spring and the tube itself were bone dry inside, the plastic plug was wet, like everything else inside the blind. It had obviously been out and handled only seconds earlier.

Halber now turned his attention to the blind, where the two other hunters stood quietly. They had neither tossed shells, nor had they tried to modify their shotguns. And all of their shells, including those in their shotguns, were the legal steel variety. Near their feet were two mallard ducks on a duck strap.

"Are these all you've got?" Halber asked.

"No," said one of the men. "There's one more over there," and he pointed down the check a ways. Sandberg walked that direction and picked up a single hen goldeneye, an undesirable duck to most duck hunters, who claim that they have a fishy taste. The wardens were certain that McRoy had intended to abandon it.

The wardens were puzzled as to why, at 11:00 a.m. on what had been a pretty good shoot day, Rascal McRoy and his two clients had taken only three ducks. But upon questioning the two clients, one an attorney and the other a realtor, both from Sacramento, the wardens concluded that this was probably the case. That didn't prevent the wardens, however, from searching every conceivable place ducks could be hidden, including the suspects' vehicles and the area surrounding the vehicles. They found nothing. A search of the blind, however, amid the clutter of candy bar wrappers and old shell boxes that had been near McRoy's feet, produced 13 shotgun shells containing lead shot. When added to the 29 lead shells recovered by Blissenbach and Libby, the total was 42.

"Those aren't mine," said McRoy. "Those were here when we got here."

"Yeah, right," said Halber. "I'll need to take a look at your guide's license, Mr. McRoy." McRoy fumbled through his wallet for a few seconds, then admitted that he had failed to renew it for the current year.

"But this wasn't a guided hunt," pleaded McRoy. "These guys are just friends of mine." The two clients, however, were in no mood to offer McRoy any support, and they readily admitted to having agreed to pay him $90 each for the day's hunt.

It was now over, but for the paperwork, which took only a few minutes. The wardens took ID information from the two clients so that they could be reached later if needed as witnesses, and McRoy received a citation. In addition to charging McRoy with guiding without a license and the use of lead shot to take waterfowl, they charged him with failure to show upon their demand the lead shells he had tossed and those that were found in his blind. And then there was the matter of his hunting with an unplugged gun. Halber was certain that McRoy had been hunting with the magazine plug out of his shotgun. But McRoy, when he had replaced the plug in his shotgun, had used his body to shield his actions from Halber's view. Halber, despite the fact that the plug had been wet and he had found the magazine cap of McRoy's gun only barely screwed on by one or two threads, wasn't sure he could make the charge stick. He would have to run it by the district attorney. There was also the matter of the three ducks.

"Mr. McRoy," said Halber, "Are we gonna find any lead

Rascal's Road to Justice

shot in these ducks?"

"Well, if there's lead shot in them we didn't shoot it. They could have been hit with lead somewhere else and still flown here."

Halber was well familiar with this defense, which was a good one. It would take luck on the part of the wardens to find lead shot in some part of a duck that would preclude any possibility of the duck having traveled after receiving the wound. The ducks would be X-rayed, and if such a wound was found, McRoy would face yet another charge, that of possessing waterfowl taken with lead shot.

McRoy looked on as Warden Blissenbach explained the citation. The wardens were in agreement that the clients were innocent.

"We'll be seizing your shotgun into evidence, Mr. McRoy," said Blissenbach, and for the first time McRoy looked genuinely pained.

When the wardens were finished, Halber turned to the two clients. "You gentlemen are free to go. We're sorry you had a bad experience this morning."

"It wasn't so *bad* as it was *memorable*," answered one of them with a grim smile.

The wardens concluded their business, climbed onto their ATVs and churned away through the flooded rice stubble. Halber rode facing aft, behind Blissenbach, who delivered him to the waiting helicopter. Chaplin had set the machine down in a farm complex near the highway. Halber belted himself in, as Chaplin's practiced hands flipped switches, turned dials, pulled levers, and the big rotor blades began to turn. Soon they were clattering away through a threatening sky, heading for Oroville Airport.

"We really appreciate it," said Halber, as they wheeled the helicopter into its hangar.

"Glad to help," said Chaplin. "That was a kick!"

* * *

Warden Leonard Blissenbach looked on with interest as

James D. Banks, wildlife pathologist at Fish and Game's research field station near Sacramento, opened the cranial cavity of the hen goldeneye duck. The two mallards lay nearby, having already been examined. Each mallard had contained both lead and steel shot, but the lead-shot wounds were not placed such that Banks could say with certainty that the wounds would have been instantly fatal. The goldeneye, however, contained but a single shot pellet. When Banks examined it under the fluoroscope, the pellet stood out in stark contrast to the flesh, bones and feathers of the duck, and it was lodged dead center in the bird's brain.

"This wound would have brought this duck down like a stone," said Banks. "Now we'll see if it's steel or lead."

Banks probed briefly with his scalpel, then reached in with his forceps and drew out a tiny metal sphere. But upon close examination, it wasn't quite spherical. Banks then applied a small pair of pliers to it and squeezed. It flattened readily.

"Looks like your friend Rascal is in more trouble," said Banks.

*   *   *

In the days following the arrest, the wardens were surprised and amused to hear that McRoy was telling anyone who would listen that he had been caught with a huge overlimit of mallards and that the wardens had used several helicopters to catch him. He was also saying that a month prior to this epic arrest, he had been foot-chased through the marsh and captured by wardens and that he had lost his shotgun during the chase. The wardens, unable to find any basis of fact in this story, were in agreement that Rascal McRoy was indeed a strange bird.

Rascal's road to justice turned out to be a bit longer than the wardens had expected. An inexperienced deputy district attorney was bullied by McRoy's veteran defense attorney who somehow convinced him to dismiss all charges against

McRoy. Halber and the other wardens, upon hearing about it, were outraged and immediately sought out Mike Ramsey, Butte County's hard-nosed District Attorney. The wardens had learned to respect Ramsey, for not only was he an aggressive and highly skilled prosecutor, a criminal's nightmare, but his father had been a game warden following World War II. Upon listening to Halber's concerns, Ramsey took steps to set things right. While he couldn't refile against McRoy in any state court, Ramsey neatly solved the problem by filing the case in federal court.

It was months later when Rascal McRoy finally faced a federal judge for sentencing. The federal attorneys, to save time and money, had combined McRoy's most recent charges with the still-pending unplugged shotgun charge filed against him over a year earlier by Agent Sandberg. And while the result was predictably beneficial to McRoy—penalties for combined charges rarely equaled the sum of what the penalties would have been had the cases been tried separately—his guilty plea resulted in a substantial fine and a lengthy probationary period. Justice, of sorts, had been done.

Upon hearing the sentence, Halber found himself thinking back over his brief acquaintance with McRoy and assessing the man. Yes, he abused the game laws. Yes, he was loud and obnoxious. And yes, he regularly stretched the truth. He was . . . well . . . he was a *rascal*—a genuine, bonafide, card-carrying *rascal*. But Halber found it difficult to dislike the man, for he was another of those colorful, one-of-a-kind characters who made life more interesting for the wardens. This, however, didn't prevent Halber from phoning a clerk at Fish and Game's License and Revenue Branch to ensure that McRoy wouldn't, in error, be issued a guide's license for the next two years. Halber provided the clerk, a young woman, the essential information, saving the name for last.

"Rascal?" said the clerk. "You gotta be kidding!"

TRUE REMORSE

A still, moonless night in the forest. A lone California black bear padded silently along a game trail on a timbered ridge, lifting his nose often to test the cool air. The scent grew stronger now, the sweet reek of molasses that drew the 200-pound animal along as surely as if by chain and collar.

The source of the scent was a pile of molasses-soaked grain inside a large steel contraption anchored to heavy steel stakes driven into the mountainside. The bear approached warily, and with good reason, but it had never before encountered a culvert trap and ultimately failed to realize the danger.

The trap was an eight-foot length of green-painted steel culvert-pipe, three feet in diameter, and equipped with a heavy steel grate on one end and a plate-steel door on the other. The door ran up and down in vertical metal guides welded to either side of the entrance end of the culvert. The raised door, when the trap was set as it was on this night, hung like the raised blade of a guillotine, held aloft by a mechanism linked to a trigger-plate on the trap's interior floor.

The bear circled the trap twice, crazed by the wondrous smell from within, tendrils of thick saliva oozing from his jowls. Upon discovering the open end of the trap and an unobstructed route to the pile of molasses feed within, he didn't hesitate. He scrambled up and in and hurried forward. He felt a slight give beneath his feet as he stepped on the trigger-plate, then the heavy door slammed down behind him with a resounding crash.

With a roar of fright and anger, the bear rammed first into the grate at the far end of the culvert, then reversed direction and rammed the door. The trap bounced and reeled as the bear fought with all his strength to gain freedom. But the steel bars were unyielding, and finally the animal collapsed in utter exhaustion.

* * *

Rays of early morning sunlight painted the interior walls of the cabin as Chester Leroy Bronk regarded his face in a mirror nailed to the wall above the bathroom sink. What he saw was a hard, angular, short-bearded visage with a cruel mouth and cold, assassin's eyes that stared back at him, totally devoid of humor, compassion, or any other benevolent human quality. While maintaining eye contact with the villain in the mirror, he took a deep drag from a half-smoked cigarette, his third for the morning, then he turned, blew a cloud of blue smoke, and strode for the cabin door.

Outside, Bronk paused for a moment, looking and listening, then headed into the forest. A faint trail and a five-minute walk took him down the ridge to a sparsely forested spot on sloping ground. He saw immediately that the trap had been sprung. He laughed to himself, a rasping chuckle, as he approached the trap. He had scored on the very first night. Upon reaching the trap, he peered inside. The bear had retreated to the opposite end of the trap and was staring back at him. Bronk chuckled again as he regarded the animal, noting the fine quality of its fur, a deep cinnamon-brown. He noted also a small patch of white fur over one eye, which was highly unusual. It wasn't a huge bear, but it wasn't a small one either. It would do nicely for his purposes. Archery bear season was just 10 days away, and he knew someone who would pay a nice price for a guaranteed shot at a bear.

He turned and started back for his cabin, with no intention of returning for a day or two. As he departed, he gave no thought to providing the bear with water, nor did he consider the fact that the August sun, which for days had baked Shasta County in 100-degree heat, would soon turn the culvert trap into an oven. Leroy Bronk didn't concern himself with such trifles.

Days passed.

* * *

The tip, when it reached Lt. Steve Callan, Department of Fish and Game, was information from a CalTIP caller who had heard it from a friend, who had heard it from another friend. But at the mention of the name Leroy Bronk, Callan was all ears. The caller went on to report that Bronk had trapped a bear a week earlier in a culvert trap and was keeping it alive in the trap, under horrible conditions, feeding it hot peppers to flavor the jerky Bronk intended to make from the animal's meat.

Callan was well acquainted with Bronk, as were a number of other northern California wardens. Bronk was the subject of a fairly regular trickle of information—whispered, anonymous tips from people obviously terrified of him. The theme of the information always involved culvert-trapped bears and dope. The wardens had also learned that Bronk, a violent and dangerous man, was already a felon, twice convicted of violent crimes and therefore could not use or possess firearms or ammunition.

But Bronk seemed to lead a charmed life. A year earlier, Callan, acting on a good tip, had obtained a search warrant for Bronk's residence in Shasta Lake City. A team of wardens had descended on the home and searched every inch of it. It was soon obvious, however, that Bronk had known they were coming and had ditched a number of firearms. The frustrated wardens later learned that a young probation officer, who had known of the warrant in advance and was apparently under the impression that the warrant had already been served, had phoned Bronk. So, Bronk was tipped off and was able to dodge the bullet.

Callan pondered the current call with keen interest, for unlike previous calls concerning Bronk and culvert traps, this caller not only knew the location of the trap, but was willing to draw the wardens a map. Callan made arrangements to meet with the man. Later that morning, Callan and Warden Dave Szody met with a highly nervous man who acted as though Leroy Bronk was watching his every move through a rifle-scope.

"They said I could remain anonymous," said the man, peering anxiously around.

"That's right," said Callan. "Did they assign you a number?"

"They did," said the man. "And they said I might get paid for my information." This was in reference to Fish and Game's CalTIP program, which offers cash rewards for tips against wildlife violators.

"What can you tell us about Mr. Bronk?" Callan asked.

"Well, he's been living in a cabin up off of Fender's Ferry Road. It's not *his* cabin, but the owner lets him stay there."

The man then described the location of the gated entrance to the half-mile of steep and rugged dirt road leading up the ridge to the cabin. He then provided a hand-drawn map of the culvert trap in relation to the cabin.

"I haven't seen the bear, but I hear it's in bad shape," the man continued.

The wardens gently prodded him for everything he knew about Bronk and the current situation, then thanked him and went on their way.

Early afternoon found them in the mountains, on Fender's Ferry Road about five miles east of Interstate 5. They were both in full uniform and in a marked patrol vehicle, but their intention was simply to locate the gate and the road leading up to the cabin. They stopped at one point and were out of the patrol vehicle, examining what could have been the gate, when they heard another vehicle coming their way. Szody quickly popped the hood of the patrol vehicle and appeared to be tinkering with the engine as a gray Datsun hatchback sedan pulled into view and stopped.

"Are you having trouble?" the driver inquired.

"I think we're OK," said Szody, approaching the driver's window. "What brings you to the woods today?"

"I have to talk to a guy about some land," answered the man, clearly studying the wardens.

"Well, have a nice afternoon," said Szody, with a casual wave as he stepped back from the vehicle. The driver nodded and pulled away, casting one last glance back at the wardens as he departed.

"That was an evil lookin' dude!" said Szody, pulling a pen and small notebook from his shirt pocket to jot down the Datsun's license number.

"Yeah," said Callan. "I think that was Bronk." A check with dispatch and DMV later in the day would confirm this.

The wardens continued up the road and had gone no more than a quarter-mile when they found the gate they were looking for. Worried that Bronk might have doubled back, the wardens drove on by, but Szody turned onto an old logging spur a short distance beyond the gate and was able to hide the patrol vehicle from the main road. He and Callan then set out on foot for a careful recon of the area.

At the gate, they examined the chain and stout padlock securing it, then walked around it and started up the dirt road beyond. They proceeded with caution, listening, careful to leave no prints. After consulting the hand-drawn map, they left the road at a point that would later prove to be about halfway up to the cabin. They side-hilled through the trees for a few minutes before a sharp odor assailed them—a rank, gamey stench. They knew instantly what it was. Adjusting their course, they now followed their noses to their destination.

As they approached the trap, the stench was almost more than they could stand. Szody steeled himself and peered through the metal grate into the trap's shadowed interior. He immediately turned away and gagged, fighting to control his rebellious stomach. Callan now joined him, his face set in a grimace, and both men took a longer look, each holding his breath. The bear was there and still alive, but in a tragic state. It lay in the terrible heat of the sun-baked culvert in several gallons of its own excrement, badly dehydrated, barely able to lift its head.

Both wardens now turned away, sickened, and their revulsion turned to anger as they thought of Bronk. Then each saw newly-born hatred appear in the eyes of the other.

"We've got to catch this guy," growled Szody. Callan, jaws clenched, grimly nodded his head in agreement.

The wardens now took a few minutes to study and photograph the trap site. It was apparent that Bronk had at some time dumped some half-rotten vegetables into the trap, and there remained a little of some kind of sweetened grain animal food, but there was no indication that the bear had been watered.

Szody pulled a water bottle from his belt, stepped to the trap and squeezed a thin stream of water through the bars, aiming for the bear's mouth. The bear shakily raised his head, licking at the moisture. Szody continued to squeeze the bottle, and the bear opened its mouth to accept the stream. But the bottle was small and soon empty, and it was all the water the wardens had.

They now discussed their options. The temptation was great to simply release the bear, but to do so would cost them their chance at capturing Bronk. No, they decided, as much as it pained them to leave the bear in the trap, they must get Bronk at all costs. They would place the trapped bear under surveillance the following day—the day before the opening of archery bear season. As they prepared to leave, Callan turned back to the bear.

"Hang in there, guy, we'll get you out of this!"

Rather than heading directly back to the hidden patrol

vehicle, the wardens decided to sneak a look at Bronk's current abode. They followed the faint trail through the trees to where the A-frame cabin perched near the ridge top. Approaching cautiously, they found no vehicles and no sign of life. They took a quick look around, snapped some photos and departed.

The following day was another hot one. Callan and Warden Dan Fehr drove in the morning to Fender's Ferry Road and stashed their vehicle on the logging spur. The surveillance of the trap area would not begin until evening, but Callan wanted to at least bring the bear some water and ease its suffering as best he could. The two wardens hiked directly to the cabin to see if anyone was there. Again, there was no sign of life. Before starting down the trail to the trap, they picked up two empty, two-liter, plastic soda bottles from the litter and garbage strewn down the slope behind the cabin. These they filled with cool water from a tiny creek.

They found the bear in much the same deplorable condition that Callan and Szody had observed the day before. Nothing had changed around the trap. It was clear that no one had fed or watered the bear. Callan approached the trap with one of the big bottles of water, stuck the mouth through an opening near the top of the trap and began dribbling water inside. The bear immediately approached and began lapping thirstily at it. Callan poured faster. The bear lapped it in. It drank . . . and drank . . . and drank. Callan tossed the empty bottle aside and Fehr poured from the full one. The bear drank . . . and drank. When the second bottle was empty, the bear clearly wanted more. Fehr hiked back to the creek and refilled the bottles. Upon his return, the bear finished off both bottles again, and only then did he appear to have had enough.

"He drank about two gallons of water," said Fehr in amazement.

Before leaving, Callan took a small sample of the sweetened grain stock food from the ground next to the trap. He and Fehr then hiked back up to the cabin, replaced the soda bottles where they had found them, and took a close look at a large sack of grain leaning against the rear wall of the cabin. It was labeled *Manna Pro Wagon Train, All-Stock Sweet Feed*. Callan examined the grain within and found it to be identical to the sample he had taken at the culvert trap. He nodded his satisfaction, then he and Fehr headed out.

The actual surveillance of the trapped bear began at 10 o'clock that night. Fehr and Warden DeWayne Little slipped into the area, equipped to spend the night. After checking on the bear and finding its condition perhaps a little improved, they crept up to the cabin. This time they found it occupied, and studying it in the green glow of a starlight scope, they could see Bronk's Datsun parked in front. Satisfied that things were going well, the wardens hiked back to a spot near the trap and settled in for the night. Not far away, wardens Szody and Scott Willems took up a position near the gate on Fender's Ferry Road. The wardens were taking no chances. They expected Bronk to be armed and dangerous and would probably have other dangerous men with him. But there would be no case against Bronk until he at least visited the trapped bear.

Dawn of the opening day of archery bear season came and went with no sign of Bronk at the trap. As the morning dragged by, the wardens grew nervous. Where was he? What was he doing? But things came together at about 10:30 a.m., when Bronk suddenly appeared at the trap without warning. The wardens had been watching the trail from the cabin, but Bronk had apparently come by a different route. But the surprised wardens reacted instantly and decisively.

"STATE GAME WARDENS!" shouted Fehr. "YOU'RE UNDER ARREST! PUT YOUR HANDS UP!"

Taken by surprise, Bronk raised his hands and frantically looked around for a place to run.

"GET DOWN ON YOUR KNEES!" Fehr shouted. "NOW!"

Bronk reluctantly knelt in the dirt, and Fehr came up

behind him, ordered his hands behind his back and snapped a set of handcuffs onto his wrists. Fehr then read the man his rights, as Szody radioed the other two wardens that Bronk was in custody. Bronk initially stated that he had nothing to say, but the wardens would later have trouble shutting him up. After first feigning some mysterious illness, at which time the wardens assisted him to the ground, into a prone position, he decided that he had recovered, and the wardens helped him to his feet. The wardens then propped him up against a tree as Fehr approached the trap to release the bear.

Standing to one side, Fehr carefully raised the door to the fully open position and engaged a metal catch which held it there. Again, the horrible stench made him gag as he waited for the bear to discover the open door. But the bear made no move to depart.

"Come on, Yogi, you're free!" said Fehr, but the bear refused to budge. The wardens now tried all manner of tactics to bring him out, but no amount of coaxing or prodding had any effect. Finally, they gave it up, figuring that Yogi would come out only when he was good and ready. That moment came about five minutes later, when the wardens had lost interest in watching the open door of the trap and were engaged in other things. Suddenly the bear bolted from the trap like a race horse from a starting gate. The startled wardens back-pedaled, and Szody crashed into Little as Yogi charged by them and vanished into the forest.

There was laughter, of course, a second or two of levity before the wardens were reminded of Bronk again and of the now-vacant culvert trap, its open door yawning wide. The smiles faded, and suddenly all four wardens were at once struck with the same thought—an intense longing to stuff Bronk into the culvert trap, into the reeking five gallons or so of urine and bear feces, and let him soak in it, slow-cook in it, through the growing heat of the summer day.

But the fantasy passed quickly, and a now talkative Bronk brought them back to reality.

"What can I do to get out of this?" he whined. "I can give you information! I know things!" But the wardens were in no mood to make any deals. Instead, they marched him up the hill to the cabin, where the first order of business was officer safety. Using a key from a key ring in Bronk's pocket, wardens Little and Willems unlocked a cabin door and took Bronk with them on a quick sweep through the cabin to ensure that no one was hidden inside. They then exited the cabin, closed the door, and sat Bronk in a lawn chair with Fehr to keep him company.

It was clear that the wardens needed to search the cabin for the weapons that Bronk was reported to have. To do so, they would need a search warrant. To obtain a warrant, they would need plenty of probable cause and good evidence to show that Bronk was in sole control of the cabin. They would also need to show a high probability that there was important evidence inside the cabin. The wardens therefore set about searching the area around the cabin for supportive evidence. This search included a search of Bronk's Datsun. This task fell upon Willems, who soon found a set of shotgun choke tubes in the vehicle's glove compartment—good supportive evidence that there was a shotgun nearby.

"What happens now?" Bronk asked from his lawn chair.

"We go for a search warrant," said Fehr. "We should have one by tonight."

"You don't need to go to all that trouble," said Bronk. "I'll give you permission to search the cabin."

Fehr quickly shared this surprising bit of information with the other wardens, and they agreed that they would first like to run it by Larry Allen, an environmental crimes prosecutor. But it might not be easy to find Allen on a Saturday. Szody, however, had Allen's home, cell and pager numbers, and it was worth a try.

At that moment, Larry Allen was in central Oregon, northbound on Interstate 5, just south of Eugene where his daughter would be attending the university. A few seconds later, his cell phone rang, and he found himself in good, clear conversation with Warden Szody, on a ridge top, a couple hundred miles away, somewhere in the Siskiyou Mountains.

Allen was a traveling "hired gun" prosecutor under the Environmental Circuit Prosecutor Project. He worked for a number of district attorneys in the north state, traveling from place to place as required. The wardens had come to respect not only Allen's knowledge and formidable courtroom skills, but his great enthusiasm for his work. When it came to the courtroom pursuit of the worst of the wildlife-destroying outlaws, Allen was a predator.

Upon reaching Allen, Szody filled him in on their success in capturing Bronk at the trap. Allen was delighted. Szody then explained Bronk's offer of consent to search the cabin. Allen gave it some thought, then assured Szody that, under the circumstances, Bronk's unsolicited consent would be acceptable, and they should proceed with the search.

The search of the cabin took considerable time, during which Fehr remained with Bronk. Bronk was seized with nicotine fits, having run out of cigarettes, and Fehr was fast becoming his hero by searching out mostly-smoked butts in the ashtrays and trash cans, placing them in Bronk's lips and lighting them. Bronk cheerfully puffed away, and, in exchange, spilled his guts to Fehr. He admitted to all kinds of helpful things, even to having trapped other bears in the culvert trap and to using the trap since about 1993.

Sometime during Bronk's admissions to Fehr, Captain Chuck Konvalin from the Fish and Game office in Redding arrived. During a lull in Fehr's interrogation of Bronk, Konvalin, aware of Bronk's ex-con status, asked Bronk what he had done to become a felon.

"I slit somebody's throat," Bronk replied.

Konvalin blinked once and exclaimed, "That'll *do* it!"

In the meantime, Szody and Little had been searching the second floor of the cabin. Upon tossing back a mattress on one of the beds, they discovered the guns. There was a .22 pistol, a .22 rifle, both fully loaded, and a 12 gauge shotgun.

"It looks like *adios* for Mr. Bronk," said Szody, examining the guns, any one of which would be enough to send Bronk back to prison for *felon in possession of a firearm*.

In addition to the guns, the wardens seized into evidence the culvert trap and considerable paper documentation indicating that Bronk was currently the sole resident of the cabin. With the search completed, the wardens locked the cabin, locked Bronk's Datsun, then paused for one last look around. And they smiled again at a wooden sign hanging above the cabin door, for carved in the wood in large letters were the words "CAMP RUNAMUCK."

As they departed, Bronk was strapped into Konvalin's vehicle, and it was Konvalin who got the honor of transporting the man back to Redding and booking him into Shasta County Jail.

The wardens dispersed, that evening, feeling mixed emotions: While gratified that they had thoroughly nailed Leroy Bronk, they were troubled over the depths of the man's cruelty and his total lack of remorse. A newspaper reporter, a few days later, was equally troubled and wrote a lengthy article describing the long, horrible ordeal of Yogi the Bear and the capture of the man responsible for it. The reaction of the public was immediate outrage. The phone lines to the Shasta County District Attorney's Office were flooded with calls from enraged citizens demanding a quick and merciless prosecution of Leroy Bronk.

Soon after the story broke, Larry Allen received a call from McGregor Scott, Shasta County's DA. Scott wanted a hand in any decisions regarding the Bronk/Yogi Bear case, which had suddenly become a high-profile matter.

"What kind of deal should we offer them?" Allen asked, "them" being Bronk's defense counsel.

"How many days did Bronk keep that bear in the trap?" Scott asked. Allen replied that it had been 10 days.

"Then offer them one year in jail for each day the bear was in the trap," said Scott.

But of course 10 years in prison was no deal at all, so the message was clear to Allen: There would be no deals for

Leroy Bronk.

Bronk was arraigned, and a court date was set, but the passage of time did little to abate public anger over the matter. People who had grown callous and non-responsive to news accounts of murderers and rapists and all manner of human suffering were thoroughly incensed over the mistreatment of Yogi the Bear. On the morning of the trial date, Larry Allen spoke with Bronk's defense attorney.

"I don't know how you're going to choose a jury that's sympathetic to your client," Allen said.

"I don't either!" admitted the defense attorney. And it was this fact and others that convinced Bronk's attorney of the folly of spending time and money defending Bronk in any type of trial. Bronk was as good as convicted, and the public wanted blood. In the end, he convinced Bronk to plead guilty to all charges and hope for the best.

"The best" turned out to be three years and eight months in state prison, and Bronk was soon to learn that life for him there would have been infinitely easier had he been a convicted axe-murderer. He would learn that convicts have their own, rather odd moral standards, and they enjoy endless methods of expressing their displeasure toward those who fall short.

A day or two following his arrival at Solano State Prison, a number of murderous-looking convicts, men who knew what it meant to be abused in a cage, converged in a tight circle around him. It was only then that Bronk felt his first true remorse over his mistreatment of Yogi the Bear—bitter, intense, gut-wrenching remorse.

* * *

With the coming of fall, it fell upon the wardens to validate bear tags. Bears taken by hunters were examined by the wardens who pulled a small tooth from each and signed off the hunter's bear tag. During previous years, the wardens had thought little of this task, thankful that there was a bear hunting season to somewhat control the problem of bear depredations which were common in many areas—bears tore up trash cans and poultry pens, broke into cars and cabins, and occasionally killed livestock. But now, at least for the wardens of Shasta County, there was the haunting memory of a starved and thirsty cinnamon-colored bear in a culvert trap. Tag validations had now become a worry for the wardens.

But when late December brought an end to bear season, the wardens were able to meet and compare notes on the harvested bears they had validated for the year. To the relief of all, a cinnamon-colored bear with a white patch over his eye had not been among them.

TURKEYS

It perched on a lower limb of a tall, slanting Digger pine, 18 pounds of meat and feathers. Black night was still upon the oak woodlands, a full hour before dawn, and yet the big gobbler, obeying some ancient instinct, felt compelled to announce the coming day. It thrust its bare, red-and-blue-wattled head skyward and delivered a full-voiced gobble that boomed across the green Sierra Nevada foothills.

Over two dozen other birds—hens, young males known as "jakes," and even another large gobbler—occupied the same tree, but the old boss gobbler was king of the woods. The hens belonged to him. Later, when the first pale glow of dawn appeared in the east, the boss gobbler launched himself into flight, his great, thumping wing-beats audible for a quarter-mile. The others followed, like a squadron of small bombers. They sailed 50 yards and landed with a fine flurry in a small clearing.

Upon reaching the earth, the big gobbler immediately went into his strut, for it was springtime. His body seemed to stiffen and puff up, and with head tucked close to his chest, wings rigid and bowed outward, his long, banded, burnished-bronze tail feathers spread in a perfect fan, he strutted first one way, then another. His long beard, which grew from his upper chest, an oddity unique to his species, nearly brushed the ground. At intervals he would lunge forward, freeze, and his whole body would quiver as he expelled breath with a sharp hissing sound. Then he would resume his strutting.

But on this morning, which happened to be the opening of turkey season, the boss gobbler's days as the dominant male in the flock came to an abrupt end. A pattern of shotgun pellets did it, the blast from a poacher's gun. A few minutes later, a blast from a second poacher's gun took the other big gobbler. The surviving birds scattered.

* * *

Not all in the woods that morning were poachers. Gary Anderson, an off duty California Highway Patrol officer, was an honest hunter. And he was good at it. He had done everything right. Not only did he have legitimate permission to hunt the Slater Ranch in Yuba County's prime turkey country, but he had done his homework. He had begun scouting the ranch several days before the season opened, and he had located a flock that included at least two large, trophy gobblers. He had spied on them enough to learn how they moved in the early morning, and he had chosen a spot from which he hoped to ambush them. To ensure they would approach close enough for a shot, Anderson had with him a selection of turkey calls.

He had hiked to his chosen spot well before dawn and set out a pair of hen turkey decoys. He then sat on the ground, fully camouflaged, his back to a tree. He heard the boss gobbler's first call of the morning, and he clearly heard the distinct flapping of many wings as the flock left the roost tree. They were coming his way. He took a deep breath, reveling in the anticipation, drinking in clean air spiced with the tang of oak leaves. At that moment, there was no place on the planet where he would rather have been. He shifted his body slightly, his eyes fixed on the spot where he now expected the birds to come into view.

Then movement caught his eye. Two jakes appeared, making a leisurely approach to the decoys. But Anderson made no move. He would wait for the big gobblers.

Suddenly a shotgun blast, alarmingly close, gave him a start. A pattern of lead shot pelted the treetop above him, and severed oak leaves filtered down. And he could hear what he knew to be the flopping of a turkey in its death throes.

Furious, he nearly stood, certain that no other hunters had permission to hunt there. But he decided to wait a bit. Turkeys, strangely enough, were often not disturbed by gunfire, even close gunfire, and there was a chance that a gobbler might still come his way. A few minutes later, however, following the boom of a second shot and the flopping of another turkey, Anderson had had enough. Despite the shooting, the two jakes were still near his decoys. Anderson brought his shotgun to bear on the larger of the two and fired. The bird flopped briefly, then was still.

Anderson rose, hurried over and picked up the fallen jake, and he immediately spotted another camouflaged man, just over a low rise, also in the act of retrieving a large, downed gobbler. Then Anderson, shotgun in one hand, turkey in the other, headed toward the other man.

"Morning!" said Anderson as he drew near. "Do you have permission to hunt here?"

The other man, small in stature, looking more like a boy in his camo face paint than a man, said that he had permission, but hemmed and hawed when Anderson demanded to know from whom. Finally he admitted that he had no permission. At about this time, Anderson spotted a second, much larger man emerging from nearby brush. He, too, carried a shotgun and a very large turkey. Anderson now asked the second man if he had permission to hunt there. This man readily admitted that he did not.

"OK," said Anderson. "We're gonna have to take a little walk. There's some game wardens just down the road."

Surprisingly, neither poacher resisted at first, both

obediently marching ahead of Anderson down the road. Anderson's reference to game wardens down the road was factual, for he was aware that the wardens were conducting a turkey decoy operation no more than a quarter-mile away. But Anderson had not gone far with the captured poachers before the smaller one began first to complain, then move as though he was about to leave the road and vanish into the forest. Anderson, chose this time to identify himself as a law enforcement officer, displaying a shiny badge in a leather wallet. The smaller man was then quiet and cooperative again for a short time, but then he began to cry real tears and beg Anderson to let him go. The larger poacher, who it turned out was the small man's employer, now spoke up in disgust:

"Shut up, Jake! Just keep walkin'."

* * *

It was a gobbler of another sort that strutted back and forth that morning on a hillside near the Slater Ranch. It had wheels instead of feet, and its innards were machinery. But it had a full suit of real feathers and looked plenty convincing from the dirt road, 40 yards down the hill. The property on which it rolled along its metal track was not only fenced along the road, but was well posted against hunting or trespassing. Hidden at strategic locations near the turkey decoy were several game wardens and a pair of U.S. Forest Service agents. All watched the road with anticipation for an outlaw-bearing vehicle, out the window of which would be thrust a shotgun barrel, and someone would take a $600 shot at the mechanical gobbler.

Warden Jerry Karnow and Agent Don McClean, hidden within sight of the fake gobbler, heard the two shots fired by Anderson's poachers and noted that the first one had been fired before legal shooting time. And they heard Anderson's shot as well. A few minutes later, they were surprised to see three men, each carrying a shotgun and a dead turkey, hiking their way along the road. They were further surprised to learn that one of the men was Anderson, whom they knew and respected, and that the other two were poachers captured by Anderson.

Anderson exchanged greetings with Karnow and McClean, then explained the situation. Karnow turned to the two poachers and asked to see their hunting licenses. The larger of the two quickly produced a valid license with the required upland game stamp. But the smaller man had neither license nor stamp. He had a driver's license, however, and it identified him as Jake Leroy Crowder, age 25.

Karnow now studied the man, taking his measure. He was young and small in stature, but something about him compelled Karnow to study him further. Was it a coldness in his eyes? Perhaps something hard and calculating in the way he spoke? Whatever it was, Karnow's well-tuned survival instincts had fixed upon it and were sending up red flags. But the man made no effort to escape, and he and his friend signed their citations and went on their way. They did so, however, without the two big gobblers they had shot. The birds now had evidence tags tied to their legs and had been stowed in Karnow's patrol pickup.

The following Monday, Karnow went to the district attorney's office in Marysville to file citations.

"Who do you have *this* time?" said a smiling young woman at one of the clerk's desks.

Karnow showed her the citations, and she plucked one from among the others and examined it.

"Jake Leroy Crowder? We know *him!*" said the clerk.

Then one of the deputy district attorneys appeared and scrutinized the citation.

"I think this guy's been in the system. I think he's done prison time."

"Great!" said Karnow. "I just gave him his shotgun back."

Karnow wasted no time in contacting Fish and Game dispatch in Sacramento to request a criminal history report on Jake Crowder. When the rap sheet came back, Karnow was staggered by its contents. It was five pages in length, and it detailed a life of crime that began when Crowder was about age 12. And he was no petty criminal. He had indeed racked up an impressive array of drug, alcohol, and vehicle-related convictions, including felony DUI, but he had an impressive history of heavy-duty crimes as well. Most recently, he had done hard time for a series of home invasion robberies during which he had brutally beaten the occupants of the target homes. And he had been charged at least once with murder. Karnow added up the numbers and determined that Crowder had spent nearly half of his young life behind bars.

The following day, Karnow returned to the DA's office and added the charge of *felon in possession of a firearm* to the original charges.

"Boy!" exclaimed the deputy DA. "You guys run into some bad dudes out there!"

"You're right," said Karnow grimly. "And we're usually alone when it happens."

A month later, Crowder failed to appear on his court date, and the judge issued a warrant for his arrest. This came as no surprise to Karnow. What *did* surprise Karnow was the news that Crowder had had a further brush with the law during the month since Karnow had cited him. And it was a memorable experience for the Yuba County deputies who arrested him.

Crowder had gotten drunk and backed his car into another vehicle in a parking lot. The collision happened to be witnessed by a Yuba County Sheriff's unit on patrol in the area. Upon seeing the deputy coming for him, Crowder leaped out of his car and fled on foot. The deputy managed to outrun him and perform a flying tackle which brought him down hard. The deputy then fought him into handcuffs and stuffed him into the patrol car. But Crowder, cuffed behind his back and seatbelted into the patrol car, managed to release his seat belt and perform the human pretzel trick, stepping through the handcuffs. The deputy, feeling the patrol car shake, checked on his prisoner. He was surprised to find Crowder now handcuffed in front.

Turkeys

The deputy hauled Crowder out of the car and unlocked one side of the handcuffs so he could cuff Crowder behind his back again. Crowder took the opportunity to again try to escape. He jerked partially free of the deputy and began flailing at him with his free hand. But the deputy had retained his hold on the still-handcuffed wrist and, with the help of a backup unit, was able to subdue Crowder and return him, securely this time, to the patrol vehicle.

Crowder was booked into Yuba County Jail, but managed to talk his way out a day or two later. Somehow the jailers had not been informed of the *felon in possession of a firearm* charge. So, Crowder was now in the wind again, and the DA was incensed. He called Karnow and asked that he go after the guy. Karnow was only too glad to comply.

Karnow knew of places Crowder could possibly be found, and he set out, with Warden Dan Duran, to hunt him down. Anticipating trouble, the wardens requested a CHP backup. By coincidence, one of two responding CHP officers was Gary Anderson, the turkey hunter.

They descended upon the first two addresses without success, but they were lucky on the third. Karnow knocked, and a young woman came to the door. Upon seeing the uniforms, she attempted to close the door. But Karnow, having caught a glance of Crowder sitting on the couch, jammed his foot in the door.

"MR. CROWDER! STATE OFFICERS! COME OUT HERE, PLEASE!" Surprisingly enough, he came out onto the porch and did not resist as Karnow applied the handcuffs. He would later tell the wardens that he would have tried to escape, but he didn't want his kids to see the attempt. Again handcuffed behind his back, Crowder rubbed foreheads with his two small sons, a gesture of farewell.

Because Karnow and Duran were together in one pickup truck patrol vehicle, Gary Anderson agreed to transport Crowder to the county jail in the CHP black-and-white. The second CHP officer now went off on another call.

Duran escorted Crowder to the black-and-white and placed him in the back seat, securing him, still handcuffed behind his back, with the seatbelt. But Duran noticed that as soon as Crowder was seatbelted in, the man had reached for the belt release and began exploring, with his fingers, the release mechanism.

"Stop that!" said Duran, and Crowder obeyed . . . for the moment. Duran would later recall that Crowder, unlike most prisoners, was intensely interested in things like the interior door handles in the back seat of the black-and-white. His eyes were never at rest, studying his surroundings. Duran was a bit uneasy about this, but then dismissed his concerns. After all, the man was handcuffed behind his back and secured with a seatbelt in a police car. What could go wrong? He would soon find out.

It is a simple fact that successful escapes by criminals usually involve very good luck on the part of the criminal and bad luck on the part of the authorities. And such was the case on this day as Anderson started for town with his prisoner, followed closely behind by Karnow and Duran in the green patrol vehicle.

It is rarely desirable for backseat passengers to be able to open the rear doors of a CHP black-and-white, so there is a locking mechanism that prevents this from happening. Unfortunately, just the day before, four smartly uniformed CHP officers had ridden to a police funeral in the vehicle Anderson was now driving, and someone had forgotten to reset the rear door locks.

No sooner was Anderson on the road than Crowder released his seatbelt and maneuvered his hands to try the door. To his surprise, the handle turned and the door opened half an inch.

"Hey, look at that!" said Duran, a car length behind in the patrol vehicle. "The rear door's ajar. Was it like that when we started?" Karnow didn't know.

It was when Anderson started over the Highway 70 bridge at the Yuba River that Crowder made his move. Anderson heard the rear door, and Crowder shouted, "I GOTTA

TRY!" as he leaped out.

The wardens were surprised when the door of the CHP unit flew open, then they cringed in horror as Crowder sprang out to go crashing at 30 miles per hour, end over end, down the asphalt roadway. Karnow stood on the brakes to avoid running over the man, then the horror of the wardens turned to astonishment as Crowder somehow rolled to his feet, hands still cuffed behind his back, and staggered to the bridge railing. He sat a half-second on the railing, terribly skinned, bruised and bleeding, then looked the wardens squarely in the eyes and rolled backwards into space.

The CHP unit and the warden's vehicle had both screeched to abrupt stops by then, their emergency lights ablaze. Karnow slammed his vehicle into reverse and sped backwards several yards down the bridge before being stopped by traffic. Duran then leaped out, sprinted the rest of the way off the bridge and scrambled down the rugged embankment.

Crowder had apparently intended to jump from the bridge into the Yuba River. He had made his move a little too soon, however, and the riverbank was still a stone's throw from where he landed. But on the bright side, he had only fallen about 15 feet, and he had missed the jumbles of sharp rocks that were everywhere and had landed on the only tiny patch of relatively flat earth around. Duran found him lying motionless, face down in the dirt. Thinking the man was dead, Duran was relieved to see him return to consciousness, the wind thoroughly knocked out of him. Ten minutes later, he was able to stand and be escorted back to Anderson's black-and-white. This time, Anderson applied a leg restraint, or "bad boy" strap, to discourage Crowder from any further thoughts of escape.

Soon thereafter, a uniformed officer at each arm, Crowder limped from the black-and-white into the emergency room at Rideout Hospital in Marysville. Having lost a quarter pound or so of his skin on Highway 70, he looked as though he'd been dragged behind a running horse.

While in the waiting room, strapped to a gurney, Crowder became quite talkative and spoke freely, not only about his life of crime, but of his escape attempt that day.

"I started planning when we left my girlfriend's apartment," he said. "Plan A was to slip my seatbelt, try the door, and if it would open, I was gonna jump out on the big bridge, then jump off into the river. I was gonna float down the river, then go to a friend's house. That's what I almost did, except that I missed the river. Plan B, if I couldn't get the back door open, and since it wasn't a cage car, was to dive into the front seat and grab the wheel to cause us to crash. I would have then grabbed the cop's gun and shot him."

Anderson, standing nearby, blinked in astonishment.

"I wouldn't have shot to kill him," Crowder continued. "But I would have shot him. If I go back to prison, I'll never see my kids again."

Anderson now stepped over and asked Crowder, "Why didn't you try to escape that morning when I caught you trespassing?"

"Because that was my boss I was with, and I didn't want to do it in front of him."

Crowder turned out to be an engaging and intelligent conversationalist, and spoke almost nonstop for the eight hours before he was taken to jail. During that time, when a doctor or nurse would come into the room, Crowder would nod at Anderson and the wardens and say, "I'm enlightening these guys." He freely discussed the home invasion robberies he had committed, various assaults and batteries he had done time for, and he even spoke of crimes for which he was never caught. It was only when Karnow asked him about the murder charge on his record that Crowder refused to comment.

As he was being taken to jail, Crowder said to the wardens, "At one time I considered becoming a game warden. But I decided to be a criminal instead."

Despite the dismal outlook for his future, and despite the painful and extensive "road rash" that would forever scar much of his body, he was cheerful in the booking cage. He greeted the jailers, one of whom asked him, "What did you do *now*, Jake?"

* * *

With the demise of the two big gobblers on the Slater Ranch, the wild turkey flock was thrown into turmoil. The surviving adult males, ranging in age from just over a year to three years, began a struggle for power. Weeks of posturing and fighting would follow, until a new order of dominance, or pecking order, was established.

They fought chest to chest, leaping skyward in flurries of feathers to strike with beaks and rake with spurs. The soft, rounded spurs of the younger birds were ineffective, but those of the older males became genuine weapons, hard with needle points, an inch or more in length. It would only be when one large male had defeated all challengers and established himself as the new boss gobbler that a sort of peace and natural order would return to the woods.

* * *

One morning, a year after tangling with Anderson and the wardens, Jake Crowder was led through a steel-barred, sliding door into a medium security unit at Solano Prison in Vacaville. He looked around with only mild interest at what was to be his home for the next few years. Nothing was new to him. The system held no surprises, for he had seen it all before.

He could feel the hard scrutiny of the other inmates as they drew their initial assessment of him. They looked for signs of weakness in him, but detected none. Crowder knew what the next few days would bring. He was prepared for those who would attempt to intimidate him, the bullies, the gangs. He was prepared, if necessary, to fight as a new order of dominance was established of which he would be a part. Only then would a sort of peace and natural order return to the unit.

He peered around at the hard faces that regarded him, some neutral, some openly hostile. And he returned their stares with eyes that were absolutely unafraid.

A WEEKEND WITH "STARSKY AND HUTCH"

They spoke quietly in an Asian tongue, three of them, dark shadows in the night. Standing waist deep in the chill waters of San Francisco Bay, in a shallow inlet on the eastern shore, they peered warily around as they worked. Wisps of fog wafted around them like smoke.

The brightly lit span of the vast Bay Bridge loomed a mere quarter-mile to the south, the toll plaza clearly visible, the drone of the late-night traffic distinctly audible.

The gillnet was homemade, crudely tied, with floats made from pieces of old flip-flop sandals and spark plugs for weights. But it was over 100 yards long and quite deadly, a fish-trapping curtain of mesh suspended vertically in the water like a net on a tennis court. Illegal to use or even to possess on waters inside the Golden Gate, it had done its work well on this night, for it hung heavy with fish.

The three netters towed one end of the net ashore, then two continued pulling while the third disengaged fish as they came in and tossed them into plastic tubs. Most of the fish were silvery striped bass weighing eight pounds or less, and most were dead. But water flew and a brisk struggle ensued when a four-foot leopard shark came in, freshly ensnared and still very much alive. Soon it lay flopping on the bank.

When the net was in, the netters lugged it and the fish to a van parked nearby. They had just begun loading their illegal gear and their catch when suddenly misfortune was upon them.

"STATE GAME WARDENS! DON'T MOVE!" came a booming voice, and the netters found themselves bathed in light.

"HOLD IT! DON'T MOVE!" came a second bullhorn voice from behind.

The violators stood like spotlighted deer, too stunned to run. And soon they found themselves sitting in the sand, hands cuffed behind their backs, as one large game warden attempted to identify them and another counted their fish.

"It looks like 37 stripers, four sturgeon, two leopard sharks and two American shad," said Warden Keith Long. "Quite a night's work."

Lieutenant Bob Wright, comparing ID photos to sullen, down-turned faces in flashlight beams, said, "Near as I can tell, two of these guys are juveniles."

Wright was the skipper of the Fish and Game Patrol Boat *Chinook*, and Long was his boarding officer. Both were tough, gutsy officers known for their exploits on land as well as sea. They had been on their way home from a hard day's work on the water when they caught a glimpse of a van, half-hidden among high bushes near the shore. In view of the place and the late hour, they had known that it had to be someone up to no good.

With the violators now in hand, Long hiked back to the patrol vehicle. Because he and Wright worked mainly on a patrol boat, their captain felt they had little need for a good patrol vehicle. So they got the bottom of the barrel, which in this case was a green, nine-passenger barge of a station wagon. On this night, as always, Long approached the vehicle with loathing. He would have cheerfully pushed it off a cliff, had there been one at hand.

Soon, however, the station wagon was stuffed full of gillnets, fish, violators and wardens and was on its way to the county jail. The wardens booked the one adult violator, but after much discussion they decided to give the juveniles a break and simply drive them home. This they did, the boys directing them through an ancient part of Oakland. The boys were brothers, and the wardens delivered them to their mother. She thanked them profusely as they departed.

While attempting to get back onto the freeway, Wright missed the onramp. The wardens again found themselves in an old part of town with tall wooden houses looming above narrow streets. Wright's mistake, however, was soon to prove the best of good fortune for others.

Not far ahead, one old wooden Victorian home had been jacked up and sat perched on massive wooden blocks. Several homeless people had camped beneath it, one of whom was feeding a small fire built in half a steel drum. Just as the wardens came around the corner, the man threw a bucketful of flammable liquid onto the fire. There was a loud CRUMP and a huge ball of flame. The homeless people scattered, singed and smoking.

"Did you see that?" said Long.

Wright had certainly seen it, and now they watched in amazement at how fast the house on blocks had caught fire. It was as though it, too, had been doused with something flammable. In seconds it was fully engulfed, flames leaping skyward. The paint on the house next to it began to smoke, then flared, and it too was alight.

Long leaped out of the patrol car to check for injured under or around the first burning house, and he now turned to its neighbor. He dashed up a flight of stairs and hammered on the front door.

"ANYBODY HOME? FIRE! YOU'VE GOT TO GET OUT!" The only response was a dog barking from somewhere within. He shouted and hammered again.

In the meantime, Wright was using the patrol vehicle's PA system to warn local residents of their peril. Every few seconds he hit his siren for effect. He was also trying to report the fire by radio, hampered by the fact that he didn't really know where he was. At one point he had to dash back to the corner to read the street names, then call them in.

Long now hurried down the stairs and ran to the next house, repeating his alarm. This time a man answered.

"Sir, the house next door is on fire! Is anybody home there?"

"Yes!" said the man, now wide-eyed. "An old lady lives there with her dog! She's kind of crazy!"

Long sprinted back to the old woman's house and was astounded how fast the fire was spreading. Her home was now fully ablaze. Again he dashed up the stairs and hammered on the door. Still no response.

Watching Long from the street, Wright happened to look up at the second-story window above which the roof and attic were intensely ablaze. A pale, elderly face was peering out.

"BREAK THE DOOR DOWN, KEITH! SOMEONE'S UPSTAIRS!" he shouted. Long took a step back and kicked the door. It burst inward with a splintering crash.

The fire was now a terrifying thing, like something alive, a giant dragon whose voice was a continuous roar. Long peered inside. The interior was hot and crackling and smoking, and it seemed likely to explode at any second. He could hear the dog's frantic barking from above. Taking a last gulp of clean air, he lunged inside, spotted the stairway and charged up the steps, two at a time. Through the smoke he found the woman still at the window, confused and terrified. She recoiled in horror at the sight of him.

"What are you doing in here? This is my house!" she cried.

"Sorry, ma'am," said Long, scooping her up into his arms. As he did so, the dog bit him on the leg. Down the stairs he lurched, the old woman shrieking, the dog snarling and snapping at him. Then from above came the crash of a collapsing ceiling. Heat, smoke, flames—it would all become a blur in his memory. Reaching the first floor, he rushed outside as flaming debris fell around him. Handing the old woman to a neighbor, he stood for a moment with Wright at the patrol car, catching his breath.

The heat was now almost unbearable on the street, and airborne burning embers had ignited the roofs of houses across the street. A utility pole had ignited and was ablaze, and just as Long was about to set out on another mission, there was a loud BOOM. The transformer on the pole had exploded, and the wardens were showered with hot oil.

They regarded their ruined uniforms, certain that they had just been drenched with the toxic PCB chemical known to be in transformers.

But there was no time to reflect on such things. Long was concerned about a burning house across the street. No one had yet come out of it. He dashed across and banged on the door. Amazingly, the young woman who answered had slept through much of the preceding drama.

"You need to get out, ma'am! Your house is on fire!" said Long. "Is there anyone else inside?"

"Oh! Oh! . . . Yes!" said the woman, on the verge of panic. "My grandmother is upstairs. She can't walk very well!"

Without hesitation, Long plunged into his second burning building of the night. But this time there was no dog, and he sensed he had a bit more time. Up the stairs he went, and he found the second old woman attempting to stand, with the aid of a walker.

"No time for this," said Long, gently disengaging her from the device. "Put your arm around my shoulder." He then grasped her around the waist and walked her carefully down the stairs.

"Oh my! Oh my!" she said, as he walked her outside, for it seemed that the whole world was ablaze.

Wright checked several other houses and was now moving the patrol car, for the tires were beginning to smoke. He parked it four or five car-lengths down the street, and he had just stepped out when there was a great crash as the burning utility pole snapped and toppled down onto the very spot where the patrol vehicle had been seconds earlier. The pole struck two other parked cars, setting them on fire, and they, in turn, ignited a third.

Five houses and three cars were ablaze when the fire department finally arrived. They swiftly set to work, wetting down houses yet unburned, and soon the spread of the blaze was halted. At one point, a fireman noticed the tails of four large fish protruding out the open rear window of the Fish and Game station wagon. The skin of the fish had bubbled from heat, and they were half cooked. He turned to Wright with a grin.

"What's this? Are you guys having a fish fry?" But before Wright could answer, Long limped up, looking horrible—singed, soiled and dog bit'.

"Are you all right?" said the fireman, genuinely concerned. "How do you feel?"

"About medium rare," said Long.

* * *

The following afternoon found Wright and Long together again, this time in San Francisco, on a mission of another sort. Two months earlier, Long had cited a 25-year-old man for fishing without a license. The man had had no ID on him at the time, but provided Long with his name, David Edward Grider, plus his address and date of birth. Long radioed this information to dispatch, and confirmed the identity, comparing the suspect's physical description to that of DMV records. Seeing no further problems, Long went ahead with the citation.

But Grider didn't appear on his assigned court date, and a warrant was issued for his arrest. Soon thereafter, Wright and Long, warrant in hand, drove to the address to pay Grider a visit. Someone looking much like him opened the door and responded to the name, but it was soon apparent that it wasn't the man Long had cited.

"That's my twin brother, John" said the man. "We don't

get along. He's always doing this to me, getting into trouble and telling the cops he's me. Here, I'll give you his *real* address. I know where he lives."

It was now a week later, and Wright and Long would again try to serve the arrest warrant on John Grider. Wearing plain shirts over their uniforms, they found the address in San Francisco, in a neighborhood of old, multistory apartment buildings. They climbed a flight of stairs leading to two apartments. Upon knocking on the appropriate door, a young woman answered. They asked to see Grider.

"He's not here right now," she said. "He went to the store."

The wardens thanked her and departed. But they didn't go far. As they were leaving, they encountered an elderly man and woman who lived in the apartment next door to Grider. The wardens explained why they were there, and the old couple invited them to wait for Grider in their apartment. The wardens gladly accepted the kind offer.

Not long after, the young woman, presumably Grider's girlfriend, left the apartment and walked to the corner where she bought a newspaper. She walked slowly back to the gate in front of her apartment and remained there, reading the newspaper. Then a bus arrived, and John Grider stepped off. The wardens recognized him instantly. As he approached the apartment, the young woman spoke to him.

"You better keep walking, John. There's a couple of guys looking for you."

At this, Grider veered away and hurried down the street. The wardens raced down the stairs to the street, and Grider glanced back over his shoulder, spotted them and broke into a run. The wardens charged after him.

Down Chestnut Street they raced, arms pumping, until Grider ducked into a narrow alley. The wardens followed, shouting for him to stop. At the end of the alley, Grider dashed up a stairway. Upon reaching the first landing, he paused to hurl trash cans down the stairs at the pursuing wardens. Trash flew everywhere as the wardens ducked and dodged, losing a second or two before scrambling after him. He did the same at the third-floor landing, and again on the fourth, trash cans flying and crashing. The wardens managed to dodge them all.

At the topmost fourth-floor landing, Grider was trapped. But not for long. As the wardens came pounding up the last flight of stairs, Grider steeled himself, then made a running leap through the air and landed on the roof of the three-story building next door. He sprinted across the roof of the second building, thinking he had escaped. Then he glanced back in time to see both wardens leap the six-foot chasm and continue the chase. In full panic now, Grider ran on, leaping to the next building. The wardens followed. People were watching now, from the street and from windows as the chase continued, roof to roof.

Finally, Grider leaped to the roof of the last three-story building within jumping range. The wardens pounded after him as he vanished behind an elevator house on the building's roof. The wardens approached this last jump, looked it over, then backed up for a running start. Over they soared, landing with great thumps on the tarred roof.

"Where is he?" said Long, as he approached the elevator house.

"I don't know," said Wright. "You go that way, and I'll go this way."

Upon meeting on the opposite side of the elevator house, they were puzzled, for Grider was nowhere to be seen. Long tried the door on the elevator house. It was locked.

"Wait a minute!" said Wright. Something had caught his eye. Four fingers were visible on the very edge of the roof, and Wright crept over for a look. There was Grider, dangling by one arm, stark terror in his eyes, three stories above the street. A crowd had gathered below to watch.

"Help me!" shouted Wright as he grabbed the man's arm. Then Grider's fingers slipped, and only Wright's grip saved him from a lethal fall. For a second or two, Wright felt *himself* being dragged over the edge, but Long caught him by the belt and stopped him. Long managed to grab the man's other hand, and he and Wright began to pull Grider up. It was an epic struggle, the wardens grunting and gasping with the effort, but finally the man tumbled back onto the roof, the wardens falling over backwards, and they all ended up in a pile. Long rolled to his knees, applied the handcuffs, and the chase was over.

"How did you guys catch me?" the man gasped. "I'm an athlete. I work out every day and run. What do you guys do to keep in shape?"

"We ride around in a boat all day," said Long.

After catching their breath, the wardens had to face the problem of getting Grider back down to the street. Their only option proved to be returning by the same way they had come, jumping from building to building. They accomplished this by uncuffing Grider and allowing him to jump, but only after one of the wardens had jumped first and was there to grab him. Upon reaching the stairway landing of the first building, they handcuffed Grider again and led him down the four flights of stairs. Out in the street, they found the area surrounded by a police SWAT team and a sizable crowd.

"Who are you guys?" one heavily armed, camo-suited cop demanded.

"We're game wardens," Wright explained. "We're serving an arrest warrant on this guy. He failed to appear."

"What charge did he fail to appear on?" the cop asked, certain the suspect must have shot at or assaulted a warden to explain the desperate attempt at escape.

"Fishing without a license," said Wright. The cop blinked in astonishment, then grinned.

"If you guys ever get tired of bein' fish cops, I can get you hired with San Francisco PD. We could use guys like you."

The next stop for the wardens was the San Francisco County Jail. As always, the place was alive with activity, for San Francisco jailers did a brisk business. Grider was strip-searched and all his possessions placed on a counter at the booking cage.

Among the things found on Grider was a half a bottle of some medication. The jailer took note of them. But a few minutes later, after Grider had been left unattended briefly, the jailer noticed that the pills were gone, the bottle empty.

"What did you do with them," demanded the jailer, confronting Grider with the empty bottle. Grider denied any knowledge of them.

"How about you, Johnson?" said the jailer, turning to face a trustee in orange coveralls who was busily sweeping the floor of the booking cage.

"I didn't see nothin', boss," said the trustee.

The wardens were nearby, filling out a booking sheet, and the jailer informed them what had happened.

"We can't take him," said the jailer. "He may have taken an overdose. He needs to get to a hospital, code three."

The wardens dropped what they were doing and were soon racing down the freeway with Grider, lights flashing, siren howling. Upon arriving at the hospital and marching Grider into the emergency room, they found themselves amid the grim results of a gang fight. Several young men sat in the waiting room, holding bloody rags to ugly knife wounds. One had a gouged eye hanging partly out of its socket.

"What's his problem?" asked a reception nurse, gesturing at Grider.

"Possible drug overdose," said Wright.

"He gets priority," said the nurse, and Grider was instantly whisked past the bleeding gang members to a treatment room.

* * *

John Grider was ultimately booked that evening, and media people who sniffed out the story had a fine time with it. Wright and Long, in reference to their Hollywood-style, roof to roof chase and heroic rescue of people from burning buildings, were dubbed "Starsky and Hutch," after a swashbuckling pair of TV-show narcs.

There was much speculation as to why Grider would have taken such risks over a fishing ticket. The best theory was that he had an overdue loan from some slimeball loan shark, and he mistook Wright and Long for goons on a collecting mission. Then again, maybe he simply wanted to avoid paying his fishing ticket. Stranger things had happened.

But for whatever reason, Grider's bad day had continued bad right up to the end when he turned in for the night on his cot in a steel-barred cell. For the wardens, there was much to think back on concerning the case, not the least of which was Grider's trip to the hospital. The wardens had been asked to wait outside as two burly, iron-pumping nurses were called in to deal with him. They strapped him down to a gurney, subduing his struggles, ignoring his shouts, screams and curses, and stuffed a big tube down his throat. Then came the whir of machinery and loud grunts of outrage as his stomach was pumped.

Peering through a crack in the slightly-ajar door, Long witnessed this procedure and offered his assessment to Wright.

"This should cure him of fishing without a license!"

THE NATURAL

One summer afternoon in the late 1950s, a lifeguard at a public swimming pool in the town of Tulare, California, was horrified to see a three-and-a-half year old girl poised on the end of the high diving board. Before he could act, the child leaped off, struck the water with a splash and disappeared. But she came up giggling, swam to the edge, scrambled out and was about to do it again when the lifeguard intervened.

Another witness to this incident was the child's father, Joe Burnett, a highly respected Fish and Game warden in the community. It was all the more surprising to him because he knew that no one had ever taught little Kathy to swim. But she could somehow swim like an otter.

During the years that followed, Burnett learned to never be surprised at anything his youngest daughter did. Not only was she highly adventurous, but she was next to fearless. Spurning dolls and dresses, she favored jeans and a cowboy hat, and one night Burnett snapped a flash photo of her fast asleep in her bed . . . clutching a football.

As a game warden's daughter, she was raised around horses and guns and game warden things, and by age eight she could pitch a tent, build a fire, clean a trout, and ride like a Comanche. And had the need arisen, she could have bested any of the other kids her age, girls or boys alike, in a fist fight. She was nine when her father gave her a shotgun, a single-shot, 20 gauge with a shortened stock, and within a week she was busting clay pigeons with regularity. At age 12, she and a girlfriend would camp in the forest, alone except for Kathy's shotgun, for as long as a week at a time.

All in all, she was a delight to her parents, and she grew into a fine young woman, slim and athletic. And it came as no surprise to Joe Burnett when, at age 21, Kathy became a cop for Hanford Police Department. Soon she was doing narcotics buys for the narcs, and enjoying the adventure.

She had been a cop for nine years when her father came to her one day and suggested that she take the game warden exam. Her green eyes sparkled as she considered this marvelous idea for the very first time.

* * *

Compared to other poachers, Pac Tran was not an imposing figure. Even with the added bulk of his wetsuit, he appeared child-like. And yet, he was one of the more destructive outlaws currently working the North Coast. Earlier in the day, he had plucked from a submerged reef a legal limit of four abalone and rushed them back to the city. He would now attempt to take limit number two.

But the weather had turned bad. A storm had blown in from offshore, bringing wind and heavy rain, and a brutal surf now pounded the Mendocino Coast. It was a nasty day for diving, potentially lethal, but Tran, like the dozen or more other divers who were preparing their gear around him, would take their chances. All were outlaws and were unable to ignore the high profits the much sought after shellfish would bring on the black market in San Francisco.

Tran looked around him. There were but six cars in the parking area at the mouth of Moat Creek, all vehicles that Tran knew. And he knew all of the other divers as well. *Good*, he thought. There would be no worries over strangers in their midst—strangers who could be undercover wardens.

Tran glanced at his watch. Only an hour of dive time remained, for legal hours for the taking of abalone ended at sunset. Tran and the others would not risk diving after hours.

After one last look around, Tran strapped on his weight belt, grabbed his float tube, and he and his companions set off down the trail from the parking area. Upon reaching the beach, they headed north along the base of the bluffs. Soon thereafter, they were a third of a mile up the beach and battling their way through an angry surf. The tide was exceptionally low, but even so the larger abalone would be in deeper water. Tran worked his way over the reef to a place where huge exposed rocks would at least partially protect them from the wind-torn breakers rolling in.

In chest deep water now, among the rocks, Tran searched by feel with his feet for the deep crevices beneath or between the rocks where the larger abalone would be. Upon finding a likely spot, he repositioned his bright yellow dive mask over his face and did a surface dive. Peering deep into a narrow space under one edge of a large rock, Tran's trained eyes spotted what he was looking for. There were a half dozen of them of various sizes, the wide, shallow-shelled snails clinging to the rock surface. In his right hand, Tran held an abalone iron—a foot-and-a-half of narrow steel bar, one end flattened, rounded and slightly upturned. While clinging to the rock with his left hand, Tran reached far beneath the rock and thrust the flattened tip of the iron under the near edge of the shell of the largest of the abalone. Then, with a quick prying motion, he deftly popped the abalone free of the rock. Dropping the iron now, which was attached to his wrist by a cord, he grabbed the abalone and surfaced. He had been underwater less than 10 seconds. He examined the abalone briefly above the surface, then slipped it into his float tube. He didn't bother to measure it with the C-shaped metal gauge he carried, as per state law, for he was quite certain it was well over the minimum size of seven inches across the widest part of its shell.

Tran ducked under a wave which rolled harmlessly over him and he emerged in time to see the same wave dash one of his friends against a rock. The man, new to ab diving, was not hurt, but there was fear in his eyes, and he quickly moved to a protected spot and appeared reluctant to leave it. But Tran's other friend, in his bright blue hood, was doing better. Tran saw him slip a large abalone into his own float tube. Tran then resumed his search, and after a couple of fruitless dives he emerged with another "keeper" abalone. As he slipped it into his float tube, he scanned the bluffs which towered over the beach, for he knew that wardens, if present, would probably be there.

Not in this weather, he thought. He then dragged his float tube with him, moved a few yards and again began diving. Soon he emerged with abalone number three.

* * *

"That's number three for Yellow-Mask!"

Fish and Game Warden Kathy (Burnett) Ponting lay prone on the cliff-top, clad head to toe in camouflage Gortex, her rain-spattered binoculars to her eyes. Beside her, Lieutenant Nancy Foley, similarly attired, jotted notes in a small notebook she held in a tiny sheltered place behind a sodden day pack. Below them on the reef, three wetsuit clad figures were risking their lives in pursuit of abalone.

"They're really taking a beating," Ponting continued. "We may end up doing a rescue." She then pulled a semi-dry handkerchief out of her parka and quickly dabbed at the lenses of her binoculars. Peering through them again, she was just in time to see another of the divers bag an abalone.

"That's number four for Blue-Hood. He's limited out. Let's see what he does *now*. Klutz hasn't gotten a one yet." This last was in reference to the third diver, obviously a beginner, who was apparently concerned more with survival than abalone diving.

Neither Ponting nor Foley had intended to work abalone

divers on this day. On assignment with Fish and Game's Special Operations Unit (SOU), their mission was to travel down the coast and look for a particular vehicle. They were in plain clothes and in an unmarked sedan. But upon passing Moat Creek and seeing vehicles there and a number of divers obviously suiting up in horrible weather with less than a hour of diving time remaining in the day, they decided to take a look.

"They've got to be up to no good, goin' out in weather like this," Ponting said. Foley agreed.

They had watched and waited until all of the suspect divers had headed for the beach, then they parked the unmarked sedan amid the vehicles in the parking area, threw on rain gear and headed out on foot. Keeping to the high ground between the cliffs and the highway, they hiked roughly northwest, leaning into the wind, eyes squinted against the rain. When they sensed they had gone far enough, they approached the edge of the cliff. From there they studied through binoculars the dozen or so divers within sight. Most had already begun to dive or rock pick. But the group of three divers farthest north immediately gained their interest, being in a more remote place particularly rich in abalone. And there was something undefinable about the three that appealed to the wardens' instincts. The wardens worked their way to a point on the cliff-top that was immediately opposite the three divers and offered some low foliage for cover.

The wind raged, the rain pelted down, and the drama on the abalone reef continued. Blue-Hood, despite his limiting out, continued diving, and Yellow-Mask, in quick succession, bagged two more abalone. He was now one abalone over his limit. Moving to the float tube of the rookie diver, the one the wardens were referring to as Klutz, Yellow-Mask transferred abalone into it from his own bag. He then resumed diving.

Another quarter-hour passed during which Blue-Hood exceeded his bag limit, passing abalone to Klutz. And Yellow-Mask took more. But due to the harsh conditions, the wardens could not be certain how many abalone the three men had kept. At one point the divers had met and appeared to be high-grading their catch, discarding an abalone or two. All in all, the wardens decided that the divers had to have kept at least 15 abalone. All three were in violation, including Klutz who was in unlawful possession of abalone illegally taken by the other two.

The daylight was now fading; the sun, invisible behind gray clouds, was touching an invisible horizon. Ponting checked her watch. "They've got about two minutes left," she said. And then, right on time, the divers started for shore, dragging their now-heavy float tubes. The wardens watched as the three men, battered and weary, emerged from the water and trudged down the trail toward the parking lot. The wardens, with considerable distance to travel, now abandoned their vigil and set off at a trot. They headed directly for the highway, in hopes of making better time back to the parking area. The wind gave them a boost from behind as they jogged along a muddy cattle trail.

Upon reaching the parking area at Moat Creek, they noted that some of the divers were already at their cars and were curious over the arrival of two women in camouflage. The wardens scanned the group, searching for their three suspects, but the suspects had not yet arrived. But then they appeared, the three of them, lugging their gear and game bags.

"State game wardens," said Ponting, stepping into their path, displaying her badge and ID, rainwater dripping off her nose. "We need to have a word with you." She had to shout to be heard over the wind and the drumming of the rain on the vehicles. While Foley covered her and kept an eye on the trail and other returning divers, Ponting questioned the suspects and checked their gear. The suspects appeared unconcerned, and Ponting was not surprised when she found that they had exactly one limit of four abalone each. And each produced a valid fishing license.

"But we've got a problem," said Ponting facing them.

"We were watching you and we saw *you*," indicating Yellow-Mask, "and *you*," indicating Blue-Hood, "take more than your limit and pass them to *this* man," indicating Klutz.

"No you didn't!" said Yellow-Mask. "You didn't see that!"

"Yes," said Ponting. "That's what we saw. And now we need to see your driver's licenses."

"No," said Yellow-Mask. "We didn't do that. You're lying."

Ponting's eyes narrowed as she squared on Yellow-Mask and again demanded his driver's license.

"Why are you picking on us?" said Yellow-Mask. "What about them?" he said, indicating the other divers. But he unlocked his car, a small brown station wagon, and located his driver's license. The other two men complied as well. Ponting collected their ID and then sat the suspects, one at a time, in the passenger seat of her unmarked sedan while she, in the driver's seat, wrote each a citation. She cited Klutz for possessing illegally taken abalone, and she wrote the other two for taking overlimits.

"We'll see you in court!" said Yellow-Mask. "We'll *beat* you in court. You're gonna lose." He and the other two then became more and more verbally obnoxious.

"You can't *do* that!" he said, when Ponting explained that she would have to seize the 12 abalone into evidence. "We'll have your *job* for that!"

By the time Ponting had loaded the evidence abalone into the trunk of the sedan, she was tight-jawed with suppressed anger. And as the three men drove away in the brown station wagon, she turned to Foley.

"I've had about *enough* of them!"

The wardens remained at the parking area at Moat Creek until all of the divers had departed. It was a frustrating thing, for both wardens knew with certainty that most, if not all, of that particular group had taken limits of abalone elsewhere earlier in the day. They would have taken them to the city, where they would have sold them mainly to individuals, one or two at a time, at the going rate of $60 each. But perhaps their day would come. The SOU wardens were making substantial inroads into this illegal and destructive industry, sending some of the worst offenders to State Prison. This type of wildlife crime was becoming very risky.

Before leaving the area, Ponting took a walk down the path from the parking area. It was still pouring down rain, and even with her powerful flashlight she couldn't see very well. She was certain that Yellow-Mask and friends had stashed some abalone somewhere, and some of the others had probably done the same thing. But she found nothing.

I wish Kodiak was here, she thought, in reference to her big Rottweiler. Among other things, he was trained to find hidden abalone.

Upon returning to the parking area, Ponting slipped into the sedan and expressed her thoughts to Foley.

"I think there's at least one stash of abalone down there, and I think somebody'll be back for 'em tonight."

"I agree," said Foley, firing the engine. They headed north on the highway, windshield wipers on high, to a spot they had noted earlier in the day. It was a turn-out of sorts, and it offered cover for the sedan and a distant, but clear view of the parking area at Moat Creek. Wind rocked the sedan as they settled down to wait.

It was a mere 15 minutes later that it happened. A northbound vehicle pulled into the parking area, and while its headlights illuminated the trailhead, a door sprang open, a figure jumped out and sprinted down the trail. The vehicle then pulled away and turned north onto the highway. Seconds later it passed the wardens, its headlights illuminating the sedan.

"It's *them*!" said Ponting. "The same *guys*! That's their vehicle!"

Faced with this unexpected turn of events, the wardens made a quick decision. They spun around and set out in pursuit of the brown vehicle. When they were a safe distance from Moat Creek, well out of sight of the parking area, Foley jammed the portable red light onto the dashboard and snapped it on. The driver of the brown vehicle reluctantly pulled to the shoulder and stopped. Both wardens then jumped out, flashlights in hand, and cautiously moved forward, one on either side of the brown vehicle.

"It's us again, guys! Turn off the engine," said Ponting.

The two occupants of the vehicle, Klutz and Blue-Hood, sat meek and silent, their bravado and bad attitudes having vanished. The wardens did a quick check for weapons, then stepped away from the vehicle to confer. The opportunity of the moment had struck them both at about the same time.

"Feel like goin' for a ride?" said Foley with a grin.

"Absolutely!" said Ponting, and within seconds they had plucked Blue-Hood from the back seat of the station wagon, and Ponting had taken his place. Sitting immediately behind Klutz, the driver, she leaned forward and spoke almost into his ear.

"*Now* . . . Mr. Vue . . . You're going to drive back to the parking lot, and you're going to do exactly as I say. Do you understand?" The man nodded his head emphatically. "And if you disobey me or resist me in any way, your night will not end well. Any questions?"

"No questions."

"OK, let's go."

Vue turned the station wagon around and headed down the highway. Upon reaching the parking lot, he turned in and drove slowly toward the trailhead. Almost immediately a figure hurried from the shadows bearing a heavy-looking black garbage bag and shouting "Stop! Stop!" Vue stopped, and acting on Ponting's instructions he turned off the engine. The passenger door then flew open, the black garbage bag was tossed inside, and Yellow-Mask scrambled in after it shouting, "LET'S GO! LET'S GO!" But Vue just sat there. "WHAT'S WRONG WITH YOU? LET'S GO!" But then a hand grabbed him gently but firmly from behind.

"Good *evening*, Mr. Tran. Guess who?"

Veteran abalone pirate Pac Tran appeared to wilt.

* * *

The conference hall in Sacramento was jammed. About 130 game wardens—roughly half the force—were there to honor their own. Before them on the stage stood the six candidates for the 1999 Warden of the Year. Among them for her second time was Warden Kathy Ponting, selected again as the Region IV candidate. As was the case the first time, upon learning of her nomination, she was deeply honored, but she never entertained hopes of winning. She was therefore astonished to hear Rich Elliott, the Chief of Patrol, call out her name.

But there was little surprise among others in the room. As one, 130 game wardens, including some of the finest wardens in California—which is to say some of the finest in the world—rose to their feet. The hall resounded with their applause.

LOBSTER JAKE

It was sunset off the Southern California coast, and the western sky was a blaze of fiery orange. The Patrol Boat *Marlin*, her twin diesels burbling softly at idle, rose and fell on the gentle swells in the protected lee of Catalina Island. Three men were at work on her aft deck, hefting the 13-foot Zodiac inflatable skiff over the side. It struck the sea with a splash, and Warden Paul Hamdorf clambered aboard.

Lieutenant Mark Caywood, skipper of the *Marlin*, then passed field packs of gear down to Hamdorf, who secured them in the skiff. The packs contained radios, basic camping gear, and enough water and supplies for two wardens for a patrol of several days. Caywood then turned his attention to Warden Ron Hoffman, who was emerging from the *Marlin*'s cabin bearing a large bundle of heavy fabric. Hoffman opened the bundle, spreading it on the *Marlin*'s deck, and when he applied an air hose to various valves, the bundle quickly inflated into an eight-foot dinghy, a smaller version of the Zodiac. The wardens then placed the dinghy on the Zodiac's cradle on the aft deck of the *Marlin*. And when Caywood lay a pair of five-gallon oil drums end-on-end behind each side of the dinghy and covered the whole thing with the tarp which usually covered the Zodiac, it appeared as if the Zodiac was still in place on the cradle.

Caywood now climbed down into the Zodiac with Hamdorf, and as he cast off he shouted to Hoffman, "We'll call you as soon as we make contact."

Hoffman then strode to the *Marlin*'s pilot house, threw the engines into gear and swung the bow toward the mainland. He gave a final wave, then leaned on the throttles. The big diesels roared, and the *Marlin* headed for her home berth in Long Beach Harbor. Caywood yanked the starter cord on the Zodiac's outboard and steered for the dark mass that was Catalina. But he was in no hurry, preferring to await full darkness before approaching the island. A half-hour later, he nosed the Zodiac's bow onto the steep, gravelly beach at Ripper's Cove.

Dawn the following morning found Caywood and Hamdorf burrowed into the shrubbery above Ripper's Cove. They had dragged the Zodiac out of the water, covered it with a pair of olive drab, military ponchos and stashed it under the low foliage of a scrub oak. Their task for the day was simply to stay out of sight. The outlaws wouldn't come until after dark, but the outlaws had many friends. Caywood's most immediate concern was to avoid detection by the helicopter-borne gunners charged with thinning out the island's overpopulation of feral goats. Caywood knew these men to be associated with some of the outlaws. Twice during the day, the rapid thumping of rotor blades sent the wardens diving for cover.

The day passed slowly, with little to do but read and think. Caywood spent many of the hours pondering the commercial fishing industry, which was his reason for being hidden out on Catalina Island on this chilly day in March. He was there to pursue the *outlaws* among the commercial fishermen—the outlaw purse seiners, the outlaw lobster men, those who ignored fishing closures and gear restrictions and fished wherever and however they chose. But Caywood was not without compassion for them, for theirs was a tough and dangerous existence in a brutally competitive industry in which *many* felt that it was necessary to cheat to compete. And it was true—many of the commercial outlaws were otherwise honest and honorable men, gentlemen under all circumstances.

Caywood smiled at the thought of one purse seiner, Salvedor Rossi, who despite Caywood's having arrested him several times for a variety of violations, would always, upon Caywood's unwelcome appearance, greet him with the words, "God bless you, Mark. Come aboard." And Caywood would always return the courtesy. Once when Caywood rode back to port with Rossi in his purse seiner, guarding a hold full of illegally taken mackerel, Rossi, upon approaching the fish docks, appealed to Caywood.

"Mark," he said, "This will be very embarrassing for me. Would you consider waiting below until we're tied up?"

Caywood had slipped below, waiting out of sight until the boat had moored and the fishermen and crew on the *other* boats had returned their attention to their own work.

But not all of the outlaws were gentlemen. Some were involved in organized crime, and some, Caywood knew, if given the opportunity, would readily knife a warden and throw him or her to the sharks. And *another* thing was sure: They all communicated through a process known as networking. They all paid attention to the *Marlin*'s movements, and they kept a close *eye* on Caywood. If one of them learned something, they all soon knew about it. It was for this reason that Caywood went to such great lengths to fool them. It was for this reason that the *Marlin* was now snug in her berth in Long Beach Harbor, the Zodiac skiff apparently secure in its cradle, and Caywood's patrol vehicle parked in front of his home. And there wasn't a fisherman on that part of the coast who wouldn't be aware of these things.

When darkness fell, following their first day on the island, Caywood and Hamdorf dragged the Zodiac from its hiding place and launched it into the cold sea, a task that left both men wet from their waists down. The outlaws, if they came, would fish the closed zone, a three-mile band of ocean extending seaward from the entire north-facing shore of Catalina Island. As it happened, a few *did* fish the closed zone that night, but Caywood and Hamdorf were simply too far out of position to have a chance at them. They searched all night, however, a good effort, despite their being wet and cold. Just before dawn they again stashed the Zodiac under the scrub oak at Ripper's Cove, changed into dry clothes and crawled into the toyon brush to sleep.

Day two was much like day one—more reading, more boredom, more dodging the helicopter. Caywood spent a good deal of time that day educating Hamdorf, a new warden, as to the ways of the outlaw fishermen. He told story after story of past victories and defeats, successes and failures, and Hamdorf learned. Caywood also speculated as to who among the outlaws was most likely to risk fishing the closure and blunder into their clutches. One by the name of Jake Franco dominated this discussion.

Jake Franco was one of the old-time poachers, having ignored Fish and Game laws for over 60 years. He was a lobster specialist and pursued nothing else. He claimed to have pioneered the poaching technique known as fishing "spreaders." Spreaders were a series of three lobster traps set in a line roughly 50 yards apart. While attached to one another by stout lines, there was no buoy line to the surface, nothing to give away their presence. The poacher would simply choose a site that he knew he could locate by means of natural landmarks such as exposed rocks or kelp beds. When the spreaders had been in place for several days, the poacher would return to the spot and drag a grappling hook until he snagged one of the traps or one of the ropes that connected them. He would then pull the traps and remove his valuable catch. The poachers would always set their spreaders at night, and they pulled them at night as well.

Franco, the undisputed king of the spreader men, had used spreaders most of his life and had always gone to great lengths to avoid the wardens. He always used two boats, a big boat, on which he lived, and a smaller lobster

Lobster Jake

skiff from which he worked his traps. He traveled from place to place driving the big boat and towing the skiff. When he was poaching, he would never bring illegal lobsters aboard the big boat unless it was moving. Working first from his skiff, he would pull his spreaders and put the lobsters into a receiver—a wire cage the size of a lobster trap. He would then toss the receiver overboard, a rope and a buoy marking its location. Next he would return to the big boat, get underway and head for the receiver buoy. As he passed the receiver buoy, he would snag it with a boat hook and pull it, using a power gurdy, while still moving. He would then transfer the lobsters to 36-gallon plastic garbage cans, placed near the gangway, where he could easily dump them overboard should wardens appear.

Franco had more than once foiled wardens by using this technique. More than once, as wardens were clambering aboard *one* side of Franco's boat, he would dump the lobsters over the *other* side. He would then turn to face the wardens, his hands raised in an open hand gesture, and say, "It's all over, guys." And he would be right, for it was quite simple—no lobsters, no case.

Franco had been frustrating wardens for decades. But he didn't always win. From time to time he was caught, his first arrest having occurred before 1940. In all, he had been convicted over 20 times, undoubtedly a record. Unfortunately, he was getting smarter in later years, harder to catch, and despite being in his early seventies he was still strong and relatively agile. And he could still handle a lobster skiff on the darkest of nights and pull spreaders by himself. In short, he was still a formidable adversary for the wardens.

Franco in his younger days had been something of a dashing figure, the perfect sea-captain type in his Greek fisherman's cap. He was, by any measure, a colorful character, and others had viewed him as such. During the 1940s and 50s, he became well known to the Hollywood set. He supplied his illegally-taken lobsters for the big celebrity parties at Santa Monica and Malibu, and he rubbed shoulders with the greatest movie stars of the day. He had bantered with Humphrey Bogart, traded sea stories with Errol Flynn and gone weak-kneed over an occasional smile from Marilyn Monroe. They were good days for him, and he enjoyed a bit of power then. When the wardens caught him once supplying lobster for a party attended by Howard Hughes and his Hollywood friends, a judge dismissed the case. It was only later that the wardens learned that the judge had attended the party.

Although Franco's Hollywood days were over, he never stopped poaching, and the pursuit of Jake Franco was always an adventure for the wardens. Once, while tracking Franco from a cliff top on San Clemente Island, a military reserve and strictly off limits to the public, Caywood and Warden Tom Jackson had to dive for cover when mortar rounds began falling around them. Neither man was a stranger to mortar attack, both having experienced heavy combat duty in Vietnam—Caywood, in fact, still carried a steel sliver of mortar round in one leg. But neither man, in his wildest dreams, expected to experience it again. They lay wedged in the rocks, shrapnel whining by overhead, until it was over. A squad of Marines later admitted to having fired a few rounds so as not to have to lug them back to their base.

Caywood smiled at the memory, then recalled another incident. While diving for an anchor off of Goat Harbor, Catalina Island, he had stumbled onto some spreaders. The rigging of the traps was unmistakably Franco's. But due to budget constraints at the time, he was ordered back to Long Beach, his supervisors of the opinion they couldn't afford the overtime necessary to lay an ambush for Franco. So Caywood, before leaving, dove down to the spreaders, released the lobsters, removed the bait, and filled each trap with about 200 pounds of rocks. His intent was simply to inconvenience Franco. He was therefore astounded to learn a week later that Franco, while attempting to pull in the rock-filled traps, had suffered an accident. A line had jammed on the spool of his gas-driven power gurdy, and before he could stop the engine, the stern of his skiff was winched under and he sank. He had to swim ashore where he was picked up by another lobster skiff. Caywood had greeted this news with mixed emotions.

Caywood and Hamdorf, at the end of their second day on the island, again launched the Zodiac, and again they prowled the closed waters along Catalina's north side. This time they went all the way to Avalon, but with no success. Their only excitement came when Caywood was grazed by a flying fish, no small hazard. These creatures would launch themselves and fly sometimes for a hundred yards or more, dangerous missiles to wardens in tiny boats. Weighing from two-and-a-half to three pounds, they flew about 25 miles per hour, two to six feet above the water, and more than one warden had been injured by them. Caywood himself had been struck hard on two occasions, for at night it was hard to see them coming.

And then there were the spotter planes to contend with. The commercial fishermen employed pilots to locate schools of fish for them. They preferred to fly at night, blacked out, a mere 300 feet above the water. Because much of the time virtually everything that moved in the sea at night left a bright trail of phosphorescence, the spotters could readily see the fish. And the more experienced spotters could identify the species of fish, simply by the nature of the glowing blue-green trail they generated. Unfortunately, the wardens in tiny boats produced phosphorescence as well, even when stopped, and the spotters were always alert for it. The wardens, therefore, had to stop often and shut down their motors to listen for aircraft. When one was about, they had to hide near exposed rocks to avoid detection. These same spotter planes often made low passes over Caywood's home to see if his patrol car was there. They were a great nuisance to the wardens.

Again, by dawn, the wardens were once more concealed in Ripper's Cove, and day three passed like the two before it. But that night, their luck changed.

Midnight found Caywood perched atop what looked like

a snow-capped rock in the middle of Isthmus Cove. But it wasn't snow on the rock. Caywood, his binoculars to his eyes, was kneeling in it, his nose wrinkled to the acrid stench of several centuries' accumulation of bird guano. Bird Rock, it was called, but the wardens felt that there had been a word left out of the name. In the distance, Caywood could see the shadowy silhouette of a purse seiner, well inside the three-mile closed area. But it had not yet made a set. Caywood ducked low upon hearing the drone of an aircraft engine. Twenty-five feet below, Hamdorf crouched lower in the Zodiac.

When the spotter plane was gone, Caywood again put his binoculars on the seiner. But a boat was pulling into Isthmus Cove, at least a 60-footer, and its deck lights were on. The glare of these lights made it impossible for Caywood to watch the seiner. He was annoyed over this turn of events until the unmistakable *pop pop pop* of an unmuffled, single-cylinder Lister diesel caught his attention. He quickly turned his attention to the approaching boat. Sure enough, it was Jake Franco's boat, the *Sweet Marilyn*. Franco was one of the last to employ the old Lister diesels to drive his power generators. Caywood could now make out the distinct lines of the *Sweet Marilyn* with a skiff in tow. At least two men were aboard. He watched as they tied off to a mooring buoy and shut down the engines. But the *pop pop pop* of the Lister diesel continued, and the deck lights remained on.

Caywood hurriedly climbed down to the Zodiac and informed Hamdorf of the situation. Soon their quiet outboard was easing them toward a barge moored in the little harbor, a vantage point closer to the *Sweet Marilyn*. Hamdorf again waited in the Zodiac as Caywood climbed atop the barge's pilot house. Caywood was just in time to see Franco and another man board the skiff. *I hope that's not Shotgun Valdez,* Caywood thought, aware that Franco had taken up with a highly dangerous low-life by that name. Valdez had done a dozen years in San Quentin for ventilating some Samoans with his 12 gauge. Caywood tried hard to get a look at the second man's face before he and Franco set off in the skiff, but the chance never came.

They're heading for the ecological reserve, thought Caywood as he watched them round a point, then he hurried back down and jumped into the Zodiac. Five minutes later, the Zodiac bumped gently against the side of the *Sweet Marilyn*, and Caywood climbed quietly aboard. *Pop pop pop* went the little diesel generator, but there was no other sound. Caywood hurried through the glare of the deck lights and scrambled up a ladder to the wheelhouse deck and relative darkness. Just aft of the wheelhouse was a large fish box, left over from the *Sweet Marilyn*'s days as a charter fishing boat. Because the fish box was well above the boat's main deck, and because it was above the main deck lights, Caywood knew that not only would the fish box provide a good vantage point, but it would remain in deep shadow. He therefore chose it for a hiding place. He climbed in amid a jumble of floats, coiled line and other gear and settled down to wait.

Acting on Caywood's instructions, Hamdorf took the Zodiac across Isthmus Cove and tied up at the Wrigley Marine Research Center dock near the ecological reserve. He then hiked to a high place above Blue Caverns Point from which he could look out over much of the reserve. From there, amid the toyon and beaver tail cactus, he watched through his binoculars as Franco and the other man in the lobster skiff pulled three sets of spreaders. An hour and a half later, they headed back to the *Sweet Marilyn*.

During his wait in the fish box, Caywood had devised a plan aimed at providing him a reasonable chance for surviving a violent encounter with Shotgun Valdez. But his plan, as it happened, was unnecessary. He would learn later that Valdez had been too drunk to come along on this trip, and Franco had instead brought along a local personality known as "the Muppet." Years earlier, the Muppet had been the loser of a bad fight during which his opponent had scrambled his face with a two-by-four. The doctor who attempted to repair the damage had either been drunk or blindfolded at the time, or perhaps there had been no doctor at all, but for whatever reason, the Muppet's face was now a comedy of damaged and misplaced features. It was his resulting resemblance to a cartoon character that had inspired his nick name. His nose had been flattened and knocked off center, one eye drooped, and one ear was lower than the other. His jaw, fractured in several places, had healed poorly, such that the sad wreckage of his teeth was always visible and he drooled a lot. He was significantly less of a threat than Shotgun Valdez, but he was still dangerous.

Peeking from the fish box, Caywood watched as the returning skiff finally came alongside, and he recognized the Muppet instantly as he and Franco came aboard into the glare of the deck lights. In short order, Franco fired the main engines, the Muppet cast off the mooring line, and the *Sweet Marilyn,* her skiff in tow, headed for the ecological reserve. Caywood didn't budge. After a few minutes of running at about two knots, Franco steered for a single float barely visible in the moonlight. Caywood couldn't see it from his position, but he knew it was there, and as he expected, the Muppet grabbed a long boat hook and stood ready at the starboard rail. Then he reached out and down with the boat hook and brought up the dripping float and attached line. Working quickly, as Franco steered for deeper water, the Muppet took a quick turn around the turning drum of the power gurdy and quickly pulled up a receiver cage jammed with lobsters. Franco now tied the *Sweet Marilyn*'s wheel and joined the Muppet on the aft deck. Together they sorted their catch. They put the legal size lobsters into two 36-gallon plastic trash cans, and the illegal "shorts" into a gunny sack. They then lugged the trash cans to the rail near the gangway and placed the sack of shorts beside them.

In the meantime, Hamdorf watched with growing concern as the *bad* guys appeared to steam away with his lieutenant. Caywood's hurried instructions when Hamdorf had dropped him off on the *Sweet Marilyn* had not covered such a contingency. Hamdorf therefore made a decision on his own. Reaching for his radio handset, he called Fish and Game dispatch and asked for assistance. He then raced down the brush and cactus covered hillside, sprinted onto the dock and leaped into the moored Zodiac. Seconds later he was underway, skipping along in the light chop toward the departing *Sweet Marilyn*. But he had the good sense to hold back at a safe distance and shadow the big boat. Had he done otherwise, 200 pounds of lobsters would have gone over the side, and the wardens would have again been out of luck.

Caywood now faced a dilemma: He knew that Hamdorf would be worried and could appear at any second and blow the case, but the Muppet had remained standing within a few feet of the lobsters, ready to dump them at the least sign of danger. Caywood was stymied for the moment. He couldn't yet risk making his move.

The opportunity, however, came just a minute or two later when the Muppet stepped to the gangway to relieve himself over the side. While he was thus occupied, Caywood slipped out of the fish box, leaped off the deck house and landed with a loud thump behind the Muppet. The Muppet let out a startled shriek as Caywood grabbed him, took him down and applied the handcuffs. Franco, hearing the commotion, came running out of the wheelhouse, spotted Caywood and stopped, aghast.

"Where did *you* come from?" he managed to ask.

"San Pedro, Jake. *You* know where I live," said Caywood, and for a while, at least, Franco believed that Caywood had ridden all the way from Long Beach in his fish box.

Only when the trash cans of evidence lobster were safely secured in the Zodiac did Caywood unlock his cuffs and set the Muppet free. The wardens then cited both suspects and departed.

"You'll never make it stick," said Franco, as the wardens pulled away in the Zodiac. The Muppet just stared, like a character from bad dream.

* * *

By the time Hamdorf was again able to get to a high place from which his radio would work, Captain Jerry Spansail had raced several miles through the city for an immediate departure with Warden Ron Hoffman on the *Marlin*. Unsure about Caywood's status, both men were highly concerned. But Hamdorf's good-news call relieved their worry just as they were clearing the entrance light on the Long Beach Jetty. They continued on, however, to assist Caywood and Hamdorf in searching for Franco's spreaders and to bring the two weary wardens home.

The hunt for the spreaders took half a day. Caywood, Hamdorf, and Hoffman donned SCUBA gear and combed the bottom. A diver from the nearby research center helped as well. By late morning, they had located and pulled four sets of spreaders, the three Hamdorf had watched Franco empty, plus another set that Franco had been unable to locate the night before. By early afternoon, the *Marlin* was again heading for home.

In the end, Franco pled guilty in the tiny courthouse in Avalon and was sentenced to six months in county jail. But he had struck a deal in advance, and the judge suspended the jail time, placing him instead on three years probation. And he was fined a couple grand and his lobster traps were ordered forfeited. But the hammer really fell three months later when the Fish and Game Commission, after reviewing Franco's past record of nearly two dozen convictions, finally said enough's enough and took the unprecedented step of revoking his lobster permit for life.

But to a man who had hobnobbed with Gable and Garbo and had been continuously poaching lobsters since long before Mark Caywood was born, permits and probation and a judge's threatening words meant little. And Caywood knew, with absolute certainty, that in the next dark of the moon, at some channel island, when the wardens were home in bed and the lobsters in the shallows were as thick as fleas on a Catalina goat . . . Jake Franco would again be there.

DIRTY HARRY AND APE ISLAND

It watched with animal eyes that missed nothing—eyes deep-set in a very human-like, old-man's face. From its perch high in its steel-barred prison, it maintained an unending vigil that had begun years earlier and would likely continue for many more. Like all gibbon apes, it belonged in the rain forests of Malaysia with other of its kind. Fate, however, had delivered it instead to California, to a small island in the very heart of the Delta—the 40-mile-wide expanse of hidden waterways, tule-berms and levee-encircled islands that lay at the confluence of the Sacramento and San Joaquin rivers.

Ape Island, as it was known among the Delta game wardens, was owned by wealthy men from San Francisco and was managed as a hunting club. A plush clubhouse and caretaker's quarters had been built on levee-high pilings at one end of the quarter-mile-long, partially forested island, and visitors could only come by boat. But it was worth the trouble. It was a pleasant place to visit any time of the year, and in the fall and winter it offered some of the finest duck hunting in the world. During duck season it seemed to exist under a permanent halo of circling ducks intent on feeding in the flooded fields of yellow corn that were planted there and left unharvested for that reason.

One brisk fall morning, a visitor of another sort made a stealthy approach to the far side of the island. Warden James Halber, Department of Fish and Game, quietly idled his 16-foot skiff toward a tule patch at the base of the levee. Patrol Dog Ruger, a shiny black labrador retriever, stood poised near the bow, where he always rode on Halber's almost daily boat patrols. Halber nosed the bow into the tules, then stepped out and planted the grapnel hook to anchor the skiff's short bow line. Binoculars in hand, a camo parka over his uniform, he now turned to face his dog, raised his hand and made the silent *stay* signal. The dog obediently lay down to wait. Halber then picked his way up the 10-foot-tall, rip-rapped levee and peered carefully over the top. He stayed as low as possible, having learned from experience that to do otherwise would immediately draw the attention of the caged ape that guarded the island. Upon spotting an intruder, the ape would sound the alarm by voicing a series of ear-splitting, high-pitched calls that were audible in the next county. The caretaker of the club would then grab binoculars and scan the island.

It was an anonymous tip that brought about Halber's visit to the island, a story of huge overlimits of ducks being taken there by the owners and their friends. And now, as Halber studied the island's interior, alive with ducks, he concluded that the report could well be true. He was aware, however, that such reports were often false, and the current report could easily be the product of some disgruntled hunter denied access to this hunter's paradise. The truth of the matter, Halber knew, could only be determined through surveillance of the club on a shoot day.

And so it was that Halber planned an operation to work Ape Island on the coming Saturday. He enlisted the help of his captain, Jim Wictum, and Warden Buck Del Nero. He also gave Jack Downs from U.S. Fish and Wildlife Service a call. Jack and a second agent, Tim Dennis, committed themselves to assist.

The day prior to the operation, Halber was again on boat patrol in the Delta. With him on this day, slouched comfortably in the passenger seat, was his friend, Officer Harry Larson of the California Highway Patrol. Larson, a highly intelligent, dedicated and virtually fearless officer, entertained himself in his black-and-white by making solo stops of squadrons of Hell's Angels on the freeways of Contra Costa County, plucking fugitives of various sorts from among them. A stout six-foot-six, he dwarfed and intimidated most criminals, but he was good natured, found humor in most everything, and had a broad grin that never really went away. Among the other traffic officers of the Concord CHP office, he was affectionately known as *Dirty Harry.*

Larson and Halber had met a year earlier when Larson had stopped Brock Peavy, a paroled drug dealer, in front of a bar in the Delta town of Oakley. Peavy, clearly intoxicated, had nearly hit another car as he pulled away from the bar. When Larson was about to handcuff the man, Peavy called to his friends in the bar. The bar immediately emptied, and Larson suddenly found himself surrounded and cut off from his radio by a disturbing collection of hostile-looking rednecks. They convened a mini-trial right there on the street and found Brock Peavy not guilty. It was about then that Halber happened by. Correctly assessing an ugly situation, Halber swung his green patrol car around for a closer look. Larson spotted him, made the cover-me sign, and Halber stepped out, ready for war. But the presence of a second fully armed and determined-looking officer unnerved Peavy's friends, who slipped away, one or two at a time, back to the relative safety of the bar. Larson and Halber had been friends ever since.

Larson, from time to time, would accompany Halber on patrol and considered game warden work a fine lark.

"It's a great hobby," he would say to Halber, flashing his grin.

Halber soon learned that it was always entertaining to have Larson along. During hunting season, Halber preferred Larson to dress like a hunter and bring a shotgun. This provided them a variety of options when approaching suspected violators in the field. Larson, looking like a hunter, was often among the suspects before they sensed danger, and being among them, he could observe their sometimes incriminating actions when they spotted Halber, in full uniform, coming their way. All in all, they were a formidable team.

But there were some adjustments Larson had to make in how he dealt with the armed public. On one early patrol he had made with Halber, they had spotted two men coming their way in a pickup, road-hunting pheasants along a levee road. The driver had a shotgun, its barrel protruding through the driver's window as he drove slowly along. The passenger was using a pistol, a violation in itself. Halber picked a suitable spot, hid the patrol car and set up an ambush. Suspecting nothing, the outlaws were driving past some high patches of blackberries when suddenly two large men, one in uniform, stepped from cover and blocked their path. Halber hurried to the driver's side as Larson confronted the passenger. The driver had hastily drawn his shotgun barrel back inside, and as Halber was directing the shaken man to carefully pass the fully loaded gun back out the window to him, he noticed that the passenger was sitting bolt upright, eyes wide, his face devoid of color. It was then that Halber noticed that Larson was holding the snub-nosed barrel of his revolver against the man's ear. Later, after Halber had cited and released the two thoroughly shaken violators, he counseled Larson against holding their customers at gunpoint.

"But he had a *gun!*" argued Larson.

"Harry, they *all* have guns," said Halber.

On the day prior to the raid on Ape Island, Halber and Larson again worked out of Halber's skiff, roaming around the Delta, checking what few hunters they could find at large on a Friday. When the patrol led them to the vicinity of Ape Island, Halber decided to take one final look. Again Halber made a stealthy approach, the skiff's engine at an idle. He tied up in the same patch of tules and again signaled for Patrol Dog Ruger to stay. The dog understood perfectly what to do, but Halber's communication with Larson soon proved to be sadly inadequate.

"Wait for me, Harry. I'll be right back." said Halber. But had he paid closer attention he would have noticed a lack of acknowledgment on the part of Larson and a distinctly predatory gleam in his friend's eyes which were locked onto the hordes of ducks circling the island, some passing low overhead.

Halber again picked his way up the rip-rapped levee, more carefully even than on his last visit, for to be spotted by the ape now and discovered on the island the day before the planned operation would be disastrous. The chatter of thousands of feeding ducks was a steady roar as he slowly raised his head above the levee-top to take a peek, carefully . . . carefully . . . but at that instant, a shotgun blast only a few feet behind him nearly stopped his heart.

Larson, with a grin, would later argue, "Hey, you wanted me to look like a duck hunter. Well, I *am* a duck hunter. I have my hunting license, my duck stamps, my shotgun, it's duck season, and I saw some ducks. And I was in a boat on state waters." But at the time, Halber was horrified, and following the shot, a number of things happened in quick succession: Not one, not two, but three mallard ducks collapsed in midair and fell lifeless beyond the levee; the ape began whooping at the top of its lungs; Patrol Dog Ruger leaped out of the skiff, raced up and over the levee-top, intent on retrieving the downed ducks; and a few seconds later Halber heard an outboard motor start up at the clubhouse dock. An angry caretaker was on his way.

WHOOOOOP! WHOOOOOP! went the ape as Halber frantically called for his dog. But Patrol Dog Ruger, intent on his mission, failed to respond. *WHOOOOOP! WHOOOOOP!*

Halber was desperate now and made a snap decision. He scrambled down the levee, pushed off the skiff and leaped aboard. He fired the engine, threw it into gear and they were off.

"What's wrong?" said Larson. "Where's Ruger?"

"I'll explain later," said Halber, casting nervous glances behind them. They ran a slalom course at full speed, careening around tule-berms and dodging snags until they were well away from Ape Island. Halber then pulled up to a small island.

"Take your shotgun and wait for me here," said Halber. "I have to go back for Ruger."

Halber peeled off his camo parka, revealing the uniform beneath. He then spun the skiff around and headed back for Ape Island. When he arrived, two men were in the act of loading Patrol Dog Ruger into a boat. Halber idled up to them and spoke.

"Good morning, men. State Fish and Game. Do you have permission to hunt here?"

"No, we're not hunting," cried one of them. "I'm the caretaker. We . . ."

"But I just heard a shot here," said Halber.

"We know, we just had some poachers. This is their dog."

"I see," said Halber. "Did you get a description of them?"

"No," said the caretaker. "They were gone when we got here. They went that way." The man pointed in the direction from which Halber had just come. "You must have just missed them."

"What are we going to do with this dog?" said the second man, who had Patrol Dog Ruger by the collar. Halber now regarded his dog as though noticing him for the first time.

"I don't know," said Halber, rubbing his chin pensively. "Well, I guess you could take him to the pound. He's wearing a license. They'll be able to find his owner."

"Would you consider taking him in?" said the caretaker hopefully. "We'd really appreciate it."

"Well, I don't know," said Halber reluctantly. "Well . . . OK. I guess I could do that. Do you think he'll stay in my boat?"

He then stepped out of his skiff as the man walked Patrol Dog Ruger his way. The dog had an unmistakably joyous look on his face as Halber took over the hold on his collar.

"Come on, doggie. Come on," said Halber, and despite

the fact that a snap of his fingers would have signaled Patrol Dog Ruger to instantly jump into the skiff, Halber picked him up and gently placed him aboard. He then turned back to the caretaker.

"When I find out who he belongs to, I'll give 'em a call and have a talk with 'em." He then pushed off and waved farewell to the two men.

When he was well away and out of sight of the caretaker and his friend, Halber released his dog's collar and scratched him affectionately behind the ears. "Hi, big boy. Are you glad to be back?" The big dog beamed, as fine and loyal a friend as a warden could want. He then trotted forward and hopped up onto his place on the bow seat. And as the skiff reached full speed, skimming over the dark water, Patrol Dog Ruger leaned forward, looking like a giant hood ornament, bright eyes shining, satin ears flapping in the wind, lips pulled back in a canine grin.

* * *

The raid on Ape Island was memorable for a number of reasons. It began three hours before daybreak at Bethel Island, where Halber moored his skiff. When the participating officers were assembled, they discussed the plan and the layout of Ape Island. They would all go to the island in Halber's skiff. Halber would drop off Wictum, Del Nero and Downs on the far side of the island, near the hunting blinds. It would be their job to slip into good vantage points without alerting the ape, and to observe the hunt. They would count the ducks that were shot, a practice wardens referred to as *counting drops*. Halber and Dennis would stay out of sight in the skiff at an adjacent island until called in by the others when the hunt was over. Halber had determined that the hunters traveled the interior of the island by boat on a system of canals, the main one of which ended at a boathouse a few yards from the ape cage and the clubhouse. The plan was for Halber and Dennis, when called, to land the skiff at a hidden, forested spot near the clubhouse, sneak in and surprise the hunters upon their return. Halber managed, with a straight face, to tell Dennis that it would be *his* job to wrestle the ape.

Wictum, Del Nero and Downs were in position an hour before shoot time, and the hunters arrived right on schedule. As expected, they had phenomenal shooting, but the observing officers, in the end, were not certain if they had taken an overlimit.

"If they shot too many, it wasn't by much," said Wictum, speaking to Halber on the radio. But the wardens decided to check the hunters anyway, according to the original plan. So when the call to Halber finally came, he ran the skiff to the chosen spot and headed on foot toward the clubhouse. Dennis followed close behind. Heavy foliage on and around the levee at that point hid them nearly all the way. But just as the clubhouse came into view, Wictum called and reported that the hunters, when nearly to the boathouse, had turned unexpectedly up another canal that would bring them to the levee an eighth of a mile or so beyond the clubhouse. Halber, puzzled over this development, tried to sneak through the clubhouse complex, past the ape, but it didn't work.

WHOOOOOP! WHOOOOOP! cried the ape, and Halber walked faster. Then a door opened and there stood the caretaker's wife.

"Can I help you?" she said, an unpleasant look on her face.

"No thank you, ma'am. I'm just passing through," said Halber, and he kept on walking. The woman immediately turned back into the clubhouse, and suddenly a deafeningly loud buzzer sounded, obviously a warning to the returning hunters. *WHOOOOOP! WHOOOOOP!* went the ape. *BUZZZZP! BUZZZZP!* went the buzzer, and Halber broke into a run.

In addition to a caged ape and lots of ducks, Ape Island also boasted a flock of two dozen or so wild turkeys, which happened to be feeding in Halber's path as he made a dash for the boat containing the hunters. Upon spotting

Halber approaching at full speed, the turkeys fled in panic ahead of him, some on foot, some flying. The three hunters in their boat watched in amazement as first the turkeys went by, then a uniformed warden arrived at full sprint. Halber's first reaction, upon sliding to a stop and finding the three men in the boat staring up at him, was embarrassment, for these were men of consequence. Quickly composing himself, he addressed one of them whom he recognized as the primary owner of the island.

"Oh, Mr. Millerton, it's you! I mistook you for a poacher."

"'Looked to me like you were exercising my turkeys," said Millerton. Halber smiled and made his way down the levee to the boat.

"How was your hunt this morning?" he asked.

"We did all right," said Millerton.

"Do you mind if I take a look?" Halber then sorted through a pile of ducks in the back of the boat. He counted. Then he counted again. "It looks to me like you've got an extra duck," he said, facing the three men.

Millerton now counted the ducks, shook his head and said, "I guess we made a mistake."

"Do you have any other ducks in the boat?" Halber inquired. As he asked the question, however, he was already searching. But there were no other ducks.

Halber checked their hunting licenses and waterfowl tags. All were in order. Convinced that they had, in fact, made an honest mistake, he decided to simply give them a warning. He selected a hen widgeon from the pile of mainly mallard ducks and faced the men.

"I'd appreciate it if you would count a little more carefully next time," he said. "Have a nice morning." He then turned, hen widgeon in hand, and hiked back the way he had come.

"Can't win 'em all," Halber said when he and Dennis picked up the other officers. But none of them really considered the operation a loss, for they had done a first-class job of investigating a report that couldn't be ignored. And while they finished the day with no captured bad guys to show for their efforts, they had shown, at least for that morning, that the hunters of Ape Island were essentially obeying the law. All agreed, however, that Ape Island deserved more scrutiny in the future.

Meanwhile, Officer Harry Larson's day had been a success by any measure. Annoyed over the fact that a serial rapist operating in the Concord area had selected a victim the night before in Larson's own neighborhood, Larson had set out to catch the man. Armed with a physical description and composite sketch provided by the rapist's eight known victims, plus a description of the suspect's car, Larson followed his instincts, prowled the back streets of the county's seedier neighborhoods, and by nightfall had located the suspect's car and shortly thereafter the suspect himself. Handcuffed in the front seat of Larson's black-and-white, the man was lulled by Larson's formidable interrogation skills into not only confessing his crimes, but to directing Larson to the home of his latest victim.

A few days following Larson's ridding the streets of the Concord Rapist, he again accompanied Halber on a boat patrol. An hour into the day they caught an outlaw duck hunter who had removed the magazine plug from his shotgun. Halber had spotted the green plastic plug protruding from the man's breast pocket. As Halber wrote the citation, Larson had a conversation with the violator's companion.

"I was cleaning a duck the other day and it was full of little-tiny worms," said the man. "What do you think they were?"

Halber, who overheard the question, had no idea what manner of parasite the worms might have been. Larson, however, had an immediate answer.

"Those were duck worms," he said.

"Oh," said the man, apparently satisfied.

Shortly thereafter the man expressed his inability to tell some ducks from others.

"I always have trouble telling a hen pintail from a hen widgeon," said the man. Again, Larson had an immediate answer.

"You can always tell a hen widgeon from a pintail because the widgeon has an inverted dihedral."

"A what?"

"An inverted dihedral."

"Oh," said the man, unwilling to admit further ignorance.

When Halber had finished the citation and the violator and his friend had departed, Halber cast a disapproving eye at Larson.

"Duck worms? Inverted dihedral?" he said.

Larson's grin was ear to ear.

COLD, COLD HEARTS

The big Alaska Airlines jet banked in the night sky onto its final approach into Anchorage International Airport. Warden John Dawson, California Department of Fish and Game, felt a prickle of excitement as he pondered his immediate future, a temporary assignment that could well turn out to be the greatest adventure of his life. In the seat beside him sat Lt. Franco D'Angelo of the Alaska State Police, Division of Fish and Wildlife. Together the two of them would spend the next several days working undercover in a remote Alaska hunting camp. If they were successful, they would bring down two ruthless and destructive outlaw guides and their underlings. If they failed, they could easily end up as grizzly bait.

As the jet's big wheels thumped down on the tarmac, D'Angelo turned with a grin to Dawson and said, "Welcome to Alaska. Are you ready for this?"

It had all started when Martin Dole, a California hunter, had phoned the Alaska State Police to inquire as to the credentials of one Doyle Kepler, an Alaskan hunting guide. Dole was considering booking a moose and grizzly hunt with Kepler, but having once been burned by a crooked guide, Dole wisely decided to check on Kepler in advance. To his surprise, he learned that Kepler was not a licensed guide, and also that the state troopers were highly interested in him. Dole immediately found his call transferred to Lt. Franco D'Angelo of State Police's Commercial Crimes Unit.

D'Angelo was frank with Dole, explaining that Kepler was a well known outlaw in Alaska with a variety of past convictions for crimes against wildlife. Most recently, he had been convicted for *guiding without a license* and *waste of game*, following his abandoning the meat of a Dall ram of which he had kept only the trophy head and cape. Kepler was said to be closely tied to another outlaw guide by the name of Jacob Radler. "Rattler," as this man was called, was also well known to the state troopers and was generally believed to be not only a committed violator, but highly dangerous as well.

"We really want to catch this guy again and put him out of business," said D'Angelo. "Would you help us?" With some coaxing, Dole agreed.

About two weeks later, D'Angelo flew to California with another Alaska state trooper, Investigator Shanahan, and was met at the Redding Airport by California warden John Dawson. D'Angelo had worked with Dawson on a previous case and had been impressed with him. He now had hopes of enlisting Dawson's help in an operation against Kepler. Dawson drove the two men to the City of Chico where they met with Martin Dole. After a brief discussion, Dole agreed to phone Kepler. Dole was to postpone his own hunting trip due to personal problems, then he was to tell Kepler about two friends of his who were looking for a hunting guide in Alaska. The wardens coached Dole on a simple scenario that would explain how he knew his two "friends." Dole made the call, left a message which included the number for a telephone that had been freshly installed in Dawson's home for this purpose. A day or two later, Dawson got his first call from Kepler, who immediately grilled him on how he knew Dole. Dawson explained, sticking to the scenario he had agreed upon with Dole. Kepler then made a pitch for his guide service, and he and Dawson began discussing tentative dates for their hunt.

But communication with Kepler would never be easy. Kepler was wary, and would never give Dawson a direct number to contact him. Dawson had to leave messages with a female associate of Kepler's, one Janice Cooper-Chance, in Anchorage. Kepler would then phone Dawson, often at odd hours, near midnight or before dawn, to discuss a possible hunt and negotiate potential business arrangements. Even without seeing the man, Dawson sensed an instability in him, something disturbing that gave Dawson the creeps.

Dawson recorded every call, labeling each tape with date and time. But for every conversation he had with Kepler, he had three or four with Cooper-Chance, and he developed a comfortable rapport with her. It was as though she thirsted for someone to talk to, and the more comfortable she grew with Dawson, the more she told him, things about Kepler, things that would have horrified the man.

"He saves bear gallbladders and sells them to somebody in Seattle," she once told Dawson. "He showed up here one time with one of those little six-pack-size ice chests full of them." Then she hastily added, "Don't tell Doyle I told you that." Dawson assured her that he definitely would not be telling the man anything about it.

Finally, Dawson and Kepler reached an agreement on a fall bear hunt.

"I usually charge $6,950 per hunter, but since there's two of you, I'll only charge you $5,500 each. I'll guarantee you each a grizzly of at least eight feet, and I'll throw in some coho salmon fishing for nothing." Dawson agreed, and the deal was struck.

A few days before the planned September hunt, D'Angelo flew to Medford, Oregon and was met by Dawson at the airport. During their drive back to Dawson's home in Yreka, a few miles south of the Oregon border, they developed a cover story, a fictional tale complete with details as to how and when they had met, names of family members and mutual friends and a variety of anecdotes concerning memorable things they supposedly had experienced together. Then they practiced it.

During the last three days before the hunt, they lived their cover story and their undercover names. They tested each other, grilling each other on details of their fictional past lives until the whole thing was second nature. Dawson went out of his way to take D'Angelo to public places, using his cover name to introduce him to dozens of people. Then they would reminisce in front of others and tell funny, "best buds" stories on each other concerning their mythical past. In a way, it was fun and games, but in a far greater way, it was in deadly earnest.

Also during the last three days, they repeatedly tested a hand-held Global Positioning System unit, or GPS, and a satellite telephone, things on which their very lives could depend. D'Angelo even insisted that they store a variety of northern California checkpoints in the GPS unit, in case Kepler should ever examine it.

Then Dawson packed his gear, the usual camo hunting clothes and accessories, into a large camo-colored backpack. Stuffed near the top of his pack was a stainless steel Smith & Wesson .357 Magnum revolver and a box of shells. He would have preferred his 16-shot, semi-automatic Glock duty weapon, but it looked too much like a cop gun. Plus, he could better justify his carrying the big-frame Magnum revolver as his "bear insurance."

Finally the day arrived. They drove to Medford, caught a flight to Seattle, then boarded the Alaska Airlines jet for the night flight to Anchorage. It was no accident that they would arrive near midnight. They felt it necessary to minimize the chance of any of the bad guys meeting them at the airport where someone might recognize D'Angelo and blow the case. Their arrival proved uneventful, and they took a shuttle bus to the Holiday Inn. They would grab what sleep they could before Kepler's planned meeting with them at 8 o'clock the next morning.

At 7 a.m. the next morning, they had visitors at their room. Two Alaska state troopers arrived to attach a surveillance wire to D'Angelo so that they could monitor the coming conversations when Kepler and possibly Rattler arrived. The State Police people were highly nervous over D'Angelo and Dawson placing themselves so squarely in harm's way, and they had carefully planned to give the two men what cover they could, at least while they were still near Anchorage.

An hour later, when it was time to meet the bad guys in the lobby, Dawson turned to D'Angelo.

"It's show time!" he said, and the two of them headed for the stairs.

Kepler turned out to be alone, and Dawson recognized him instantly from the booking photos he had studied. He wasn't a big man, but there was something both formidable and unforgettable in his appearance, and he appeared highly nervous. He was popping Tums antacid tablets, one after another, from a large bottle he kept in his jacket pocket. To Dawson, he looked like a bad-tempered mountain man from a different age. There was something sinister in his narrow, beard-stubbled face, and when he smiled, his mouth assumed the shape of a smile, but the rest of his face somehow didn't join in, certainly not his eyes, which to Dawson looked like those of a church-bomber.

"Let's go up to your room and check out your gear," said Kepler following introductions. In their room, under Kepler's direction, Dawson and D'Angelo emptied their packs on the beds, laying everything out for Kepler's scrutiny. It was obvious that he was looking for some clue that his two "clients" might be something other than what they claimed to be.

The wardens made no attempt to hide the satellite phone, the GPS unit or Dawson's pistol, for they knew that Kepler must be accustomed to clients bringing such things. Kepler, in fact, paid them little attention, instead snatching up the box of .357 Magnum cartridges Dawson had brought. He studied them, and what followed was the first of a series of nerve-jangling incidents that over the next three days would gnaw at the stomachs of the wardens like feeding rats.

"Where did you get these?" Kepler demanded, fixing his unblinking gaze on Dawson. Dawson was afraid that he had somehow brought a box of for-cops-only ammunition that Kepler had recognized and the case would be blown.

"I don't know, BiMart or someplace," Dawson answered.

Kepler glared at Dawson for a moment, then tossed the box of cartridges aside. Dawson would later learn that Kepler was an expert in reloading ammunition and was an authority on bullets, primers and powder. For now, at least, the man was satisfied with Dawson's explanation, and he turned his attention to Dawson's pack, checking that nothing had been left in any of the many pockets. Kepler then popped a couple of Tums and turned to D'Angelo's gear. Dawson took a deep breath, vastly relieved.

But his relief was short lived, for suddenly the room's telephone rang, sounding to Dawson like a fire alarm. Dawson hurried over and picked it up, said hello, and the answering voice was that of one of the other state troopers.

"Is Franco there? His wire's not working."

Dawson was horrified, but didn't miss a beat.

"Yes . . . I see . . . Don't you have his credit card number? . . . I see. All right, I'll send him down," Dawson said, then hung up the phone. Kepler had stopped what he was doing and was watching Dawson.

"It's the front desk," said Dawson, addressing D'Angelo. "There's some problem with the bill. They want you to go down there and talk to 'em." Kepler's eyes then followed D'Angelo as he headed for the door.

"I'll be right back," said D'Angelo. Kepler returned his attention to D'Angelo's gear. Somewhere near the front desk, the other state troopers found D'Angelo and hurriedly corrected the problem with the wire.

"We couldn't risk leaving you in there with the wire not working," one of them explained. But to D'Angelo, in view of the total isolation he and Dawson would soon share with Kepler and his associates, the call to the room had been a great and unreasonable risk. But soon he was back in the room, and it appeared that no damage had been done.

Following the gear inspection, Kepler ordered them to pack their gear again and carry it out to the parking lot. As he did so, he popped two more Tums, and his hands were shaking so badly when he replaced the cap on the bottle that D'Angelo was highly concerned.

"Hey, man, are you gonna be all right to fly today?" said D'Angelo.

"I'll be OK, just as soon as we get going," Kepler replied.

They piled their packs and rifle cases into the back of a battered, four-door Dodge pickup, and the three of them climbed in. Kepler drove them first to the home of Janice Cooper-Chance. Kepler introduced her as his bookkeeper and baby sitter, and Dawson now had a face to go with the name and voice of the friendly woman he had spoken to so many times while arranging for the hunt.

Next, Kepler drove them to his apartment to pick up his own gear, which included a large .44 Magnum revolver and two rifles, one of them a big .50 caliber piece. While there, he showed Dawson and D'Angelo a Dall sheep head in his freezer.

"A doctor client of mine shot this ram, but my dog ate the cape off of it," Kepler explained. "I'll have to go shoot another one to get a cape to send to the taxidermist."

Soon they were on the road again, heading north. The plan was to drive to some distant airstrip near Trapper's Creek, and from there Kepler would fly them on to the hunting camp. During the drive north to the airstrip, Kepler made two stops, each one a worry to the wardens. They were concerned that they would encounter someone who would recognize D'Angelo, who had been a narcotics officer earlier in his career. It was also on the drive north that Kepler launched into a discourse about how much he hated wardens, or "fish cops" as he called them.

"Y'all ain't fish cops are you?" he inquired at one point, turning to study their reactions to the question.

The wardens made appropriate responses to the contrary, and Kepler seemed satisfied.

The first stop was at Birchwood Airport, not far out of Anchorage. There, Kepler obtained a second pickup, this one a four-door Chevrolet. He then informed Dawson and D'Angelo that he would be driving separately from there on and that they were to follow him in the Dodge. Soon they were on the road again, the two wardens following behind Kepler's pickup.

Passing through the City of Wasilla, they made a stop at a market, during which Kepler pushed a shopping cart down the aisles and instructed Dawson and D'Angelo to toss in whatever they wanted to eat for the next few days.

Finally they made a stop at a roadside lodge along the way. Kepler said that he needed to meet with some friends. It was another chance for D'Angelo to be recognized, and Dawson was concerned enough about it to plan for such an event while Kepler was inside. Because his pistol was buried deep in his pack in the bed of the pickup, he looked for more readily accessible weapons. He found what he needed on the rear seat of the pickup. There were two .22 caliber firearms, one rifle and one pistol, loaded.

"If things really go bad, we can use these," he told D'Angelo.

From the time they had left the motel that morning, they had been tailed and monitored by undercover Alaska State Police. Dawson had looked for them and occasionally spotted them, but they were good, and Kepler never caught on.

It was early afternoon when they arrived in Trapper's Creek, and Kepler led them off the highway to the little airstrip at the place known as Potato Pete's. His plane was hangered there, a small, high-winged Maule, which looked to Dawson much like a Super Cub, a commonly used single-engine bush plane in the north country. They loaded D'Angelo's gear first, Kepler explaining that he would have to fly them in one at a time. He also explained that there was a larger airport nearby and that for safety reasons they would actually be flying out of there. He instructed Dawson to drive D'Angelo to the larger airport where Kepler would pick him up.

Dawson drove to the larger airport, and soon Kepler's little yellow and white airplane appeared and touched down on the runway.

"Do you think we're crazy?" said Dawson to D'Angelo as Kepler was taxiing toward them, for he and D'Angelo were about to go flying with a dangerous, jittery man who had no pilot's license and at least one crashed airplane to his credit.

"If not crazy, we're close to it," said D'Angelo.

As D'Angelo was climbing into the little airplane, Kepler instructed Dawson to drive back to Potato Pete's and wait for him there. But Dawson remained where he was long enough to watch Kepler taxi to the far end of the runway, gun the engine and take off.

Dawson watched until the plane was but a speck in the sky, then turned the pickup around and headed out. As he did so, he noticed several men standing near the gas pumps watching him. He at first thought they were undercover state troopers, but they were too obviously scrutinizing him. Upon leaving the airport, he looked for the tail that he knew was nearby, and sure enough, a white pickup appeared far behind in his rear view mirror. Dawson then spotted a church, just off of the highway. He turned into the vacant parking lot and drove to the rear of the building. The white pickup soon joined him.

State Trooper Matt Dobson introduced himself and inquired how things were going. Dawson gave him a summary, plus Kepler's apartment number and the tail number of the Maule airplane. Dobson took notes.

"Were those your people at the gas pumps back at the airport?" Dawson asked.

"Not hardly," said Dobson. "Those were friends of Kepler's. In fact, one of them was the one they call Rattler."

Dawson drove back to Potato Pete's, and while awaiting Kepler's return, he did a quick search of the pickup. What he found sickened him. In a storage pouch sewn into a lower part of the seat covers, he found a small tape recorder.

Its switch was in the *record* position, the tape had run to its end, and the batteries in the machine were dead. Had it been recording when he and D'Angelo had been alone in the pickup discussing the operation? He thought back over his private conversations with D'Angelo. He was certain they had discussed things that would alert Kepler, should he listen to the tape. It was a serious dilemma, and Dawson pondered his options. Should he take the tape? *Damned if I do, damned if I don't*, he thought. He again considered his options and made his decision. He hit the eject button, plucked the tiny tape from the machine and put it in his pocket. He then replaced the recorder where he had found it.

Kepler flew back after a little more than an hour. They loaded Dawson's gear and Kepler's rifles and duffle bag, then Kepler sent Dawson back again to the bigger airport from which they would depart. Soon thereafter, the two of them sat in the tiny plane at one end of the runway.

"Here we go!" said Kepler as he pushed the throttle lever to full power. The little engine roared, and the airplane rolled forward, gathering speed. Down the runway they raced, faster and faster. Dawson's already substantial worries increased as the far end of the runway drew nearer and nearer. Finally Kepler drew back on the control yoke, the nose of the plane pitched skyward, and with great reluctance the machine left the ground. They cleared the nearest of the black spruce trees beyond the runway by a mere 10 feet.

As the earth fell away and Dawson gradually recovered from their white-knuckle takeoff, he peered out over a vista he would never forget. Through a hundred miles of crystalline air in all directions, he marveled over a jagged skyline of rugged, snow-capped mountains, surrounded by thousands of forest-rimmed lakes and rivers, a vast expanse of what was still some of the wildest, most beautiful country on the planet.

After a half-hour, Kepler began descending toward a tiny dirt strip near a river. As they drew nearer, Dawson made out the name, *Rifle Creek*, spelled out in white-painted stones along the quarter-mile-long landing strip. He noted a two-story cabin and several outbuildings at one end of the strip and a single cabin on the other.

Kepler may have lacked a pilot's license, but he was an experienced pilot, and he brought the little Maule in for a good landing. D'Angelo was there with his camcorder, filming the arrival. Dawson was relieved to see him safe and healthy.

They spent the remainder of the day test firing their rifles and otherwise preparing for the next day's hunt. Kepler even gave them a demonstration firing of his .50 caliber rifle, the monster gun that fired the same sausage-size cartridge as the U.S. military's heavy machine gun.

At one point, they were introduced to three of Kepler's "friends," villainous looking characters who studied Dawson and D'Angelo with barely disguised suspicion. Bob and Tex were a sullen pair in their early forties. Skip was a wild-eyed, 20-year-old whom Dawson sensed was on the verge of insanity.

"Show 'em your moose, Skip," said Kepler, in reference to an animal the kid had killed the evening before. Skip led them to an outbuilding where huge quarters of red meat hung from a beam. The head and antlers were nowhere to be seen, and the wardens suspected that it had been a sub-legal animal. When they returned to the main cabin, Kepler asked Skip if he had put out any bear bait nearby. Skip replied that he had hung two sacks of meat scraps in trees, in plain sight of and within rifle range of the cabins. The wardens were amazed that they would speak so freely about the baiting of bears, a highly illegal practice.

That night, following a dinner of moose heart and potatoes, Kepler played the role of the grand story-teller, relating tale after dubious tale of the adventures and misadventures of his past clients and of the giant bear and moose they had bagged. Then it was time to sleep, and Kepler showed his two "clients" to their sleeping quarters in the cabin at the far end of the airstrip. Even though Kepler slept in the same room with them, his .44 Magnum under his pillow, Dawson and D'Angelo, who had endured a long day of almost constant tension, slept like the dead.

They arose the next morning to a magnificent red sunrise, the sky filled with pink-tinged purple clouds. Following breakfast, they dressed in hunting camo, grabbed their rifles, and Kepler, Dawson and D'Angelo climbed onto a six-wheeled Polaris all-terrain vehicle. Bob drove them a couple of miles to the place where Skip had killed the moose two days earlier. They found what remained of the carcass buried beneath a pile of brush.

"A bear's been on it," said Kepler, as he began pulling brush off of the kill. When the kill lay uncovered, Kepler led Dawson and D'Angelo to a rise of higher ground about 50 yards away.

"We wait here," said Kepler. From this spot they would have a good chance of seeing any bear that might come to feed on the moose carcass. "Now, as soon as a bear shows up, I want you to shoot. If the bear has cubs, shoot those too. There's too many bears around here. They're hurtin' the moose population."

Both wardens were struck by Kepler's cold heartedness. They had expected him to liberally violate the game laws, but the killing of bear cubs went well beyond their worst expectations.

It was midmorning when they began their vigil near the moose carcass, and seven hours were to pass before they got action. This gave the wardens plenty of time to contemplate what lay before them, the sad fact that they were going to have to kill a grizzly bear in order to build a strong case against Kepler. But it boiled down to the simple fact that sacrificing one would ultimately save many. Kepler had chosen Dawson to take the first shot, and Dawson mentally prepared himself.

They sensed the presence of the big bear before they heard or saw it. Then there was a crashing among the willows as the bear made for the bait. Next came the disturbing sounds of the bear ripping at the carcass, animal grunts and the cracking and crunching of breaking bones. It was an old boar grizzly, large and battle-scarred. One ear had been ripped and was freshly scabbed, the results of a brief battle with a sow grizzly two days earlier. The sow had fought in vain to protect her single, half-grown cub which the old boar had killed and eaten.

Dawson caught an occasional glimpse of golden brown fur, but the willows were a little too high to allow him a good shot. But suddenly something alerted the bear, and it stood up, facing the three men.

"Take him," whispered Kepler, and Dawson centered the rifle-scope's crosshairs squarely in the middle of the bear's chest and squeezed the trigger. The rifle bucked sharply as the shot boomed out, and the bear went down, crashing and thrashing among the willows.

"Shoot him again! Bore another hole in him, boy!" shouted Kepler.

Dawson, however, could not see the bear, just the violent shaking of disturbed willows. But Kepler kept shouting for him to shoot again, so he sent one more bullet blindly into the brush. Finally all movement in the willow thicket ceased, and Kepler made a stealthy and careful approach, rifle at the ready. He found the bear dead. In the meantime, D'Angelo had filmed the whole event.

There followed considerable posing and picture taking with the dead bear, then suddenly Kepler froze, peering skyward, listening. A small plane was flying low, not far away, and Kepler frantically ordered Dawson and D'Angelo to hide their gear in the brush and stay out of sight. Kepler then began skinning the bear, pausing often to look and listen for airplanes. When this task was completed, he strapped the head and hide onto his pack frame.

Dawson then asked Kepler for the bear's gallbladder. "I have a friend in Los Angeles, a Korean guy, and I told him I'd bring him a gallbladder."

"Well, you can't have the gallbladder," said Kepler. "The gallbladder's mine. It's my bonus."

"But it's my bear," Dawson complained.

"Yeah, but the gallbladder's mine. Why do you think I like to hunt bears so much?"

Dawson then offered him $500 for the gallbladder, and Kepler just laughed and said, "No way!" He then sliced from the bear's liver the greenish-colored organ, the size and shape of an avocado. Enlisting Dawson's help, he tied the bile duct closed with a piece of twine. Then he handed it to Dawson to store in his pack.

"Be careful with that," he said. "That's gold."

They hiked out to where Bob had come to meet them with the Polaris. They piled aboard and soon were on their way back to camp. But they hadn't gone far when a floatplane came buzzing by at low altitude. Bob shook his fist at it. He was highly angered by the incident and when back in camp he explained that it was the plane flown by guides from another hunting camp.

"They're not supposed to hunt in our territory. We agreed on that."

Dawson then asked, "Well, what are they doing by flying? Are they spotting game?" Both Bob and Kepler assured him that they were spotting game, and that it was illegal. It was true: Alaskan law forbade the use of aircraft for spotting game, even forbidding hunters or guides from hunting the same day that they flew.

"But I guess we do it, too," said Bob. "How do you think we found that moose the other day? It's like having an aerial tree stand."

"You spotted that moose from the air?" Dawson asked.

Bob nodded with a smile, and Skip put his finger to his lips, indicating that Dawson and D'Angelo should keep quiet about it. Inquiring further, Dawson learned that the technique was for a pilot to spot a bear or moose from the air, then, so as not to have to use radios, the pilot would turn on the plane's landing lights and fly a tight circle directly above the animal. Hunters on the ground would then race on ATVs to that spot.

The following morning, Kepler decided to fly Dawson's bear hide and the gallbladder back to Potato Pete's.

Dawson immediately remembered the tape recorder in the pickup there, and he was sickened anew. D'Angelo, too, was worried, Dawson having told him about the recorder. Would Kepler check the recorder while he was there? Time would tell.

Before leaving, Kepler instructed Dawson and D'Angelo to deny having hunted, should any wardens appear in camp. He then instructed Skip to take them salmon fishing. He and Bob then climbed into the Maule, taxied to the end of the airstrip and took off.

From an array of heavy fishing gear on the wall of an outbuilding, Skip selected two snagging outfits, stout rods with heavy reels and line. He then led Dawson and D'Angelo to a spot on the bank of Rifle Creek, from which they could see over 100 pinkish-red coho salmon finning in the shallows. Skip took one of the snagging outfits, cast the weighted treble hooks beyond the salmon, then ripped the hooks through the mass of fish by means of a great sweeping jerk of the rod. The hooks impaled themselves in a nice salmon, and it leaped and flipped as Skip horsed it in with the heavy line.

"Now, you try," said Skip, handing the outfit to D'Angelo. It took D'Angelo only seconds to snag another salmon. He reeled it in, tail first, then released it.

"Looks like you've got the hang of it," said Skip. "Fish as long as you want. I'll be back at the cabin."

Dawson watched him depart, then followed him a short distance until it was certain that the man was returning to the cabin. Dawson then hurried back and advised D'Angelo that they were alone. D'Angelo pulled out the satellite phone and dialed State Police Headquarters. He had made one other call on the night of their arrival, telling Kepler that he wanted to check in with his wife to let her know that they had arrived safely. Walking out onto the airstrip, well away from the cabins, he had called State Police and advised them of the GPS coordinates of the hunting camp, plus he gave them a brief description of the layout of the cabins and the number of people present.

Upon again reaching State Police headquarters, D'Angelo informed them about Dawson's bear, the illegally killed moose and the bear baiting. And he was telling them about the salmon snagging when the sudden and unexpected snarl of an aircraft engine stopped him midsentence. Kepler's Maule raced by, alarmingly close, right over their heads.

"What's he doing back?" said Dawson.

"I don't know," said D'Angelo. "But I hope my phone call didn't bleed over onto his radio." The two men faced each other as this very real possibility sunk in, the chance that Kepler had, through some quirk of electronics, heard some or all of D'Angelo's report to Anchorage. They hurried back toward the cabin as Kepler made his approach and dropped the little airplane onto the dirt strip.

The wardens watched with alarm as Kepler emerged from the cockpit looking thoroughly enraged and stalked toward them, the big .44 Mag pistol in his hand. Dawson discreetly unsnapped the safety strap on his holstered pistol, ready for war, and D'Angelo, unarmed, looked for a place to dive. As Kepler drew near, he was muttering curses under his breath, and it was all Dawson could do to keep his own hand still, away from his pistol.

"I couldn't make it," growled Kepler. "Ran into fog at Potato Pete's."

Dawson and D'Angelo glanced at each other with vast relief, able to breathe again. Kepler's dark mood then seemed to brighten as he told them about an unusually large black bear and two very large bull moose that he had spotted, not far away, when he was flying. He also told them that a bear had already been feeding on the skinned carcass of the bear Dawson had killed the previous day.

"It'll probably be a grizzly sow with cubs," said Kepler. Then turning to D'Angelo, he said, "You have to be ready for that, OK? If there's one cub, we shoot it. If there's two cubs or three cubs, we shoot them all. Do you understand?" D'Angelo was able to hide his revulsion and nod his head in understanding.

That afternoon, they left camp for their second hunt. Again they traveled on two ATVs driven by Bob and Skip, who dropped them off near the place where Dawson had killed his bear. Bob and Skip then drove away to search for the moose Kepler had spotted earlier from the plane.

Kepler and his two clients watched and waited for a couple of hours before they got action. But the action, when it came, was not in the form of a hungry bear, but rather a helicopter flying not far away. Kepler was instantly in a panic, leaping up and gathering up his gear.

"Hurry! Hurry!" he ordered. "Get your stuff under that tree and cover it with camo." Dawson and D'Angelo did as they were told, and peeking out from their hiding place they spotted the helicopter not far from their camp.

"Those are fish cops," said Kepler, highly upset. Then he added, "But you're not doing nothin' wrong. I just don't want them ruining y'all's hunt." The wardens found this curious, the fact that Kepler had them engaged in an illegal "same day" hunt following his flight earlier in the day, and he had directed them to shoot cubs should the opportunity arise, and yet he was now playing this lame charade of telling them they were doing nothing wrong.

He was right, however: The helicopter had contained fish cops. They had landed at camp and asked Tex about some ATVs that had been reported stolen from a mining camp a few miles away. It had been a simple ruse by the wardens to enable them to get a look at the layout of the landing strip and hunting camp, knowledge that would be valuable when the time came for the take-down.

When Kepler and his clients heard the helicopter depart, they resumed their watch over the carcass of Dawson's bear. But Kepler was in such an agitated mental state that it was obvious that the hunt wouldn't last much longer, and when a float plane appeared and began buzzing around at low altitude, Kepler called it quits. They grabbed their gear and began hiking out.

They hadn't gone far when they met Bob and Skip on the ATVs. They, too, had decided that it was a bad time to hunt. As Dawson and D'Angelo loaded their gear onto the machines, Bob suddenly called to Kepler, "Hey Doyle!" Everyone looked at Bob, who was pointing at something in the distance. A bull moose had just walked out of the brush, apparently frightened by the floatplane that was still buzzing around. Kepler reacted instantly, grabbing his rifle and throwing it to his shoulder. Giving no thought to his clients, he peered at the moose through his scope.

"What do you think, Bob? Should I shoot it?" In answer, Bob stepped over to Kepler and invited him to use his shoulder as a rifle-rest. Kepler, however, declined and hurried a few steps to his left. Again he aimed the rifle and this time he fired, just as the moose was disappearing into a thicket. The moose instantly went down, legs flailing.

"Good shot, Doyle," said Bob, inviting a high-five from Kepler. Dawson and D'Angelo offered their own congratulations on what had indeed been a good shot. Dawson then leaned close to D'Angelo and whispered, "I got the whole thing on film."

Upon approaching the downed moose, Skip pulled a Magnum pistol from his belt and fired a shot into the animal's head. The wardens made mental note of this, due to the fact that they had learned from Bob that Skip was a convicted felon and could not use or possess firearms. The wardens had also noted, earlier in the day, that Skip carried a second pistol, a two-shot, .38 caliber derringer, in a front pocket of his pants. When Dawson asked him why he carried the derringer, a pitifully inadequate weapon for protection against big game, Skip had answered that it wasn't for bears, but for fish cops, should any appear.

As they were preparing to skin the dead moose, which was too small to be legal, D'Angelo was astounded to see a grizzly bear stroll into sight about 300 yards away on a hillside. D'Angelo alerted Dawson, who pointed it out to Kepler. Kepler immediately began shooting at the animal and yelled at D'Angelo to do the same. Kepler got off three shots, one of which sent the bear spinning in circles before it crashed away into dense brush. Kepler, in a rage, then turned to face D'Angelo.

"Why didn't you shoot?" he implored. "You should've been shootin'."

"You were in front of me," said D'Angelo.

"Don't worry about me, just shoot! Shoot 'til you're empty!"

Kepler then directed D'Angelo to accompany him to the place where the bear had been, and they searched for several minutes for any sign of a blood trail. But the light was poor, the sun low on the horizon, and they headed back. D'Angelo was relieved that Kepler would apparently not be trying to trail a possibly wounded grizzly into thick brush.

The light failed them entirely, long before they finished the labor of skinning and quartering the moose and packing the meat into meat bags. They then worked by the light of two flashlights. They piled the meat into the Polaris. Dawson, using D'Angelo's camcorder, had filmed much of this operation until Skip had glared at him, an unmistakably hostile look. Dawson had then stuffed the camera into his pack.

A tense situation arose when D'Angelo, riding behind Dawson on the Polaris, noticed that Dawson had failed to turn off the camcorder, and a red light on it glowed visibly inside the pack. D'Angelo was afraid Kepler or one of the others would see it and suspect that Dawson had done it intentionally to record their conversations. And then, as if D'Angelo's rising blood pressure could go yet higher, Kepler, who was riding up ahead on the quad-runner, stopped and stalked back to address D'Angelo, who was in the act of turning off the camcorder in Dawson's pack.

"Give me your rifle," Kepler demanded.

D'Angelo hesitated a moment, then handed his cased rifle to Kepler, who turned and carried it back to the quad-runner. Had he intentionally disarmed D'Angelo? Again Dawson's mind turned to the reassuring bulk of the big pistol on his hip. But nothing came of the incident.

The following morning, Kepler and Bob piled moose

meat and Dawson's grizzly hide and gallbladder into the Maule. Again they would attempt to fly these things to Potato Pete's.

"If wardens show up, tell 'em you're moose hunting," said Kepler. He and Bob then climbed in and were soon airborne and away.

Dawson and D'Angelo took this opportunity to get away from the others and walked down to the creek. There they found the head of Skip's moose, nailed to a tree for bear bait. They also inspected what they determined to be a bear trap of a particularly cruel and disturbing design. The top of a 55-gallon drum containing meat scraps had been modified with a cutting torch. A large, star-shaped piece of metal had been cut from the top of the drum, leaving sharp, triangular-shaped teeth pointing towards the center. These steel teeth had been bent slightly downward, such that a bear could squeeze its head past them, bending them downward, but they would spring back, grab and hold when the bear tried to pull its head out. And it this wasn't horror enough, the wardens found large treble hooks on stout steel leaders tied to trees. The hooks were baited with pieces of meat intended to attract a wolf or wolverine.

"All right, that does it!" said D'Angelo with disgust. "We need to call this off now before we lose anymore wildlife." Dawson agreed. They had plenty to convict Kepler and the others on a variety of serious charges. D'Angelo pulled out the satellite phone and made the call.

Kepler and Bob returned around noon in the Maule, having successfully stashed the meat, hide and gallbladder at Potato Pete's. Kepler wolfed down a sandwich, complained of being tired and stalked away toward his cabin at the far end of the airstrip. This presented a problem for the wardens, who had hoped to keep all four suspects at one place for when the take-down team arrived. But it wasn't to be. No sooner had Kepler reached his cabin when D'Angelo, who was standing outside of Bob's cabin, detected the thump of approaching rotor blades. He stuck his head inside the door and caught Dawson's attention.

Dawson caught the signal and knew then that action was imminent. He remained with Bob, Tex and Skip while D'Angelo headed for the far cabin where Kepler had gone.

The take-down team of five heavily armed State Troopers arrived, three in a helicopter and two in a Cessna airplane. They stormed out of the two aircraft, weapons at the ready, and were met by Bob, thoroughly outraged, who at first ignored their commands to lie down on the ground. One trooper on the arrest team spotted D'Angelo, rifle slung over his shoulder, midway down the airstrip. Not recognizing him at first, the trooper ordered him onto his belly as well. D'Angelo complied.

Tex's reaction to the arrival of the arrest team was highly disturbing to Dawson. Upon identifying the new arrivals as wardens, Tex turned, dashed back into the cabin, grabbed from the wall an SKS assault rifle with a large 30-round banana clip and dashed up the stairway to the second floor. Dawson, thinking the man intended to fire on the troopers from an upstairs window, followed him up, ready for battle.

"Hey, man, what are you doing?" Dawson implored. "We need to get outside!"

"Wait a minute! Wait a minute! I have to stash this," said Tex, stuffing the weapon beneath a mattress. Dawson exhaled in great relief, and soon he and Tex were outside with the others, where a shotgun-wielding trooper ordered them onto their bellies. A whispered word or two by Dawson to a trooper prevented his being handcuffed. A search of the bad guys followed, and a trooper, tipped off by Dawson, plucked from Skip's pants pocket the two-shot .38 caliber derringer.

In the meantime, D'Angelo and one of the troopers approached Kepler's cabin. The trooper carried a shotgun, and D'Angelo was now armed with the trooper's handgun.

"STATE TROOPERS! COME OUT WITH YOUR HANDS UP!" shouted the trooper. No response. The trooper then carefully pushed the door open and shouted again. Still no response. Weapons at the ready, D'Angelo and the trooper now rushed inside. The cabin was empty.

Kepler had apparently heard the helicopter coming and had slipped away into the woods.

D'Angelo made a quick search of the cabin and located all of Kepler's guns. His parka and fanny-pack survival kit were also there. Kepler had apparently left in a hurry, fleeing with no coat, gun or survival gear, and was now alone and on the run, unarmed in grizzly country. Soon the helicopter was searching for him, but without success.

Kepler's escape was a depressing development for Dawson and D'Angelo, but both men knew that he couldn't last long in the bush, ill-equipped as he was. If he survived, he would turn up soon, and the troopers would hear about it. But even with the initial escape of Kepler, the operation had been a resounding success. All four outlaws were in serious trouble. For Skip, a convicted felon in possession of firearms, it meant a quick return to prison, and Kepler would undoubtedly face substantial jail time, plus huge fines and the loss of all his guns.

The following day, back in Anchorage, Dawson's work was over. He bid farewell to D'Angelo as he prepared to board a jet for Seattle.

"Thanks again for the help, John. You're a real pro," said D'Angelo as Dawson headed for the boarding gate.

"Thanks for the adventure," answered Dawson.

* * *

The big sow grizzly lay in a willow thicket, licking the wound where a bullet had creased her flank the day before. Hungry, in pain and still suffering from the loss of her cub to a boar grizzly a week earlier, she was in an ugly, ugly mood.

She caught wind of the man-scent before she saw or heard the man. Then she spotted him, hurrying through the brush a hundred yards away. She watched as he moved along, peering nervously from side to side and sometimes behind him. She had feared men in the past, but not on this day. There was something in the way this man moved, something in his scent, something that told her that this man was in distress and weakened and posed no threat to her.

Then she looked at him in a *different* way. She heaved herself to her feet, fixed on him with her tiny, close-set, hungry eyes . . . and began to follow.

Author's note:

"Doyle Kepler" (not his real name) survived the ordeal that followed his escape from the state troopers at the hunting camp on that September day. Two months later, a State Police SWAT team arrested him at the cabin of an acquaintance near Anchorage.

DAVIE CROCKETT AND THE BUSH BABY

Charles "Davie" Crockett knew it was going to hurt. He just didn't know how much. He was clinging to the side of a speeding truck when he spotted a robed and bearded man rushing onto the roadway ahead, a rocket-propelled grenade launcher over his shoulder. Just as the man took aim and fired, Crockett leapt, and as the truck exploded in a ball of flames, Crockett landed hard, flipping end over end before coming to rest in the dirt.

He lay there for a few seconds, knocked half senseless, as others rushed to his side.

"Are you OK, Davie?"

"I'll tell you in a minute," said Crockett, slowly sitting up, tentatively testing each of his extremities. Then he rose unsteadily to his feet, dusted himself off, flashed a smile to the director and limped toward his trailer. He was battered and bruised, but about $10,000 richer. Just another day in the life of a stunt man.

But he had taken his last tumble for a while. He now planned to kiss L.A. goodbye for a couple of weeks and head for Oregon. Elk season was about to open there, and he intended to do some serious hunting. As always, he would illegally purchase a resident Oregon hunting license, using his sister's Oregon address in Bend. And because he had fraudulently registered his big dually pickup in Oregon, there would be no California plates on the vehicle to catch the eye of the Oregon game wardens.

At dawn one brisk morning a week later, Crockett lay prone on a high-desert ridge top, his rifle rested on a juniper root. The bull elk in his crosshairs was not a large one, but big ones were tough to find, and even a smaller one represented a lot of good meat. But the major factor in Crockett's decision to pull the trigger was his reputation. He was known for always bringing home the bacon. *A bird in the hand,* he thought as he began his squeeze.

The big .338 Winchester Magnum boomed, and the elk went down in a heap. Crockett rose to his feet, rubbing his recoil-bruised shoulder, which like most of his anatomy had taken more than its share of abuse. By noon, he had the elk tagged, field dressed, skinned, quartered and packed out to his pickup. Soon thereafter, he was heading south to California. Upon crossing the California border below Klamath Falls, he gloated a bit, for it appeared he had successfully thwarted the law yet again.

*   *   *

"Where are you coming from? Do you have any live plants, fresh fruits or vegetables?"

Inspector Kevin Gleason, California Department of Food and Agriculture, stood in his booth at the Dorris Agricultural Inspection Station, querying motorists driving south on Highway 97 from Oregon.

The fact that Gleason had already asked these same questions to over a hundred motorists on this day bothered him not one bit, for he knew well the vital importance of his mission. The ag stations were California's first line of defense against the introduction of potentially devastating threats to agriculture and wildlife, be they plant, animal or insect. Gleason took his job very seriously, and he had a good eye for problems.

He knew, for instance, that a harmful insect was destroying cherry trees in Washington, an insect not yet found in California. Cherries were therefore high on the list of forbidden things the ag inspectors hoped to intercept at the border.

During the preceding summer, Gleason had felt uneasy about a pair of nervous-looking farm workers traveling south from Washington. A check of the trunk of their sedan revealed nothing. Casting a flashlight beam into the back seat, Gleason had spotted what appeared to be a sleeping man, on his side under a blanket. But something didn't look just right about it. Upon opening the back door and checking under the blanket, he was surprised to find nothing but cherries, carefully heaped and arranged in the shape of a sleeping man.

Gleason was now working the swing shift, and it was dusk when he watched a shiny black Dodge dually pickup pull into his lane. The driver and sole occupant was a man in his early thirties. Gleason asked him the same questions, but added another, something he reserved for people in pickups and SUVs, people who looked like they could be hunters.

"Any live animals or any fish or game meat to declare?"

"I've got a quartered elk in the back," said the driver of the big Dodge. "I got it up near Condon."

Gleason asked him to pull off to one side and fill out a Declaration of Entry form for the elk. The man did as he was directed, without complaint, filling out the form on a clipboard. He then handed it back to Gleason who waved him through, noting the pickup's Oregon plates. When the vehicle was gone, Gleason examined the declaration form, noting that the man had given a Bend address for his residence.

Why is he heading into California with a whole elk if he lives in Bend? Gleason pondered. There could be legitimate answers to this question, but it struck Gleason as unusual. Grabbing a pad of Post-It notes, he scribbled on one, pasted it onto the Declaration of Entry form, and tossed the form into a box with others of its kind. The note read, "Rennie, you might want to take a close look at this one," and was intended for Rennie Cleland, the local Fish and Game warden. Cleland took a keen interest in these forms, followed up on the ones that looked suspicious, and made good arrests every year as a result of them, people smuggling illegally-taken fish or game into the state.

An hour or so after the departure of the elk hunter in the big Dodge pickup, Gleason noted the approach of a U-Haul moving van pulling a small red car on a towing dolly. Gleason spoke to the driver, a young man crowding 30, and a slightly younger woman. He learned that they were coming from Redmond, Oregon, moving to Palm Desert, and no, they had no fresh fruits or vegetables. Noticing what appeared to be a cage covered with a towel on the front seat between them, Gleason asked them, "What kind of a pet do you have?"

"It's a bush baby," said the man. Noting Gleason's bewildered look, he explained, "It's a little primate from Africa, sort of like a cross between a monkey and a lemur."

At Gleason's request, the man pulled the towel off of the cage, revealing the animal within. It was the size of a small raccoon and had big, radar-like ears, a black button nose, and it peered out at Gleason with enormous, soft-brown eyes that were perfectly round.

"Do you have a permit for this?" Gleason asked.

"We do, but I'm not sure where it is right now," said the man. Gleason directed him to pull the truck off to one side and come into the office with him. The man did as he was told, without complaint, and he and the woman were helpful as Gleason looked through his regulation book on prohibited species in California. The bush baby was there, among the others, clearly illegal to import into the state except under special circumstances.

"I'm sorry, sir, but I'll need to see your permit before I can allow you to pass through."

"Not a problem," said the man. "We'll just go back to Klamath Falls and stay in a motel for the night. We'll find our permit and come back tomorrow."

Gleason then issued them a *Notice of Rejection* slip for the bush baby and sent them on their way. As they turned around and headed north, Gleason jotted down the license plate numbers of both the truck and the car. He was feeling a growing suspicion that they had no intention of staying in Klamath Falls, but intended instead to make an end run to some other border crossing, maybe one of the ones that were closed at night. But he would give them the benefit of the doubt and leave a note for the morning crew to watch for them. If they didn't show up, he would know they had slipped across the border elsewhere. To be on the safe side, he decided to alert Rennie Cleland.

Warden Rennie Cleland, California Department of Fish and Game, had just finished a late dinner when the call came in. He listened with interest as Gleason explained the situation concerning the bush baby and, as an afterthought, the suspicious circumstances surrounding the elk hunter. Cleland took notes, asked a few questions, then agreed to contact Gleason again in the morning.

The next morning, at the start of office hours, Cleland phoned Fish and Game's Licenses and Revenue Branch and had them check the names Marvin and Debra Trask, the names given to Gleason the night before by the bush baby people. The records clerks found nothing under either name, and they assured Cleland that there was no way that the Trasks could have a permit to keep a bush baby for a pet.

About the time Cleland cleared his call with the records people, his phone rang, and it was Gleason.

"They never showed up!" said Gleason. "They must have crossed the border somewhere else."

Cleland agreed, and began formulating a plan to run them down. He first phoned Highway Patrol dispatch and ran Marvin and Debra Trask in both California and Oregon for driver's license information. He learned that Debra Trask had a valid license in Oregon, showing an address in Redmond. Marvin Trask, on the other hand, was licensed in both California and Oregon, but both licenses had been suspended for multiple drunk driving convictions. His records showed previous addresses in Palm Desert and Cathedral City, desert communities not far from Palm Springs.

Cleland now phoned the first of two U-Haul dealerships in Redmond, Oregon, and was immediately lucky. The dealership's owner remembered the Trasks.

"They were a pain in the neck," said the man, who was able to confirm the Trask's destination as Palm Desert. He also informed Cleland that there were two U-Haul dealerships in Palm Desert, to either of which the Trasks could return the moving van.

Cleland next phoned Warden Tom Stenson, of Indio, the closest available warden to Palm Desert. Cleland filled him in on the bush baby smugglers, and Stenson readily agreed to help. Stenson located the two U-Haul dealerships and planned an ambush for the Trasks. But when the expected time of arrival for the Trasks was long past, Stenson decided to phone the U-Haul people in Redmond for more information.

"You ain't gonna believe this!" said the U-Haul man. "I just got a call from them. They're broke down in Bishop. The brakes went out. They're demanding that we pay for their motel room and meals."

Stenson wasted no time in phoning Lt. Art Lawrence, who supervised the wardens in the Bishop area. Lawrence, in turn, notified the Bishop Police Department. Within minutes, the moving van with the attached red car was spotted, and the Trasks were captured.

Later that day, Cleland received a call from Lawrence.

"We've got your bush baby," said Lawrence. "Debra Trask claims she paid $2,400 for it in Portland. And she's an unemployed waitress. Marvin Trask is in the slammer. The feds were looking for him. There was a federal no-bail warrant out for his arrest. In addition to smuggling bush babies, he apparently dabbles in mail fraud."

With the bush baby case now wrapped up, Cleland turned his attention to the southbound Oregon elk hunter. He examined the declaration form, considering the name, Charles D. Crockett. Phoning dispatch, he requested a California DMV check on the name. The computer search revealed no records that fit.

Cleland then phoned the Oregon State Police. Senior Trooper Mike Cushman, of his agency's wildlife division, received Cleland's call and was interested. By checking Oregon DMV records, Cushman quickly learned that Crockett held an Oregon driver's license, showing a residence address in Bend. Cushman next checked license records and learned that Crockett had purchased resident hunting licenses and elk tags for five of the preceding seven years. But Cushman agreed with Cleland and Gleason that an Oregon resident taking an entire elk into California was unusual behavior. Cushman decided to dig a little deeper, and he phoned a state trooper stationed in Bend.

The following day in Bend, Mrs. Lora Crossman was surprised and worried to find an Oregon State Trooper at her door.

"I'm looking for a Charles Crockett, ma'am. Is he here?"

"That's my brother," she said. "He's not here right now."

"Does he live here?" the trooper asked.

"Yes, he lives here, but he's not here very much," she said, not meeting the trooper's eyes. "He works a lot in California."

The trooper continued with the questioning, more and more convinced that the woman was lying to protect her brother.

"Why would he take an entire elk to California?" the trooper asked.

"He has a lot of friends down there," she said.

Before leaving, the trooper gave her a card with Cushman's name and phone number on it.

"Please ask your brother to call Senior Trooper Cushman. It's important."

Crockett must have immediately received an urgent call from his sister, for he tried to phone Cushman that same afternoon. But Cushman was not in the office. The trooper who fielded the call suggested to Crockett that he leave a phone number, but Crockett made some lame excuse not to do so.

The following day, Crockett tried again to phone Cushman, and again Cushman was out. When asked to leave a phone number, Crockett claimed he was traveling in Arizona. This happened yet a third time, and Crockett again refused to leave a number, actually hanging up abruptly. Cushman concluded that Crockett didn't want to leave a number because it would have been a California number. When Cushman reported this information to Cleland, Cleland's response was, "Looks like we've got him on the run."

"Here's an interesting footnote," said Cushman. "The word around Bend is that this guy Crockett is a Hollywood stunt man."

Cushman continued his investigation and soon learned that Crockett had two vehicles and two trailers registered to him in Oregon. Pressing further, plugging everything he knew about Crockett into Oregon State Police's excellent Resource Data System, Cushman wasn't really surprised to find out that Crockett owned property near Saugus, California. Cushman was even able to come up with two California phone numbers for the man. Again, Cushman passed his information on to Cleland.

Turning up the heat on the investigation, Cleland contacted Warden Mike Stefanak in the Saugus area. It was time to pay Crockett a visit. Stefanak easily found Crockett's residence, a nice ranch home on scenic property near Castaic Reservoir. Crockett wasn't home, nor was his live-in girlfriend, with whom he owned the home. Stefanak peered around at obvious signs of wealth, and wondered why somebody like Crockett would take such a risk and falsify a license application just to save a few bucks. And why would he take an even greater risk to fraudulently license all his rolling stock in Oregon?

Before leaving the area, Stefanak visited the homes of two of Crockett's neighbors.

"He's lived here for years," said one of them. Another said the same thing and added that Crockett went hunting at least once each year in Oregon.

Stefanak returned to Crockett's home the following day and *this* time got lucky. Crockett rolled into his driveway in the big black Dodge pickup about the time Stefanak stepped out of his patrol vehicle. Crockett climbed out looking like a whipped dog, knowing he'd finally been caught.

In the end, Crockett, who was born and raised in Oregon, based his defense on his strange contention that Oregon was his heritage, that in his heart he had never left there. But judges in both Oregon and California were soon to see things quite differently, as would the California Highway Patrol. The CHP's assessment against Crockett for vehicle sales tax, back license fees and penalties would cost him thousands. When all was said and done, the stunt man's latest stunt would end up costing him about 10 grand.

Months later, Cleland would recall the cases of the bush baby smugglers and the elk-hunting stunt man with a certain satisfaction. These were not the crimes of the century, but those involved had intentionally ignored state law. They needed to be caught, and Cleland, with Inspector Gleason's help, had seen to it that it happened. Cleland made a mental note to stop by the Ag Inspection Station and thank Gleason and the other inspectors again for their good work.

* * *

Back at the Ag Inspection Station in Dorris, it was business as usual. Inspector Dave Bienenfeld was about to go off shift one night when a heavily loaded sedan pulled up to his booth. Leaning down to address the driver, his nose was assailed with the unmistakable smell of swine. Shining his flashlight into the back seat, he was astounded to see two large hogs about 200 pounds each sitting there, apparently enjoying the evening.

"That's Bob and Sally," said the driver, a large woman who looked vaguely like Miss Piggy. "They're our pets." A much smaller man in the passenger seat nodded his agreement.

Searching for something appropriate to say, Bienenfeld commented, "They seem to ride pretty well in the car."

"They usually do," said the woman. "But on long trips, they quarrel a lot!"

TIGER'S REVENGE

Ronald Wayne Pender, his mouth stuffed full of rib eye steak, eyed the Fish and Game warden sitting at an adjacent table with his wife. The Steelhead Lodge, in the community of Klamath Glen, was busy as usual, it being not only an excellent restaurant and bar, but the *only* restaurant and bar for a good many miles around. Recognizing an opportunity to impress his friends by needling the warden—by pulling the tiger's tail, so to speak—Pender spoke.

"Hey, Rick!" he said, addressing the warden. "If I'd known you were gonna be here, I'd have been out catchin' salmon with my gillnet." He grinned now, revealing crooked teeth and a gob of half-chewed food. As others at the table chuckled, Warden Rick Banko looked up from his meal and regarded the man with disgust.

"I'll be sure to tell you the next time I intend to *be* here," said Banko. More chuckles.

But to Banko, it was no joke. His suspicions that Pender was a serious violator were fast being confirmed through recent information from a variety of sources. The most detailed account was passed to Banko by a Del Norte County Sheriff's deputy who had received it from a reliable informant. The informant claimed that Pender was using a gillnet on the Klamath River to catch salmon and that he was selling the salmon. Because much of the lower Klamath River flowed through the Yurok Indian Reservation and only card-carrying Yuroks could legally fish with gillnets, Banko had checked with the Bureau of Indian Affairs people in their office in Klamath. There he learned that Pender was definitely not a Yurok tribal member. As to the alleged selling of salmon, no one, not even Yuroks, could legally sell river-caught spring-run fish.

There were other allegations against Pender as well. He was a pilot, and he flew to Klamath Glen in his own light plane. He claimed he was a contractor, but the story never rang true, and few believed him. It was rumored that he was a drug smuggler, flying occasional forays into Mexico. This seemed more plausible, particularly since a U.S. Customs officer had been nosing around asking questions about him.

In addition to owning a plane, he owned an expensive boat as well—a beautiful Design Concepts inboard jet-drive, one of the Cadillacs among river boats. With such expensive toys, Pender had to be receiving considerable cash from time to time.

Because Pender was thought to be living somewhere along the river, Banko had made jet-boat patrols specifically to learn what he could about the man. On two different occasions, Banko had spotted the big jet-boat beached in front of what was known as the Elle Wolcott cabin, a remote spot a good 20 miles upriver. On one of these occasions, he actually spotted Pender there, but there had been no sign of a gillnet. This, however, was not surprising, for even in such a remote part of the river, Pender would have to be crazy to use a gillnet in broad daylight. He was, Banko concluded, probably fishing at night.

On the day following Pender's comments to Banko at Steelhead Lodge, Banko set out to do some serious surveillance of the Elle Wolcott cabin. This would require a stealthy approach to some vantage point on the opposite side of the river from the cabin. But getting there would be a problem. Early May in the redwood forest was a tough time to get around. The timber company roads, many of which were behind locked gates, were poorly maintained and often too muddy to travel. But Banko set out anyway in his four-wheel-drive patrol vehicle, and after a grueling, slippery, two-hour drive, he reached his destination.

It was a gray afternoon, an hour before dark when Banko arrived at the heavily wooded mountainside on the south side of the river, opposite the cabin. He parked his vehicle a safe distance away and walked down a muddy road to a hidden place from which he had a clear view of the cabin and the river in front of it. At first glance, Banko could see the big jet-boat pulled up on the gravel bank below the cabin. He then examined the scene through his binoculars and was surprised to see what looked like net floats no more than 15 yards upriver from the beached jet-boat. Sure enough, a gillnet was set, one end secured to something on the bank and the other end anchored straight out from the bank. It had been the white Clorox bottle floating the far end of the net that caught Banko's eye.

Banko was puzzled at first. Here it was, still daylight, and the net was set. How could Pender be so brazen? Then he understood. Pender, aware of the one-hour or so jet-boat run the wardens would have to make in order to reach Elle Wolcott's cabin from Klamath Glen, was counting on the wardens not coming late in the day. He knew they would allow at least an hour of daylight to make the return run down the river back to town. Assuming all this to be true, Pender would know he had at least an hour of relatively safe daylight netting time on either end of each day. And now, as Banko studied the situation through his binoculars, he felt certain that the net had been set only a short time before his arrival.

Banko sat tight as daylight faded to dusk. The river rolled and whispered in its granite bed, and the forest creatures prepared for night. Then Pender was on the move. The cabin door flew open and he and another man emerged. Banko easily recognized Pender, but the other man, shorter and considerably greater in girth, was a stranger to the warden. Banko watched as they hiked the path, 50 yards or so down the water's edge. They climbed into the jetboat, and the engine fired with a roar. Pender then applied a burst of power in reverse thrust, and the boat slid backwards into deep water. Pender's companion, armed with a boat hook, walked forward and waited as Pender maneuvered toward the net. A quick jab with the boat hook brought in the Clorox bottle, then the man began pulling the net hand over hand.

The sodden net came aboard, then finally the silver, torpedo-shape of a fresh-from-the-sea spring-run salmon came aboard. Pender hurried forward and helped disentangle the 15-pound fish from the net. Seconds later he helped again as another salmon slid aboard. Finally a third fish appeared, this one still alive, and Pender dispatched it with blows from a small club. He now maneuvered the boat such that they could again stretch the gillnet out into the river. At the appropriate time, Pender's companion dropped the net anchor and tossed the Clorox bottle over the side. They then beached the boat and lugged the three fish up the trail to the cabin.

With barely enough light to see, Banko hiked back to his vehicle and headed for home. He had intended to stay all night, if necessary, but he had gotten lucky almost immediately. What he now had was probable cause for a search warrant for the cabin. Hopefully he would recover not only the three salmon Pender and his companion had netted that day, but others they had taken earlier and maybe even evidence as to where they were selling the fish.

Banko arrived home, grabbed a quick dinner and began writing the affidavit for the search warrant. Luckily it was a simple case, and he had made a perfect observation of the violation, so the affidavit was neither long nor complicated. He managed to have it before a judge that same night.

In the meantime, Lt. Steve Conger, Banko's supervisor, had notified three other wardens to help serve the warrant. He also enlisted the help of Dale Miller, a patrolman for the Simpson Woods Timber Company. Miller had an extensive background in police work and was highly respected by the game wardens who regarded him as one of them. He had keys to the locked gates and knew the most direct route through the confusing maze of backcountry roads to get the wardens to Elle Wolcott's cabin.

At dawn the next morning, Banko and Conger eased into position on the south side of the river, where Banko had been the previous day. On the north side, in the forest near the cabin, Lt. Martin "Marty" Hauan and wardens Nick Albert and Mike Maschmeier awaited orders with Dale Miller. The first thing Banko noted upon his arrival was an International Scout vehicle parked at the water's edge near the beached jet boat.

"That wasn't there yesterday," he whispered to Conger. "It was parked up by the cabin. They must have gone somewhere in it sometime during the night."

"They could have sold the fish," said Conger.

"You're probably right," said Banko. "And I'll bet they drove down to the water when they got back and checked the net again. Look! Can you see that white float? The net's still out."

Conger nodded, reached for his radio handset and called the wardens across the river. He apprised them of the situation, then he removed a camcorder from his day-pack and filmed the entire scene.

"I'll bet they pull the net before long," said Banko. "I don't think they'd risk leaving it out much longer."

Sure enough, a short time later Pender and his companion emerged from the cabin, hiked down to the boat, shoved it most of the way off the beach and climbed in. The big engine roared. Again, Pender handled the boat while his companion pulled the net, and again the net contained three salmon. Conger filmed it all with the camcorder. When finished pulling the net, Pender and his friend did not reset it, but brought it ashore and loaded it and the three salmon into the International Scout. They then climbed into the Scout, Pender at the wheel, and started driving up the hillside toward the cabin.

"We should take 'em now," said Banko.

"I agree," said Conger, and he spoke the command into his radio.

Pender pulled the Scout to a stop at the cabin and was stepping out when a stab of terror pierced his heart, stopping him dead . . . for he had suddenly found himself surrounded by the law.

"State Game Wardens," announced one of them. "We have a search warrant."

The wardens then removed the two men from the Scout and found to their surprise that the shorter of the two, upon closer scrutiny, was a woman—an enormously pregnant one. Lucille Theola Mullenax, upon finding herself captured, immediately began waddling in a tight circle demanding to use the bathroom.

"I'm gonna wet my pants!" she threatened.

Lt. Hauan, suspicious of this sudden emergency, sent Warden Maschmeier into the house to check the bathroom for weapons or drugs. Hauan then did a quick pat-down search of Mullenax and checked her pockets. He found nothing of concern. He then escorted Mullenax into the house and waited just outside the bathroom as Mullenax stepped in and closed the door. By the time she emerged, the wardens had shown Pender a copy of the search warrant, patted him down for weapons and brought him inside the cabin. They then searched one corner of the living room and directed Pender and Mullenax to sit there and remain.

In the meantime, Warden Albert had hiked down to the big jet-boat and driven it across the river to pick up Conger and Banko.

"One of them is a woman," said Albert, as Conger and Banko stepped in.

"No way," said Banko.

Not long into the search of Pender's lair, Banko found a small pane of glass on which was a razor blade, a short section of a drinking straw, white powder residue and a bindle of white powder. He immediately radioed the sheriff's office and requested that they send in some narcs. About this time, before anyone could stop her, Mullenax walked across the room to a table and unzipped a pink, plastic makeup bag. Her back was now to the closest warden, Maschmeier, who quickly escorted her back to the sofa on which she had been sitting.

"Hey, Marty," said Maschmeier, summoning Hauan. "She just got into that zipper bag on the table."

As Hauan was receiving this information, Mullenax complained of morning sickness, jumped up and again hurried for the bathroom. She made it inside and closed the door, but Hauan followed her in and found her bending over the toilet. He rushed over to prevent her from flushing the toilet, and as she stepped back, he noticed one corner of a plastic bag protruding from a pocket of her hooded sweatshirt. It had not been there before. He removed it and found it to contain white powder.

"I guess I screwed up," said Mullenax.

Mullenax had indeed screwed up, as had Pender, and both of them soon found themselves in handcuffs. Next came thorough searches of their persons. A thick wad in Pender's pants pocket turned out to be almost $2,000 cash. The search of Mullenax, reluctantly performed by Conger, revealed nothing new; however, her purse with her driver's license, found in the bedroom, contained about $500 cash.

Also in the bedroom, Banko found a Realistic Pro-33 radio scanner. He turned it on, and it began scanning a number of channels. Banko keyed his radio handset, and the scanner instantly locked onto one of the channels which was set to Fish and Game's frequency.

"I'm glad they didn't have this on this morning," said Banko to no one in particular, as he placed the scanner with other things that would be seized into evidence.

The narcs arrived with a DA's investigator, and the search continued. The narcs soon found more drugs and paraphernalia. As to the Fish and Game violations, the wardens located a total of seven salmon bearing gillnet marks, and they found a second gillnet hidden in an ice chest. Plus, they found some scribbled records of salmon sales, a suspicious-looking address book and other incriminating paperwork. Because the case would now involve felony drug charges, a rifle and pistol found in the cabin were also seized into evidence by the wardens.

Pender was understandably glum as he pondered the misfortune that had befallen him, but he became totally distraught when Banko explained to him that his big, beautiful Design Concepts jet-boat was being seized as well. Being well aware of the asset forfeiture laws related to drug cases, he knew there was a good chance he would never see his boat again. When he and Mullenax were seat-belted, still handcuffed, into Fish and Game patrol vehicles, about to leave for the county jail, Banko directed one last comment to Pender.

"Oh, by the way, Mr. Pender, I'm gonna be at the Steelhead Lodge tonight. I told you I'd let you know." Pender just blinked his eyes and said nothing as the patrol vehicles headed out.

Conger now climbed into the big jet-boat with Banko, fired the engine and dropped Banko off on the opposite bank. He then blasted away, heading down river.

That night, Banko and the others had the satisfaction of knowing that they had prevailed over a pair of substantial outlaws who had been killing a lot of salmon and selling a lot of dope. Now it would be up to the courts, but Banko knew better than to count on heavy penalties. The courts, he had found, were largely unpredictable, and when the lawyers stepped in, anything could happen. He therefore was not surprised, weeks later, when Lucille Mullenax pled guilty to the drug charges, taking complete responsibility for all of the drug-related evidence. In doing so, she saved Pender's bacon, for he had a prior drug conviction and would have gone to state prison. When Mullenax pled guilty to the felony drug charges, the Fish and Game charges were dropped. So when the District Attorney decided to grant her DA's diversion, which meant a freebie, she got off scot-free on the whole thing. She paid not one dime for her part in gillnetting salmon, not one dime for drug use and trafficking, and she paid no price for jeopardizing the life of her unborn child. Pender, at least, was convicted of gillnetting salmon. For this he received a $1,200 fine and lost all of the equipment seized by the wardens. All, that is, except for the big jet-boat which a sympathetic judge returned to him.

But the public at large was not so sympathetic. Not long after the case was completed, someone tried to torch Elle Wolcott's cabin, and someone sabotaged Pender's airplane. Fortunately for Pender, he spotted the damage before takeoff. But he took the hint. Soon thereafter, he pulled entirely out of the Klamath area. Not only did he want to flee those who bore him grudges, he wanted to put some miles between himself and Warden Rick Banko. So, he moved his operation far away, to sunny Lakeport, California.

* * *

It was a few years later when Warden Rick Banko stood one night before a mixed crowd of admirers at the Elk's Lodge in Crescent City. The occasion was a going away party in his honor. He was being promoted to the rank of patrol lieutenant and would be moving to a new duty station. The great hall was packed with people whose lives he had touched and who respected his fairness, compassion and dedication to his work. There were even a number of past customers there as well, people who had been arrested for various wildlife-related crimes. Their presence that night was the ultimate expression of respect for a warden.

It was an evening of fun and laughter, enjoyed by all, with Banko roasted by his friends and past adversaries alike. In the end, they all wished him good luck and happiness in his new duty station—sunny Lakeport, California.

SMOOTH OPERATOR

San Francisco Bay, October, 1989

The 26-foot urchin boat, *Sculpin*, rolled gently on the incoming tide, her engine at idle. Her owner, Delbert Rupp, a smug look on his face, stood watching from the wheelhouse door as Warden Danny Reno, boarding officer of the Fish and Game patrol boat, *Chinook*, rummaged through mesh bags of brick-red, long-spined sea urchins in her hold. It was the third boarding of the *Sculpin* by Fish and Game in as many months, and as was the case with the other two, the wardens had found nothing amiss. Rupp found it amusing that only a few nights earlier, had the wardens been clever enough to catch him, they would have found his hold full of illegally taken abalone.

Lt. Keith Long, at the controls of the *Chinook*, deftly maneuvered alongside the *Sculpin* and recovered his boarding officer. He then spun the patrol boat around and sped away. Rupp watched until the patrol boat was a good quarter-mile off, then turned with a smile to a boom-box radio in the wheelhouse. He pushed the "play" button on the tape deck, and the air was suddenly filled with music, the haunting, driving melody of the song, *Smooth Operator*, by the velvety-voiced singer, Sade. Chuckling now, Rupp grabbed the mike of his marine-band radio, held it to the speaker and keyed the transmit button. Sade's song now boomed out over the airwaves.

"Smooth operator . . . . . He was a smooooooth operaaator . . ."

Aboard the *Chinook*, Long gritted his teeth, forced to endure this insult yet again. Rupp seemed to enjoy playing cat and mouse with the patrol boat, dangerous business in view of his outlaw ways, and he did indeed consider himself a smooth operator. He had, several times, during the past few weeks, given Long the slip by ducking into fog banks or losing himself and his boat in some confusing maze of North Coast marinas. And each time, he had followed his maneuvers by playing the song, *Smooth Operator,* over the marine band radio frequency which he knew Long would be monitoring aboard the *Chinook*.

Having come to regard himself as uncatchable due to his cunning and the apparent predictability of the Fish and Game wardens, he would have been stunned to know the truth. He would have found it chilling, for instance, to know that Lt. Long, during each of his last three boardings of the *Sculpin*, had been neither surprised nor disappointed over the lack of incriminating evidence to be found there. Long had known in advance.

* * *

October 17, 1989

Wardens Mark Lucero and Joe Knarr clung like reptiles to the weathered granite of the cliff top overlooking the cove at Elephant Rock. They had belly-crawled to the very edge of the cliff and were peering down at the urchin boat, *Sculpin*, anchored a mere 70 yards offshore below them. The sun hung low in the west, the ocean calm on this peaceful afternoon. Elephant Rock was covered with resting seabirds, which sat glutted after a day of easy fishing. Several dozen sea lions lay at ease on the rugged shoreline, enjoying the last hour of daylight.

Lucero and Knarr were red-eyed and drunk with fatigue, a condition well known to those assigned to Fish and Game's Special Operations Unit, or SOU as it is known. Following weeks of little rest, Lucero's day had begun well before dawn at Spud Point, Bodega Bay, where he had posed as a fisherman with rod and reel, an unbaited line in the water. Other wardens were stationed nearby, all part of *Operation Ab Eyes*, which targeted the suspected worst of the worst of the commercial abalone poachers who were the scourge of the northern California coast.

The hours passed slowly for Lucero and the others, and it was nearly 10 a.m. before their patience was rewarded. It was then that Delbert Rupp and his deckhand appeared at the marina and hopped aboard the *Sculpin*, which was moored there. Rupp fired the engine, the deckhand cast off the lines, and they were underway. A few minutes later they rounded Spud Point. Lucero watched as they gained open ocean and made their turn.

"They're headin' south," said Lucero into his handset radio.

Knarr, already south of town, raced down the coast in an unmarked sedan. His destination was Tomales Point, a logical place from which to spy on the *Sculpin* for some indication of Rupp's intentions. But it was a long trip on slow roads, and by the time Knarr parked his car and jogged a half-mile to the cliffs overlooking the ocean, an hour had passed. As he arrived, panting, the ocean now in full view, his heart sank, for the *Sculpin* was nowhere to be seen. He had apparently arrived too late. He scanned north and south. Nothing. Then he walked closer to the edge of the cliff, revealing more of the cove below. Suddenly his heart gave a leap, for there, no more than 70 yards offshore and immediately in front of him, lay the *Sculpin* at anchor. Overjoyed at this good fortune, Knarr hurriedly passed this information along by radio. Soon he was joined by Lucero.

It was an opportunity beyond belief for the wardens. Here they were, perched some 300 feet above the ocean, the perfect vantage point, peering right down the throat of one of the most obnoxious and destructive outlaws on the coast. Rupp was in diving gear, busily at work on the ocean floor, clouds of bubbles dancing to the surface. A hooka compressor aboard the *Sculpin* provided him a steady supply of air. But was he harvesting abalone or sea urchins? Rupp was licensed for both, but there was no commercial abalone harvesting allowed north of the Golden Gate, and Elephant Rock was 25 miles into the closed zone.

"He's gettin' abs," said Lucero, checking his watch. "He's been down at least 30 minutes."

Lucero's opinion was based on his knowledge that urchin divers usually take no more than 20 minutes to fill one of their large, nylon-mesh urchin bags. Abalone divers, however, often stayed down an hour at a time.

The wardens hardly moved all day as Rupp and his deckhand went about their illegal work. Twice Rupp had surfaced and taken breaks, and twice he had descended again, remaining down the better part of an hour each time. Finally, without ever having brought anything to the surface, Rupp climbed aboard his boat and stripped off his wetsuit top. After wolfing down two enormous sandwiches and most of a six-pack of beer, he and his deckhand broke out a deck of cards and started a game.

"They're gonna wait 'til dark," said Lucero.

And so it was that Lucero and Knarr maintained their vigil as evening approached. Rupp had snapped on the radio on his boom box. Forty miles to the south, at Candlestick Park, the Oakland As and the San Francisco Giants were preparing for game three of the World Series. Rupp tuned in the appropriate station as the teams were in warm-up. The wardens could catch bits and pieces of the commentary.

And then something strange happened. Lucero had just checked his watch at 5:04 p.m. when suddenly every bird within sight took flight, squawking noisily, and the sea lions began a frantic barking. Rupp and his deckhand leaped up and peered around with alarm.

"What the . . . " said Lucero, but then they felt it. Or perhaps they *heard* it first as the earth began to move, a low and ominous rumble. The wardens then looked at one another with alarm.

"Earthquake!" they said in unison. The ground now bucked and swayed as the wardens clung to their perilous perch, wishing to be anywhere but there. They cringed as bits of the cliff-top crumbled and tumbled into the sea.

"We're gonna end up down there with *them*," said Lucero. But it was soon over, and the wardens grinned at one another. Both men had lived their entire lives in earthquake country, and they soon forgot about the quake and ignored the aftershocks that followed, returning their attention to the *Sculpin*.

As darkness approached, Rupp pulled on his wetsuit top again and strapped on his mask and weight belt. After carefully scanning the horizon for boats, he jumped over the side and disappeared. His deckhand now swung the hoist-davit outboard and lowered the cable-hook. Seconds later he powered the hoist and a huge mesh bag of illegal abalone emerged from the depths. He swung it aboard, dripping, and lowered it into the hold. At this moment, Lucero, high above, propped himself up on his elbows and carefully snapped a low-light photo. The deckhand then lowered the cable into the sea again, and again he brought up an enormous bag of abalone. As he was stowing yet a third mesh bag full of abalone, Rupp surfaced and scrambled aboard. Almost immediately he fired the engine, pulled anchor and headed out to sea. Upon clearing the rocks, he headed south. The wardens were astounded at how little time it had taken the outlaws to recover their illegal catch and depart.

The wardens jogged back to their vehicles and headed south. Traveling down Highway 1 toward San Francisco, the wardens were curious over the condition of the highway.

"I don't remember it being this bad," said Knarr into his mike, as he bounced over yet another spot where the asphalt had apparently buckled. At one point, it appeared as if the highway had sheared in two and shifted, the yellow center lines of the two parts now misaligned. At another, it appeared as if the ground had fallen away beneath the road, resulting in a sizable dip.

The wardens continued on, full darkness now upon them. Their destination was the north end of the Golden Gate Bridge, a vantage point from which they hoped to spot the *Sculpin* and follow her to whatever berth Rupp had in mind. On Highway 101 now, southbound on the Marin Peninsula, a strange feeling came over them as though something was terribly wrong. Yet they were so focused on their mission that they failed to notice the reasons why—the unusual darkness of the communities through which they passed and the deteriorating condition of the highway. While they were not yet to a place from which they could directly see the magnificent skyline of San Francisco, the bright glow of the millions of electric lights that normally painted the night sky *above* the city was ominously absent, a strange red glow in its place. Then the wardens rounded the last bend, took a dirt road up onto a high knob, stepped out of their vehicles and were stunned by what they saw.

The city was dark except for large fires burning here and there and the searchlights from rescue helicopters and the flashing red and blue lights of emergency vehicles. The Marina District was in flames, which cast a ghastly glow over the bay and the great bridge. It could have been a scene from wartime Europe, for the city looked as though it had been freshly bombed.

"Take a good look," said Lucero. "We're witnessing history, here."

They stood mesmerized by what they were seeing, doing their best to come to grips with the enormity of it all. Then they remembered their business. In their vehicles again, working their way past stalled traffic, they made it to their lookout point and forced their attention onto the ocean outside the Golden Gate. They scanned with binoculars and checked their watches, calculating Rupp's running time. Then suddenly he was there, rounding Point Bonita, right on time. The *Sculpin* hugged the Marin Peninsula, passing beneath the wardens and under the darkened Golden Gate Bridge.

"He's going to Sausalito," said Knarr. Lucero agreed and informed the other *Ab Eyes* wardens by radio.

Sure enough. Rupp soon made a careful approach to the blacked-out marina at Sausalito, crept to a vacant berth there and tied up. He and his deckhand then hurried ashore and vanished. Lucero and Knarr, both dead-tired, were now stuck with the chore of babysitting the *Sculpin* with its cargo of illegal abalone through the night. They took turns, one on watch while the other cat-napped in the car. Lucero, on watch at about 4 a.m., fought a desperate battle to keep his eyes open. He was so crippled by fatigue that when his eyes told him the *Sculpin* had begun to move, he nearly convinced himself that he was hallucinating. But then the unmistakable silhouette of the urchin boat turned into the channel and Lucero suddenly snapped wide awake.

"He's comin' out," said Lucero into his radio, then he watched as the boat gained open water and turned, making a bee line for San Francisco. Lucero then radioed the two wardens on watch at Pier 45, on the San Francisco waterfront.

"He's all yours," said Lucero, who then stumbled back to his unmarked sedan, crawled into the back seat, lay his head down and was instantly asleep.

* * *

Lucero's "handoff" of Delbert Rupp and the *Sculpin* that early morning went to Lt. Art Lawrence and Warden Lisa (Luhnow) Curtis, whose last dozen hours had been eventful indeed. They had spent the preceding day, prior to 5:04 p.m., in typical *Ab Eyes* fashion—tailing suspects and covertly monitoring activities among the waterfront fish businesses. But their primary objective was Rupp and the *Sculpin*.

Because Lawrence was presently the lead person in the field operation of *Ab Eyes*, he was advised of everything. He had therefore known when the *Sculpin* was at Elephant Rock, under the close scrutiny of Lucero and Knarr, which meant that he and Curtis had time for a nice dinner. Because they had had little to eat all day, they were anxiously looking forward to a meal at a Chinese restaurant they had found near the waterfront. A flight of stairs took them to the second-story dining area. While Lawrence went in search of a telephone, Curtis stood admiring a large aquarium of tropical fish. The clock on the wall behind the cash register read 5:04 p.m.

Suddenly Curtis was startled to see the water sloshing from the aquarium. Then the floor bucked beneath her feet and the old wooden building began to shake and creak and groan.

"EARTHQUAKE!" shouted Lawrence, thundering towards her. "Let's get outta here."

Down the stairway they raced as windows shattered, walls collapsed and buildings were knocked from foundations. They ran to the middle of the street where people were screaming and wringing their hands in terror as the lights of the great city flickered and died. Across the bay, the upper level of the Cypress Street section of the I-880 freeway collapsed onto the lower level and a section of the Bay Bridge did the same. Then it was over. That is, the initial quake was over, but here and there parts of the city had caught fire, and ruptured water mains sent small rivers rushing down twisted, broken streets.

The wardens attempted to aid local residents, but there was little they could do. Confusion was complete, especially when darkness fell and there was no electrical power. It appeared to the wardens that no one was seriously hurt in their immediate area, but they would later learn that there was pain and suffering no great distance away, and over 60 people had lost their lives.

Shops, restaurants and other small businesses simply locked their doors, and employees could be seen leaving with great arm-loads of food, anticipating days or weeks of privation. This reminded the wardens that they themselves, ravenously hungry and trapped as they were by duty as well as earthquake damage, were in danger of going hungry indefinitely. This sobering realization prompted them into action. They set out in search of food. But there was none to be found. Everything was closed down. Finally, however, Curtis encountered the chef of a small restaurant departing through the back door of the establishment, and he reluctantly sold her two loaves of bread.

A harrowing night followed in the darkened, wounded city. Sirens wailed continuously as flames licked at the smoky sky. The wardens remained near the waterfront, prepared for a radio call from Lucero should one come, snacking on bread and water. If their calculations were correct, and Rupp wasn't spooked by the earthquake, he would be coming to Pier 45 to sell his load of abalone to Bounty Seafoods.

And so it happened. Lucero called at 4 a.m., and 20 minutes later, Lawrence and Curtis spotted the *Sculpin*, running without lights, cautiously approaching the twisted, but still useable, Pier 45. Rupp and his deckhand quickly moored the boat, then hopped onto the pier and strode purposefully toward a large warehouse known as "the shed." The fires in the Marina District provided the only light.

Then something astonishing happened. As the wardens waited, Lawrence noticed headlights flash in the parking lot above the pier, some kind of signal. Then two shadowy figures in dark clothing emerged from the shadows and trotted toward the *Sculpin*. One hopped aboard while the other hurriedly cast off the mooring lines. A tiny light then appeared in the wheelhouse, followed seconds later by the engine firing. Then the wardens watched in amazement as the *Sculpin* backed away from the pier, swung around and headed for open water. Now Rupp came pounding down the pier at full sprint, highly distraught.

"MY BOAT! SOMEONE'S STEALING MY BOAT!"

The wardens could only look on in disbelief as the *Sculpin*, bearing her valuable cargo of abalone, critical evidence against Rupp, was swallowed up by the vast, post-earthquake darkness that shrouded San Francisco Bay.

The wardens of *Operation Ab-Eyes* dealt with the theft of the *Sculpin* and the apparent loss of their evidence as best they could, hampered as they were by poor communications, difficult surface travel around the Bay Area, and other earthquake-related problems. They began a systematic search, and ultimately it was a pair of wardens in a Fish and Game aircraft who located the missing boat. It was moored in the tug yards in Richmond, across the bay and 10 miles to the north of Pier 45. It had been stripped of its expensive electronics gear, but the abalone were untouched.

Now that the wardens had located the stolen boat, they faced the problem of how to inform Rupp without arousing his suspicion. This dilemma was solved, however, when Rupp somehow located his boat on his own. Upon finding it still operable and its cargo of abalone alive and intact, he got underway and headed straight for Pier 45. Lawrence and Curtis again watched his arrival, and soon he was in negotiations with a tall, rugged-looking man in a refrigerated Bounty Seafoods van. They apparently struck a deal, and the wardens were able to document the offloading and weighing of the abalone, followed by Rupp's strolling back to the *Sculpin* with a fist-full of cash.

The man from Bounty Seafoods, after his purchase of Rupp's 16 dozen abalone, punched numbers into his amazing new cellular telephone. Deputy Chief Greg Laret, Department of Fish and Game, at his desk high in the Resources Building in Sacramento, took the call.

"We made the buy," said the Bounty Seafoods man, who was actually Warden Eddie Watkins of the *Ab Eyes* operation. Bounty Seafoods was an SOU front painstakingly set up over a period of many months to trap Delbert Rupp and others of his kind.

"Good news!" said Laret. "I was beginning to think *this*

one wasn't meant to be. Now, if we can just get one *more* on him." This was in reference to the District Attorney's instructions to make at least two buys from any of the bad guys before taking them down. His contention was that a single buy, it could be argued, could be simply an isolated bit of bad judgment. Two or more buys, however, made for a strong case.

Following his sale to Bounty Seafoods, Rupp took the *Sculpin* up the coast to his home port of Bodega Bay. There he remained for a few days due to bad weather. Then one morning he and his deckhand took some supplies aboard, fired up the engine and idled over to the fuel dock. They topped off the fuel tanks, then headed out of the harbor, paying no attention to the lone fisherman on Spud Point. An hour later they dropped anchor in Horseshoe Cove, near Fort Ross.

* * *

It would have taken a keen eye to spot the two wardens peering from the blind they had built amid the low branches of a stunted, wind-ravaged pine. Wardens Lucero and Knarr were peering down at the anchored *Sculpin* in Horseshoe Cove and were again documenting the evil-doings of Delbert Rupp and his deckhand. As before, the outlaws were obviously engaged in the illegal harvest of abalone, again using their sea urchin gear as a front. They brought aboard an occasional bag of urchins so as to appear legitimate, but the wardens knew exactly what they were doing.

By midafternoon, Rupp was finished for the day, and when he pulled anchor and headed south the wardens were certain he had left a hidden cache of abalone on the ocean floor. To test this theory, warden divers Mervin Hee and Steve Morse, clad in wetsuits and diving gear, arrived an hour later in an outboard-powered Zodiac inflatable to take a look. Responding to radioed directions from Lucero and Knarr, they tossed out an anchor, pulled on their masks and tanks, and rolled over the side. No more than 10 minutes later, Hee erupted through the surface, both fists raised in a thumbs-up victory signal. He had found several hundred abalone stashed in nylon urchin bags. Before leaving the area, the two divers marked the shells of many of the abalone for later identification.

In order to maintain an unbroken "chain of evidence" of the hidden abalone, Lucero and Knarr chose to maintain their vigil. They remained in their blind, taking turns sleeping, curled up on the cold ground like coyotes.

As expected, Rupp returned to Horseshoe Cove the next morning and resumed diving near the cache of abalone, and the day passed much like the day had passed at Elephant Rock over a week earlier. Lucero and Knarr watched as Rupp was obviously engaged in abalone picking, but as before, Rupp brought none of them to the surface. Just as before, Rupp finished his diving well before sunset, then he and his deckhand again played cards and waited for dark. When barely enough daylight remained for him to dive, Rupp went over the side, and the deckhand winched in great sacks full of abalone, hundreds of them. They then pulled anchor and headed south.

Lucero and Knarr, after 34 hours in their blind, wearily tailed the *Sculpin* down the coast as Rupp steered for the Golden Gate. As before, Rupp passed under the great bridge and veered north to Sausalito where he spent most of the night. The *Ab Eyes* wardens moved into position for what they expected to be another run by Rupp to Pier 45 and the crucial second sale to Eddie Watkins. Sure enough, Rupp got underway in the *Sculpin* about an hour before dawn and headed for Pier 45.

But someone blundered.

Among the 20 or so *Ab Eyes* wardens, one who was assigned to watch the marina in Sausalito made a serious mistake. He somehow tuned his radio handset to the wrong channel, choosing the regular Fish and Game operating frequency instead of the secure channel in use by SOU. When he observed the *Sculpin* pulling out of the marina and heading for San Francisco, he made his report by radio over this insecure channel which was scanned by every outlaw on the North Coast—including Delbert Rupp. Lucero and Knarr were horrified when they heard it, and the damage was instantly apparent. The *Sculpin* suddenly made a hard right turn and accelerated toward the Golden Gate Bridge and the open ocean beyond.

Within seconds, Art Lawrence had Greg Laret on the phone at his home in Sacramento. Lawrence hurriedly explained the sudden crisis, and Laret briefly considered the options.

"Take him down," said Laret.

Lawrence didn't have to be told twice. Lt. Long aboard the *Chinook*, however, didn't believe his ears. Prowling the harbor entrance, his mission to be ready for anything, he found it difficult to believe that his fondest dream had suddenly come true.

"TEN-NINE?" roared Long into his mike, requesting Lawrence to repeat the order.

"Take him down," said Lawrence again. Long cheerfully acknowledged, jamming *Chinook*'s throttles to the stops. The engines roared and the patrol boat raced ahead. Closing on the tiny blip that was the *Sculpin* on his radar screen, Long soon had the boat in sight. The *Chinook* then came dashing in, her red and blue lights flashing, Long's voice blaring over the bullhorn.

"STATE FISH AND GAME! STAND BY TO BE BOARDED!"

Rupp was horrified, desperate to escape, but there was no way. With no options, he reluctantly throttled back and brought the *Sculpin* to a stop. Long pulled alongside, and Danny Reno hopped aboard.

*   *   *

As it turned out, the failure of the *Ab Eyes* wardens to get the second abalone sale on Delbert Rupp was of little consequence. Rupp and the deckhand were convicted on all charges, and an unsympathetic judge hammered them with brutal fines and several months in jail. The worst part for Rupp, however, was that he would never again see his beloved *Sculpin*, the $40,000 craft having been ordered forfeited. Rupp, as time would tell, would never commercial fish California again.

As for the *Operation Ab Eyes* wardens, they would recall those weeks and months with mixed emotions—the long boring hours of stakeouts, the crippling fatigue, balanced on the other hand by the fast action and high adventure that occasionally befell them. Mark Lucero would never forget his wild earthquake ride on the cliff-tops above Elephant Rock, and he would always remember the long but pleasant hours he worked with Joe Knarr, the superb young warden who would later leave California to become a warden in Montana.

But perhaps the most satisfying memory of all would be Keith Long's recollection of his final capture of Delbert Rupp, who had become his nemesis over the months, taunting and teasing him. Rupp, upon seeing the *Chinook* bearing down on him, emergency lights ablaze, had sensed immediately that the jig was up, that the wardens somehow knew *exactly* where he had harvested the 600 or so abalone in his hold. He was in a daze as he was taken into custody and the wardens drove the *Sculpin* to Sausalito for offloading of the abalone.

It was at the dock at a launch ramp in Sausalito that Long would experience what would become his fondest memory. As nearly a ton of abalone was hoisted from *Sculpin*'s hold, Danny Reno happened to notice the boom box in the boat's wheelhouse. On impulse he pushed the "play" button on the tape deck. Instantly music filled the air.

"Smooth operator . . . . . He was a smoooooooth operaaator . . ."

But outlaw Delbert Rupp, awaiting transport to county jail, staring at his feet, his hands cuffed securely behind his back, was feeling anything but smooth.

TIME BOMB

A distinctly uneasy feeling crept over Bob Tonelli Jr. as he regarded the two rough-looking characters standing near a green pickup. They watched as he drove past them, following him with their eyes as he continued down the country road. He was certain they were up to no good.

Tonelli had just left his home, a little ranch house amid the sage and junipers bordering Sam's Neck, a small valley that opened into the much larger Butte Valley, in northern California's Siskiyou County. It was a sunny afternoon, the mountains of southern Oregon clearly visible a few miles to the north as he headed for town. He had spotted the pickup parked on the shoulder of the gravel road, less than a quarter-mile from the gate to his driveway. He was on his way to work, with no time to investigate, but at least he could alert his father, Bob Tonelli Sr., whose home was just three miles farther down the road. His father's alfalfa fields occupied a sizeable portion of Sam's Neck. Upon arriving at the farm, he located his father and explained the situation. His father considered the information.

"That sounds like the same two men I ran into at your place a while back," said the elder Tonelli. This was in reference to an incident that had occurred two weeks earlier. Checking his alfalfa fields while riding a dirt bike motorcycle, he had spotted a green pickup pulling into his son's driveway. Aware that his son was not at home, he had investigated. He found two unkempt-looking men sitting in the vehicle, scrutinizing the house and barn. When he approached them, he found them reeking of alcohol, and neither appeared sober enough to drive. He inquired as to their business there.

"We're lookin' for owl puke," said the driver, the slightly younger of the two, a man of about age 40. The other man laughed at his companion's comment as though it were a fine joke.

Tonelli discerned from this that the men were seeking owl castings, the gobs of indigestible fur, feathers and bones coughed up periodically by owls. There was a market for them, the ultimate consumer usually being schools, where students carefully pick them apart and study them, the tiny skeletons within revealing information about creatures that had met with violent ends. Castings were worth about 50 cents each to the finder, and a good roost site could yield hundreds of them.

"Well, I can't help you," said Tonelli. "This is all private property, and the owner doesn't appreciate visitors."

"Could we just look in the barn?" the man persisted.

"Sorry," said Tonelli. "I'll have to ask you to leave."

The man's eyes narrowed, fixing Tonelli with a hostile stare, then he fired the engine and turned the pickup around. He shot Tonelli one last venomous look as he started down the driveway. Tonelli watched until they were out of sight.

The incident had disturbed the elder Tonelli, for he sensed that he had not seen the last of the two men, and now his son was clearly worried as well.

"I'll go check on them, Bobby. You go ahead and go to work," said the older Tonelli. Tonelli Jr. then departed, heading for the little town of Dorris.

Tonelli immediately climbed onto his motorcycle and headed toward his son's place. He soon spotted the parked pickup, and he could see several deer in the alfalfa field, apparently fleeing the area. The two men stood near the rear of the vehicle, in deep grass beside the road. They watched him as he approached, obviously displeased over his arrival. As he pulled to a stop, one of them hurried over to intercept him.

"What's going on?" said Tonelli. "Why are you guys here?"

"We had a flat tire. We just changed it," said the man, whom Tonelli recognized as one of the drunken men he had encountered before in his son's driveway. He was a large, rangy-looking man of at least six-foot-three, in filthy Levis and a white t-shirt. And to Tonelli's surprise, he was barefooted.

"Well, like I told you before, this is all private property around here," said Tonelli. He then put the bike in gear and pulled away, continuing the 300 yards or so to his son's driveway. There, he closed and locked the gate. As he returned to the motorcycle, he looked down the road to where the two men and the pickup were still there. He was surprised to see them carrying something heavy up from the roadside ditch. It was large, brown and limp, and they hurriedly hefted it into the back of the pickup. They then closed the back of the pickup and walked forward.

Even at nearly a quarter-mile, Tonelli could see that the object was a deer. He jumped on the motorcycle and started towards the men as they climbed into the pickup and drove away. Tonelli closed rapidly on them, attempting to get a look at their license plate, but the dust they raised made it difficult. He kept up his speed and passed them, but he was not far ahead of them when the driver accelerated, closing to within a few feet of his rear tire. He, too, accelerated, highly uneasy, but the driver did the same, crowding him dangerously close. He went faster still, his uneasiness turning to fear, but the pickup kept pace. He could hear its tires crunching gravel right on his tail. Then his driveway appeared, and he veered onto it. The pickup sped by, missing him by inches.

Tonelli lay the motorcycle down, dashed into his house

and grabbed the phone.

*   *   *

Warden Rennie Cleland, Department of Fish and Game, was on patrol when the call came in on his cell phone. He found himself talking to a highly excited Bob Tonelli Sr.

"Hello, Bob. What's the problem?"

Tonelli hurriedly told the story, and when he mentioned that he thought the suspects' pickup had Oregon plates, Cleland spun the patrol vehicle around and headed north for Dorris. He also radioed the Highway Patrol and the sheriff's office and asked them to watch for the "Forest Service green" pickup with Oregon plates Tonelli had described. Then he picked up the cell phone again, resuming his conversation with Tonelli.

"You gotta be kidding," said Cleland at one point. "One of them was barefooted? And they weren't kids?" Tonelli assured him this was the case.

Upon reaching Dorris, Cleland drove through the small community and took up a position north of town where he could watch all Oregon-bound traffic. He knew that the suspects could not yet have reached this place. He waited there a while, worrying over the possibility that the suspects, despite their Oregon plates, might live in California. If so, they would not likely pass his way. When it was clear that they had not headed straight for the border, Cleland drove back through town, checking the likely spots they might have stopped.

Upon approaching Pace's In and Out Gas and Convenience, he spotted a milk-green Ford pickup with a dark-colored camper shell. It matched Tonelli's description perfectly. Because no one was visible in or near the vehicle, Cleland pulled into the rear of the business to wait. He took the opportunity to run the Oregon license number through DMV. Dispatch reported it registered to one Troy Alvin Lottman, a resident of Klamath Falls, Oregon.

Soon a large man emerged from the store, an unkempt-looking individual carrying a 12-pack of beer. He wore a dirty white t-shirt and Levis. And he was barefooted. It made Cleland's skin crawl to see a grown man, in public, walking across dirty asphalt in his bare feet. As the man opened the rear door to the camper shell, Cleland stepped out and approached him.

"State Game Warden, sir!" said Cleland, noticing as the man turned to face him that his t-shirt was stained with a crimson splotch of fresh blood over his right chest. "I'm Warden Cleland, sir, and I'm investigating a report of a deer poaching in the Sam's Neck area."

The man regarded Cleland with unblinking eyes, his face flushed, his breath reeking of beer. Even barefooted, he stood at least three inches taller than Cleland, who was a solid six-footer.

"The vehicle involved is similar to yours, sir. Have you been in the Sam's Neck area this afternoon?"

"No!" answered the man, almost shouting the word. "I just drove down from Klamath Falls." His speech was noticeably slurred.

"How did you get that blood on your shirt?" said Cleland, pointing to the red stain.

The man looked down at the blood, swaying unsteadily, then answered, "My niece's pit bull bit me when I was wrestling with it." He then showed Cleland a scabbed-over wound on his forearm.

"Sir, can I see your identification?" said Cleland.

"For what? I didn't do nothin'," said the man, growing more agitated, a wild look appearing in his eyes. Cleland took a step back, ready for anything.

"Do you have any firearms or deer in your truck?" Cleland asked. The man answered with an emphatic no. "Would you mind if I take a look?"

"Sure! Go ahead!" said the man confidently, moving to the rear of the pickup and raising the camper shell lid.

Cleland looked inside and found no deer. What he *did* find, however, was fresh blood smeared on a carpet and various other items inside and some deer hair. He made no mention of these things, however, and intentionally showed no indication he had seen them. He turned to the man and again asked for identification. Despite the man's growing agitation, he finally produced an Oregon driver's license. He was, indeed, Troy Alvin Lottman.

Cleland then walked to his patrol vehicle after directing Lottman to stand by his pickup. He radioed dispatch and learned that Lottman's Oregon driver's license had been suspended. He then radioed for a Highway Patrol backup. The nearest CHP unit was 10 miles away in Macdoel, but would be on its way.

Returning to Lottman, Cleland asked him for permission to look in the cab of the pickup. In truth, he needed no permission at this point, but he asked anyway as a courtesy.

"No way!" said Lottman.

"I need to take a look," said Cleland, moving closer. "Please move to the front of your truck."

"No way!" said Lottman, blocking Cleland's path. "You ain't lookin' anymore in my truck!"

"Move to the front," said Cleland, gently grasping Lottman's arm to turn him, but Lottman jerked away and assumed a fighting stance. Then a hard look came into Cleland's eyes, something Lottman, even in his semi-drunken state, recognized instantly. And when Cleland then ordered him to turn around and put his hands behind his back, he complied.

"This is for your safety and mine," said Cleland as he applied the handcuffs. "I have plenty of evidence to show that you and somebody else killed a deer out of season. You'll have to stay with me until I complete my investigation."

Shortly thereafter, Officer Degraffenried of the California Highway Patrol arrived and stepped out of his black-and-white patrol car. Cleland briefed him on the situation, and he then kept an eye on Lottman while Cleland searched the cab of the pickup. Cleland found a can of owl castings on the front seat, but no guns or ammunition.

Lottman, in the meantime, was becoming loud and

verbally abusive. He was growing angrier by the minute, his face flushing redder and redder as though ready to burst, and as his anger grew, his sanity seemed to leave him. Cleland was thankful he had handcuffed the man when he did, for Lottman now reminded him of a time bomb, ready to explode at any second with lethal results. Degraffenried had by now heard enough from the man and crammed him into the caged back seat of the black-and-white patrol car.

Cleland grabbed his cell phone and called Bob Tonelli Sr., requesting that he come to town to take a look at Lottman. Hopefully, Tonelli would recognize the man. Tonelli agreed to come. Cleland also contacted his supervisor, Lt. Alan Matthews, and advised him of the situation. Throughout these phone conversations, Cleland was hampered by the fact that Lottman was shouting obscenities and attempting to kick the windows out of the CHP patrol car. But Degraffenried intervened again, opening the door and having a quiet word with Lottman. Cleland couldn't hear what Degraffenried said, but whatever it was had a remarkable calming effect on Lottman.

Cleland now photographed and secured evidence from the pickup, labeling each blood-spattered object with an evidence tag. When this was done, he consulted with Degraffenried about what to do with Lottman. There were a variety of things that would have justified booking Lottman into county jail, but the jail was over 70 miles away in Yreka, and neither officer was anxious to make that drive. Plus, Lt. Matthews was in favor of citing and releasing the man, since he seemed to have good identification. At one point Cleland asked Lottman if there was someone in Klamath Falls who could drive down and pick him up.

"I don't live in Klamath Falls. I live about two minutes from here in a trailer park." This came as a surprise to Cleland, but it was welcome news.

About this time, Tonelli arrived and immediately identified the pickup as being the vehicle he had reported.

He also got a brief look at Lottman, still in the back seat of the black-and-white, and advised Cleland that he was almost certain that Lottman was one of the two he had confronted at Sam's Neck.

When Cleland was finished with Lottman's pickup, Degraffenried parked and locked it near the rear of the parking lot. Cleland then followed him as he drove Lottman to the man's residence at the mobile home park. But before they could release Lottman, Cleland had one last bit of business to attend to.

"Mr. Lottman, I have to take your clothes. You have blood on your t-shirt and blue jeans, and I need them for evidence."

But Lottman's mood had brightened somewhat when he had learned he was going home instead of to jail, so he was ready to cooperate.

"And I'll need to go with you when you go inside to change," said Cleland. This was to prevent Lottman from arming himself when he went inside, should he be so inclined. Cleland freed Lottman of the handcuffs and followed the man inside the single-wide mobile home. And while Cleland, on hair trigger, watched his every move, Lottman shed the blood-stained garments and pulled on other clothes. He also stuffed his blood-spattered feet into a pair of running shoes.

While inside Lottman's trailer, Cleland spotted a deer-size object wrapped in a bloody bed sheet. Unfortunately, the object was only a sleeping bag, but the bloody sheet, to Cleland's trained nose, had a gamy, fresh venison smell to it. Cleland seized it and the bloody clothes into evidence. Cleland questioned Lottman thoroughly, but despite his best efforts, he could not get the man to admit to anything. Lottman tenaciously stuck to his pit bull story to explain the blood. Cleland went ahead and issued Lottman a citation for the illegal killing and possessing of a deer and instructed him that he would be notified when to come to court.

With or without a confession by Lottman, Cleland had a good case against the man, and it was sure to get better.

Upon leaving Lottman to contemplate his misfortune, Cleland drove to Sam's Neck where Tonelli Sr. showed him the place where the pickup had been parked. Beyond the shoulder of the gravel road and the grassy ditch beside it ran a barbed wire fence. A line of junipers grew along the fence, beyond which was a vast alfalfa field.

"The deer like to bed down under these trees along the fence," said Tonelli. "They're almost tame. We drive by 'em all the time, and they don't even get up."

In seconds, Cleland knew the whole story: Three feet of skid marks on the road clearly marked the spot where the pickup had abruptly stopped. Splatters of blood in the roadway led to bloody drag marks through the grass from the fence. Cleland located a small area of flattened grass against the fence where one or more deer had been lying. A small pool of blood marked the spot where a deer had been killed.

Cleland photographed and measured, meticulously documenting all evidence at the scene before concluding his business there and heading back to Dorris. As he drove, he considered the case and concluded that he had plenty of good evidence to send to the Wildlife Investigations Lab in Sacramento. Technicians there would surely be able to match DNA blood samples from the kill site to the blood from Lottman's clothing and pickup. But where was the deer? Who was the second suspect, and where was the rifle?

The following afternoon, as Cleland was returning from patrol, driving through Dorris he passed a place from which he could see Lottman's residence in the mobile home park. As it happened, Lottman's pickup was just pulling away. Shadowing from a distance, Cleland saw the vehicle drive to the Dorris Lumber and Moulding Mill. The day shift had just ended at the mill, and employees were heading to the parking lot for their vehicles. Cleland saw Lottman get out of his pickup and meet with two men. They stood briefly in conversation, then Lottman approached the rear of his pickup, opened the lid to his camper shell and pulled out a small-caliber rifle. He handed it to one of the other two men, who placed it in the cab of a small tan pickup with Oregon plates. Each man then climbed into his own pickup and departed.

From Cleland's vantage point, a half-mile from the parking lot, he had no direct route by which to get there. But because it was highly likely that the three vehicles would pass through Dorris, Cleland took up a position where he could intercept them. He wanted to at least get a look at the rifle. As he waited, two of the vehicles approached, but the tan pickup was not with them. It had apparently turned north on Highway 97 and would soon be across the Oregon line. Cleland, with a pressing engagement elsewhere, couldn't pursue the matter.

As part of his followup on the Lottman case, Cleland contacted a friend of his, Deryl Hess of the U.S. Forest Service, and filled him in on the case. He then asked Hess to keep an eye out for a dead deer dumped somewhere between Sam's Neck and Dorris. Three days later, Hess called Cleland, reporting that he had found a deer that could well be the one they were looking for. Cleland responded immediately, hurrying to an abandoned pole barn south of town.

The deer was a small buck, its spike antlers in velvet. Cleland first noted that the animal had been partly field dressed, then abandoned. He noted also what looked like a small-caliber bullet wound at the base of the skull, near the animal's ear. Cleland felt reasonably certain that it was Lottman's out-of-season kill. Two days later, Warden Herb Janney ran his metal detector over the carcass, got a signal, and Cleland was able to dig two bullet fragments from the first vertebra of the deer's spinal column.

During the weeks that followed, Cleland completed his investigation, compiling another of the first-class, highly professional investigative packages that had earned him a reputation as one of the finest investigators in the state. Compiled in a thick binder, it contained everything pertinent to the Lottman Case, including a report by ballistics experts at the U.S. Fish and Wildlife Forensics Laboratory in Ashland, and a report on the blood evidence submitted to California's Wildlife Investigations Lab in Sacramento.

The federal lab in Ashland had identified the bullet fragments as originating from a .22 caliber bullet. They further identified the bullet as to brand and manufacturer, and they provided a short list of rifles that could have fired it. The report on the blood evidence from the Sacramento lab was but a preliminary report, for the DNA tests were not yet completed. In this report, however, Senior Wildlife Pathologist James Banks was able to say conclusively that all of the blood samples submitted were of fresh deer blood.

Cleland now submitted the case to the Siskiyou County District Attorney's Office, verbally summarizing it to John Quinn, the deputy district attorney who would be prosecuting it.

"Did you know that this guy is a convicted felon?" said Quinn, to Cleland's surprise. "He has a long criminal history of drug-related stuff, assaults and at least one felony conviction for manslaughter. And you're telling me that you saw him with a gun?"

Cleland confirmed that he had indeed seen Lottman with a rifle, despite the fact that Lottman, as a convicted felon, was prohibited from using or possessing firearms. This crime in itself would be enough to send Lottman back to prison.

When Cleland left the DA's office on that day, he was absolutely certain that Lottman was as good as convicted and that he would pay dearly for his misdeeds. But Cleland was wrong. Time would prove that Lottman would ultimately be convicted of nothing. He would pay not one dime for his crime of killing a young, half-tame deer in its bed, and he would spend not one single day in jail for ignoring his felony conviction and illegally possessing a rifle.

Cleland learned of Lottman's escape from prosecution one afternoon as he was reading a particularly disturbing headline story in the local newspaper. Suddenly the name Troy Alvin Lottman leaped out at him from the printed page.

Cleland read on in horror how Lottman, the walking time bomb he had confronted at the mini-mart months earlier, had finally exploded. He had detonated squarely in the face of his stepfather, the 33-year companion of Lottman's 72-year-old invalid mother, a kind and gentle man who looked after her every need and who worked two jobs to support her. In a fit of drunken rage, Lottman had pulled a pistol and killed the man.

But Lottman would even dodge the charge of murder. He would never serve so much as one day in jail for it. He would never even be arrested for it, for when the police came to take him into custody, he stared them square in the eyes, put the pistol to his head and killed himself.

CHEATERS

At first glance, they might have appeared to be honest fishermen, but they were anything but honest. Ankle deep in the Sacramento River, at a wide and shallow riffle near the town of Princeton, the two of them stood poised with rod and reel, waiting, studying the shallow riffle that whispered over a cobbled bottom before them.

Suddenly a disturbance in the water caught their eye. A striped bass the length of a baseball bat was thrashing its way up the riffle, the top of its body clearly visible above the surface. Gregory Atwell, a relentless poacher of game and fish for most of his 32 years, was the first to react. He dipped his long rod-tip low behind him, then powered it forward, launching a heavy, finger-length torpedo sinker which rocketed in a low arc across the riffle. The sinker and the three large treble hooks tied just behind it struck the water forward of and well beyond the fish. Flipping the reel into gear, watching the fish and timing his move perfectly, he took three swift turns on the reel handle and made a mighty jerk with the rod. The hooks ripped through the water, and the point of one of them found its mark. It struck the moving fish and buried itself in flesh behind the spined dorsal fin.

The fish, a female of about 38 pounds, was no stranger

to fish hooks. During the 18 years of her life, which included 13 round-trip journeys from San Francisco Bay to the upper Sacramento River to spawn, she had survived and bore the tiny scars of several near-fatal encounters with fishermen, legal and otherwise. The fact that she still lived was miraculous, a measure not only of her remarkably good luck, but also of her keen survival instincts.

She had begun her life as one of over 3 million tiny eggs spawned by her mother in the open water of a deep drift in the river and fertilized by a host of males that followed her. Each egg, nearly weightless in the water, was no larger at first than a pinhead and floated free, borne along by the current. She had no sheltering nest and no parent on guard to protect her. From the very first, she and the others had been on their own, adrift in an exceedingly hostile world. Over a million of what would have been her siblings perished on the first day, feasted upon by predators or victims of all manner of other lethal hazards. It was a miracle, in fact, that she survived her first year. By her sixth year, she alone had survived out of the millions. But now, yet again, her survival was very much in doubt.

At the first bite of steel into her flesh, she reacted instantly. The water exploded as she drove ahead with her powerful tail, thrashing the shallow water, propelling her swiftly over the riffle and into the deeper water above.

Atwell's reel screamed as the heavy line smoked away. Afraid that the big fish would strip the reel bare, he turned a wheel and tightened the drag. The added pressure swung the fish and by chance she was drawn around the bare roots of a long-dead, long-submerged cottonwood. She completed a full circle around the roots, then another, and Atwell felt the difference and sensed his problem.

The fish, feeling the unyielding pull of the fouled line that drew her ever closer to the tree-roots, reacted with another burst of power. The line pulled banjo-string tight, and the hook ripped free from her back, leaving a ragged wound. But she was free. She glided into the depths of a deep hole to rest and regain her strength. She had cheated death yet again.

Atwell cursed his luck, the big fish gone, his line hopelessly snagged. Grumbling, he clamped down with his hand on the spool of his reel and walked backwards, the line tightening until it finally popped. Still grumbling, he tied on another torpedo sinker and three more large treble hooks.

While the big female striper rested in a drift above the riffle, another large fish swam onto the riffle from downstream. This one would not be so lucky. Atwell's companion, John Mar, another outlaw of renown, had first crack at the second fish and made his cast. Like Atwell, his aim was unerring, his timing perfect, and with a powerful jerk of the rod he buried two points of a treble hook deep into the fish's back, just behind its head. Again the water's surface erupted as the second fish now fought for its life.

This fish, another female, was even larger than the first, her swollen gut jammed with eggs. She fought hard, but her luck had left her. After 15 minutes her strength was gone, and Mar dragged her, feebly flopping, onto a gravel bar.

"This one should do it!" said Mar, staring down at the fish. Atwell agreed. Using a pair of pliers, Mar pulled the hook from the fish's back, then using one of the hook points grasped in the jaws of the pliers, he made a wound inside the fish's lower jaw. If later he was accused of snagging, Mar could point out a hook wound in the fish's mouth.

Four hours later, in the town of Knights Landing, at the weigh-in station for a weekly striped bass derby, Mar and Atwell entered the fish into the competition. The attention of a suspicious judge was immediately drawn to the snag wounds on the fish's back. The judge looked first at Mar, then at Atwell, whom he remembered as being the winner of the derby two weeks earlier. And he clearly recalled the snag marks he had seen on Atwell's fish as well.

"What did you catch this fish on?" the judge inquired, unsmiling, studying Mar's eyes.

"A Rebel," said Mar, unable to meet the judge's gaze.

"She really slammed it!"

As it happened, Mar's fish, at 41 pounds, was by far the largest fish of the week's contest, and despite the judge's suspicions, Mar walked away with first prize, an expensive rod and reel outfit. But the judge had no intention of letting the matter drop. As Mar and Atwell drove away, the judge studied their vehicle, Atwell's lift-kitted, gray primered, 4X4 Ford pickup with oversize tires, and he jotted down the license number.

* * *

Warden Bruce Greer, California Department of Fish and Game, was in a quandary. On his belly on the east bank of the Sacramento River, propped up on his elbows with his binoculars to his eyes, he studied the actions of two men across the river from him on a shallow riffle a quarter-mile downstream. It wasn't the first time he had watched them, and it wouldn't be his last, for he knew they were up to no good. He was certain they were snagging stripers, but they were careful, always keeping their snag gear hidden between casts. Despite his best efforts, he had so far failed to catch them.

With little more than a year on the job, Greer had much to learn. Like most wardens, he had a hard-won, four-year college degree to his credit, but the real learning for wardens, he knew, came on the job. And he was now beyond his experience in dealing with the two striper snaggers. He had tried to surprise the two men, to catch them with their illegal gear, but they were vigilant, and a vast gravel bar protected them, providing simply too much open country for a warden to cross unseen. When Greer had tried it, the two men had quickly cut the snag gear from their lines and tossed it away into the river. When Greer got to them, they were the picture of innocence, tying legal lures onto their cut lines.

On this frustrating occasion, Greer had checked their fishing licenses and tackle boxes. He had found torpedo sinkers and large treble hooks among their gear, but it was not against the law to possess these things, and each, in fact, had legal applications. Before leaving the men, however, Greer had filled out field identification cards on them, recording their names and dates of birth. But despite the implied threat of this action by Greer, there had been a smirk on the face of Atwell and a look in his eyes that clearly said, "Forget it, stupid. You'll never catch us."

So now, with the two outlaws at it again, Greer had to decide what to do. As he pondered this question, he heard Lieutenant James Halber make a call on the Fish and Game radio, and Halber wasn't far away. Greer picked up the microphone and gave him a call. Halber, a veteran of many years, agreed to meet with Greer a few miles to the north at Butte City.

Upon learning the identities of the two suspects, Halber's eyes narrowed, and he listened with complete attention. He had only tangled once before with Mar, but Atwell, and his older brother, Robert, had for years been steady customers of the Butte County wardens. The Atwell brothers typically ignored fishing and hunting laws and had been trouble for Halber from his first day in Butte County. Not only did they regularly exceed bag limits, fish or hunt during closed hours and take things out of season, but they usually trespassed to do so. And they always ran when threatened by wardens, which often resulted in dangerous vehicle chases through the farm country. Because of their wild and reckless driving in their hopped up and elevated Ford 4X4, and because of their willingness to push the chase to breakneck speeds over ground no sane person would travel, they sometimes escaped. This of course did nothing to endear them to the wardens.

On one moonlit night, Captain Dave Nelson, Halber's supervisor at the time, witnessed someone shoot into a huge flock of feeding ducks, killing dozens of them. Nelson had been unable to catch up with them, but was able to radio Warden Gayland Taylor to intercept them. Taylor, upon seeing their headlights coming his way, had attempted to set up a roadblock. But he didn't have a big enough vehicle to block the entire road. So he stood in the open space between patrol vehicle and ditch, in hopes that the oncoming outlaws would yield to his red light and physical presence. They did not, of course, and following an initial slowing, the driver hit the gas. At the last instant, Taylor leaped for his life as an elevated pickup with big wheels nearly flattened him.

Two days later, word reached the wardens through informants that Greg Atwell was crowing about making a game warden dive for cover. Soon thereafter, Halber stopped Atwell and Mar in the rice country, got Greg Atwell aside and advised him of some grave misfortunes that would befall him should he ever again endanger the life of a game warden.

But the wardens sometimes got lucky, and it was always an expensive experience for the Atwells. Halber had a clear recollection of the last time he had encountered them. Having spotted them driving down the Cherokee Creek Levee east of the little farm town of Richvale, shooting out of the windows of the big truck, he had worked his way ahead of them, stashed his truck, and hurried on foot to set up an ambush. Hidden near a bridge over Cherokee Creek, he had watched them come. When they were no more than 100 yards away, he saw them shoot first a coot, then a beautiful white egret before they suddenly wheeled their truck around on the levee top and sped away in the opposite direction. Halber was furious with himself, for they had apparently spotted him.

Sprinting back to his patrol truck, he attempted a wide end run to head off the fleeing outlaws, but they simply vanished. He fumed over it for a minute or two, then had an idea: He had clearly seen both Atwell brothers, Greg driving and Robert doing most of the shooting, and their big pickup was unmistakable. So, he decided to simply wait for them at their home near Chico. This he did, having memorized their address, and he was sitting there in his patrol truck when the two surprised brothers pulled into their driveway. They were enraged, loud and abusive, accusing him of violating the rules of fair play. But Halber, unaware of any such rules, wrote them each a citation and seized their rifle into evidence.

It had been an important case, having illustrated to the Atwells that they needn't be actually caught in the field to be prosecuted. But while it may have somewhat slowed their illegal game-poaching activities, it apparently had little effect on their abuse of the fishing laws.

Halber listened with interest as Greer explained the situation, including the problems as he saw them—the impossibility of sneaking up on the suspects, the surety of their clipping off and tossing their snag gear. Halber then asked Greer to draw him a map, which Greer did, on the back of a citation book. Halber studied it briefly.

"OK," he said. "Here's what I think we should do. I think I can make 'em hide their snag gear, and you should be able to watch 'em do it."

Halber then stepped to his vehicle and withdrew a spotting scope mounted on a tripod.

"Take this," he said, handing it to Greer. "Get as close as you can to them, then use it. Tell me when you're settled in and have them in clear view."

Following a few more words of instruction from Halber, they parted company, and Halber crossed the Butte City Bridge to the Princeton side of the river and headed south. He chose a spot a mile north of Princeton to pull over and wait. About 10 minutes later, he heard from Greer.

"I'm ready," said the younger warden. "I can see 'em really well with this scope. They're just standing there, watching the riffle."

"Let's wait until you see each of them cast at least once," said Halber, and it was a good quarter-hour before Greer finally called again.

"Good!" said Halber. "I'm on my way."

Halber drove south, through Princeton, then took a dirt road to the east, through a prune orchard. Seconds later, a vast expanse of river-bordered gravel came into view. He immediately spotted the big 4X4 pickup, a third of a mile or so down river. Scanning with his binoculars, he soon made out the two men standing in shallow water, near a tiny island in the riffle. Things were perfect for his purposes. He could have chosen another road which would have emerged from cover much closer to the suspects, but that wouldn't do. He was where he needed to be.

He started the engine, but before heading out he turned to the big German shorthair pointer sitting upright in the passenger seat next to him.

"How about it, Boone, feel like a little run?"

Boone's ears perked up and he stood expectantly. Halber then held open the driver's door while the eager, brown and white dappled dog cheerfully scrambled across his lap and leaped out.

"Find a bird!" said Halber, addressing Boone, as the patrol vehicle started forward.

The outlaws spotted the green pickup immediately, but they saw little menace in it, for it wasn't a warden making a banzai charge at them from a hundred yards away. What they saw was a warden away off in the distance, running his dog—a totally unthreatening situation. True, they would have to ditch their snag gear, but there was no need to toss the two or three bucks' worth of sinkers and hooks. They had time to hide the stuff. And hide it they did. They clipped their lines above the snag gear, walked a few feet to the shallow water near the island and buried the illegal rigs in the sand, beneath a few inches of water. Only an inch or two of heavy monofilament line was visible above the sand. They then returned to their original spot and tied large Rebel lures to their cut lines. They were busily casting and retrieving the Rebels when the patrol truck rolled to a stop.

"It was just like you said!" said Greer excitedly over the radio. "They cut off their gear and stashed it! I know exactly where it is!"

Taking his handset radio, Halber stepped out and walked through the shallow water to speak to the two men. Boone took advantage of the situation to take a swim. Near the shore, Halber noted a large striped bass on a rope stringer. He noted also a tiny wound near the fish's dorsal fin.

"Mr. Atwell! Mr. Mar! What are you guys up to today?"

"Just fishing," said Atwell, regarding his old enemy.

"Well," said Halber. "I'll need to see the gear you were using a few minutes ago."

Both men stiffened.

"We've been using Rebels all morning," said Atwell.

Halber then explained that he was *demanding* to see the gear they had been using. He further explained that their failure to show it to him would mean an additional charge on the citations they were about to receive. Certain they were being bluffed, the two men stuck to their story.

"One last chance," said Halber. "I'm demanding to see what you took off of your lines a few minutes ago." But they stuck to their Rebel story.

Halber now called Greer on his handset, and Greer guided him toward the hidden snag gear.

"Keep going! Keep going!" said Greer as Halber waded toward the island. "Now come towards me a little. Hold it! Look right there!"

Studying the bottom, Halber first saw a faint disturbance in the submerged sand. Looking closer, he then made out a tiny leader of monofilament line. Reaching down, he grasped it and pulled. Out popped the series of treble hooks and a torpedo sinker. Looking further, he spotted another tiny leader, and soon he was carrying both snag rigs to the little island.

"We've never seen those before," said Atwell.

Ignoring him, Halber radioed Greer and advised him to come on around. Soon, not only Greer appeared, but also two other wardens who had monitored the radio traffic. Warden Steve Owen, upon his arrival, called Halber aside.

"Are these the guys who were entering snagged stripers in derbies?"

"They're the ones," said Halber. "The bigger of the two is Greg Atwell. I've been chasing him around since he was a teenager."

During the 15 minutes of paperwork, Atwell and Mar stood sullenly, forced to accept the grim fact that they had been outsmarted by the game wardens. When finally allowed to go, minus their heavy snag rods, the big striped bass and their snag gear, they climbed into their truck, each bearing the pink copy of a citation.

Greer ended his day a little wiser than he had begun it, firmly committed now to consulting the older, more experienced wardens whenever he faced a difficult problem.

Two months later, Atwell and Mar again faced the wardens, this time at the Colusa County Courthouse. Both men had pled not guilty, and Halber and Greer were there to testify in their trial. The judge in the proceeding, upon hearing Greer's testimony that he had actually watched the two defendants clip off and bury their snag gear, quickly found them both guilty. And upon hearing about their cheating to win the striped bass derbies, he was outraged and hammered them with heavy fines and many hours of public service work. Ironically, but certainly appropriately, Halber would run into Atwell a few weeks later in Oroville, doing hard labor on behalf of fish, working off his public service hours at the Feather River Hatchery.

* * *

One warm May afternoon, in a long drift in the Sacramento River near Princeton, the water's surface suddenly came alive with fish—hundreds of them, striped bass of all sizes. The water seemed to boil with them in what to some could have appeared to be a feeding frenzy. But in fact it was a *reproductive* frenzy, with hosts of males competing for position among the thrashing females.

Among them was a 38-pound female with a wound on her back. She released clouds of eggs near the surface, six pounds of them, nearly 4 million in number, to be fertilized by clouds of milt exuded by anxious males. On it went, for several hours, the river's surface churning with activity, until finally it ended, the exhausted fish retreating into the depths.

Two days later, swept along by the current, the vast numbers of tiny eggs began to hatch. But many didn't make it this far, for those borne into quiet water simply sank to the bottom and died. The survivors lived on yolk sac for a week before learning to feed on their own. Less than a quarter-inch long, they were prey to all manner of predators, but they were now tiny predators themselves, feeding on small aquatic animals known as zooplankton.

By early summer, the lucky ones had reached the Delta, where they would live and grow in the brackish water for two or three years before pressing on to their ultimate destination, San Francisco Bay. Most would remain there, in the food-rich waters of the bay for most of their lives, but some would even venture into the Pacific Ocean. By age four or five for the females, younger for the males, a strong urge would come upon them and they would be drawn by the magic of instinct to return up the great river, to the place where their lives had begun. And there, on some other warm spring day, in a river alive with their kind, the cycle of life would begin anew.

* * *

A few months following the convictions of Atwell and Mar for various fishing crimes, a large striped bass was hooked from a boat and fought to exhaustion near Alcatraz Island. As the fish was netted and hoisted aboard, the happy angler, a young woman, let out a whoop of delight, then knelt to look closer at the fish.

"Look at this!" she cried, pointing to a half-healed wound just behind the fish's dorsal fin. "Something tried to *get* this one!"

One of the men on board reached for a small club to dispatch the fish.

"No, wait!" cried the young woman. "I don't want to hurt it!"

"What?" said the man incredulously. "This is a trophy

fish!"

"I know, but I don't want to hurt it! Get my camera!"

As one man readied himself with the camera, another pulled the hook from the fish's jaw. The woman then struggled to pick up the great, flopping fish, ultimately cradling it in her arms like a huge loaf of bread. She smiled broadly as the shutter clicked, then awkwardly, but somehow with great tenderness, she carried the fish to the side, hoisted it over and slipped it into the water.

The big fish lay there for a moment near the sun-sparkled surface, her gills pulsing. Then with a flip of her big tail, she shot away into the depths. She would live again in the blue waters beneath the Golden Gate, perhaps even spawn again. But from this moment on, her life would mean something much more, for she was now irreversibly bound to a smiling young woman . . . with a photograph to be treasured for a lifetime.

A CALCULATED RISK

The foothills of western Merced County

Darkness had fallen. William Anton Bartos, his callused hands clenching the wheel of his four-wheel-drive poaching rig, guided the aging vehicle up the twisting band of asphalt that was Dinosaur Point Road. Dark, sodden clouds had rolled in from the sea, extinguishing the stars over the coastal mountains and smothering an already dying moon. It would be a wet night, Bartos concluded. His pickup's headlights, and those of a second pickup not far behind, cast great arcs of light over the rolling, oak-forested hills until the vehicles turned onto a dirt road and stopped at a heavy steel gate.

Bartos stepped out, moved to the rear of his pickup and pulled out a pair of heavy bolt cutters as long as his legs. Lugging these, he approached the padlocked chain on the gate, selected a link well away from the padlock, and applied the bolt cutters. His biceps bulged and he grunted with effort as he muscled the tool's handles together, the steel jaws biting into steel. The chain link parted with a metallic *chink*. The chain fell away as Bartos pushed open the gate. Seconds later, both vehicles passed through the gate onto forbidden ground.

Bartos hurried back and dragged the gate closed. He then dug into a front pocket of his Levis and drew out an object he had crafted in his garage. At first, it appeared to be a single chain link, like the one he had just destroyed with the bolt cutters. But this one was in fact quite different. Cleverly built, it was hinged. It could be opened and closed. As one of his companions held a flashlight, Bartos wrapped the chain again around the gate and secured it by adding the hinged link to the chain where he had removed the old link. The gate now appeared as it had when Bartos had first approached it. But Bartos was not yet satisfied with the job. From his jacket pocket he removed a small plastic bag containing a piece of dark-colored modeling clay. This he applied with his fingers to the hinged link, filling in all gaps and seams until the hinge was all but invisible. He stood back and surveyed his handiwork, grunted with approval then trotted back to his pickup. Soon the taillights of the two vehicles were out of sight beyond the first ridge.

Five crooked miles later, large raindrops began to fall just as the poachers approached a second gate. Bartos again used the bolt cutters to get through the gate, but *this* time he cut the padlock. He then picked up the destroyed lock and hurled it into the brush. When both pickups were through this gate, Bartos closed it behind them, and secured the chain with a large padlock of his own. It was raining steadily as they continued on.

The pigs were where they always were, on the back side of Mt. Ararat, and the poachers cornered a big boar in an ancient stand of bay laurel trees. The half-dozen pig dogs, fierce pit bull crosses, did their job, lunging, snapping, frantically barking, occupying the boar until Bartos and his friends could arrive to end the battle. But the fearless old boar didn't go easily. It repeatedly charged the dogs, ripping and slashing with curved ivory tusks that had disemboweled other dogs on other nights. But on this night its luck ran out. Bartos dashed in and touched the sawed-off barrel of his 30-06 "pig killer" rifle to a spot behind the boar's left ear and fired. The shot, though muffled by the body of the pig, was deafening under the bay tree canopy. The old boar dropped instantly. A half-hour later, it lay gutted and lashed to the top of the dog boxes in Bartos' truck.

"Do you want to try for another?" Bartos asked, turning to his long-time poaching buddy. Dominic "Vince" Vincenti, always the clearer thinker of the two, considered the question as the rain beat down on them. It was only a little past midnight, plenty early, but they were all pretty wet, especially the boy. Vincenti regarded the boy, age 16, shivering in his sodden jacket. *If his grandpa only knew*, thought Vincenti, for the boy was the grandson of a retired game warden captain. And the boy's father, standing next to the boy, rainwater dripping off his nose, was the retired warden's ex-son-in-law.

"I don't know, Bill," said Vincenti. "We may have trouble gettin' outta here. The roads are gettin' pretty bad."

"I agree," said a fourth man, who sometimes accompanied Bartos and Vincenti on their illegal forays. He was riding with Bartos on this night, and the father and son team were with Vincenti.

It took little more to convince Bartos that it was time to leave, and the two pickups were soon sloshing their way toward the valley, far below. But they had not traveled far when they came to a bad stretch of road crossing a small meadow. Bartos, in the lead, nearly bogged down, but his heavy mud and snow tires got him through—barely. Vincenti was not so lucky. He mired axle deep less than halfway across. They struggled for an hour to free it, knee-deep in mud, sopping wet, jacking, stuffing brush under the wheels, pushing, cursing, but to no avail. Finally, they agreed to wait until daylight or until the rain stopped, which ever happened first.

Dawn found the five of them cramped and uncomfortable in the two pickups, but it appeared that the storm had passed. Following another hour of hard labor, they managed to free the mired pickup, but only after Vincenti had apparently damaged the transmission. More cursing. The vehicle could travel, but it was clear that it would not be able to do so until the roads dried out a bit.

"It's too risky to travel now anyway," said Bartos. "We'd probably run into one of the ranchers or maybe even a warden."

So they found a hidden spot, off the main road, and settled down to spend the day. By midmorning the sun came out, and the roads had begun to dry.

*   *   *

Fish and Game Warden Ryan Broddrick, his brow wrinkled with concentration, studied the rain-faded vehicle tracks at the gate off of Dinosaur Point Road. *These weren't here last night*, he thought, peering down at the faint impressions. Studying them further in the morning light, he detected the presence of two distinct tread patterns. He had checked the gate the previous evening shortly before dark and there had been no visible tracks. But now, it appeared as if two vehicles had entered the gate sometime during the night. With his eyes, he followed the tracks through and beyond the gate and verified that there had, in fact, been two vehicles and that there were no return tracks.

Trespassing and poaching on the larger ranches was no new problem. It had been happening for over a century. But in recent years, the poachers were becoming more bold and were doing property damage as well as damage to wildlife. It was now common for outlaws to cut through a fence to enter private property at one point, then cut the fence elsewhere to exit. And they would often leave the fences down behind them. Landowners were furious.

Broddrick now examined the locked chain on the gate. At first glance, it appeared intact, but Broddrick had learned a variety of tricks relative to poachers and gates. He was about to learn another. A slight color variation caught his eye and drew his attention to one link in the chain different from the others. "Well, I'll be darned," he muttered as he examined it closer. He opened the hinged link and removed it from the chain. *Pretty clever*, he thought, then tossed it once in his hand and slipped it into his pocket.

Assessing the situation, Broddrick concluded that the chances of the bad guys still being around were slim. They had probably left by another route hours earlier. But then again, it had rained hard during the night. They could have gotten stuck somewhere. It was a small chance, but still it was a chance. Broddrick made up his mind, pushed the gate open and drove his patrol vehicle through. As he was closing the gate behind him, the sun suddenly broke through the retreating rain clouds and painted the world a dazzling gold. Broddrick paused for a moment, drinking it in with his eyes and breathing deeply of cool, clean air that smelled of wet earth and oak leaves. And he was reminded again of the wondrous good fortune of his being a game warden.

Deer watched him from the higher slopes as he topped a saddle and dropped down into a hidden meadow containing a decaying barn and a maze of wooden cattle corrals and loading chutes. It was here that the road and the tracks he followed passed through another locked gate in a taut, four-strand barbed wire fence. Upon examining the lock, for which the rancher had given him a key, he found it had been changed. It now appeared that the poachers had cut off the old lock and replaced it with one of their own. It also meant that there was a greater chance that the poachers were not only still out on the private property, but that they would return through this gate.

With the increasing probability that he might soon be facing two truckloads of heavily armed pig poachers, Broddrick decided it was time to call in some help. He reached for his radio microphone, made the call, and an hour later Lt. Roger Reese rolled onto the scene. Broddrick had already backed his patrol vehicle into the old barn and out of sight, and Reese now did the same. It made for a perfect ambush.

As Broddrick briefed his lieutenant on the situation, Reese listened attentively. Reese supervised the wardens in that part of the state, and Broddrick, four years into his career, had been a welcome addition to the squad. With his ready smile and infectious laugh, he was instantly likable, and yet he was relentless in his pursuit of wildlife violators. By any measure, he was a fine warden. Reese had concluded early on that Broddrick had the talent and the intellect to rise to whatever level he chose in Fish and Game.

Respect between the two men was mutual. Broddrick had found Reese to be an excellent supervisor who, despite his lieutenant's bars, was a tireless worker and had remained game warden through and through. Many saw Reese as reserved, maybe even a bit cold, but Broddrick soon discovered that beneath his facade of the serious, no-nonsense professional lurked a dry sense of humor that was a delight to those who knew him well.

Hours passed as the wardens awaited the return of the poachers. Both men agreed that it was unlikely to happen, but they couldn't ignore the possibility. So they waited, and they spent the hours in continuous, amiable discussion. And inevitably they had to laugh again about an eventful evening that had occurred the previous Fourth of July, not far from where they now stood. They had responded to a CalTIP report that someone had been spotlighting deer or pigs on one of the big foothill ranches and that the suspects were staying in a mountain cabin in the area. Reese, Broddrick and Reserve Warden Ed Ayres headed out that night to have a look. Upon locating the cabin, which was down in a small, bowl-shaped valley, they found that there was no safe place to park the patrol vehicle nearby. Reese therefore decided to remain on foot and watch the cabin while Broddrick and Ayres took the vehicle elsewhere to wait.

The suspects had arrived an hour before midnight. Reese watched their headlights as they drove directly to the cabin. About this time, Broddrick, slouched behind the wheel of the patrol vehicle, shifted position in an attempt to get more comfortable. And as he settled his six-foot-three, 205-

pound frame lower in the seat, a couple of things happened: First, one of his size 13 feet, seeking a more comfortable nook up under the dark recesses of the dashboard, became entangled in a spaghetti of electrical wiring. The resulting damage disabled both his emergency red light and his siren. Second, his relaxed right knee came to rest firmly against the transmit button on his radio microphone. Suddenly Reese and others for miles around were treated to an animated conversation between Broddrick and Ayres which boomed out over the radio waves.

It would have been funny had it not been for the urgency of the situation, for the suspects had departed the cabin in their vehicle and had immediately begun spotlighting. Reese watched helplessly, trying repeatedly on his radio handset to break through to Broddrick and Ayres. But it was no use. The conversation in the patrol car firmly controlled the airways.

"Say, I'm gettin' hungry, let's break out those nachos!" *Rustle rustle . . . ripping cellophane . . . rustle rustle . . . munch munch.* "These are great!" *Munch munch.*

Reese was getting frantic. The suspects, still working the spotlight, appeared to be heading in the general direction of Broddrick and Ayres, and Reese had no way to warn them. A quarter-hour later, the situation had not changed. The suspects were still spotlighting, and Broddrick and Ayres were still chattering away. At one point, Reese himself became the topic of discussion, specifically his obsession with neatness and order.

"I can't believe that guy," said Broddrick. "He organizes everything. I think he arranges all the paperclips in his desk drawer so they're facing the same direction."

Reese was beside himself with anxiety. The suspects were nearing the top of the ridge. If they turned one way, Broddrick would probably never see them. If they turned the other way, they would probably blunder right into the wardens, and if they ran for it, the wardens would have to pursue them in heavy dust, a highly dangerous practice.

As it happened, Broddrick and Ayres did get a warning of the approaching outlaws, a rather spectacular one. They were still deep in conversation in the patrol vehicle, the windows down to the pleasant summer-night's breeze, Broddrick's knee still depressing the transmit button on the microphone, when suddenly Ayres let out a shriek and nearly jumped into Broddrick's lap. Having sensed a presence to his right, Ayres had turned and found himself face to face with a visage so horrible that it nearly stopped his heart. It was big and black, its lips pulled back in a hideous grin, its murderous fangs yellow in the moonlight. It was the nightmare face of Satan . . . Satan the pig dog.

Satan was a rottweiler/pit bull cross of over a hundred pounds. It stood on its hind legs, forelegs braced on the side of the patrol vehicle, peering hopefully into the open window.

"Give him a nacho," said Broddrick. The stricken Ayres recovered his composure and did so. Satan inhaled it. "Give him another," said Broddrick. "We don't want to make him mad."

Then things happened fast. Because Broddrick's knee was no longer keying the microphone, Reese was able to warn them by radio. It came just as the wardens caught the first flash of approaching lights. Two outlaws in an open jeep, unaware that their dog Satan was having nachos with the game wardens, continued to shine the spotlight around as they topped the ridge. As they pulled into sight, Broddrick snapped on the headlights and sped the patrol vehicle towards them. As he did so, he hit the switch to the red light. Nothing happened. He then hit the siren switch. Nothing. There was nothing he could do but continue his charge and stop only when the suspects were a few feet away, full in his high-beams. There followed a tense couple of seconds as Broddrick and Ayres leaped out of the patrol vehicle and half expected the suspects to start shooting or at least make a run for it, confronted as they were by an unidentified vehicle. But the two terrified outlaws sat transfixed in Broddrick's headlights like spotlighted bucks.

The wardens made the arrests without further incident.

Looking back on it now, eight months later, it seemed all the funnier, and Broddrick and Reese shared a good laugh. But Broddrick, at the time, had been mortified upon learning of the open microphone and his half hour of private conversation going out over the air. He and Ayres had wracked their brains afterward, trying to remember what they had said during that half hour, who they might have offended. Had they said anything about Reese? But Reese had never said a word. Offended or not, he maintained his silence.

The afternoon passed slowly for the two wardens, maintaining their vigil in the old barn. With each passing hour it seemed more likely that the poachers had left the area by a different route, that the wardens were wasting their time. But neither man was willing to suggest calling it quits. It wasn't until dusk, when the sun had vanished behind Mt. Ararat, that Broddrick suddenly froze, his hand raised for silence.

"Wait a minute," he said. "Do you hear something?"

"I believe I do," said Reese.

* * *

The pig poachers had spent the day simply killing time. And they were nervous. The problem with Vincenti's transmission had denied them a variety of options. Their choice now was whether or not they should take a longer but safer alternate route out of the big ranch and risk Vincenti's transmission giving out completely, or should they take a calculated risk and leave the way they had come in. The latter option would be much easier on the ailing transmission, but it greatly increased their chances of running into trouble.

"I think we should risk it," said Vincenti. "I don't want to have to leave my pickup in here somewhere."

Bartos finally agreed, but he insisted that they wait until at least sunset, when the ranchers would be home at supper, and any game wardens who may have spotted their tracks would probably have long since given up waiting them out. And so it was that dusk found them topping the ridge overlooking the little valley with the loading chutes and the old barn. Bartos studied the complex through binoculars. No sign of life. They started down. They reached the valley floor, then pulled up to the gate. Bartos jumped out, ran forward, unlocked the padlock and dragged the gate open.

Out of necessity, Vincenti was in the lead. This would allow Bartos to give him a push should the transmission start slipping too badly. So as Bartos was closing the gate, Vincenti drove on ahead, hoping to build speed to help deliver him over the next ridge that loomed before him. As he sped by the old barn, he never spared it a glance, and he failed to notice in his mirror as a green pickup came careening out of the old structure and started after him. He failed also to notice as it gained rapidly on him and fixed itself on his rear bumper. But he *did* notice the battery of lights that suddenly lit him up, one of them a bright red, and a siren's banshee wail which nearly sent him through the roof. He hit the brakes and lurched to a stop.

"STATE GAME WARDEN!" shouted Broddrick, stepping out. "STAY IN THE CAR AND KEEP YOUR HANDS WHERE I CAN SEE THEM! DRIVER . . . DROP YOUR KEYS OUT THE WINDOW!"

Broddrick took no chances with the pig poachers, for like most wardens, he considered them to be among the most dangerous people on the planet. He carefully removed the suspects from the pickup, one at a time, disarmed and handcuffed them. When he was finished, he had an impressive pile of weaponry on the hood of his truck. Both adults had been carrying .44 Magnum pistols in shoulder rigs. The driver, in addition to the big handgun under one armpit, had a sheathed 10-inch Bowie knife under the other. And there were two fully loaded shotguns and two fully loaded big-game rifles in the pickup as well, plus enough ammunition for a major fire-fight.

Reese had made a similar stop on Bartos' vehicle. There was a huge boar lashed on top of the dog boxes, and Reese found both the pickup's occupants to be armed to the teeth. But the poachers didn't resist, and no one was hurt. Bartos, in fact, was quite talkative. In addition to admitting to cutting the gates the preceding day, he confessed to cutting many gates and fences on many other days. He appeared to be proud of the fact that he had been poaching on the big ranches since he was a kid.

"This is the first time I've been caught," said Bartos. "I took a calculated risk, and you guys got lucky."

It wasn't until the citations had all been issued, the guns and pig seized into evidence and the now unarmed poachers sent on their way that the wardens could breathe easily again. Reese led the way back out to Dinosaur Point Road, and while Broddrick closed and chained the gate behind them, Reese walked back for a few words with him.

"I was glad to see that your red light and siren worked tonight," said Reese. Broddrick smiled at the obvious reference to the July night eight months earlier.

"And I was happy that you had no radio problems either," Reese continued, his face totally neutral. "It was a good lick, tonight. Those guys needed catching." Then he bid Broddrick good night and turned and started back to his vehicle. And as he did so, without looking back, he said, "I need to get home and organize my paperclips."

Broddrick, puzzled at first by this statement, stared after his departing lieutenant.

Then the realization struck him. And it wasn't until Reese was in his vehicle and accelerating away that he shot a glance back at Broddrick . . . and flashed him a grin.

KILLER JOHN

There was no good reason for John Drudik to shoot a bear. There *were*, however, some *excellent* reasons for him to leave the animal alone. Not only was bear season closed, but the two-year-old animal on which the cross-hairs of Drudik's rifle-scope now rested was little more than a cub. It had bothered no one. Its only offense was to amble into a freshly vacated camp site and root for meat-bones tossed into the fire ring by careless campers. And it wasn't like Drudik was alone, for an occupied camp was less than a quarter-mile away.

Dawn had come to the forest, the August sun not yet topping the wooded ridges to the east. But Drudik had been wide awake for hours. It wasn't that he was an early riser, for in fact, he had not yet gone to bed. Like many meth-using dopers, and like the young bear he studied through his rifle-scope, he was largely nocturnal. But unlike the bear, he was in no way a hunter. He was simply a killer. Some defect in his dope-numbed brain compelled him to put a bullet into any creature that crossed his path.

Many who knew Drudik, including his parole officer and a number of cops and game wardens who had tangled with him, believed that his lust for killing didn't stop with animals. And all who wore a badge approached him with the same caution due a venomous reptile.

Drudik now assumed a steady shooting position, leaning across the hood of his pickup, his rifle to his shoulder, peering through the scope. He lifted his head briefly as he considered the threat posed by the potential witnesses in the nearby camp. But he quickly dismissed this concern, for good judgement rarely colored his decisions. He again settled his cheek against the walnut stock, and again he squinted through the scope. His finger tightened on the trigger.

*   *   *

George Yates, a retired fireman, was just emerging from his tent when the loud boom of a rifle gave him a start. *That was close*, he thought, as his wife voiced her concern from inside the tent.

"It's OK, hon'," said Walsh. "Someone just fired a gun. I think it was those people in the other camp."

"Pretty inconsiderate, I'd say," said his wife. Yates agreed, but suspected that it was more than that. His experienced ear had detected, he believed, another sound, almost one with the shot, but a millisecond later—the *thump* of a bullet striking flesh. A half-hour later, after pulling on his boots and downing a cup of coffee, he grabbed a pair of binoculars and stalked into the forest. He took his time, staying out of sight, and worked his way to a rock formation that provided an elevated vantage point.

From the rocks, he found he had a good view of the other camp. And he had no sooner adjusted the focus on his binoculars when he spotted the straggle-haired man and teenage boy he and his wife had spoken to the day before. They were dragging something from the woods behind camp. At first it looked like a big dog, then Yates realized it was a bear. They dragged it to the rear of the pickup, opened the camper shell, dropped the tailgate, and hefted the bear inside.

Aware that bear season was a good two months away,

Yates now turned his attention to the rear license plate on the pickup. A trailer hitch blocked part of the number, but he committed the rest to memory. He then yielded to the tiny warning voice in his brain and slipped back to his own camp. A half-hour later, the pickup passed his camp, but the dust cloud it raised prevented his reading the rest of the license number. He peered after it as it rattled down the mountain toward Oroville. It was nearly a week later when he finally got around to calling CalTIP.

"I don't want any money," said Yates to the CalTIP operator. "I just want to get this information to a game warden." He then agreed to leave a number where he could be reached. Ten minutes later, his phone rang and he found himself talking to Lt. James Halber, Department of Fish and Game. Halber was highly interested and questioned the man carefully. He learned that Yates and his wife had taken a walk the evening before the incident and had passed the suspect's camp and had actually spoken briefly to the suspect and the boy.

"Can you remember anything that would give us a clue as to where they live?" Halber asked. Yates hesitated a few seconds, and Halber could hear him querying his wife.

"My wife thinks she remembers the boy saying something about Oroville," said Yates.

Halber continued with the interview until he felt he had gleaned every tiny detail he could get from Yates. He then thanked the man for calling.

"I don't know if we'll be able to do anything with this, but we'll give it our best shot," said Halber. "We'll let you know what happens."

A few minutes later, he radioed Warden Leonard Blissenbach, the Oroville warden, and arranged to meet with him. They met in Oroville, on a levee overlooking the Feather River. Halber watched as the other warden arrived and stepped out of his patrol truck. Blissenbach was a formidable-looking man, a defense tactics instructor, built like a linebacker. And with his full head of curly blond hair and large walrus mustache, his was a memorable appearance. In addition to being bad news to game-law violators, he had a nose for drug cases and made more felony arrests than most narcs. But it was his computer-like memory for past customers—their names, arrest records, vehicles, accomplices, and dwellings—that Halber hoped to employ on this day. Halber quickly filled him in on the reported bear killing.

"The witness said the guy looked about 40, long scraggly black hair, mustache, slim build, about five-ten. He was in a tan Ford Ranger with a white shell. The RP said there was something about the guy's eyes that really bothered him, made him feel uneasy."

Blissenbach thought for only a second or two, then said "That sounds like our friend John Drudik." Halber searched his memory, then it came to him.

"Is that the guy we got poppin' pheasants out of his truck over on Nelson Road, the one they call Killer John?" Halber asked.

"That's him," said Blissenbach. "I think he was driving a tan Ranger with a shell that day. Remember? He's the same guy Fred Brown got down by Gray Lodge. Fred watched him crawl up on a flock of snow geese and kill 15 of 'em. And I think Fred and Bob Orange got him another time spotlighting deer up out of Feather Falls." As always, Halber was amazed at Blissenbach's powers of recall.

To check out Blissenbach's hunch that Drudik was their man, Blissenbach radioed dispatch and had them run Drudik through DMV records to see what vehicles were registered to him. With luck they could get a match on the vehicle and partial license number provided by the witness. But it didn't happen.

"Wait a minute," said Blissenbach, rubbing his chin pensively, "I think he might have been driving his *father's* truck that evening out on Nelson Road. Yes, as I recall, his father lives in Oroville, not far from *him*." Blissenbach then called dispatch again, and within a few minutes, the dispatcher had found records on another Oroville man by the name of Drudik, this one about 20 years older than their suspect. The dispatcher then ran the older Drudik for vehicles, and DMV records revealed that he owned a small Ford pickup. As she read the license number, the wardens anxiously compared it to the partial license number provided by the witness.

"Bingo!" said Blissenbach with a grin.

"I'm really impressed," said Halber, and he meant it.

Soon thereafter, Halber and Blissenbach, in an unmarked vehicle, located the residences of both John Drudik and his father, William. They lived in the Oroville district known as Thermalito, about three blocks from each other. And the wardens were not surprised to find the Ford Ranger parked at their suspect's house. After thoroughly assessing the situation, Halber began calling other wardens in his squad for help. By midafternoon he had assembled a team which included, in addition to Blissenbach, Wardens Will Bishop and Wade Johnson, plus two very capable reserve wardens, John Christofferson and Jack Teagarden. Seated at a long table in the conference room at the Feather River Hatchery, Halber briefed them on the case and set about refining a plan.

"We don't think the bear is at John's house. It's a brand new double-wide mobile with nothing around it—no garage, no other outbuildings, clean as a whistle. But his father's place is a regular rat's nest. There are at least three outbuildings there, well hidden from the street. Lots of trees and bushes, a screened-in porch on the house. We think that at least *part* of the bear will be there, and probably *all*. Any comment?"

What followed was a lively discussion as to how best to proceed. It was of the utmost importance that the wardens somehow come up with a piece of the freshly killed bear. Without this "corpus," there was little chance for a prosecution of the bear killer. Even if the wardens were to find fresh bear blood in the back of the tan Ranger, the best they could hope for would be a search warrant for John Drudik's home, and none of the wardens expected the bear to be there. What they needed was a warrant to search the father's home, but even the unanimous opinion of a squad of highly experienced wardens meant nothing when it came to the necessary probable cause to obtain a warrant to search a man's home. This left the wardens with but one choice: They would resort to trickery.

The plan was put into effect late that afternoon. It began with Lt. Halber being dropped off at a wooded lot a block up the street from the elder Drudik's home. No one noticed as he burrowed into shrubbery there where he had a good view of the front of the residence. Next, wardens Will Bishop and Wade Johnson arrived in plain clothes, in an unmarked vehicle. They parked nearby and immediately split up and began knocking on doors across the street from the elder Drudik's house. When people answered, the wardens displayed their badges and identification and delivered a carefully prepared interview.

The questioning was intended less to gain information than it was to inform the residents that the wardens were investigating a wildlife crime and had focused their attention on one the nearby neighbors.

"Have you heard anything about one of your neighbors perhaps shooting a bear about a week ago?" they would ask. "Do you know of anyone nearby who might have done such a thing?" They would follow this with a glance toward the Drudik house and the question, "How well do you know the people across the street?"

When finished with the interview, they would thank each resident for their time, then turn to leave. But then, as an apparent afterthought, the warden would turn again to the resident and add, "Just so you won't be too worried, in about a half hour some Fish and Game vehicles will be pulling up out front. It's no big thing, so don't let it scare you, but it would probably be best for you to stay inside for the first few minutes." The warden would then depart.

Of the four of William Drudik's neighbors contacted by Bishop and Johnson, one interviewed by Johnson showed promise. Johnson had the distinct impression that the man was a friend of the Drudiks and may even have known about the bear. This proved to be the case, for immediately after Bishop and Johnson had driven away, Halber saw the man in question walk out into his front yard, peer off in the direction the wardens had taken, then trot across the street to the Drudik house. He was there less than a minute before he again appeared, walking back across the street to his house. Halber spoke low into his radio handset as he advised the other wardens.

Less than three minutes later, Halber was delighted to see the tan Ford Ranger come careening around a corner and slide to a stop in front of the elder Drudik's house. The man Halber recognized as John Drudik leaped out and dashed toward his father's house, out of Halber's sight. He was gone but a minute or two before he reappeared, hurrying out with a large cardboard box heaped with what looked like paper-wrapped packages of meat. He stuffed the box inside the camper shell, then ran back and returned with another large box of similar packages. This time his father was with him, bearing an armload of loose packages of what Halber was sure was meat and a burlap bag containing a lump the size of a basketball. They dumped it all inside the camper shell, then the younger Drudik leaped behind the wheel again and sped away.

Halber, speaking into his handset radio, had given the other wardens a running account of all of this, and they were all prepared for anything when John Drudik departed with what had to be a load of bear meat. The wardens had expected Drudik to head out of town and dump the meat somewhere, but he surprised them all by simply driving back to his own home, three blocks away. And when he jumped out and ran into the house, Blissenbach and Johnson were but a half block behind him.

By the time Halber arrived, the other wardens had surrounded the house, but repeated attempts to convince Drudik to answer his door had failed. Halber approached the tan Ford Ranger and peered inside the camper shell. The two boxes of wrapped meat were still there, as were the few loose packages and the burlap sack. By straining his eyesight to the utmost, Halber was able to read handwritten labels on a few of the packages. Most of them were marked with a large letter B, followed by whatever cut of meat was inside.

"Guess what," said Blissenbach, approaching Halber. "I just ran a rap sheet on him. He's a convicted felon. He's done time for burglary, assault, arson and a variety of drug crimes."

"So he can't possess a firearm," said Halber.

"That's right," said Blissenbach. "And come take a look at this." Halber followed him up the front steps of the house, peered through a living room window, and there, in plain view, was a five-foot marijuana plant growing in a pot.

The wardens now held another quick discussion. There was doubt, under the circumstances, as to whether or not the wardens could legally open the closed camper shell on the pickup and recover the meat. And there was the problem of their suspect's refusal to answer his door. There was even the possibility that the suspect could have bolted out the back door before the wardens had it covered.

"We need to get a search warrant," said Halber. "We've got plenty of probable cause, and it's the only safe way to deal with this. I'd hate to lose the whole thing in court on some technicality." The others agreed. So Halber took a patrol vehicle and raced home to his computer and began hammering out a search warrant.

For Halber, writing a search warrant was not a particularly difficult task, but it was time consuming. The affidavit had to contain the whole story of the case, beginning with the witness observations and containing every little bit of evidence that contributed to what the attorneys referred to as *probable cause*. Nothing could be left out. But on this day, a Saturday, Halber knew that the process would be much more difficult to complete. The problem was to first locate someone from the DA's office to *review* the warrant, then to find a judge to *sign* the warrant—no small feat on a weekend.

Two hours flew by. As Halber worked at his computer,

his growling, complaining stomach reminded him that it was well past dinner time, and he had missed lunch as well. Picking up his radio handset, he called the wardens and suggested they send someone out for hamburgers. He then printed the necessary pages and headed out the door. Then began a series of wild goose chases that took him to the far ends of the county. When finally he located a deputy district attorney, the even more difficult task of locating a judge still lay ahead. In the end, it was nearly midnight when he rolled into the driveway of Judge Brian Rix in Paradise.

Despite the hour, Judge Rix greeted Halber pleasantly and invited him in. As Halber walked through the door, an incredibly wonderful aroma washed over him, the smell of things fresh baked, just out of the oven—wondrous things made with real butter, sugar and cinnamon. Then his famished stomach gave an audible groan as Judge Rix seated him at a kitchen counter within reach of dozens of the biggest, plumpest, most scrumptious looking sugar cookies he had ever seen. Some were still warm on the cookie sheets, and others were piled on a great platter. Halber lusted for them, felt himself drawn to them as if by some strong magnetic pull.

Oblivious to Halber's intense hunger, the judge took the warrant documents and began poring through them. Halber was left to stare longingly at the sugar cookies, salivating like a hungry pup. At one point, the judge directed Halber to add some verbage to the document, writing it in, longhand, and initialing it. Then finally it was done. Halber raised his right hand, as per instructions, and swore to the accuracy of the document. Then the judge signed it, endorsed it for night service and handed it to him. *This is where he gives me a cookie*, Halber thought, but Brian Rix, an excellent judge and a fine man by any measure, simply didn't think of it. Halber cast one last mournful glance at the sugar cookies as he went out the door.

Back at Drudik's house, the other wardens had maintained the vigil. But absolutely nothing had happened to indicate that anyone was inside the house. No lights, no voices, no toilet flushing, no sounds of any kind. The wardens were beginning to think that no one was home, that Drudik had in fact escaped out the back door right at first. But now, Halber was on his way with the warrant, and the mystery would soon be solved. Blissenbach began considering how to gain entry into the house without breaking in a door, and it was then that he noticed that there were no screens on any of the windows. *That's odd*, he thought.

Then Halber arrived. Aware that he was about to force entry into a house probably containing an armed felon, he pulled the 12 gauge riot gun from its lock. Following a brief discussion with the other wardens, Halber stuffed the warrant into a shirt pocket and mounted the front steps.

BOOM BOOM BOOM, Halber hammered on the front door. "STATE GAME WARDENS! WE HAVE A SEARCH WARRANT! OPEN UP!" shouted Halber. Silence. *BOOM BOOM BOOM*, on the door. "SEARCH WARRANT! OPEN UP OR WE'LL BREAK IN YOUR DOOR!" No response from within. Halber was about to kick in the door when he decided to try one last thing. Making a big deal out of it, he pumped a round into the chamber of the 12 gauge riot shotgun, an action which produced a loud, ominous-sounding, unmistakable *CLACK CLACK* sound that was audible a block away. Results were immediate.

"Hold it! Hold it!" came a voice from a rear bedroom of the home. "I'm comin' out!" Soon thereafter, as the wardens stood back, weapons at the ready, the door opened, and there stood Killer John Drudik. Within seconds he found himself wearing Blissenbach's handcuffs.

The search of Drudik's lair was memorable for a number of reasons. The wardens were surprised to find three other adults, plus a 10-year-old boy in the house they had begun to think was empty. One or two women present complained that Drudik had made them spend the whole time on the king-size bed in the master bedroom and would not even allow them to flush the toilet. And to make matters worse, the air conditioning had been on high during the warmth of the afternoon, and Drudik wouldn't let them turn it off when it got cold. By the time he finally opened the door for the wardens, he and his friends were nearly frozen, and the place felt like a meat locker.

In addition to the heavy chill in the house, the wardens were surprised to find the house full of empty beer cans. They were everywhere. Every horizontal surface was jammed with them. Every floor in the house was nearly covered with them. There were literally thousands of them. The wardens had to kick through them as they walked from place to place in the house. When Blissenbach asked Drudik "Why all the beer cans?" Drudik answered, "That's my retirement."

A search of a cluttered bedroom produced a number of large M-80 firecrackers and a homemade bomb—a fused film canister stuffed with black powder and taped to a large steel bolt. When Blissenbach asked Drudik what they were for, he said that he used them for fishing.

In the closet of the same bedroom, Blissenbach learned the secret of the missing window screens. They were all there, in the closet, stacked with beer can spacers between them, a fan blowing across them, covered with drying marijuana leaves and buds. It was obvious that Drudik had some source of the weed other than the three live plants that the wardens found in the house. A triple-beam scale provided the last element necessary to charge Drudik with *possession of marijuana for sale*.

And of course there was the meat in the Ford Ranger pickup. Not only were there parts of a bear, but there was some suspicious-looking deer meat and some ducks and pheasants as well. The burlap sack contained the hide of one small cinnamon-colored bear with a white spot on its chest. All of this was potential evidence, and it was all therefore seized, along with a variety of other things from the house. There were nine rifles and shotguns and a pistol, none of which Drudik could legally possess, and there was considerable evidence of hard drug use, all of which the wardens seized into evidence. All in all, it was enough to send Drudik away for a while, and his journey began with a ride to the Butte County Jail in Blissenbach's patrol vehicle.

Because of the boy, the wardens chose not to book Drudik's wife. The other man and woman, who claimed to be only visiting, were ultimately released. But it was time-consuming business sorting it all out and determining, through paperwork found at the house, who actually lived there. By the time the wardens were finished, it was but a couple of hours before dawn. Halber left an evidence receipt and a copy of the warrant on the table, then took a last look around and departed.

As was their custom following an all-night investigation, the wardens met for breakfast at an all-night restaurant before heading home. Despite their fatigue, they were all hungry, especially Halber, who could have eaten his belt.

"No," said a puzzled waitress, "We don't have sugar cookies," so Halber had to settle for a large stack of pancakes, which were at least the right shape.

Sitting around the table that morning, discussing the case, Halber had to brag again to the other wardens about Blissenbach's incredible memory, without which there would have *been* no case against Killer John.

"Then how come he can't remember to get a haircut?" said Wade Johnson with a grin, for Blissenbach was known to look a bit wild in between haircuts.

"Good point," said Halber, turning to face Blissenbach with mock gravity. "How 'bout it, Leonard? When was the last time you got a haircut and trimmed your mustache?"

"I can't remember," said Blissenbach. "My mind's a complete blank."

EPILOGUE

John Drudik was found guilty of shooting a bear out of season, sale and cultivation of marijuana, possession of an explosive device, and felon in possession of firearms. He was sentenced to a year in jail, of which he served about six months. But on a winter day a year and a half later, he had another brush with the law. Special Agent Joe Sandberg, U.S. Fish and Wildlife Service, found him parked where several thousand geese had seconds earlier taken to the air in fright. When Sandberg approached the vehicle, he found Drudik and a young woman inside. Both appeared to be high on drugs, and Drudik was concealing a pistol under his leg. Sandberg, drawing his own pistol, promptly disarmed Drudik. And when he ran warrant check on the man through Butte County Sheriff's Office, Warden Blissenbach overheard and quickly warned him by radio about Drudik. Blissenbach then made a code-three run to backup Sandberg. Drudik didn't fare well in the court proceedings following this encounter. A superior court judge apparently felt he had been coddled enough and promptly sent him to State Prison.

NEW TALENT

Manny Mesick, a deer rifle in each hand, couldn't shake the feeling of foreboding that had suddenly come upon him as he hiked down the brushy slope. Following close behind, the two Pedri brothers, hands and arms smeared with blood, each dragged a freshly killed buck. Missing on the antlers of both deer were the deer tags required by state law.

Mesick peered nervously down the mountainside, past the Gilman Ranch headquarters, to State Highway 1, half expecting at any second to see a Fish and Game patrol car turn into the ranch driveway. And then, as though summoned by his fears, one appeared and did exactly that. Terrified, Mesick stood frozen for a moment, then reacted.

"Wardens!" he shouted, as the green pickup approached the ranch headquarters. "Quick, get the deer out of sight."

The Pedri brothers didn't ask questions, but immediately set out at an awkward, bent-over trot, dragging the two untagged deer into a dense thicket of coyote brush. Mesick followed them in.

"Did they see us?" Mark Pedri inquired, chest heaving from exertion.

"I doubt it, but it's possible," said Mesick. "They're a long ways away. They'd have to have awful good eyes."

The three men peeked out of their hiding place, studying the patrol vehicle as it passed the ranch complex and disappeared behind the barn.

"What do we do?" Mark Pedri asked.

"We stay put," said Mesick, his face a mask of worry. But the Pedri brothers wanted no part of waiting and slipped away into the brush.

*   *   *

Fish and Game Warden Jack Edwards was in a fine mood as he motored south on the coastal highway out of Half Moon Bay. It was a beautiful fall morning that had begun, for Edwards, with a magnificent country breakfast prepared by his visiting grandmother. It was also the second weekend of deer season, and Edwards looked forward to a day of concentrated game warden work. He was just beginning his third year as a warden, and he found every day an adventure.

Riding with Edwards on this morning was Keith Long, a rookie warden still in his first year. But veteran wardens had already noted that Long had considerable talent, not the least of which was a particularly sharp mind and the eyesight of a falcon. He was currently the boarding officer assigned to the patrol boat *Minnow*, and because his boss, the boat lieutenant, was on vacation, he would be spending the day with Edwards, another talented young warden, who would give him a taste of what land wardens do. Long, like Edwards, was looking forward to every minute of the day ahead, and he listened attentively as Edwards explained what they would do.

"We'll check some deer camps first. Maybe you'll get to validate your first buck," said Edwards, and a few minutes later he turned off the highway onto the gravel road leading to the Gilman Ranch. They had gone but a few yards down the gravel road when Long leaned forward and pointed to a spot high on a brushy mountainside beyond the ranch house complex.

"There's somebody up there," said Long. "I see one . . . two . . . three guys . . . and they're dragging something . . . looks like a couple of deer."

Edwards stopped the patrol car, squinted in the direction indicated by Long and groped for his binoculars. Then he saw the tiny specks high on the mountainside.

"How in the world did you see *them*?" said Edwards in amazement, focusing his binoculars.

"They're running," said Long, just as the image sprang into focus in Edwards' binoculars. *Sure enough*, Edwards concluded. They were indeed running, but he was astounded that Long could determine these things with his unaided eye.

"Keep 'em in sight," said Edwards as he fired the engine and drove forward again. He proceeded through the ranch headquarters complex and stopped beside a barn. He jumped out with his binoculars, fired some hurried instructions at Long, and headed toward the suspects. This required him to first scramble down a steep descent into a small canyon, cross a creek bed, then hike up the mountainside beyond. It was a good 15 minutes before he neared the spot where Long had last seen the suspects. Because the wardens lacked a portable radio, they communicated through hand signals. Responding to Long's gestures far below and homing on the outraged scolding of a disturbed scrub jay farther up the mountain, Edwards finally cut the trail of the dragged deer and followed it into a thicket. Uneasy over the possibility of ambush, he drew his sidearm, a .357 Magnum revolver.

Slipping along quietly, he spotted the guns first, scope-equipped, bolt-action rifles, hidden under a coyote bush. Then, he saw the two untagged deer where they had been stashed with two plastic bags he suspected contained their livers. He was approaching the deer when he heard a rustling in the brush. He spun around, his pistol at the ready.

"Don't shoot, Jack! It's me, Manny!" came a frightened voice. Then out crept Manny Mesick, cautiously, hands in the air. Edwards was not pleased to see him, for Mesick was the manager of the hunting club there on the Gilman Ranch. Edwards had always had a bad feeling about the guy, and now his instincts were proven correct. Mesick got no consideration from Edwards who quickly patted him down for hidden weapons.

"Where are your friends?" demanded Edwards.

"I don't know," said Mesick. "They ran off."

"Well, you'd better call 'em back. They're in enough trouble. Call 'em back . . . *now*," said Edwards.

Mesick hesitated only a moment, then cupped his hands around his mouth and shouted, "HEY, MARK! HEY, MATT! COME ON BACK!" and Edwards now had their first names. But the two missing suspects didn't respond. In a few minutes, Keith Long appeared, having made short work of the substantial climb. Following a fruitless search for the departed suspects, Edwards picked up the two rifles and the plastic bags of deer livers, then turned to Mesick.

"Grab one of those deer," said Edwards. Mesick obeyed as Long grabbed the second buck, and soon they were on their way down the mountain. Back at the patrol car, as Edwards issued Mesick a citation for *possession of untagged deer*, Edwards was able to extract from him the last names of the two missing suspects. Mesick would never say who had actually done the shooting, but he did explain how it came about.

"We were down at the clubhouse waiting for another guy to get here to hunt, and we spotted these two nice bucks up on the mountain. We figured we'd go ahead and shoot the biggest one and tag it with the other guy's tag when he got here. But we ended up shooting both of 'em. I know, we shouldn't have done it, but that's what happened."

Mesick signed the citation, then the wardens loaded the deer and the two evidence rifles into the patrol car. "Tell the Pedri brothers they'll be hearing from the DA's office," said Edwards as he and Long climbed into the patrol car and headed out.

"We'll file formal complaints on the other two," said Edwards, as he and Long left the Gilman Ranch behind.

"When Craig Gilman finds out about this, Manny Mesick will be lookin' for another job. Gilman is a good sportsman and plays by the rules."

Back in Half Moon Bay, the wardens hung the deer in Edwards' garage. Edwards' grandmother, still very much the Michigan farm girl, was surprised that her grandson had left only a short time earlier and yet was already back with two big deer. "Oh, my!" she exclaimed, a twinkle in her eye. "Are these for dinner?"

"No, Grandma," said Edwards. "We don't eat our evidence."

As Edwards made a phone call and arranged for the deer to be picked up by church people for use in a local soup kitchen, his grandmother circled the hanging animals, snapping photos with an ancient little camera.

"The girls in my travel club will find this interesting," she said.

With the deer taken care of, the two wardens headed for the door, anxious to resume their patrol.

"You boys be home by six," Grandma Edwards called after them. "I'm gonna fix you a real nice dinner."

"We'll try, Grandma," said Edwards. Turning to Long he said, "That's a meal you don't want to miss."

Soon they were on their way again, southbound out of town, cheered by the fact that the day was still young, and yet they had already struck a sound blow against wildlife crime. As they traveled along, Edwards shared "war stories" with Long—tales of his past adventures and those of other wardens, things intended to add to the new warden's education. Many were humorous, and they laughed a lot.

"I want to hear about the time you fell off the pier," said Long with a grin.

"Who told you about *that*?" said Edwards, feigning outrage.

"It's already legend," said Long. "But I want to hear it from you."

Edwards then told the story of a day over two years earlier when he had gone to the pier at Half Moon Bay. He was there to check deep-sea anglers on a returning charter boat. He had stayed out of sight until the 50-foot boat was about to moor, a deckhand poised with a mooring line. Edwards had then strode into view and offered to receive the mooring line from the deckhand. The deckhand's first toss of the line was short, the boat still several yards from the pier. Edwards didn't even try for it. The deckhand quickly coiled the line and tossed again, and again the toss was short. But this time Edwards grabbed for it anyway and immediately regretted it, for in his zeal to catch the line, he reached out a little too far. His arms windmilled briefly as he tried to regain his balance, but it was too late. Off the pier he plummeted, accompanied by a chorus of gasps and groans from onlookers. He fell 12 feet into the bay, struck feet first with a colossal splash, and vanished. Weighted as he was by heavy boots and gun belt, he might well have remained under, but a series of powerful strokes brought him up. As he burst into the sunlight, gasping for breath, the first thing he saw was the means for his deliverance. Someone weeks earlier had tied a stout rope to a cleat on the pier, and it now dangled down to the water just a few feet from him. Following three more powerful strokes, he grabbed it. The concern of the onlookers, including the returning anglers on the boat, then turned into astonishment as Edwards ascended the rope hand over hand like a gibbon ape.

Less than 30 seconds after toppling off the pier, Edwards was back on top again, poised to receive toss number three of the mooring line. This time, he caught it and secured it to a mooring cleat, and had he not been sopping wet, witnesses to the event might well have concluded that they had only imagined it. When the gangway was secured and the anglers started ashore, Edwards was there to greet them, grinning, dripping seawater, his sodden uniform festooned with bits of seaweed.

"Good afternoon, sir. State Fish and Game warden. How was the fishing today?" He set about counting rockfish in burlap bags, checking fishing licenses and bantering with the amused anglers.

"I ain't givin' you my license," said one elderly fisherman, "You're all wet." Unable to argue this point, Edwards checked the license while the man simply held it up for him to see.

Edwards chuckled over the memory of that day, and Long was thoroughly amused. "Hee-hee-hee ... ha-ha ... You're lucky you didn't drown," said Long.

"I probably would have," said Edwards. "but I was just out of the Academy and in real good shape." Edwards, in fact, was *still* in good shape, built like a gymnast, a shorter version of Keith Long who stood well over 6 feet.

Early afternoon found the two wardens prowling along Gazos Creek Road, again in the coastal mountains. Edwards was in mid-war story when they rounded a bend and encountered a foreign-made pickup coming their way. The two occupants stared straight ahead as they passed the patrol car.

"Those guys are up to no good," said Edwards, continuing on, but looking for a spot to turn around. "Did you see how they had their eyes glued straight forward as they passed us? That's not normal behavior. Most innocent people look us over real good when they see us." Long, although inexperienced, had made much the same observation. "And they were road-hunting," Edwards continued. "The passenger had a shotgun between his knees."

Edwards wheeled the patrol car around at a wide spot and set out in pursuit. The suspects in the little pickup, suspecting their peril, were now traveling away at a good clip, but the wardens soon caught up with them. Edwards snapped on his red light. The little pickup slowed, pulled to the right shoulder and stopped, the patrol car close on its rear bumper. The wardens stepped out and cautiously walked forward, one on either side of the suspects' vehicle.

"State game wardens," Edwards announced, crouched slightly to better see inside as he drew near the driver's window. The driver peered out, his hands white-knuckled on the wheel. "We noticed you had a shotgun, sir. Have you had any luck?" Edwards inquired.

"No, we're just drivin' around," said the driver, a surly man in his mid-thirties.

"Well, I'll need to take a look at your shotgun," said Edwards. "Is it unloaded?" But he already knew the answer to this question, having spotted three 12 gage rounds loose on the floor around the passenger's feet. The shotgun had been hastily unloaded. Nevertheless Edwards handled it with great care when the driver passed it through the window to him. It was indeed unloaded. He sniffed the muzzle briefly. The unmistakable odor of freshly burnt gunpowder told its own story.

"This gun has been fired, sir," said Edwards. "What did you shoot today?" The driver's lame reply that he had shot at a rabbit had a distinctly false ring to it.

"Would you two mind stepping out please?" Edwards asked, but it was no question. The two suspects reluctantly climbed out and moved, as per Edwards' instructions, to the front of their car. Edwards peered into the vehicle's interior again, then approached Long.

"Look on the floor on the driver's side and tell me what you see," said Edwards. Long did as instructed, and at first he saw nothing of interest. Then he spotted it. It was the tiniest of feathers, almost weightless, a barely visible bit of fluff. Long retrieved it and held it to the sunlight.

"That's either a pigeon or a dove feather," said Edwards, who then turned to face the suspects. "Are you sure you didn't shoot anything today?" But the suspects stuck to the rabbit story. Edwards then asked if he could take a quick look through the car. The driver, although highly nervous, shrugged his shoulders and said, "Go ahead." Edwards began his search, and upon reaching well back and under the passenger seat he felt a paper bag. He drew it out, and was not surprised to find that it contained a pair of freshly killed bandtail pigeons.

"You're startin' the season about a month early on these," said Edwards, again facing the suspects. But they had nothing to say. Each warden scratched out a citation this time, and soon they were on their way again, the evidence pigeons stowed in the trunk.

"Is it always like this?" said Long, in reference to the two good cases they had made in just half a day.

"No," said Edwards. "Most hunters we check are honest. We just got lucky today." The wardens, however, were to end the day with luck of another sort.

They were heading home when it happened. Traffic was light on Highway 1, and they thought nothing of the oncoming white sedan until it was almost upon them. It contained two young men, and as it approached, the one on the passenger side thrust his hand out the window bearing a green object about the size of a football. This he hurled, or rather hook-shot, over the top of his own vehicle, aiming it at the oncoming green car. The wardens saw it coming, straight for their windshield, and both men ducked, expecting the windshield to shatter. But there was just a loud thump as the object struck and splattered into mush and bits of green skin.

"What was it?" Edwards exclaimed as he sat upright again.

"Some kind of a melon," said Long.

Edwards chose a break in the traffic, swung a U-turn and set out in pursuit, teeth clenched, eyes narrowed, gas pedal to the floor. Long, too, was in grim humor as they sped along, hoping fervently to overtake the white sedan. Then they caught a glimpse of it far ahead and knew they were gaining on it. Finally Edwards hit the red light and siren, and the white sedan pulled over and stopped, terrified eyes in its rear view mirror. The wardens sprang out and within seconds they had dragged the two frightened suspects out and had them spread-eagled against their own vehicle.

"We're sorry! We're sorry!" one of them cried as Long patted him down, none too gently, for weapons. "We didn't know you were cops."

"You could have killed somebody," growled Edwards.

"No! No! It was just a big zucchini!"

"You could have blinded somebody or caused an accident," Edwards added.

"I know. I know. It was dumb."

In interrogating the suspects, the wardens learned that they were college students on their way home for the weekend. The zucchini bombing had been just a prank, albeit a dangerous one, and the anger of the wardens soon subsided.

"Now we've got to figure out what to charge these guys with," said Edwards, after calling Long aside.

"How about assault with a vegetable?" said Long. "Hee-hee."

"*Deadly* vegetable," Edwards added. "Ha-ha."

"Brandishing a zucchini?" said Long. "Hee-hee, ha-ha." And so it went.

The wardens pored through the Penal Code, then turned to the Vehicle Code where they finally found the appropriate section that forbade the throwing of objects at moving vehicles. It was a serious charge, but they reasoned that a judge would take into account the age of the zucchini bombers and the fact that there was no apparent intent on their part to hurt anybody or do any property damage.

"Kids do dumb things," said Edwards, summing it up. "Always have, always will."

The afternoon sun was low over the Pacific Ocean as the two wardens returned to Half Moon Bay where Edwards' grandmother eagerly awaited an account of the afternoon's events.

"Oh, my!" she said, upon hearing about the pigeon poachers. "Oh, my!" she said, in a different tone, bristling now over the news that someone had flung a large vegetable at her grandson. "Did you catch them?"

"We caught 'em, Grandma," said Edwards. "They won't do *that* again."

Long added, "You should have seen the looks on their faces, Mrs. Edwards, when they passed us and spotted our uniforms. Pure horror!"

It had been a memorable day, and Keith Long was still

grinning when he left for home that evening, stuffed full of Grandma Edwards' home cooking. But it was Jack Edwards who would most ponder the day's events, amazed over certain aspects of Long's performance on that day. The man's eyesight, as he had demonstrated at the Gilman Ranch, was amazing enough, but the most remarkable demonstration of his powers of observation had occurred during the zucchini-bombing incident. Despite the fact that the patrol car and the white sedan had been closing at a combined rate of well over 100 miles per hour when the zucchini was hurled, Long, upon seeing the thing coming, had somehow managed to assess the danger and instantly react, folding his sizable body down and into the irregular-shaped space beneath the dashboard of the patrol car. This, to Edwards, was impressive enough, having never seen anyone so big move quite so fast. But what happened next was astonishing: Long, upon unfolding himself from beneath the dashboard, had plucked his pen from his shirt pocket and scribbled something on the palm of his hand.

"What's that?" Edwards inquired.

"Make, model and license number," said Long.

SLOW LEARNERS

A star-filled night in the foothills. Two does and a buck descended a brushy slope, threading their way through chamise and poison oak thickets to a near-dry creekbed below. From a granite pothole there, they drank sweet rainwater left over from the first storm of November.

The buck, a coastal blacktail, wasn't particularly large for his breed, but he had survived four years in an increasingly hazardous world, and his perfect, tri-pointed antlers spread high and wide. He was aware of an approaching vehicle on a nearby road, and having narrowly avoided a number of near-collisions with vehicles, he was aware of a certain danger. For the moment, however, he sensed he was a safe distance from the road. But he was wrong.

The approaching vehicle was an older pickup, its blue paint peeling off in strips. Its driver, Rocco Deluca, drove slowly, leaning forward in the seat, searching for game on the hillsides illuminated by the pickup's headlights and roof-mounted spotlight. The spotlight, operated by his friend Sammy Noia in the passenger seat, cast arcs of bright light first on one side of the road, then the other.

While Noia was a slightly villainous-looking character, Deluca was mildly handsome, with the lean, hard body of an athlete—which he was. Or at least had been. He had been born with a gift. He could hurl spherical objects with astounding velocity and accuracy. As a pitcher on his high school baseball team, his ability to blow sizzling fastballs past frustrated batters had caught the eye of at least two major league teams, and he had been signed by one of them. In practice, during that one year on a minor league team, he did well. It was said that he could deliver 95-mile-per-hour pitches that foiled the team's best batters. But it soon became apparent that he couldn't handle stress, that he suffered a serious and hopeless loss of control when facing real batters in real games. When under game pressure, his wild, potentially lethal fastballs were a danger to everyone.

When baseball bid Deluca a grateful farewell, he turned bitter and surly and became a danger of another sort. He soon found himself arrested and convicted of assault. When released from jail, he continued to get into trouble, and he turned to a variety of illegal pursuits to entertain himself. One of these was poaching, and on this moonless night in western Tehama County, a week after the close of deer season there, he had set out not only in search of illegal game, but to experience the excitement and risk of pitting his wits against those of the game wardens. He had reasoned, on this night, because deer season was still open in the opposite end of the county, 40 miles to the east, that the game wardens would be elsewhere. He too was wrong.

Shortly after crossing a bridge, the pickup's spotlight beam fell upon three sets of reflective eyes.

"There!" said Noia, as Deluca hit the brakes. The deer froze where they stood in the creek bottom, a long stone's throw upstream from the bridge.

A scoped and fully-loaded deer rifle rested butt-down against the seat between the two men. Deluca snatched it up, thrust the barrel out the driver's window and jammed the butt against his shoulder in a single practiced motion. He leaned close, peering through the scope, and he placed the cross-hairs on the buck, on a point midway between its eyes. He took a deep breath, let half of it out and carefully squeezed the trigger. The shot was the clap of doom inside the pickup, and both men were temporarily deafened. But the bullet found its mark, and the buck collapsed.

When satisfied that the buck was dead, Deluca drove on across the bridge and accelerated down the road. Earlier in the evening, he and Noia had planned what they would do if they killed a deer. They now put the first part of the plan into action, putting distance between themselves and the dead buck. But they drove only a few miles before pulling up in front of a tiny home on the outskirts of the city of Red Bluff.

Jane Mandy wasn't surprised to hear a commotion in her front yard, followed by a distinctive knock on her door. Deluca, her boyfriend of about seven months, had informed her earlier in the night that he and Noia were off to do a little night hunting. She knew from past experience that this could mean his return at some late hour to enlist her help. She bundled her robe tightly around her and opened the door. Noia was waiting in the truck, but Deluca, rifle in hand, barged past her and took command.

"Get some clothes on, babe, we're goin' for a ride!"

Mandy, unsmiling, stood there for a moment, brushed a lock of blond hair from her eye, then turned toward her bedroom. As she dressed, she thought of Deluca and their unpromising relationship. Not only was he becoming more and more controlling, but he lacked ambition. And, of late, she had found herself a little afraid of him. Worst of all, she greatly resented his involving her in activity on the wrong side of the law. But she was not at the moment prepared to make an issue of these things. She dutifully grabbed her coat and headed for the door. Deluca stashed the rifle behind the couch, then he and Mandy stepped out into the night.

* * *

Warden Tyler Young, Department of Fish and Game, sat

in his darkened patrol vehicle, windows down, enjoying the brisk but beautiful starry night. He had acted this night on a hunch, nothing more. His well-honed warden's instincts had urged him to suit up and take a drive up into the foothills above Red Bluff. Upon spotting deer feeding in a meadow along Lowery Road, he had driven the patrol vehicle out of sight behind a cattle loading chute and corrals. There he waited. With the deer serving as a tempting bait for night hunting outlaws, his trap was now set.

It was around 11 p.m. when he heard the shot. It wasn't a loud report, just a boom in the distance, but it was unmistakably a large-bore rifle. Young thought for a moment then concluded that it had to have come from at least two miles to the northeast. He sat there in the darkness, listening for more, but all was silent.

In deciding what to do, Young took into account some things he knew for sure: He knew that if a deer had been killed and the poachers had chosen to immediately load the animal and flee with it, he would have no chance of catching up with them. But if the poachers had chosen to initially leave the animal for a while so as not to risk an encounter with a responding warden, then he would have a chance at them. With these things in mind, Young set out, working his way northeast, driving with only his low beams. He was all too aware that poachers under these circumstances would often watch from hiding to determine if a warden was in the area. He therefore stopped often and killed his engine and lights to listen.

Upon reaching Redbank Road, he turned right, toward Red Bluff, its glow visible 10 miles in the distance. He had gone no more than a mile when he rounded a bend and spotted a vehicle ahead, also driving toward Red Bluff. Unfortunately, due to the lay of the land and a bend in the road, it was likely that the driver of the vehicle had seen Young's headlights. Young therefore continued on. Although he was traveling at a leisurely speed, it soon became apparent that he was gaining on the vehicle, which he didn't want to do. He slowed down, but he still gained on the vehicle. It now appeared as if the driver of the vehicle wanted Young to pass him, which of course would mean that the patrol vehicle would be identified. Young therefore slowed even more, keeping well back. But he was close enough to identify the vehicle as a dark-colored pickup, and he could see what he believed to be three people in the cab, their heads and shoulders silhouetted against their own headlights.

Finally, the pickup turned onto a side road, and Young, taking advantage of the opportunity, gunned his engine and sped on by. The occupants of the pickup craned their necks looking back, but could see little. Young continued on for a quarter-mile or so then cut his lights, turned around and crept back to a vantage point from which he could see the side road. He was in time to see the pickup turn around and head back the way it had come on Redbank Road. Young didn't follow, but found a place to pull the patrol vehicle off the road and wait.

No more than 10 minutes later, the pickup returned, continued on beyond the side road and passed Young in the hidden patrol vehicle. Young trained his binoculars on the rear window after it passed and noted that it now contained only the driver. "All right!" he said under his breath, for he now knew that two of the suspects had been dropped off by the third. This meant that they were probably out field dressing a deer or maybe even a beef, for wardens occasionally blundered onto cattle rustlers. He considered the matter briefly, then fired the engine and set out after the pickup.

Jane Mandy, at the wheel of the blue pickup, felt growing apprehension as the headlights in her rear view mirror rapidly drew nearer, and when the bright red light suddenly flashed on behind her it was as though a huge hand had applied a crush-hold on her heart. She pulled to a stop, quaking with apprehension, and watched in her mirror as a uniformed officer approached.

"Good evening, ma'am," said Young, peering in the

driver's window, his flashlight illuminating the young woman and the interior of the pickup. "Can I ask what you're doing out here tonight?"

"Uh . . . I'm just out for a drive," Mandy answered, avoiding his gaze.

"Where are your two friends?" Young inquired.

"Friends? What friends?"

"Look, ma'am, I know you dropped two people off back there. Now, listen to me. You need to be honest and give me some answers." As he spoke, Young directed his flashlight beam into the back of the pickup, and it fell upon something furry. Looking closer, he found that it was a dead raccoon.

"Where'd the raccoon come from?" Young asked.

"I don't know," said Mandy with complete honesty. "This is my boyfriend's truck."

"And where is your boyfriend?"

Mandy responded with a series of lame answers, and Young became more and more certain that the boyfriend, and whoever he was with, had been the source of the rifle shot he had heard. He sensed also that Mandy had not been a willing participant in whatever crime had been committed, and he set about exploiting her growing resentment.

"You know, he put you in a real bad spot," said Young. "Here you are, by yourself in his pickup with a raccoon in back, and raccoons are out of season. They can't be hunted this time of year, and it's a crime to even have one in your possession. And you're in possession of one right now!"

"But, I . . ."

"Wait a minute, listen to me," said Young. "Your boyfriend and his buddy are as good as caught tonight. Now, do you want to be part of the crime? Do you want to end up in front of a judge to explain all this? You have only one good option, and that's to cooperate with me and get this all behind you." And within a few more seconds he had her firmly convinced that if she failed to cooperate, the world would end and the sky would fall.

Slow Learners

"All right," she finally said in a low voice. "What do you want me to do?"

"Well, to start with, tell me what happened tonight," said Young. Mandy then took a deep breath and began talking. Young soon had the whole story.

"OK," said Young when she was finished. "Here's what we're gonna do. You're gonna scoot over and let me drive, and we're going back there in this truck. And you're gonna tell me where to stop."

Mandy looked horrified at first, then thought about it for a moment and finally nodded her head in consent. Young made a quick radio call from the patrol vehicle, locked it, and slipped in beside Mandy in the blue pickup. He started the engine, swung a U-turn and headed back up Redbank Road. As he drove, he engaged Mandy in conversation designed to keep her from thinking further about what she was doing. They had traveled no more than five minutes when Mandy suddenly said, "Here! Stop here!"

Young stopped, leaving the engine running, the headlights on high-beam. About four car-lengths ahead, the road passed over a concrete bridge spanning a dry creekbed. Young scanned what he could see in his high-beams, seeing nothing at first. Then suddenly a man appeared, scrambling up the bank from under the bridge. His sleeves were rolled up past his elbows, his forearms smeared with blood. Upon reaching the road he motioned for the pickup to be driven the remaining distance to him. Young, however, sat tight. The man motioned again, obviously annoyed. Still Young sat tight.

"He's gettin' mad," said Mandy.

Rocco Deluca was indeed getting mad, and when he emphatically motioned again, mouthing the words "COME ON!" and still got no response, he stomped toward the pickup with pure rage in his eyes. Upon reaching the vehicle, still half blinded by the high-beams, he grabbed the driver's door and yanked it open. Expecting to find his slim little girlfriend there, he was astounded when a six-foot-one game warden sprang out. He staggered back as though electrocuted, and Young grabbed him, muscled him up against the pickup and handcuffed his wrists behind his back.

About this time, Noia appeared from beneath the bridge, blinking into the high-beams. Unaware of any of the events of the past few seconds, he, too, approached the pickup, and he, too, received one of the major shocks of his life. He suddenly found himself gripped by a large game warden, his arm twisted back in a come-along hold.

With the second man now captured, Young spoke into the microphone of his handset radio, and a few minutes later, his lieutenant, Walt Mansell, and a Tehama County Sheriff's unit rolled onto the scene. They had been waiting at Young's patrol vehicle, as per Young's earlier request. Upon seeing the suspects, Mansell walked up and addressed Noia.

"Mr. Noia? You again already?" This was in reference to an incident that had occurred a mere two weeks earlier. Mansell had responded to a midnight spotlighting call and had encountered the culprits about the time all their lights mysteriously went dead. One of the two suspects, Sammy Noia, had acquired a super-powerful handheld spotlight that he had wired to plug into his pickup's cigarette lighter. Unfortunately, while using the big light that first fateful night, it had overpowered the vehicle's electrical system, sucked the battery dry, and left them stalled in the middle of a mountain road. Mansell had cheerfully cited the two men for spotlighting and seized their rifles and the big light into evidence. Luckily for them, however, they had not yet killed a deer.

"I have to say, Mr. Noia, you're a bit of a slow learner," said Mansell, shaking his head.

With the suspects in good hands, Young hiked down the bank to the creekbed below the bridge. There he found a field dressed, three-point buck which he dragged back up onto the road. When he returned to the others, he found Deluca in a hot argument with Mandy.

"You just couldn't keep your mouth shut!" said Deluca,

glaring at the woman.

"Don't blame *me* for this, Rocco! *You* did this! This is all *your* fault!" said Mandy, and so it went.

Mansell then stepped in and said, "Back off, Mr. Deluca, she didn't have any choice."

For a variety of reasons, not the least of which was concern for Mandy's safety, the wardens chose to book both Deluca and Noia into county jail. The deputy agreed to take Mandy home and recover Deluca's rifle. Young transported Deluca, handcuffed and seat-belted in the passenger seat of the patrol vehicle, and during the ride back to town, he sought answers to other questions.

"Who shot the raccoon?" he inquired.

"Nobody," said Deluca. "I hit it with a rock."

"Yeah, right," said Young, not buying it.

"No, really!" said Deluca. "It ran across the road in front of us and I threw a rock and hit it."

"Yeah, sure," said Young.

At county jail, the jailers gave Deluca and Noia a warm welcome.

"Hey, Rocco! Hey, Sammy! Where've you been? What's it been, now, about a month?"

*   *   *

Exactly one week later, Young responded to a call reporting someone hunting pheasants in a hillside olive orchard behind the old hospital near the city of Corning. Pheasant season was open; however, the orchard was within the city limits and shooting was prohibited. Young agreed to go to the lower end of the orchard, while a Corning policeman went to the upper end. Young hid his patrol vehicle and stepped out in time to hear shotgun fire coming from the orchard. Upon approaching the orchard, he spotted a familiar-looking blue pickup with peeling paint. At about that time he heard the policeman's P.A. system on the hillside above the orchard.

"THIS IS THE POLICE! COME ON OUT!"

Soon thereafter, Young heard the pounding of running feet coming his way. He stood perfectly still beside a tree as Rocco Deluca came sprinting by, a shotgun in one hand, a pair of pheasants in the other. As he passed, he tossed the pheasants, which landed under a tree only a few feet from the warden. He was at his pickup, stashing his gun, when Young walked up behind him.

"Hey, Rocco, how're you doin'?" Deluca spun around, color draining from his face.

"Oh . . . uh . . . I didn't know I couldn't hunt in here . . . uh . . . but I didn't get anything!"

"You didn't get anything? We need to go for a little walk, Rocco," said Young, beckoning, and Deluca reluctantly followed. Young led him into the orchard to the olive tree beneath which lay the two pheasants, one rooster and one hen. Young picked up the hen and held it up.

"Don't you know you're not supposed to shoot the brown ones?" said Young.

"I . . . er . . ."

"I'll need to see your ID again," said Young, and Deluca dug for his wallet. Deluca was again busted, this time for shooting in the city and the illegal take of a hen pheasant. Young did the paperwork and sent him on his way.

In view of Deluca's two arrests in just a week, Young figured that the man had most likely learned his lesson and would not be a problem again. But Young also knew that the really slow learners have a way of showing up again and again. This proved to be the case with Deluca, for a few months later, as Young was driving across a bridge over the Sacramento River, he spotted a blue pickup near the water's edge. Taking a closer look, he could see a man with a fishing rod near the pickup. Young doubled back under the bridge and approached the pickup. There he encountered Rocco Deluca in the act of stowing his fishing gear.

"Good morning, Rocco. How's the fishing?"

"Well . . uh . . . I don't know. I haven't started fishing yet. I just remembered I don't have a license."

Young walked over to the pickup and looked inside the bed. There, amid the clutter, were two fish—a large catfish and a Sacramento pike. The catfish had been dead for a while, maybe even from the day before. The pike, however, was not only fresh, it was still alive.

"Hey, Rocco," said Young, pointing at the fish. "What do you think this means?"

Deluca studied the fish for a moment, then replied, "I think it means I get another ticket."

*   *   *

As time went on, Tyler Young learned that other wardens had caught Deluca at various misdeeds, that he was indeed one of the slowest of the slow learners. To his credit, however, he never resisted his many arrests, and the wardens bore him no particular ill will. In fact, they found him a rather interesting character, his being a failed baseball player turned poacher. Young, upon learning of Deluca's former experience as a minor-league pitcher, had to look back on the man's racoon-killed-with-a-rock story and admit that it could actually have happened. The story became all the more credible when Young, at some later gathering of wardens, encountered a warden who had once cited Deluca for killing a gray squirrel in a game refuge.

"I wouldn't have believed it if I hadn't seen it," said the warden. "The squirrel was in a tree over 30 yards away. It would have been a good shot with a rifle . . . but *Deluca* nailed it with a rock!"

PREDATORS

Butte County, 1986

It would have taken a keen eye to spot the homemade pipe bomb lashed about knee-high on the trunk of a small oak tree. Keener vision *still* would have been required to detect the monofilament trip-wire stretched ankle-high across a trail adjacent to the oak. This was unfortunate for Lance Troy Lomas, whose dope-clouded vision was definitely not up to either task.

Night was approaching, and darkness came early in the narrow, upper reaches of Butte Creek Canyon. Lomas, however, was in no hurry. As with most days of his life, he was looking to steal something, and darkness usually worked in his favor. The fact that his probable victim on this day would be a pot-growing criminal much like himself made no difference, for there was little honor among his breed of thieves.

He crept along through the oak forest, on a trail above the river. All was silent but for the soft murmur of moving water below. Upon reaching a cross trail leading upslope to several ramshackle buildings, he made the turn. He had gone but a few steps when he felt his foot contact the trip wire. His next conscious thought occurred a day later in a

Chico hospital. The blast blew his hat 30 feet, shattered his left leg, blew out his left eardrum, and sent jagged shards of hot steel into various parts of his body. He fell bleeding and unconscious beside the trail.

A few days later, reliable sources in the upper canyon contacted the Department of Fish and Game with chilling news: The bomb had been intended for Warden Will Bishop.

* * *

On a June afternoon a few days later, as the sun began its slow descent in the west, Warden Will Bishop strode onto a great slab of dark basalt rock overlooking a deep drift on Butte Creek. Peering into the clear water, shading his eyes with his hand, he made out the dark shapes of three spring-run salmon holding near the bottom. He was cheered by the sight of the fish, and yet he felt a sadness as well, for there should have been many more of them.

More a river than a creek, Butte Creek has one of the last remaining runs of spring-run salmon. A strain of king salmon, these fish spend most of their life at sea, then, bright-silver, plump and heavy with stored fat, they leave the ocean in late winter or early spring to journey to the upper reaches of a few of California's rivers to spawn. But they don't spawn in the springtime. They spend the summer months in deep holes and drifts in the rivers and spawn in the early fall. Unfortunately, they're vulnerable to a variety of hazards during their several months in the rivers. Dwindling summer flows and water diversions sometimes strand them, and in all but the most inaccessible areas they're easy prey for poachers. In Butte Creek, spring-run salmon were losing the battle to survive. The run that had once numbered many thousands of fish per year had dwindled to fewer than 200.

It was clear that the Butte Creek spring-run salmon needed serious protection, and Bishop had made it his business to do just that. The task was complicated, however, by a gradual influx of criminal-type people over the years who sought refuge in shacks and old trailers in the remote upper reaches of the canyon. This place, beneath the towering canyon walls, had been the site of a wild Gold Rush community known as Helltown. So intimidating were many of the current residents of the area, the Butte County Sheriff's Office didn't patrol there, and upon receiving calls to respond there, they would do so only in force.

However, Bishop patrolled the Helltown area regularly, day or night, despite the grim fact that radios simply didn't work in the upper canyon and that he would have no chance of summoning help should he need it. He often did so by motorcycle so he could travel the trails far beyond where a pickup could go. His strategy was simple: He wanted to be unpredictable. He wanted the Helltown outlaws, particularly those with a taste for spring-run salmon, to never know when he might show up. He was the perfect predator, absolutely unafraid. He would skulk the trails and river haunts, often in the dead of night, a camo shirt over his uniform. Occasionally he got lucky and snapped up a salmon-snagging outlaw or two.

Bishop, on several occasions of late, had crept up on a remote habitation consisting of several old buildings near Helltown. He had been hearing disturbing rumors about the owner of the place, and he had the distinct feeling that bad things were occurring there, things far more serious than the poaching of fish. The owner, it seemed, a man in his early forties, always had several young boys staying there, suspected runaways, and Bishop was not alone in feeling that it was an unwholesome, if not dangerous, environment for the boys.

One night close to midnight, as Bishop was studying a collection of several hundred obviously stolen road and highway signs hanging on a tall fence behind this troubling place, one of the older of the boys had come walking down the trail. Bishop, who could have easily remained hidden from the boy, chose instead to step out in front of him. The boy's shock and terror were complete, but remarkably he didn't run, apparently frozen in place. Presently he found his voice.

"Wh . . .who are you?" he gasped.

"I'm Warden Will Bishop, Department of Fish and Game. I'm just out for a walk."

Bishop then went on his way, and when the boy's story was circulated among the local pot growers, dope cookers and fugitives, it caused quite a stir. It had, in fact, exactly the effect Bishop was striving for: It put a real scare into the bad guys who wanted anything but this kind of attention. But Bishop hadn't banked on someone setting an explosive booby-trap for him on one of the trails.

And now, on this sunny day a week after the booby-trap incident, Bishop was again in the canyon, on his way to Helltown. After spotting the three fish, he walked back to his motorcycle, swung his leg over the Honda 250 trail bike, and headed out.

Memorable in appearance, Bishop was in his late thirties, with the body of a gymnast and movie-star good looks that turned the heads of women wherever he went. In dark glasses, on a motorcycle, he cut a particularly dashing figure.

Up the canyon he sped, leaning into the turns, enjoying the wind in his face. Upon reaching the upper canyon, he passed through landowner Robb Cheal's gate and thumped and rattled across the old, wooden Helltown bridge over Butte Creek. The bridge was unsafe now for public traffic, a major reason why Cheal had installed the gate. Across the bridge now, Bishop continued on. Finally he stashed the motorcycle and spent the afternoon hiking trails and checking some of the deep holes on the river, the holding-water for spring-run salmon. He found no one threatening the salmon, but he saw disturbingly few fish.

It was shortly before dusk when he straddled the motorcycle to ride straight into one of the most dangerous encounters of his career.

* * *

On a level bench of land, just off of the road leading

over the Helltown Bridge, two men sat in discussion on the lowered tailgate of a pickup truck. Landowner Robb Cheal, owner of the Old Helltown Ranch, the 760-acre parcel of land on which the pickup was parked, was discussing with his friend, Ed Churnside, building plans for a ranch headquarters. A few weeks earlier, Cheal had assisted sheriff's deputies in raiding some of the squatters in the Helltown area, some of whom had been cutting his fences, stealing wood and whatever else they could carry off, and illegally driving across his property. A number of people were picked up on warrants and others were forced to move away. It was a successful operation, but it hardly made a dent in the population of undesirable criminal-type people living in the upper canyon. Unfortunately, during the process, Cheal had made dangerous enemies.

As Cheal and Churnside were talking, movement caught Cheal's eye, and he turned in time to see two armed men, crouched low, sneaking across the dirt road toward his property.

"What the . . . ," said Cheal as Churnside followed his gaze.

The two men approached the gate, aware now that they had been spotted. One had a dense black beard and wore a sleeveless black t-shirt over which he carried a pistol in a shoulder holster. The other, a particularly villainous-looking character with a large mustache and a prominent scar near his chin, wore a filthy, sleeveless Levi jacket and carried what looked like an assault rifle. They had a distinctly dangerous look about them and appeared anything but friendly.

"Who are these guys?" said Cheal.

"I don't know," said Churnside. "But I'll find out! Wait for me here."

Adopting a pleasant demeanor, Churnside waved a friendly hand and walked toward the gate. As he approached the two men, his eyes went to the rifle the man with the scar carried, a Ruger 10/22 with two long "banana" clips taped together. A third such clip was taped to the stock.

"Can I help you?" said Churnside.

"Not unless you want to make *your* business *our* business," said Scar Face, swinging the weapon to bear on Churnside's stomach.

Churnside took a step back, raised his hands in supplication. "OK, fine," he said, as he turned and hurried back to the pickup. Cheal now stood on the far side of the vehicle, at the driver's window. Churnside, looking very grim, went to the passenger window, reached inside and grabbed a holstered pistol off the seat.

"What do they want?" asked Cheal, as Churnside hurriedly strapped the pistol to his belt.

"I don't know," said Churnside, "But they're up to no good."

In the meantime, Scar Face and Black Beard had been in discussion. Scar Face now turned and ducked into the brush. Black Beard shouted for Churnside to return to the gate. Churnside gave hurried instructions to Cheal.

"Stay behind the truck so they can't see that you're unarmed."

Churnside then started for the gate again, painfully aware that he had fired his pistol earlier in the day, and at best it contained but two live rounds. He was in serious trouble and knew it.

Black Beard launched into a tirade during which he claimed to be an attorney representing an adjoining landowner. Churnside would have more readily believed him had he claimed to be an astronaut. Black Beard's tirade, however, in view of what happened next, proved to be only a delaying tactic.

Cheal, feeling genuine fear now, was peering from behind the pickup when he heard a sound behind him. He whirled around and was shocked to see that Scar Face had circled behind him and was now advancing toward him, the rifle leveled at his chest. Cheal was no coward. He had stood up to all manner of dope-growing squatters and other criminals on his property. But at the sight of this incredibly evil-looking man, in whose cruel eyes he saw only death, a mind-numbing terror struck him like a dagger through his heart.

"Who . . are you?" he quavered. But Scar Face said nothing as he moved yet closer. Then he paused as though listening, looked quickly into the cab of the pickup, then left Cheal and strode toward Black Beard who was still haranguing Churnside. Cheal, at that moment, thought, *They're going to kill Ed, then come back for me.*

But then a sound came to Cheal's ears, a sound Scar Face had apparently detected several seconds earlier. Turning, he was in time to see Warden Will Bishop, in camo, crossing the bridge on his motorcycle. Afraid to look back, Cheal hurried to meet Bishop, covertly holding his right hand against his stomach, index finger extended like a pistol barrel, his thumb moving as though cocking the imaginary pistol. This pistol-shooting gesture, along with the look of sheer terror on Cheal's face spoke volumes to Bishop.

"What's wrong, Robb?" said Bishop as he rolled to a stop and killed the engine. Cheal, so crippled by fear that he could not form a sentence, surreptitiously pointed toward the armed men and mumbled something about guns.

Bishop now locked his eyes onto Scar Face and Black Beard, and without breaking eye contact he stepped off the motorcycle and slipped off his camouflage shirt. When he peeled off the camo shirt revealing the khaki shirt, blue and gold arm patches, shiny badge and gun belt beneath, looking magnificent in his uniform and totally formidable, to Cheal it was the equivalent of Superman stepping out of a phone booth. He knew his deliverance was at hand.

Bishop advanced toward the armed men, focusing on Scar Face, who carried what looked like an assault rifle and was ducking through a fence, his intent unclear. Bishop walked through the gate and confronted first Black Beard. Upon Bishop's approach, Black Beard backed up against the fence and held his hands up in a gesture of non-resistance.

"I'll need your gun," said Bishop, reaching out and plucking the loaded revolver from the man's shoulder holster. "And I'll need to see your ID as well," he said as he stuffed the pistol into his belt. As Black Beard fumbled for his wallet, Bishop turned his attention to Scar Face, who was now about 50 feet away, on the far side of the fence.

"Sir!" said Bishop. "Come back over here, please."

Scar Face hesitated, then bent to slip between the top and middle strands of barbed wire. As he was doing so, he lowered the muzzle of the rifle until it was pointed directly at Bishop.

"Watch that muzzle! Point it up!" said Bishop, as the thought occurred to him, *He's going to shoot me and claim it was an accident.*

Scar Face complied briefly, then again pointed the rifle at Bishop as he finished stepping through the fence.

"POINT IT UP!" shouted Bishop. Through the fence now, Scar Face stood, cradled the rifle in his left arm so that it was again pointed at Bishop, and started walking toward the road.

"STOP," shouted Bishop, but Scar Face continued walking. Bishop now drew his sidearm, a Colt .45 automatic, walked toward Scar Face, training the weapon at the man's head. Scar Face now stopped and turned to face Bishop, shouting profanities. Bishop continued to advance, his pistol trained now on the man's chest.

"Give me the rifle," said Bishop, reaching out with his left hand to take it, but Scar Face backed away, holding the rifle over his head, still shouting profanities. Bishop briefly considered holstering his .45 and wresting the rifle from the man, but he felt certain that the man would immediately shoot him. Again Bishop demanded the rifle, and again Scar Face stepped back, holding the rifle out of the warden's reach. Bishop then stopped and commanded Scar Face to put the rifle down. Scar Face ignored him, still shouting profanity, and he brought the rifle back down to port arms, the muzzle again pointed nearly at Bishop. Bishop now took a two-handed grip on the .45 and refined his aim on Scar Face's chest.

"PUT IT DOWN OR I'LL SHOOT!" commanded Bishop,

and none present had any doubts that he meant it. Scar Face stood frozen, his wild eyes locked onto Bishop, calculating his chances, his finger finding the trigger.

"LAST CHANCE!" said Bishop.

"Wait a minute! Wait a minute!" said Black Beard. "Put it down, Lee!" And at this, Scar Face bent, placed the rifle on the ground, and began backing away.

"Now, I'll need to see your ID," said Bishop, stepping over the rifle and attempting to approach the man. But Scar Face continued backing away. "Hold it right there, you're under arrest!" Scar Face now shouted a vile insult at Bishop, turned and loped away down the road.

"SHOOT ME IN THE BACK AND IT'LL BE MURDER!" shouted Scar Face.

Bishop started to give chase, then remembered the rifle lying behind him and Black Beard, who could easily get to it. Giving up on the fleeing suspect, Bishop now went back, snatched up the rifle, unloaded it and Black Beard's pistol and laid the weapons near the gate.

"Watch these," he said to Churnside, then turned and confronted Black Beard. Cheal and Churnside remained on the far side of the gate.

"Who was that guy?" Bishop demanded, but Black Beard, it seemed, had a defective memory. "OK, I need your ID now."

Black Beard now began to protest, challenging Bishop's authority. He still had his wallet in his hand, but refused to give Bishop his ID. Bishop demanded it again, stepping closer. Again the man refused. Bishop now made a swift grab for the man's wrist, but the man jerked his hand away, his wallet flying out of his hand, spinning upward, disgorging a shower of business cards and paper matter. In anger, Black Beard now pushed Bishop into the fence.

"That's it!" said Bishop. "You're under arrest." He pulled his handcuffs, caught a hold on the man's arm, and the battle was on.

Cheal would later describe it as the most violent fight he had ever seen. Black Beard became a maniac, cursing, spitting, biting, arms flailing with Bishop struggling to gain control. Down they went, into the dirt, a tangle of arms and legs. Then into the fence they fought, the barbed wire ripping a large gash on Bishop's arm. Finally Bishop managed a good hold on the man, spun him around and captured his head from behind in a choke hold. With Black Beard's neck now scissored in the crook of Bishop's muscular arm, he bucked and kicked all the harder. Then Bishop applied a careful, calculated pressure. Both of Black Beard's carotid arteries were pinched closed and the blood flow to his brain immediately ceased. He struggled violently for two more seconds then went limp, totally unconscious.

Bishop lowered the man onto his stomach, grabbed his right arm, pulled it behind his back and snapped a handcuff onto his wrist. But then, as Bishop was going for the other arm, on which the man was lying, Black Beard suddenly came back to life. Again he went berserk, kicking, screaming like an animal and flailing at Bishop with the loose handcuff dangling from his right wrist. Bishop ducked under the blows and captured the flailing right arm, wrenched it back, then pinned the left arm, pitching the man onto his face. Then it became a contest of strength, Bishop gritting his teeth with the strain, Black Beard emitting strained, guttural grunts, but slowly . . . slowly, Bishop muscled the man's left arm rearward. Slowly . . . slowly, until the two wrists came together and Bishop snapped the loose handcuff onto Black Beard's left wrist.

Both men were exhausted, gasping for breath. Bishop remained on his knees for a few seconds then stood, dusty and bloody, his uniform ripped and missing buttons. Upon regaining his breath, he reached down and unsnapped the military web belt Black Beard was wearing, grabbed him by one arm and dragged him over to the fence.

"YOU'RE DEAD!" shouted Black Beard, spittle running down his chin. "YOU'RE DEAD!"

Using the web belt, Bishop strapped the man by his handcuffed wrists to a fence post. Turning now to Cheal and Churnside, who had stood, spellbound, through the whole thing, he spoke:

"Go to a phone and call the sheriff's office. Have them send a unit up here code two," he said. Churnside hurried toward his pickup, for the nearest phone was at least a mile away.

Asked later why they had failed to assist Bishop during the fight, both Cheal and Churnside stated that it hadn't occurred to them to help him, because it never appeared that he *needed* any help.

With Black Beard strapped to a fence post, Bishop conducted a spirited search for Scar Face, but could find no trace of him. Peering up at the high, brooding, basalt canyon walls, Bishop could see a hundred hidden nooks from which the man could be watching his every move from hiding. Frustrated, Bishop returned to the gate in time to help a Butte County deputy stuff Black Beard into the back seat of a patrol unit.

As the sheriff's unit disappeared down Helltown Road, Bishop received heartfelt thanks from Cheal and Churnside, followed by a short summary of what had occurred prior to Bishop's arrival.

"They were going to kill us," said Cheal with certainty. Churnside nodded his head in agreement. Weeks later, this theory would be proven when a district attorney's investigator would learn from informants that Black Beard and his companion for two weeks had been planning and talking about killing Cheal and Churnside.

Following hand-shaking and more expressions of gratitude, Bishop slipped on his camo shirt and climbed onto the motorcycle. Cheal and Churnside watched him motor away, the man to whom they most certainly owed their lives.

*   *   *

A few weeks later, Bishop was contacted by a lawyer from the Attorney General's office. It seemed that Black Beard, whose real name was Edward James Daxton, was suing the State of California, claiming Bishop had brutalized him. Bishop was astounded to see copies of color Polaroid photos, taken by Daxton's girlfriend, of Daxton, covered with blood and bruises that certainly had not been there when Bishop had booked the man into county jail. The matter was to be settled in a court in the town of Paradise. For Bishop, however, help arrived from an unexpected quarter.

* * *

One morning, about the time Bishop received news of Daxton's lawsuit, residents of the Helltown area were disturbed to hear screaming in the upper canyon, a series of agonized shrieks and cries that continued for over 15 minutes. At the time, no one had the nerve or inclination to investigate, but the following morning a local resident made a horrifying discovery: He found the nude, mutilated body of Richard Eggett, 44, tied to a tree and tortured to death. The man had been pistol-shot in both feet with snake loads, stabbed several dozen times and had large fish hooks impaled in various of the more tender parts of his body.

Fortunately, and to the particular relief of the residents of Butte Creek Canyon, the sheriff's office made an arrest almost immediately. One Lee Max Barnett, 43, was taken into custody on charges of kidnaping and first degree murder. Two witnesses had come forward to swear that he had committed the crime.

Special Investigator Tony Koester, of the Butte County DA's office, was assigned the case and became more and more amazed over what he learned about Barnett. As answers to his inquiries began to pour in from law enforcement agencies all over the United States and Canada, Koester realized he had a super-criminal on his hands. Barnett, it seemed, had over 60 felony arrests, had used over 60 aliases and had escaped from custody 14 times. His most noteworthy escape had involved a head-first dive, while handcuffed, through the unbarred, plate-glass window of a bus traveling at 60 miles per hour down some Canadian highway. He next surfaced somewhere in the Lower 48 when he was shot in the leg during his armed robbery of a donut shop. His list of crimes went on and on.

About a month after Bishop learned of the lawsuit by Edward Daxton, he received a handwritten note that immediately piqued his interest. The writer of the note claimed to have first-hand knowledge of a plan Edward Daxton had pursued to make a phony injury claim against the state. The note was signed, Lee Max Barnett, Butte County Jail.

The following day, Bishop and Warden Wade Johnson were granted an interview with Barnett at the jail. Immediately upon seeing the man, Bishop had the feeling he had seen him before. Barnett launched into a tale during which he described how Edward Daxton's girlfriend had used mascara to paint phony bruises on his face and body and how Daxton had used a hypodermic needle to draw blood which he smeared over various parts of his body prior to being photographed.

"He really overdid it," said Barnett. "And after his girlfriend took the pictures, he realized he would need scars to go with the blood, so he cut himself with broken glass. Then he realized that the cuts didn't match the blood smears on him in the pictures, but it was too late, because he had already turned in the pictures."

As Bishop listened, he noticed a scar near Barnett's chin, and this, along with certain facial expressions of Barnett's, further tugged at his memory. Then it struck him: *It's him.* Bishop realized then, with certainty, that he was facing a shaved and sanitized version of the scar-faced man who had been with Daxton at Robb Cheal's place, the one he had nearly shot and who had escaped.

"Why are you telling us all this?" said Bishop, curious why Barnett would betray a former friend.

Without hesitation, Barnett said, "Because when I got arrested, Daxton moved in with my girlfriend." *So*, Bishop thought. *It's as simple as that!*

Before leaving the jail on that day, Bishop advised Barnett that he recognized him as the guy with the rifle with Daxton on that near-fatal day. Barnett denied it, but the denial was without conviction and Bishop never had the slightest doubt. The question for Bishop was what to do about it. He could certainly file charges against the man for *resisting arrest* and *assault on a peace officer*, but would it be worth it? The man would soon be tried for murder. Bishop decided to let the DA make that decision. The important thing, aside from Edward Daxton's dream of deep-pocket wealth being now in the toilet, was that a loose end that had been bothering Bishop was now tied in a neat bow. There was no longer a mystery man who had escaped from him, and the man responsible for his weeks of frustration was now in a high-security cell awaiting trial for his life.

Works for me, thought Bishop.

* * *

The passage of time did much to set things right in Butte Creek Canyon. More good people chose to live there, and more of the criminal element were forced out. As for the spring-run salmon, the unflagging efforts of a few dedicated people had done much to wrest them from the very brink of extinction.

On another sunny afternoon in early spring, 15 years following the incident on Robb Cheal's property, Warden Will Bishop strode out onto a great slab of dark basalt rock overlooking a deep drift on Butte Creek. Outwardly, he looked much the same as then, only the lines around his eyes perhaps having deepened. Inwardly, however, he was weary, change and adversity having taken their toll. But he still cared deeply for the things that counted. Peering into the clear water, shading his eyes with his hand, he made out the dark shapes of nearly two dozen plump spring-run salmon holding near the bottom. He watched them for a while, delighted over their numbers, feeling something very much akin to paternal pride.

As he turned and walked away, he was for the moment content—aglow with the special satisfaction known only to those who have laid life, limb and happiness on the line to wear a badge on behalf of wildlife.

Author's Note

Lee Max Barnett was tried for the torture-murder of Richard Eggett and convicted of first degree murder. At the time of this writing, he is on death row at San Quentin State Prison, awaiting execution. Will Bishop, to this day, is haunted by the possibility that had he dealt differently with Barnett on that day in Helltown, Richard Eggett might have been spared his horrible death.

THEN CAME SPEEDY

Sheepherder Eduardo Estrella knelt in the growing darkness to examine the torn body of yet another bear-killed lamb. Over a dozen of them, lambs and ewes, lay strewn about the mountain meadow where they had fallen.

The attack had come at dusk, a quarter-hour earlier, when a black bear sow and her two grown cubs had charged from the forest, slashing with teeth and claws, killing or maiming every animal within reach and scattering the great flock.

The sheep dogs had sounded the alarm, and Eduardo had come running with his rifle. His warning shots had driven the bears away, but not before they had taken a dreadful toll on the sheep. And he knew, with growing dread, that they would return. He looked to the east where a cold, three-quarter moon was rising, and suddenly he felt more alone than ever before in his life.

But he was *not* alone, and feeling a soft brush against his leg, he bent down to stroke the soft-furred head and neck of Speedy the sheep dog, a border collie mix. The dog peered up at him with bright eyes alight with intelligence and affection.

"Gracias, mi amigo," said Eduardo softly, regarding the loyal companion he had learned to love, the friend who responded instantly to commands in either Spanish or English, who anticipated most commands before given and who regarded the sheep as his personal responsibility.

Behind them loomed the higher peaks of the Sierra Nevada, dark bastions against a cobalt sky. Far below, to the east, gleamed the cluster of distant lights of some small town. Eduardo drew in a deep draught of cool air, spiced with high-country sage and the pungent smell of sheep. It was an aroma as common to him as breath itself, and if he closed his eyes, it would carry him back to the rugged slopes of the Peruvian Andes, to the tiny village where he had been born and raised.

There had always been sheep. His earliest memories were of sheep, tended in the mountain camps by his father. He had learned at an early age to care for sheep, to doctor them, to assist them at birth, to apply the lessons learned by his ancestors over centuries of sheep raising, the bits and pieces of hard-earned knowledge that would keep the flocks healthy and productive. Now at age 35, Eduardo knew all that was practical to know about sheep, and it was this knowledge and experience, along with his willingness to live the lonely life of a sheepherder, that had been sought by a sheep rancher in America.

Fred Fulstone was a second-generation sheep rancher in Western Nevada. He was active and capable at age 80, and he knew the sheep business inside out. He had known for years that the best available sheep and herders came from Chile and Peru, and he had arranged a visa for Eduardo and had sent him a one-way plane ticket to the U.S. Eduardo had arrived, anxious to begin his three-year contract, anxious to begin earning seven times the pay he could earn in Peru.

He had begun in the spring, driving nearly 2,000 head of ewes and lambs west from Fulstone's ranch in Wellington, Nevada, across miles of sage and juniper flats, into California. He had walked with the sheep the whole way, six to eight miles per day, his ears tuned to the continuous bleating and blatting and the tinny clinking of bells which hung from the necks of one in every 200 of the sheep. His tent, camping gear and food were packed on a single burro.

They had crossed Highway 395, stopping traffic as the sea of wooly bodies flowed across, and the occupants of the cars and trucks had marveled over a sight from a different age. They had continued on, gaining altitude, continuing west, ever higher, until reaching the alpine meadows and the sweet summer grasses of the eastern Sierra Nevada. And the sheep had thrived under his care.

Always nearby was faithful Speedy, restlessly patrolling the trailing edge of the huge flock as they traveled. His coat, a mottled black and white, appeared as a grey blur as he raced first one way, then another, nipping at the heels of any foolish animal that would wander off course.

There were other dogs on the drive as well, for dogs were essential to sheepherding. There were two all-business Australian shepherds, and a third one, little more than a pup, learning the trade from his elders. And there was a huge Great Pyrenees, the guard dog of the flock, whose job it was to keep marauding coyotes at bay. But it was Speedy who had adopted Eduardo for his own, and the others kept their distance.

The first year had gone well, but now, as summer of the second year was upon him, he was troubled. Black bears were becoming more numerous and more aggressive. It was a problem new to him, for he had never encountered bears in the Andes. Bears were fast, powerful predators, and they could kill many sheep in a short time. He brooded over the problem, longing to seek the wise guidance of Fred Fulstone. At least he was comforted to know that Julio Gorriz, Fulstone's camp tender, was due in a day or so to bring him supplies. He could discuss the matter with Julio.

As he crawled into his sleeping bag that night inside his tent, with Speedy bedded down nearby, he couldn't help but mourn the loss of the murdered sheep. But then he turned his mind to happier things, and as sleep came over him, his last thoughts were of the smiling faces of his wife and children a half a world away.

It was just before dawn when it happened. He was preparing to cook his breakfast, when a sudden cacophony of noise brought him up short. It was the frantic barking of Speedy and the other dogs accompanied by the braying of the burro and the loud, combined dissonant voices of almost 2,000 frightened sheep. Eduardo grabbed his battered 30.30 rifle and hurried toward the commotion.

The eastern sky had begun to lighten, and there was just enough grey light for Eduardo to see the flock of sheep surging first one way, then another, and parting as large, dark shapes charged among them. He hurried closer, to within rock-throwing range of the bears, then threw his rifle to his shoulder and fired a shot. He then fired again, his aim being to frighten, not kill, and three of the bears immediately fled for the forest. But a fourth one, a large male, was unmoved by the shooting and struck down and killed a lamb right before Eduardo's eyes. Eduardo felt he had no choice. He jacked another live round into the chamber of his rifle, took aim in the dim light and fired.

The bear bellowed with rage, spinning circles as though chasing whatever it was that had struck him. Eduardo doubted that he had made a killing shot on the animal and attempted to shoot again. But he had forgotten to reload the night before, and there was just the metallic snap of the firing pin striking an empty chamber.

At that instant, Speedy dashed in, snapping at the bear's heels, and the bear, with astounding swiftness, turned and swiped at the dog, hooked him with his great claws and drew him to his chest. Speedy screamed as the huge teeth sunk into his body, and Eduardo, horrified, charged in, clubbing the bear with his rifle. Once, twice, three times he swung with all his might, shattering the weapon over the bear's skull. The bear now dropped Speedy and turned on Eduardo. It was on him like an avalanche, driving him to the ground, biting, tearing, grunting savagely, its hot, putrid breath engulfing him.

In the midst of this nightmare, Eduardo closed his eyes

and tried to protect his throat and face, and when the bear lunged for his throat, it got his forearm instead, the great canine teeth sinking deep into his flesh. The bear then shook him violently, and when Eduardo opened his eyes briefly, he found himself staring straight into the fierce, pig-like eyes of the animal, mere inches away.

Eduardo lay drenched in blood, a mixture of his and the bear's, and he turned to his faith and prayed, convinced he was about to die. But then the violence of the bear's attack began to slow. It was as though it were succumbing to some drug. It moved slower and slower, its labored breath slowing, until it simply stopped. The great weight of the animal then settled onto Eduardo, who found himself pinned beneath 300 pounds of dead bear.

Using all his strength, Eduardo rolled the dead animal aside but found that his forearm was still locked in the death grip of the animal's jaws. With his free hand, he tried to force the large jaws apart, but to no avail. Then, using the back of his good hand, he wiped blood from his eyes, looked around and spotted the broken Winchester. He was just able to reach it, and he used its barrel to pry the bear's jaws open enough to withdraw his mutilated arm. He then collapsed on his back, heart pounding, his breath coming in ragged gasps.

It was the presence of Speedy that brought him back to his senses, the little dog hurt and bleeding, but alive. Speedy had limped to him and was licking his face. Eduardo raised a shaking hand and petted him.

Eduardo rose painfully to a sitting position and assessed his own injuries. They were many. He had oozing puncture wounds and ripped flesh all over his body, but surprisingly he could detect no broken bones. Being in shock, he felt very little pain, but he knew this to be a temporary condition. He therefore forced himself to rise, found he could stand, then he and Speedy staggered back to the tent. There, using rolls of gauze from the first aid kit that Fulstone insisted his herders carry, Eduardo bound, as best he could, his and Speedy's wounds.

By the greatest of good fortune, Julio arrived shortly thereafter. Eduardo and the sheep had not yet reached the isolation of the really high country, and there was still the rudiment of a dirt road on which Julio was able to drive a pickup. Julio was shocked to see Eduardo in tattered, bloody clothing, roughly bandaged and he wasted no time in getting the injured man loaded into the pickup. Eduardo, however, wouldn't leave without Speedy, so Julio gently lifted the dog onto the seat and slid in after him. Julio now slipped the pickup into gear, and Eduardo's pain began in earnest.

At the hospital in Bridgeport, 60 miles to the south, doctors worked for hours on him, cleaning, stitching, and pumping him full of antibiotics. Only then was he allowed to rest. He would spend three days there before finally being released. But even then, Fulstone would have to drive him the 120-mile round trip to Bridgeport every other day or so to get his dressings changed. It would be a full month before Eduardo would be able to move without substantial pain.

In the meantime, Speedy had been treated and was making his own recovery, and it was a happy reunion when Eduardo finally saw him again. The dog seemed to understand perfectly that he owed his life to the quiet man who had rushed to his aid and had paid so dearly for it.

When fall arrived, Eduardo was able to work again, mainly around the ranch in Wellington. But he was able to help with the sheep in October, when the lambs were driven down from the high country to be grain fed and readied for market, and he cared for the ewes in November, when they were trailed down to the high-desert flats near the ranch.

One brisk November day, as Eduardo was out on the flats, watching over a large flock of ewes, a green Fish and Game patrol vehicle drove his way from the ranch headquarters. When it arrived, out stepped one of the largest men he had ever seen. Lt. Art Lawrence, who stood a beefy six-foot-four, was indeed an imposing figure, particularly in uniform as he was on this day. Lawrence supervised the game wardens in Inyo and Mono counties, and he took his mission of protecting the state's wildlife very seriously.

Lawrence had heard, from Nevada game wardens, the story of the Peruvian sheep herder who had been mauled by a wounded bear. Because the bear had been shot out of season, Lawrence felt compelled to investigate. As he approached, Eduardo watched his coming with considerable apprehension, and Lawrence noticed that a small black and white sheep dog had moved protectively to the man's side. Lawrence also noted several large rents in the coarsely knit wool sweater the man was wearing. The damage appeared to Lawrence as though it could easily have been done by an angry bear, which in fact it had.

Despite the language barrier, Lawrence's friendly, easy manner soon set Eduardo's fears to rest, and through crude communication, Lawrence was able to piece together the story and determine for himself that the bear had in fact been legally killed while attacking a flock of sheep. Eduardo showed Lawrence some of his many fresh scars, then, at Lawrence's request, produced the old Model 94 Winchester rifle with which he had shot the bear.

Lawrence inspected the rifle and was both amazed and amused over its condition. Not only was it ancient, an early example of its type, but it had obviously kicked around sheep camps for most of a century and had suffered horrible abuse. The metal receiver had been broken and crudely welded back together, and the scarred wooden stock had been shattered more than once and pieced back together with glue and wire. Someone had cut a nickel in two and welded half of the coin to the end of the rusted barrel to replace a missing front sight, and the rear sight had been pegged into place with part of a toothpick.

Lawrence chuckled as he hefted the remarkable weapon in his hands, fascinated by it, then he handed it back to Eduardo.

Preparing to leave, Lawrence shook Eduardo's hand, then turned to give Speedy a pat on the head.

"You're one lucky dog!" he said.

*   *   *

Late the following spring found Eduardo again trailing a huge flock of ewes and lambs toward the high-country summer ranges. He again led his pack burro, and Speedy and the other dogs were on duty doing most of the work driving the sheep. As they gained elevation and entered the forested areas, Eduardo felt a growing apprehension concerning bears. As it happened, his fears were well founded, for the flock was soon attacked, and the first losses occurred.

But losses to predators were part of the sheep business, and Fulstone would lose over 500 sheep on an average year, with coyotes and mountain lions doing most of the damage. But it was the bear problem that bothered Eduardo the most, for he was plagued by the recurring nightmare of his near-death experience of the year before.

His worst fears came to pass almost a year to the day after his ordeal of the preceding summer. Again he was preparing his breakfast, just before dawn, when the burro began to bray, followed by the frantic barking of dogs and the cries of the terrified sheep. He grabbed the same battered Winchester and dashed toward the sheep. It was as before, with at least three bears rampaging through the flock. He fired his warning shots, and the bears fled, running up a hillside above the meadow. But *this* time one of the bears, a large male, clambered up a tall fir tree as the others continued running.

The sheep dogs, now in pursuit of the bears, ran right by the tree containing the large male. Speedy was with them, but only as a half-hearted participant. He trailed behind the others, having gained a healthy fear of bears.

When Eduardo arrived at the tree, he could see the large black mass of the big male bear, 30 feet above him, and he could hear the diminishing barking of the dogs as the chase led them farther away. It was growing lighter now as the new day began, and Eduardo was faced with a decision: Should he let this bear live and gamble that it would stay away from the sheep? Or should he end its marauding days right then and there? But he already knew the answer. The bear would surely return to kill more sheep.

Now, Eduardo was an expert in caring for sheep, and he was a highly experienced outdoorsman. But he was no hunter. In Peru he had never fired a rifle. True, during the preceding two years in America he had learned the rudiments of rifle shooting, but he was a marginal shot at best. And his judgment was not the best when it came to hunting-related things like the choosing the best spot from which to shoot.

In *this* case, the bear was high in a tree growing on a fairly steep hillside. Because the bear was clinging to limbs on the downslope side of the tree and was most visible from the ground at a spot almost directly beneath it, Eduardo chose to shoot from this spot, unmindful of the hazards it presented. He drew a shaky bead on the animal, aiming for its heart, and jerked the trigger.

The rifle boomed, but the bullet missed the heart, ploughing instead into the animal's abdomen. The shock dislodged the bear from its perch, and down it came, bellowing, crashing through branches until it struck with a great thump a few feet in front of Eduardo. But due to the slope of the hillside and the remarkable resiliency of all bears, the animal bounced, deflected by the sloping ground, and struck Eduardo squarely, knocking him flat. The bear recovered instantly and tore into Eduardo, who unbelievably found himself reliving the worst horror of his life, again being torn apart by a huge, highly-enraged animal.

Again Eduardo did his feeble best to protect himself against the killing onslaught of teeth and claws, clutching the rifle barrel to protect his throat, gagging over the rotten bear-stench. The large teeth repeatedly sunk deep into his flesh and the animal shook him like an old rag, ripping, tearing, its loud guttural grunts hammering at Eduardo's ears.

The ferocity of the attack was even worse than the year before, *this* bear even larger, and in the midst of his horrible ordeal, Eduardo knew all too well that *this* bear would not die in time to save him. It was he, Eduardo, who would soon die and would never again see his home or his family. And with this sad realization, despite the continuing violence of the attack, a sort of calm came over him as he awaited his death.

* * *

It was mid-afternoon when Fish and Game Warden Eric Wang received the call. A sheepherder had been mauled by a bear and was being treated at the hospital in Bridgeport. Wang and Tim Taylor, a Fish and Game biologist, drove to the hospital and looked on in amazement as emergency room doctors worked on the poor, mutilated man, applying dozens of sutures to close his ghastly wounds.

When the initial treatment was over, the doctors allowed Wang, through an interpreter, to speak to Eduardo. Wang's concerns were now the possibility of a wounded bear wandering around in the high country where some backpacker could stumble onto it. Although Eduardo was drugged and barely conscious, he was able to confirm that the bear was indeed wounded and alive when last he had seen it. The interpreter, Isadoro Luna, who was a ranch foreman for Fred Fulstone and Eduardo's immediate boss, offered to guide Wang and Taylor to Eduardo's camp.

The camp, it turned out, was above Swauger Canyon, the mouth of which was 13 miles northwest of Bridgeport. Upon approaching the canyon, the three men drove past the remote residence of Bret Emery, the man who had spotted Eduardo staggering out of the canyon. Emery had driven Eduardo to Luna's home, which was nearby. Luna, who was fluent in Spanish, questioned Eduardo as they drove him to the hospital. Eduardo, in a broken, quavering voice, had told his remarkable story.

Emery was surprised to learn that Eduardo, following the bear attack, had first made his way back to his camp, in deep shock, and had dressed his wounds, using toilet paper when he ran out of gauze. He had changed his shoes, which were full of blood, and his pants, which were ripped and bloody, then he had set out down the canyon to reach help. He had begun not long after sunrise, walking and sometimes crawling, and it wasn't until early afternoon, seven hours later, that he had come upon Emery. By then, he had nearly bled to death.

Wang and Taylor, as they four-wheeled up the canyon in the patrol vehicle, were astounded at the distance and rugged terrain Eduardo had traversed, in his horrible condition, to make it out. Wang parked the patrol vehicle when the poor excuse for a road gave out, and the men hiked another half-mile before arriving at Eduardo's camp. They searched an ever-expanding radius around the camp, searching for the dead sheep or the wounded bear, but found nothing. Darkness forced them to call it quits for the night.

The following day, Wang and Taylor returned to the area, this time with the aid of a pair of federal trappers. The well-armed team searched all day, and while they found many fresh bear tracks, the wounded bear continued to elude them. It was on the third day that the team encountered a large bear, well over 300 pounds.

"Well, *this* one won't be hurtin' anybody!" said Wang, peering down at the animal, for it had apparently died a day earlier from gunshot wounds.

* * *

To Eduardo, the world now seemed a somehow brighter place. True, he had the pain and inconvenience of another healing and recovery to endure, but it felt so good to be alive. Fred Fulstone had again brought him home from the hospital, this time a full 10 days after the attack, and again there followed weeks of antibiotics and round trips to

Bridgeport to have his wounds checked and dressings changed.

Back at the ranch in Wellington, when he was feeling up to it, he worked in the cook house, baking bread and generally assisting the camp cook. He felt terrible that he was again unable to finish the work he had been hired to do, and he chastised himself often for his carelessness in putting himself in such danger, but he couldn't change what had happened.

On the bright side, however, he would be going home for Christmas in four months, back to his family and the little village in the Andes. And he would take home with him a lot of money, for he had spent little of his earnings during the past two-and-a-half years. He would remain with his family for three months, then, hopefully, Fulstone would ask him to return the following spring for another three-year contract.

It would be a great sacrifice to spend another three years away from his family, but he could not ignore the huge rewards. When he would ultimately return home, he would have enough money to buy a big sheep ranch in Peru and be wealthy for the rest of his life.

As the weeks passed, Eduardo was often reminded of that horrible day above Swauger Canyon, but much of what had occurred eluded his memory. Mercifully, he recalled little of the attack itself or the miles of pain and torture he had endured hiking out from his camp to the Emery place far below. And he had but a vague memory of Bret Emery and Isadoro Luna, who had driven him to the hospital, and of the doctors and nurses who had initially treated him there.

But there was one vivid memory of that day that he would not forget, that would always be with him, a recollection so powerful and moving that for a time it would bring tears to his eyes each time it came to mind. It had occurred during the attack, when he had lost all hope of survival, when he was certain that the enraged bear would maul him until he was dead. It was at that moment of his deepest despair that his hopeless situation had suddenly changed, for the bear was suddenly struck from behind by a 35-pound, black and white rocket on legs, a concentrated bundle of raw courage and sharp teeth. Speedy had arrived.

The bear dropped Eduardo and spun around, roaring with rage. Speedy nipped him again, then dodged the swift blow from a claw-studded paw. The little dog circled the bear, nipped at it, worried it, all the while drawing it farther from Eduardo. The bear charged, Speedy dodged, to circle and nip again. Over and over, Speedy attacked, darting in then away, evading the lethal blows that followed. Finally, the bear had had enough and lumbered away.

Eduardo recalled the incident, as always, with a strange mixture of pride, inexpressible gratitude and sadness, for after it happened he had been in too desperate a condition to express his gratitude to the dog. He was even forced to order Speedy to remain with the sheep when he had set out on his torturous walk out of the mountains. And now, months later, he had yet to see Speedy since that day.

But his chance came one cold November afternoon as he stood on the wind-torn sage flats near the ranch headquarters at Wellington. A large flock of ewes was trailing in, driven down from the high-country by another herder. As they drew near, Eduardo spotted the familiar black and white shape of Speedy coursing back and fourth behind the rearmost of the ewes.

Eduardo called out to him. The little dog stopped, his ears pricked with attention. Eduardo called again, kneeling down to dog level. Speedy approached tentatively, then a light of recognition flashed in his eyes and he joyfully dashed straight into the Eduardo's arms, licking his face. Eduardo hugged him, stroked the soft fur of his neck and whispered into one silken ear.

"Gracias, mi amigo! Gracias!"

DELTA GHOSTS

"To protect the fish . . . many wise laws have been passed, and there is a fish patrol to see that these laws are enforced. Exciting times are the lot of the fish patrol."

Jack London

The tiny canoe surged ahead as yet another powerful gust of wind struck it from behind. In the stern seat, Warden James Halber leaned into his paddle-stroke, the first feelings of dread beginning to gnaw at the pit of his stomach. Most of Grizzly Bay, a great bight of Delta waters over four miles across, still lay ahead. *Should I call it off?* Halber considered the danger. A large body of water was no place to be caught in a canoe in a strong wind. If he acted now, he could still abort the operation and radio the skiff to pick them up. He started to reach for the radio, but changed his mind and hunkered a little lower on the seat as he paddled on.

In the bow, Warden Carl Jochums paddled with a steady rhythm that Halber matched, stroke for stroke. They had become a team, the two of them often prowling the Delta waters by canoe on the darkest nights, in silent search of the most elusive of the Delta outlaws.

Halber glanced to the west. The sun had sunk beyond the Carquinas Strait, and its last glow was fading fast. They were right on schedule. About three miles ahead, on the tule-choked southeastern shore of Grizzly Bay lay the tiny, protected inlet known among the wardens as Rat Catcher Cut. The cut, with its ramshackle collection of a dozen or so wooden shacks built on stilts, was miles from anything and had served as a haven for outlaws for decades. The outlaws in this case were gillnetters who knew that Grizzly Bay was a natural fish trap. They knew that king salmon, migrating by tens of thousands up the combined waters of the Sacramento and San Joaquin rivers, were often fooled on a flood tide into entering the bay where they were highly vulnerable to the illegal practice of gillnetting.

Rat Catcher Cut was a problem for the wardens. Not only did it lie in a remote part of the Delta, but it was difficult to approach. It was all but inaccessible by vehicle during the winter, and because sound carried so remarkably well over the bay itself, it was difficult to approach undetected by motorized boat. Plus, the outlaws had many allies, and when the wardens launched boats or traversed the usual approaches to Grizzly Bay, telephones would ring. But the perimeter of the bay itself, except for Rat Catcher Cut, was uninhabited, a fact that the wardens now intended to exploit.

The plan was simple: Halber and Jochums would cross Grizzly Bay by canoe from the north side, just before dark. They would land and hide the canoe a half-mile or so west of Rat Catcher Cut. They would then proceed through the dense tules to some point from which they could watch the mouth of Rat Catcher Cut. Hopefully, sometime during the night, outlaws would leave by boat and set a net. The wardens would then wait until the outlaws returned to pull the net, at which time they would call in the two wardens in the skiff who would race in and pounce on the outlaws when their boat was full of incriminating evidence. It was a reasonable plan, one that had worked elsewhere, and Jim Wictum, the highly respected captain of the Delta Squad, had endorsed it and committed six wardens to the operation, including himself.

They had met for a briefing in midafternoon, then launched the skiff at a remote ramp far to the northeast of their destination. Next came the nine-mile run by skiff down Montezuma Slough, hauling the canoe with its bow actually lashed on top of the skiff's transom, its stern trailing in the water. They reached Grizzly Bay at sunset. They hurriedly piled gear into the canoe and Halber and Jochums carefully climbed aboard and set out.

It had been smooth going at first, the breeze only moderate, but conditions began to change fast. They were no sooner well committed when the wind freshened considerably, and now it was gusting a light gale. Fortunately for the wardens the wind was right at their backs, propelling them along in exactly the direction they wanted to go. The problem, however, was the increasing size of the wind-driven waves coming from behind. The waves were now reaching alarming heights and would have been dangerous even for the skiff.

Halber paddled grimly on, for there was now no other choice. He eyed the life jackets lying uselessly at his feet. He and Jochums had known from experience that to wear them during the long, hard labor at the paddles would leave their bodies and inner garments soaked with sweat, a poor condition in which to begin a chilling winter night in the marsh. So they had chosen to ignore their safety gear, a decision Halber was beginning to regret.

The waves had now grown high enough that the canoe was being caught up by them and would slide down the faces of waves like a surfboard. It was all Halber could do to keep the craft going straight, a condition on which their lives now depended. A wave would catch them and begin to turn them broadside to it, a turn which if unchecked would result in instant disaster. Halber would dig deep with the paddle and muscle the canoe straight again until its bow dug into the wave ahead and the process would begin anew. But while Halber was fighting a desperate battle for their lives, Jochums, less aware of their peril, was having a fine time, enjoying one of the better rides of his life.

The wardens were being flung along in the dwindling light through a vast expanse of white-capped waves, but now, barely visible ahead, loomed the dark band of tule flats that was their destination. Visible as well were the roofs of the shanties at Rat Catcher Cut. *Maybe we'll make it yet*, thought Halber, and during the minutes that followed he became more and more confident that he could keep the canoe upright until they reached shore. But he knew that even if they reached the wave-battered shore, their landing wouldn't be pretty. At best, they and their gear would get a good soaking.

The last quarter-mile was the worst, the canoe tossed by waves growing yet higher as Halber, nearing exhaustion, noted the shoreline racing toward them at an alarming rate. Just when a wreck seemed inevitable, he spotted a tiny cove almost dead ahead. Making a slight course adjustment, he skinned a narrow point jutting out into the bay and veered into the few yards of protected water beyond. He then skidded the canoe broadside, its momentum sliding it neatly up onto the shore. He and Jochums stepped out without even getting their feet wet.

"Wow! That was *great!*" said Jochums as they dragged the canoe back into the tules.

"Yeah, great," said Halber without conviction. He was not yet ready to tell Jochums how many times he had nearly lost control of the canoe during the crossing, how very close they had come to capsizing which could have easily resulted in their deaths by drowning or hypothermia.

Halber advised Wictum of their safe arrival, then he and Jochums grabbed their gear and set off on foot in the direction of Rat Catcher Cut. By keeping to the water's edge and dodging the incoming waves, they were able to avoid the thick tules and make good time. They reached their destination in the last dim light of day. Amid the driftwood and debris they found a wooden shipping crate that had washed ashore during some high tide. It was large enough to provide them a place to sit, and it offered a good view of the entrance to Rat Catcher Cut, a hundred yards to the east. They had no sooner settled in to wait, when Jochums suddenly froze, listening hard.

"I hear a boat," he said. Halber strained his ears, but could hear nothing but wind and waves. He didn't doubt for a moment that Jochums had heard an engine, for Jochums, Halber had learned, had remarkable powers of sight and hearing. "It's like he has radar," Halber was fond of saying about his friend.

The wardens no sooner got their binoculars to their eyes when a boat appeared, leaving Rat Catcher Cut. It was about an 18-footer with a small cabin and covered wheelhouse. It pitched and bobbed in the rough water and traveled no more than a hundred yards offshore before it slowed. Its occupants then engaged in some kind of activity near the stern of the boat.

"They're puttin' out a net," said Jochums. Halber strained his eyes, but could see little more than the dark shape of the boat against the water. He knew, however, that there was no other reason for people to be out at dark under such conditions. Sure enough, after only about eight minutes, the boat returned to Rat Catcher Cut. Jochums now studied with a starlight scope the water where the boat had been. "I see at least one float," he said, knowing that there would be floats strung along the top of a gillnet, some more visible than others. Halber radioed the information to Captain Wictum.

"Now we wait," said Halber.

With the coming of darkness, the wind subsided somewhat, but grew colder, and the wardens pulled on gloves and down parkas. Knowing that the outlaws would allow the net to fish at least through the flood tide and slack water, a matter of several hours, the wardens had time to relax for a while. They chatted quietly concerning the promise of their situation, the prospects for making a really good arrest, and they planned for every contingency. Would the outlaws run? Would they beach their boat and attempt to escape into the dense tules? Would they fight? Whatever happened, the wardens would be prepared.

Halber turned to Jochums. "If you were half a man, you'd swim out to 'em when they pull the net, like Gene Durney did." This was in reference to a celebrated exploit of one of the tougher of their predecessors some 25 years earlier. Warden Gene Durney had indeed swum a hundred yards one dark Delta night, clambered aboard a net boat and captured two astonished gillnetters.

"No thanks," said Jochums. "But I'll hold your coat while *you* do it."

This led to a discussion of other of their predecessors who had worked the Delta and distinguished themselves in the gillnetter wars—tough, dedicated men like Ken Hooker and Artie Brown, particularly effective wardens, and Charlie Sibeck on the old patrol boat, *Rainbow*. Sibeck had even teamed up a few times with "Ol' Sabertooth," Gene Mercer, with great success. But a few wardens had not survived their struggles with gillnetters. Edward Raynard was beaten to death by outlaw fishermen. Alan Curry died by shotgun blast. Richard Squires and Ray Hecock had been found shot to death, adrift in their boat.

"I wonder how *that* happened?" said Jochums, in reference to the mystery deaths of Squires and Hecock.

"I don't know," said Halber, grimly. "But I wish I'd *been* there."

The discussion now turned to the most famous of all of the Delta wardens, or fish-patrolmen as they were known in the early days. He was a man who had left a legacy bigger than life: Jack London, the famous author, as a young man early in the 1890s, had served two harrowing, adventure-packed years in what was then known as the Fish Patrol. He had plied San Francisco Bay and the lower Delta in his boat, *Reindeer*, a swift little gaff-rigged sloop, and had hounded the oyster pirates, the shrimp draggers and the outlaw gillnetters. Many of the outlaws of his day were in fact the grandfathers and great-grandfathers of the same men Halber and Jochums now pursued in the same waters.

London had written about his experiences in his book, *Tales of the Fish Patrol*, which Halber had read several times. Halber, in particular, felt a kinship to London and often pictured him aboard *Reindeer*, in the ancient days before power boats, his hand on the tiller, racing across Grizzly Bay before a stiff breeze.

Hours passed. The discussion continued, despite the damp cold of the marsh which began to take its toll on the wardens. At one point, in reference to the packing crate on which they sat, Jochums said, "This would be a good place to hide a gillnet." He had then reached behind them, into the open end of the box, and explored its interior with his hand. To his astonishment, he found a gillnet.

"You're kidding!" said Halber, scrambling around to take a look with a tiny pen light. He studied for a moment the pile of nylon mesh and floats inside the box. He and Jochums had searched often for nets, and they had found a couple, but it was a rare thing. And now they found that they had been literally sitting on one for the last few hours. "Well, at least *this* one will never fish again."

When it was time for vigilance again, the wardens began standing half-hour watches. One would huddle down, bundled in a Space Blanket, while the other would peer through the night-vision scope, alert for the return of the net boat. And so it went, hour after teeth-chattering hour until about 4:30 a.m. when Jochums nudged Halber and announced, "They're comin' out!"

Halber reached for his radio and made the call to alert Wictum and the skiff crew. Lieutenant Jim Dixon and Warden Bill Slawson, the skiff crew, had spent the night at a deserted waterfront cabin on a tiny island near Buckner Point. Slawson, during the night, had assumed a prone position on the dock in front of the cabin, scanning Grizzly Bay with his night-vision scope rested atop a rolled life vest. Unfortunately, his new handset radio slipped from his coat pocket at one point and somehow was knocked into the water. Without hesitation, Slawson, who had been a paratrooper during World War II and was still tough as a combat boot, stripped off his clothes and dove into the frigid water to recover the radio. Despite his valiant effort, he emerged empty-handed, tight jawed, and a delicate shade of blue. But he was ready for action when Halber called, and he and Dixon immediately jumped into the skiff and made a quiet departure.

Following the south shoreline of Grizzly Bay, they proceeded at low speed in the direction of Rat Catcher Cut, two miles to the northeast. They had gone but a short distance, however, when Dixon groaned and began fiddling with wiring behind the instrument panel. The engine warning light had suddenly appeared, a brilliant red, and soon thereafter, the engine began to miss.

"Pretty bad timing," said Slawson. Dixon just shook his head in frustration.

*   *   *

Salvador Carboni, one hand on the throttle, the other on the wheel, aimed his outboard-powered net boat at the white marker-float he could barely see tossing in the pre-dawn darkness on the still-troubled waters of Grizzly Bay. As he brought the float alongside, his nephew, Anthony, hooked it neatly with a boat hook and began pulling in the gillnet to which it was attached. It was immediately apparent that the net hung heavy with fish, and as Anthony dragged the first one aboard, a shiny, 18-pound male, fresh from the ocean, a third man on the boat, Nicholas Baldo, went into action with a small, gaff-like tool called a fish pick. He grabbed the fish's head with one hand and with the fish pick in the other he raked the nylon mesh entangling the fish. By doing so he was able to draw the fish on through the net. This single fish, he noted, would sell for over $60 at the going price.

Baldo, like his friend Carboni, had gillnetted salmon most of the 60-some years of his life. He had learned the trade from his father prior to 1957 when gillnetting was still legal. Like Carboni, and many other descendants of the original immigrants who had begun gillnetting the Delta long before 1900, they had defied the law, unable to resist the high profits. But there was a price to be paid. Both Baldo and Carboni had been been caught several times and had lost their boats and expensive nets. But the profits were worth the risks, and a $5,000 fine could often be paid off with the profits from as few as two nights of gillnetting. The fines and the cost of seized boats and nets were therefore considered simply the price of doing business.

One after another the big fish slid aboard and were pulled from the net and tossed onto the deck. Soon the deck was covered with fish and it became difficult for the men to walk, but still the fish were hauled in. At one point they pulled a five-foot sturgeon aboard and soon thereafter a large striped bass, but the take was mainly salmon, dozens of them. The boat settled lower and lower under the weight of the illegal catch.

Then it was over. The last of the net snaked aboard and Baldo removed the last fish. Carboni swung the boat around and added power, but he didn't head for Rat Catcher Cut. Instead, he paralleled the shoreline, in the direction of Buckner Point. The fish and the nets would be stashed elsewhere.

*   *   *

"They're comin' your way," said Halber, radioing the skiff crew.

"We'll do what we can, but we're still havin' engine problems," answered Slawson. Dixon had managed to keep the skiff running, and they were not far from Rat Catcher Cut. But it was touch and go. He now held his thumb over the engine warning light to prevent it from being seen by the outlaws.

To Halber and Jochums, unsure of the location of the skiff, it appeared as if the suspects and their load of fish and gillnet had a good chance of escaping unchallenged. They were absolutely beside themselves with anxiety as they watched the net boat pass in front of them in the darkness and continue on. But then, inexplicably, it turned shoreward.

"They're comin' in," said Halber. "Let's go!"

Sure enough, the net boat was indeed heading for shore, and it appeared that it would land at a point within reach of the wardens. In fact, it appeared to be heading for the little cove where the wardens had stashed the canoe. Both wardens were now at full sprint, crashing through the tules in a mad dash to get there first. But they didn't make it. The driver of the boat drove its bow up onto the beach, and others aboard began offloading burlap sacks containing panels of gillnet. Fortunately, due to the noise of the wind and the waves pounding the shoreline, the outlaws didn't hear the wardens coming.

Upon spotting the boat beached dead ahead, Jochums continued directly for it. Halber, however, who expected one or more of the outlaws to bolt into the dense tules to escape, veered away from the shoreline, still at a run, and crashed through the tules to a position where he could deny them this option.

Halber, still at a run, bellowed, "STATE GAME WARDENS! DON'T MOVE!" almost simultaneously with Jochums' shouted, "STATE OFFICERS! YOU'RE UNDER ARREST!"

The reaction of Carboni and his nephew was instant flight. They leaped off the boat and dashed into the jungle of 10-foot-tall tules. Jochums, however, grabbed the nephew before he could go far, and Carboni, upon hearing a shout ahead of him and what sounded like a rhino coming his way, crouched and hid. About this time the skiff nosed ashore next to the net boat, and Slawson leaped off.

"One went that way!" said Jochums, pointing out the direction Carboni had taken. Slawson hurried in pursuit, casting the beam of his flashlight ahead of him, following a trail of freshly disturbed tules. Jochums escorted the nephew, Anthony, back to the net boat where Nicholas Baldo sat quietly in the boat, his days of running from wardens long past. Slawson hadn't gone far when he spotted a splash of bright red ahead. Investigating further, he found it to be Salvador Carboni hunkered down in a red and white sweater.

"You should wear *green* when you're gonna hide in the marsh," said Slawson helpfully, as he marched the man back to the others.

Halber now strode out of the tules and took in the scene of the three suspects standing dejectedly near their boat with Jochums and Slawson. He then peered into the boat for his first look at the illegal catch that would later be determined to consist of 67 salmon weighing a total of 1,288 pounds, plus one striped bass and a sturgeon.

With the arrests made, the *real* work began. The fish had to be counted, sacked and tagged, the gillnet panels inventoried, a trailer found on which to haul the seized net boat and motor, and a stake-bed truck arranged for to haul three-quarters of a ton of evidence. And the suspects had to be transported to Contra Costa County Jail. On top of that, there was a disabled skiff which ultimately was towed in by the seized net boat. It was early afternoon by the time the wardens were finished, and they were exhausted. It had been a long, bitter-cold all-nighter, and they were all in serious need of sleep. Halber, in fact, could not trust himself behind the wheel, and upon being returned to his patrol car he crawled in, rolled his parka into a pillow and lay his head down upon it on the seat.

As he closed his eyes, he reflected again on the events of the previous night, of their near brush with disaster, of the outlaws and the huge catch of salmon and the tiny chapter he and the others had written in a continuing story that had begun nearly a century earlier. And as he drifted off, his thoughts turned again to the brave wardens who had preceded him in the Delta, of the sacrifices they had made. Then sleep was upon him like a warm blanket.

But all at once he was there again, on the gale-torn waters of Grizzly Bay, this time aboard a trim little gaff-rigged sloop heeled sharply over, her sails billowing, her rigging singing in the wind. A tousle-haired young man, half-drenched with spray, leaned into the tiller, his sharp eyes alight with excitement. And Raynard was there, and Curry and Squires and Hecock, all peering ahead and poised for action.

On they sailed, into the night, bound for adventure.